intelligence

SUSAN HASLER

intelligence

THOMAS DUNNE BOOKS • ST. MARTIN'S PRESS ☎ NEW YORK

THOMAS DUNNE BOOKS.
An imprint of St. Martin's Press.

INTELLIGENCE. Copyright © 2010 by Susan Hasler. All rights reserved.
Printed in the United States of America.
For information, address St. Martin's Press, 175 Fifth Avenue, New York, N.Y. 10010.

www.thomasdunnebooks.com
www.stmartins.com

Design by Meryl Sussman Levavi

Library of Congress Cataloging-in-Publication Data

Hasler, Susan.
    Intelligence / Susan Hasler. — 1st ed.
        p. cm.
    ISBN 978-0-312-57603-5 (alk. paper)
    1. Women intelligence officers—Fiction.   2. Terrorism—Prevention—Fiction.
3. Political fiction.   I. Title.
    PS3608.A847I58 2010
    813'.6—dc22

                                                                    2010002340

First Edition: June 2010

10   9   8   7   6   5   4   3   2   1

For my former colleagues

Acknowledgments

Over the years, many people have provided support, guidance, and inspiration for my fiction writing. I would like to thank a few of those, in particular, for helping me with this novel: my husband, Stephen White, for everything; my agent, Liza Dawson, for making things happen; my writing partner, Janice Lierz, for combing over multiple drafts; Phil Richardson and Cindy Storer for reviewing an early draft; Ron Rash for his critique of the first chapter and words of encouragement; Chris R. for brainstorming what Alan Monroe might do in Iran; and Anne Jablonski for reminding me how the CIA values good people. Special thanks go to Judi Hill for being a friend and introducing me to the Wildacres magic mountain.

intelligence

1. Maddie

I can't decide which is worse: the lucid dreams or the muddled reality. I have no one to blame but myself. I paid sixty-five dollars an hour for a "sleep consciousness therapist" to teach me how to be aware while dreaming. The idea was to learn to alter the outcome of my nightmares. So, for example, if I dreamed of an explosion and I was aware that I was dreaming, I could confront that negative image, engage it in constructive dialogue, and turn it into something helpful and pleasant. I could say, "Hey, you nasty old explosion, wouldn't you be happier and more fulfilled as a bouquet of flowers?" Then it would turn into a dozen peonies. I would sniff them and say, "Ah, how lovely. Now isn't that better than ripping people to bits?" The therapist told me it would be great fun, that I could even learn to fly freely about the dreamscape.

As it turns out, I was a natural at the "lucid" part, but I never quite mastered the "altering the outcome" part. So I fall asleep and I know I'm dreaming. I know shit is about to happen and I can do absolutely nothing to stop it. I confront the explosion, and the explosion says, "Fuck you!" and blows my brains out. I'm fully conscious that I'm dreaming and fully conscious that my brain bits are flying freely about the dreamscape and, frankly, it's no fun at all.

So now I hate, hate, hate going to sleep at night.

The Mines wouldn't even pay for the sleep consciousness therapist. They did pay for the psychiatrist—a security-cleared psychiatrist—who told me I had post-traumatic stress disorder and prescribed a series of selective seratonin reuptake inhibitors, or SSRIs. Nice little druggies when they were working, but the effect never lasted for long. The woman at Special Employee Services who doled out the checks for the psychiatrist balked at the sleep therapist. She said it was "a little too new age-y" for the Mines' taste. So I had to shell out my own hard-earned bucks, even though the debilitating nightmares were and are legitimately work related.

I'm a bomb dissector, which is Mines jargon for "counterterrorism alchemist." *Alchemist* is Mines jargon for "analyst." Intelligence analyst is just another way of saying intelligence failure. And I most certainly am an intelligence failure. I was one of the people who failed to stop the Strikes five years ago.

I'm terrified of failing again. Everything—my nightmares, my instincts, and the deadly lull in the chatter—is telling me that something is about to happen. I can stop it or I can screw it up. If I fall off this wall, I don't think all the Mines' drugs and all the Mines' shrinks will be able to put Madeleine James back together again.

I'm back home after an excruciatingly long and utterly useless day in which I tried and failed to warn. No one would listen, so now I address myself to the one being in my world who will listen.

"What do these people have for brains?" I ask. "'Intelligence community?' What intelligence? I tell them something's going to blow up and they look at me like I'm hallucinating. I ask you, what do these astounding, arrogant, arbitrary assholes have for brains?"

What do I have for brains? I'm talking to a rabbit as if I fully expect him to answer. I've had Abu Bunny for five years, and he's a great little pet, but leaves something to be desired as a conversationalist. He only blinks. He stares at me, then goes back to foraging for crumbs among the pillows on my bed.

I finish undressing, but I don't bother to hang anything up. Hangers are for anal retentive assholes and administrative personnel. Fuck 'em. I toss my skirt and jacket over a chair, lob my shoes in the direction of the closet, and collapse face-forward on the bed without the will to do battle with my pantyhose.

"Damn the FEMWIP." FEMWIP stands for Fucking Evil Misogynist Who Invented Pantyhose. I've been with the government for my entire adult working life, so creating acronyms is as natural as seething.

"What does the FEMWIP have for brains?" The pillow muffles my voice so I make a supreme effort and turn over, which sends Abu Bunny hopping across the pink-flowered meadow of the comforter. I hate this comforter. Mom bought it for me even though I've told her a hundred thousand times I hate pink. And I hate flower prints. And I most emphatically hate ruffled bedding.

But here it is and here I am. "What do I have for brains, Bunny? It's all mush inside my skull. Tired disgusting mush. Yep, that's what's inside my head instead of gray matter. Another seventeen-hour day that yielded nothing but frustration. Would anybody listen to me? No. And I'm talking to a rabbit. No offense, Bunny-Poo, but you are a freaking rabbit."

Bunny pauses in his foraging, blinks at me, then turns his fluffy ass in my direction.

I'm too tired to be logical or fair or to care that I'm lecturing a rabbit. I want to kill someone at work, but I don't have the energy. I need to sleep, but the monsters under the bed are bigger, nastier, more serious than the ones who lived there when I was a child. I look at the clock and see that it's already Tuesday. What time of the year is it? Spring sometime I think. Last time I checked on Mother Nature, the Bradford pear in my townhouse yard was blooming. Spring sometime and past midnight. The alarm will ring in too few hours to get a decent rest even if I fell asleep instantly. I'll be a zombie tomorrow at work.

I'm afraid, afraid, afraid to go to sleep.

I've been having the wizard nightmare recently. Wizard as in *Wizard of Oz*. In the nightmare, I'm Dorothy and Abu Bunny is

Toto. I'm thirty-eight. How long do I have to deal with being trau-
matized by flying monkeys when I was six? What scares me is that
the wizard nightmare always comes before terrorist attacks. I don't
believe that dreams come true; however, I know for a fact that
nightmares do. I've had the wizard nightmare before the bombings
of embassies, nightclubs, and planes. Seventeen years now I've been
working terrorism in the Mines and having that dream, with different variations for each attack. Before the Strikes I dreamed of
two huge flying monkeys colliding with the Emerald City.

I had that dream three times before the planes hit the towers.
The terrorists have dreams, too, but their terrorist colleagues take
them seriously. Mine would have me put away.

"Seriously, Bunny, I can't sleep in these pantyhose." I lift my butt
to wriggle out of the nylons and have a brief, poignant flashback to a
time when I was wriggling out of pantyhose in the backseat of a
Camaro parked outside a military base. Can't remember which one
now. I'm still attractive, I think, but lately I just scare men off.

"Must not think about sex, Bunny. Must not think about sex.
Pointless. Bombs. Must think about bombs, because something is
about to go off. I know it."

I cut off the lamp and mutter myself to sleep. I maintain a white-
knuckled grip on my comforter, but that doesn't stop me from getting blown away by a tornado and touching down on that asinine
yellow brick road. I stomp my feet on the butter yellow brick. "Cliché!" I yell. "You're a fucking cliché!" I know I'm dreaming, but I
can't wake myself up and it makes me really mad. I pinch my arm
hard, but I'm still standing on yellow brick stretching into infinity.
So here I am, waiting for the Munchkins, who will all look like former blind dates, if earlier dreams are any indication.

I can't stop this dream, but I can look around the dreamscape
for clues. Maybe I can at least learn to use these dreams. Maybe
they can help me stop the awful thing before it happens. I can be a
good bomb dissector. I can be a professional. But I look down and
I'm wearing patent leather Mary Jane shoes, a dirndl with puffy

sleeves, and pigtails tied with bows. Abu Bunny is wearing a dog collar. Would it be too much to ask to have some dignity in the dream world? I'd rather be naked. Of course, the Vice President is wearing a tin suit and my boss, Harry Esterhaus, is covered with cat fur and fondling his own tail. Is that the President with straw sticking out of his jacket, singing "If I only had a brain?" Right, good luck with that brain thing.

Here come the poppy fields and they're crawling with Munchkins. Look over there. It's Wesley Marshall with the appalling halitosis. It's going to be a poppy field dream, which has got to be better than a flying monkey dream. Right? I sniff the air and it smells like Wesley's breath mixed with the scent I wore on that blind date: Emeraude. Does smelling halitosis and Emeraude mean we're going to have a chemical attack? I try to pick one of the poppies so I can have it analyzed by one of our chem experts, but when I bend over, the thing starts flapping like a bird and flies away. Flying poppies instead of flying monkeys? Then the whole field of poppies takes flight, hovering in a dense mass before exploding in bursts of petals and blood. Dead Munchkins everywhere.

I wake up thinking, *This can't be good.*

2. Doc

We, the disgruntled, are legion in the Mines. We inhabit forgotten side shafts, hidden pockets, the underside of dislodged stones. By our own stubbornness, audacity, or foul luck, we've condemned ourselves in perpetuity to scuttle laterally through the vast intelligence bureaucracy, kept away from the controversial accounts, from the glass-walled upper reaches of management. We wallow in supposed moral superiority and thumb our noses at the eager climbers, glib accommodators, ass-licking yes-men and -women who pass us on the stairs. We're bitter, wise, and irreverent. We know where the bodies are buried and have the don't-give-a-damn gall to joke about it. They never let us brief the Esteemed Legislative Body. They would fire us, but we might write books.

They call me "Doc," which is not a tribute to my Ph.D. in international relations—we do not use titles of respect in the Mines. Indeed, respect has disappeared from our tunnels. Doc, which I suppose should properly be written DOC, is an acronym that stands for Disgruntled Old Coot or Disgruntled Old Cuss or Disgruntled Old Codger or Disgruntled Old Chuck (my name, once upon a time). As is often the case in a world filled with acronyms, I cannot remember the original words.

To descend into the Mines you take the elevator up, a contradiction you soon cease to notice. The vaults have a subterranean feel, even if you're lucky enough to have a window, which you can't open. The windows were sealed back in the eighties, around the time they medivacked the stiffening corpse of Vaughn Sutter Wayne off the roof. The events were unrelated, so they claim. The man collapsed at his desk, falling forward into a large powdered doughnut filled with raspberry jam.

The doughnut never made it into the press stories, but Wayne's secretary told me about it. She was taking dictation when the legendary Boss of Mines stopped in mid-sentence and said "Uh." She looked up, surprised, having never known the great man to hesitate. Then his head pitched forward into that eternal darkness. His titanic nose landed dead center of the doughnut, raising a puff of powdered sugar. Over the years I have thought often about that sugar, how the morning sun streaming through the large windows of the executive suite must have lit the sparkling cloud as it settled on the mahogany of the boss's desk. It is ironic that such a hard, sour life would end in a puff of sugar, a moment of silence for a man fond of bluster.

"He was such a messy eater," his secretary said.

Among other things.

It was Vaughn who derailed my career in its early stages, but his death didn't put my career or the Mines back on track.

I shake my head to dispel Vaughn's ghost as I pass a handful of miners in our low gray tunnels. No one is flattered by the fluorescent lighting. The young look prematurely haggard, and the old look ready to be taken out and shot. There's Ed Boswell, also known as "Assman." He was the logistics officer responsible for acquiring donkeys to carry Stingers into Afghanistan. His overseas career was cut short by a swift kick to the groin.

Ed and I nod stiffly, a ghost of a sheepish smile, the standard greeting in the Mines.

"Got a bead on the Chieftain yet?" he says.

"He paces his tunnels, we pace ours."

"Gotta kill that bastard. Flies on the eyeballs."

I nod, and he limps on.

I take the elevator to the fifth gallery. As I step out, I come face-to-face with a sour-visaged woman of roughly my own age: my ex-wife, Rebecca. She smirks.

"Good morning, Doc. Any bombs about to go off?"

"Probably."

"Lovely. Have a nice day." She pushes past me to the elevators, and the doors close. I let out a sigh of relief.

I may not have a window, not even a sealed one, but I have family here: ex-wife, a son, and an ex–daughter-in-law. Had a brother until he hit the doughnut, which is Mines slang for "died." The Main Shaft is fond of calling the Mines a family. Hell, if we don't stop inbreeding, we'll have our own discrete gene pool. Scary thought.

I arrive at the door of my vault. All of our offices are vaulted. The heavy metal doors are equipped with cipher locks for the day and combination locks for any time when there are no cleared personnel within line of sight. An electronic keypad inside controls the alarm system, motion detector, steel traps, trip wires, deadfalls, spring snares, et cetera. I have called this particular vault home sweet home since last May's reorganization. My fingers punch in the required numbers on the cipher and I enter.

A noisome odor permeates the vast, low-ceilinged space: mildew from the ventilation system, someone's charred bagel, a half-full container of General Tso's chicken left in the trash can overnight. The place looks as if it had been sacked and abandoned. As the reorganizations and sector moves have accelerated over the years, fewer people bother to unpack their boxes. They rise here and there in dusty stacks. After our subshaft secretary left in the latest paring down of support staff, her desk became a repository for boxes, old three-ring binders, defunct equipment, broken umbrellas, crumb-covered foil trays from hasty, fifteen-minute birthday celebrations. Beyond the secretary's desk, the decor is what I would call sado-eclectic, comprising terrorist mug shots, link charts, maps, souvenirs from liaison trips, a gas mask, newspaper clippings, and Afghan war rugs (picked up cheap in Kabul) in shades of ochre and dark red like dried blood. By the copy machine is a yellowed, life-size cardboard cutout of someone called Buffy the Vampire Slayer. Paper signs hanging from the ceiling identify the various subshafts. More signs name the passageways between the cubicles. Sarindipity Street is where the chem subshaft lives. To get to the nuclear experts, you follow Yellowcake Road.

I hear fingers tapping keyboards. At seven thirty in the morning everyone is either at a meeting or preparing for one, sifting through the mountains of slag—what we call the daily take of raw intelligence—looking for nuggets of interest.

A fluorescent tube in the ceiling blinks on and off, buzzing with the persistence of a dying fly. I see Maddie James's head appear above the cubicle partition immediately below the faulty light. Maddie's my former daughter-in-law, but I feel closer to her than I do to my blood relatives. Her young colleagues introduce her as "the aptly named Maddie James, not mad as in crazy, but mad as in really pissed off, all of the time." She hasn't always been that way. She's a small-boned thing, a former high school ballerina, graceful even in pique. Her jaw is narrow and sharp as the prow of a ship, as is her nose. She's dark eyed and emphatic, with fast-moving hands that sweep, clench, and jab in time to her words. She must be standing on her chair. She wobbles and I move anxiously into the cubicle, thinking of her back surgery last year.

"Fuck this," she says, as she directs an obscene gesture toward the blinking tube. "It's driving me batty."

The Mines—and a childhood spent on various military bases—have turned her into a foul-mouthed little ballerina.

"Good morning to you, too, Maddie."

"When is the last time we had a good morning in the Mines, Doc?" She removes the tube from its sockets and begins to gesture with it as she speaks. "You know I spent all yesterday afternoon trying to get this light fixed while at the same time trying to warn of a terrorist attack?"

"I know. I heard. We all heard," I say. Maddie kept screaming expletives at the computer as it rejected her efforts to submit an Automated Repair Supplication Entry. Then she would scream the same expletives at the telephone, after hanging up on some editor upstairs.

"Then I spent all evening trying to rewrite my PIU while that fucking light blinked, buzzed, blinked, buzzed, blinked, buzzed. So today I brought in my own desk light."

PIU stands for President's Intelligence Update. I almost ask Maddie if they published her PIU article, but I bite my tongue. She has the look of someone who has just wasted a day of her life.

"The shift boss said I was 'hyping the threat' and BLIPed it." To translate: The night manager found her article too alarmist and judged it Below the Level of Interest of the Policymaker, thereby relegating it to the burn shaft, the brimstone hell where Mines paperwork turns to ash.

"Do you think you should be climbing over chairs with your back?" I ask as she wobbles.

Maddie waves me off. "If I had any concern whatsoever for my health or sanity I would not be working in this pit."

"Maddie," I say. "Put the tube down and have a cup of coffee with me. I just made a fresh pot."

"I have some digging to do before the morning production meeting."

"You were here late last night. They'll give you a break. You need to take a breath."

Maddie puts two fingers on my arm and steps down from her chair like a diva descending the stage. She deposits the tube gently in the trash can, and slips on her well-scuffed shoes. I remember a time when Maddie wore high heels and short, tight skirts. I labored as the senior alchemist in her subshaft back then. I was her mentor. I worried that management wouldn't take her seriously, despite her talents. I couldn't say anything, of course. Soon, she was dressing more conservatively of her own accord, as most young women here do. Today her big doe eyes are underlined with circles and she looks downright shabby in a wrinkled blue suit with a sprinkling of rabbit hair on the skirt—she bought a rabbit to replace my son after the divorce.

"Don't forget a coffee mug," I tell her.

Maddie looks over her selection of mugs—mostly souvenirs from various military commands.

"You see this?" She points to one from the 101st Airborne. "It's covered with dust. Dust!" She seems genuinely distressed, which surprises me.

"I've never known you to be that concerned with housekeeping."

"You don't understand. These aren't just mugs, they represent men, affairs, hookups if you will. This mug from the hundred-and-first is the last one I've collected, and that was over a year ago. I don't even remember his name. Mark, Matt, Mork . . . I don't know. How depressing is that?"

"I don't think I want to even know about this," I say. Maddie is one of those women who will tell you absolutely anything, no matter how private.

Maddie sighs deeply. "I'll just use this one. I bought it myself." She chooses a red mug depicting a horse lying upside down with all four hooves sticking straight in the air. REALLY I'M FINE it says.

We get our coffee and retire to the subshaft's tiny windowless conference room, which served as its large closet before the reorganization. Maddie plops into a chair as I close the door. She groans because she has forgotten to mind her back. Then she tries to give me a malevolent stare. "I suppose you're going to tell me I'm too young to join the ranks of the disgruntled?"

"Nonsense, you're not that young. You'll be forty in a couple of years, won't you? I was about to tell you to take a vacation."

"Before I flip off some senior official?"

"Precisely." I have always felt a need to protect her, a feeling strengthened by my lingering guilt over introducing her to my lout of a son.

"What are they going to do, fire me?" Maddie says. It's a standard joke around here, always accompanied by a maniacal laugh. "It would be the best thing that ever happened to me."

She's probably right. It would be the best thing for her, but they would never do it. She's prickly and hard to deal with, but experienced counterterrorism experts are in short supply. Maddie takes a sip of her coffee and gags theatrically.

"Ugh! You make wretched coffee! You could weaponize this stuff."

"I make excellent coffee. If you had ever had excellent coffee you would recognize it."

Maddie spies a bowl of gummy bears on the far end of the conference table and lunges for it, grabbing a generous fistful.

"This will take the taste out of my mouth. I love to bite off their little heads," she says.

"You spend too much time here," I tell her. "It's not healthy. Are you getting enough sleep? A good ten-hour sleep is what you need to refresh your spirit."

Maddie narrows her eyes. "I am not refreshed by sleep. I don't give a crap what Shakespeare said, sleep does not—I repeat, not—knit up the raveled sleeve of care."

I love those lines, but I resist a strong urge to declaim the entire passage. "You spend too much time thinking about this job. It will make you old or drive you crazy."

"It already has."

"Maybe you should take a vacation."

"Can't. Something big is about to happen." Maddie takes a red gummy bear, twists it in two, and pops both halves into her mouth. Her eyes wander about the room, as if searching for the direction from which that "something big" will come.

"An attack? Attacks are always being planned. And always being delayed."

"We heard a possible go signal a week ago."

"And we wrapped up the cell three days ago." Too late, I remember the subject of Maddie's PIU article. I've hit a nerve and she bristles.

"Isn't anybody listening to me? Did you read my article? The Lahore cell wasn't it. It was a distraction, not the big success the administration is touting. There's another cell out there directly involved in planning an impending attack. We just haven't found it yet. That go signal is still in effect. I'm certain of it. The Lahore cell was just providing logistical support. Not a single individual arrested fits the profile of an operative. They're all facilitators."

"Two of them confessed."

"After waterboarding and sleep deprivation, you'd tell us whatever we wanted to hear, too. You know how reliable that type of confession is. I wish they could have kept the arrests under wraps for a few days to give us a chance to find out more about who those guys were working with."

"Keep a success under wraps when the administration needs successes? You must be joking."

"The chatter has been dead quiet for the last three days. That's what worries me. The Lahore arrests may make them move the attack forward."

She's right on all points. They have me doing long-term research work on Islamic ideology, so I'm not tuned in to the daily flow of intelligence, but I've felt an uneasiness myself.

"Any theories on what or where?" I ask.

"It could be any one of dozens of places, multiple sites, perhaps multiple countries. There's a tanker truck full of acid missing in the U.K. An operative has advised family members to leave the 'city of the broken promise.' Three facilitators flew out of Paris. There's talk of a 'prayer meeting' in the 'land of mad dogs.' A 'package' is ready by 'the poison river.' Some really troubling references to 'holy swarm,' 'red cloud,' and 'dance.' A truck full of fertilizer is missing in Idaho. A whole damn cargo plane disappeared in Canada. Other indications suggest activity in Indonesia, Italy, L.A., D.C., and Baltimore. Then there's been recent talk about planes, trains, buses, and boats. A menu of plots to choose from."

"As always," I say.

"Connect the dots." Maddie rolls her eyes. "The page is black with dots."

"A lot more people are working terrorism now. A lot of young people to do the all-nighters. Let them."

"The thing is, I can't convince anybody else that something big is up. Nobody sees beyond the usual threat. It's not in the interest of their careers. But the quiet is driving me over the edge. You know what it means: The operatives are in place. They have their marching orders. They're not risking any further communication before the attack."

"You won't do anyone any good if you make yourself sick."

"Don't worry, I'm all set. I've stocked my bottom drawer: Zoloft, Nexium, ibuprofen, Maalox, muscle relaxants, vitamins, gummy bears, anvil-size hunk of extra-dark chocolate, bottle of Scotch, toothbrush, toothpaste, change of underwear, towel, and a bar of soap. Everything one needs for good health and hygiene in the Mines."

"I remember when we kept files in our desk drawers."

"You're showing your age. We have those computer thingies now." Maddie finishes chewing her gummy bears and starts in on her fingernails, which are already gnawed to the quick. The table is shaking from Maddie's bouncing foot. She's always been incapable of sitting still, but now the physical ticks and obsessive habits are getting out of control. It's painful to watch.

"You had the wizard dream again, didn't you?" I lower my voice. I know I am only one of two people Maddie has confided to concerning her dreams, the other being her friend Vivian.

"Yep."

"Did the Emerald City blow up?"

"No, the poppies exploded."

"Um," I say. I have never been able to make head nor tail of Maddie's dreams. I just try to look concerned and thoughtful. Then I change the subject.

"Is anything else wrong?" I ask.

Maddie covers her face with her hands and peers through her fingers. "I could use help."

"Maddie, you know I will do anything I can to help. No matter how trivial or menial. Name traces, searches, you name it."

"I need you to go down to the cafeteria and tell Mom that I can't make lunch today, but you'd be happy to join her for a short meal."

"Ask me something else."

"That's what I need." She looks at me with imploring eyes, but to no avail.

"If you had listened to me, you would have sent your mother packing years ago." I stand up to make my escape. "When you get back from lunch, think of something else I can do to help. Give my regards to Gladys. Then tell her I've retired and moved to Costa Rica."

Maddie stomps off, and I turn to my screen and scroll down the list of cables from the last twenty-four hours. She's right, there's nothing here but routine reports. Not a word from the most notorious of the planners or facilitators. It's dead quiet on the screen, but in the vault I hear the renewed chatter of young alchemists who, having reviewed their morning traffic, are pleased to find it yielded no pressing assignments. Foolishly, they look forward to another quiet day.

3. A Voice with Many Names

I trace my fingers over their wings. They're elegant. I worked on them through the night, because they have to be ready sooner than planned. Now the sun is high in the sky, and I should sleep for a few hours, but I can't take my hands from them. By the time the pear blossoms outside the window are gone, they will soar on the updraft of our prayers. Blue planes, white trails of smoke, red clouds blooming below—what a patriotic show! I've planned it like a stage set. My entire life has been preparation for the approaching moment.

My life would count for nothing without this.

I resemble neither a Frenchman nor an Arab, although I'm both. My skin was dark enough to earn me insults along the streets of the nineteenth arrondissement. My mother kissed the tears from my eyes. I swallowed the slurs along with chocolate crepes, *soupe au pistou*, and my favorite, her marvelous *blanquette de veau*.

My father was a halal butcher, and taught me to kill the calf for this dish according to the method of *dhabh*, as was practiced by the Prophet, peace be upon him. The knife must be large and clean, the blade sharp to ease the pain of death. The animal should not see the sharpening, for it would cause distress. The slayer must be gentle, respectful. Both the slayer and the animal should face Mecca. The slayer says, *"Bismillah Allahu Akbar"* before making the cut to the right side of the neck, to skin, muscles, esophagus, trachea, jugular, carotid. The spinal cord should remain intact. They did a study in a German university, using an electroencephalogram to record brain impulses. For the first three seconds, the machine indicated that the animal had no reaction consistent with pain. In the next three seconds a state of sleep unconsciousness occurred, due to the rapid loss of blood. Sleep. Ease. No pain. This is the merciful way of the Prophet, peace be upon him. Helping my father with the butchering and dining on the results brought me the only peace in my life.

My father's holy profession and my mother's culinary flair made for delectable fare, but a poor marriage. They had different backgrounds, different religions. They fought with a wild, grim, futile passion. And I loved them both with the blind, helpless devotion of a child.

When I turned fifteen, I awoke one night to feel my father's moist palm clamped over my nose and mouth. I couldn't breathe. He gestured for me to be silent, to get dressed. He had already stuffed a few of my clothes into a paper bag. He thrust it into my hands. I was confused and groggy. I didn't understand what was happening, but I didn't dare disobey my father. As we left my room, my mother met us in the hallway and grabbed for me, demanding to know what was going on. My father's hand was so quick, I had no time to think. My mother's face was surprised, then blank. She staggered back, hit the wall, slid to the floor as the Sèvres plates that had hung there rained down around her. I remember the shattering of porcelain and then the silence. She lay slumped among the pastel shards of her beloved plates. Blood dripped from a cut on her lip. I wanted to cover her. She was wearing a thin lace nightgown and had a silver cross around her neck. My father shoved me out the door, and I never saw her again.

He took me to Yemen, where we lived with my grandmother, who scolded me severely for my accent, my Western ways, and even for the color of my skin, which was for the first time in my life too light. When my father came home, he listened to her complaints and flogged me with a knotted rope that hung by a peg next to the door. Three knots. It was the largest, at the end, that hurt the most.

I quickly learned to speak like a native and discovered I had a talent for mimicry and languages. Two years later, I left for jihad. I trained near Jalalabad with brothers from all over the world. I made them laugh by speaking to each brother in the same accent in which he spoke to me. We learned to pray, fire weapons, obey a leader. I excelled and went on to more advanced lessons: how to build bombs, surveil buildings, poison dogs, withstand torture. But my spoiled stomach had yet to grow accustomed to the food. I spent many hours suffering for it. I was still uncertain. I hadn't truly learned piety.

One night I had dropped my flashlight in the latrine and was trying to make my way back to my bed in the darkness. I tripped and fell, and my knee hit a sharp stone. Tears came to my eyes. Then, as I knelt on the rocky ground, I smelled something sweet on the breeze: attar of roses. I saw him. He was walking with a half-dozen others. I knew it was him. The Chieftain. He carried a staff like the Mahdi. He radiated a soft light. I'm not lying or exaggerating. I saw it with my eyes. He raised his hand, a long, slender, dark hand like mine. He spoke to me, called me "brother." The gentleness of his voice, his manner, stunned me. My doubts fell away. I had no more trouble with the food. I no longer hated my own skin. I had come home.

It's not often that I stop to think about my past, particularly my childhood. For what I must do, my individual, personal life has to be abandoned like the useless trivia that it is. I only think about it because yesterday I once again practiced slaughter according to the holy method of *dhabh*. It was all done properly, and such was my skill that I did not allow a drop of his blood to touch my skin or clothing. I have nothing to regret, except that it might call attention to the operation.

4. Doc

My little friend Maddie should get out of the Mines before she becomes like me: disgruntled and sour. But leaving the Mines is easier said than done. The place exerts a stranglehold on people like us. It has warped our outlook and minds until we don't fit anywhere else. We're wearied by the endless sparring of intellects and overwhelmed by the flow of information, but we couldn't live without it.

What would I do without the Mines? I have few acquaintances above ground. Somehow I've never been able to get close to anyone who didn't possess a Top Secret White Damp (TSWD) clearance (White Damp is the name of a compartment of information related to especially critical terrorist threats). When talking to Uncleared Personnel (UP), I always suffer that moment of hesitation. I try not to let them know where I work, but I'm not allowed to make up a cover story, because I'm not officially under cover. How does one make small talk or any talk inside the Beltway if one can't talk about one's job? Neither can I talk about the things that absorb my interest—politics and international affairs—because my opinions are informed by classified information. The Mines claims that part of my brain. So in social settings, I end up nodding, bobbing my head until I have nearly shaken my brains loose, smiling blankly, waiting for the earliest possible moment to make my escape.

Generally I avoid social situations and keep to my own kind. We have our own unique language, customs, history in the Mines. At one time I thought outsiders didn't have the right to know about us, but my opinion is beginning to change. The public has been too happy, too carefree, too complacent in its ignorance. Too willing to let hard moral choices be made behind closed doors, where they will not prickle the general conscience. Americans think they're safe. They've sold a few civil liberties for safety. Surely vast efficient armies of protectors—with nothing but their welfare in mind— hover over them.

The public is not safe and, furthermore, there is no such thing as safety. It is a delusion, much like the other great delusions of life: the free lunch, the Easter Bunny, and efficient government.

As an intellectual exercise, I'm working on a syllabus for a course I call Mines Anthropology 101.

The course would focus on the four distinct castes which have evolved deep within our tunnels, far below the bosses. These castes are as follows: sharpers, smithies, alchemists, and drones. Inter-marriage among castes occurs now and then, but more often than not it is unsuccessful and seldom produces normal offspring.

The sharpers work in the Black Mines. They dig for ore. They wander far and wide searching for veins of information, talking fast, cutting deals. They run foreign assets or "groupers" as we call them, people who give us information in exchange for money or other favors, or for ideological reasons. Sharpers are disdainful of those who haven't spent a lifetime in the field, assuming that real knowledge can only be acquired in a seedy bar or bomb-pitted back alley. They prefer action to thought, which sometimes produces a rockslide, Mines slang for an unfortunate incident that becomes public, like the time a sharper was caught trying to plant a listening device in the brassiere of a foreign premier's mistress. A hotel security guard found him up to his elbows in her lingerie drawer just as he came across a love letter to the busy woman from a senior senator from Mississippi, who also sits on the intelligence oversight committee. My, that was ugly.

The smithies make whatever tools are needed for the trade: listening and concealment devices, disguises, what have you. They are astoundingly good—akin to magicians—and tend to be more cheerful than the other castes, because they are generally given problems they can solve, and because it is fun to make fake dog poop and exploding cigars.

The alchemists work in the White Mines. They take the raw intelligence—called slag—and attempt to purify it, sifting away the half-truths, self-serving dross, and downright lies. They transmute the rest into nuggets of insight, or so they hope. Like meteorologists, they are regularly asked to predict the future. Their job is to tell the policymaker what he needs to hear, whether he wants to hear it or not. Alchemists speak more slowly than the sharpers and often hesitate and stare at their feet. The old joke is that an extroverted alchemist is one who stares at *your* feet. Given their head, they would never act, but only think.

The drones run things. They range from the wonderful admin assistant who lights your way through the tunnels, to the rank obstructionist bureaucrats who cling to the walls like bats.

I'm an alchemist, as is Maddie. Early in my career I worked on the Evil Empire, our old Slavic nemesis. After my career imploded—no small thanks to Vaughn Sutter Wayne—the bosses shunted me off to work with an underclass of alchemists and sharpers known somewhat disparagingly as BDs or bomb dissectors. Counterterrorism experts. BDs have never gotten much respect in the Mines.

The BDs want to keep the Grand Old Democracy safe, but they can't. Things have gone too far.

Why did I never raise my middle finger, hoist up my well-larded ass, and leave? I can't stop asking myself that question. I'm certainly old enough to retire. Old enough to die. I thought about retiring four years ago in the face of yet another feckless reorganization.

Breaking into my vast stash of unused leave, I took a reconnaissance trip to my home state of Georgia with the idea of finding an estate to buy with the proceeds from my overvalued Reston hovel. I stayed with some cousins who talked of nothing but golf and duck hunting. I take it that both golf and duck hunting are intended as forms of recreation, but the allure escapes me. The entire mindless concept of recreation escapes me. The idea of spending countless hours and dollars obtaining special equipment and clothing to put a ball in a hole or a hole in a duck—to what purpose? So one can make oneself boring and unpopular by boasting "I put a ball in the hole" or "I put a hole in a duck"? When I tried to relieve the tedium by introducing a meatier topic—the remarkable similarity in the use of eschatological imagery among Salafi jihadists and certain evangelical Christians—I received only blank stares.

"You a liberal or something?" one cousin asked.

"Are you talking about shit?" said another.

I didn't bother to explain the difference between eschatology and scatology. I went into another room, closed the door, and sat down with the local news rag. I imagined it as my window to the world. I promptly packed my belongings. If I had stayed the full week, I would have become a drooling, blabbering idiot.

So I remain in the Mines, possibly until my own nose, like a smart bomb, finds the center of a powdered doughnut.

5. Maddie

Oh shit, I'm limping. At first I assume it's either an old ballet injury acting up or else it's psychosomatic. I'm going to meet Mom for lunch, and it would be just like my body to react by going gimpy. Then I look down and see that my shoes don't match. They're both black—nearly all my shoes are black—but the heels are a different height and the toes a different shape. Also, one pair is shiny and the other matte. Not that I would care, except that wearing mismatched shoes probably looks as unprofessional as wearing Mary Janes and a dirndl. Must get that dream out of my mind. . . .

I look up from my feet and see Harry Esterhaus coming toward me with that straight-shouldered, puff-chested, manager's gait. He's the boss of the BD Sector, now officially called the Central Counterterrorism Supersector. He has a head of thick, badly cut gray hair and a mustache. He looks like a tall, skinny Captain Kangaroo, but without all the pockets or the good will. He's going to try to slither right past me like the sleazy, slime-sucking snake that he is, but I sidestep directly into his path.

"Harry, I need to talk to you."

"Sorry, Maddie, I'm deeply busy. I'm on my way to the Main Shaft for a meeting." He starts to edge around me, and I make a move to block him again.

"Give me a time when we can talk. I need to brief you on a threat."

"Again, Maddie?" He shakes his head and gives me an indulgent smile. "Unfortunately, the BOM is testifying before the Esteemed Legislative Body tomorrow. I do the prebrief this afternoon and I have to attend an offsite tomorrow. I won't have a moment until the day after tomorrow."

"Day after tomorrow then."

"Early, the rest of my day is booked."

As I try to block his exit again, I stumble over my mismatched shoes, my back rewards me with a white-hot thrust of pain, and Harry escapes.

As I stand frozen with pain and watch him go, Kristin Russell appears from a side tunnel. Harry gives her a big smile and a hearty hello and they end up walking down the tunnel together and I know, just know he's telling her how well the policymakers liked the article she wrote for the PIU the other day. Kristin is what I was fifteen years ago: the pretty, sexy, brainy young thing. You can tell from the bouncy way she walks that her self-confidence is still intact. Her skirt fits perfectly over her skinny butt. Her pantyhose are free of runs, and she's wearing those high, high heels with the extremely pointy toes. Fifteen years ago I knew the names of the latest shoe styles and wore them and had a great butt. I was the one who wrote the PIU articles that got the great reviews instead of the ones judged to be Below the Level of Interest of the Policymaker—BLIP.

I inch my way to the nearest wall and lean against it, waiting for the pain to subside. I close my eyes to keep them from tearing over and remember what it felt like to be the one striding down the hallway feeling strong, capable, and confident. What happened? It's not a mystery. I can put my finger on it, the freaking moment that my life skipped its orbit and went caroming off the walls, the windows, the ceiling.

• • •

That moment was in September of 2001, but not the date you would guess. Not the day we all stood gaping at the television. We looked like hungry baby birds with our heads up, mouths open, faces blank and stupid as newborns.

"This is it," someone whispered.

This was *the big thing*. We had known it was out there, even though there were no direct references to what or where. We sensed it from what wasn't being said: a black hole in the slag. The words eddied around it. Now everything made sense, and nothing made sense. We had warned, warned, warned that the Base might commit "simultaneous mass-casualty attacks" directed against U.S. interests, but we didn't really understand what that meant. Our world was all cables scrolling down the screen, code words, a Carl Sagan–scale million bazillion slivers of information we tried to piece together like a mosaic. The words were monochrome. Now we were shocked by the colors that bloomed on the screen, orange-and-yellow flame, gray cloud, blue sky.

"All those people in the upper floors are dead," someone else said. "They're dead."

My life didn't go off track that day, it went into automatic. The squishier parts of my brain—those responsible for empathy, sorrow, and despair—froze, while the logical side took charge. I watched for a few moments, then returned to my computer to do the essentials: search the names on the passenger manifest, monitor the incoming slag, task the sharpers, build the intelligence case against the Base. I heard the guttural expiration of air when the towers collapsed. I didn't get up to look, but kept running searches.

"The Pentagon is on fire," someone said.

"I don't feel good about sitting in this building."

The announcement went out that the Mines were evacuating, except for the BDs—it felt like a punishment to us. "You failed, you stupid little bomb dissectors." *Slap.*

Vivi Fields, my best friend, was eight and a half months pregnant with a child she and her husband had been trying to conceive for a decade. She waddled up to our boss, Ben. "If you don't mind, I'd like to get out until the planes are out of the air, an hour maybe. I have a child to think about now."

"What's an hour? You want to lose most of the country's terrorism expertise in one blow?" someone else said.

Ben assumed a stern, righteous, TV-hero tone. "This is your job. Nobody's going anywhere."

The Boss of Mines and his senior staff had already retired to a low, inconspicuous building nearby, but it wouldn't have looked good to have the BDs leave the main building, even for an hour.

Technicians began to take up sections of the floor panels, stretching the wires and cables needed to turn the main conference room into a crisis center. Their activity transformed the tunnels—our avenue of escape should a plane hit our building—into an obstacle course. I imagined our low ceiling collapsing down on us, burning jet fuel. . . .

A plane crashed in Pennsylvania.

Someone said, "The President's on the phone." Several of us jumped up to be available to provide what little we knew. I saw Ben mouth the words "Oh, fuck" as he took the receiver.

I remember that time as one long day that stretched for weeks. The year before, a fast-moving cancer had cut down my father. I was there for the last month of it, helping my mother take care of him at home. I had no control over anything. I moved according to the instructions of doctors, the whims of the disease, and the continually changing schedule of medication: 3:00 A.M. Ciprofloxacin, 5:00 A.M. tube feeding, 7:00 A.M. morphine. This felt just the same. I had a 3:00 A.M. crisis report, 5:00 A.M. talking points, 7:00 A.M. teleconference. No time to acknowledge the grim reaper who hung over my shoulder, no time to watch the apocalypse bloom again and again across the television screen.

We didn't have time to eat in the cafeteria, which closed after 4:00 P.M. anyway, and logistics told us that regulations forbid the government to provide us with food. Several senior managers chipped in for cartloads of croissants, fruit, and coffee. Spouses sent in casseroles, brownies, and bags of tortilla chips. Someone from logistics donated sample sizes of toothpaste, deodorant, soap, etc., and laid them out on a conference table. The Mines provided cots and blankets.

The ladies' room might as well have been atop Mount Everest. Every time I tried to reach it, someone cut me off with a question or tasking. I needed coffee to stay awake, but that complicated the problem. Once I finally got there, the cleaning crew had one of those orange NO ENTRY cones in front of it. I must have kicked that fucker fifteen feet down the hall before I went in.

After forty hours, I went home for fresh clothes. That's when I found out Rick, my charming but mendacious sharper husband, hadn't been home either. I shouldn't have been surprised, he hadn't responded to any of my messages. In hindsight, all the indicators were there: the frequent so-called language immersion weekends at an off-site facility, the designer silk briefs that abruptly appeared to replace his frayed boxers, the vague whiff of someone else's perfume that emanated from the cushions of our couch. I'd filed it all away in my "read later" folder. And I call myself an intelligence officer.

But that wasn't the moment that I lost it, either. I remained calm, logical. Divorce was the obvious choice, not because he'd had an affair, but because he was so tacky as to take advantage of the Strikes for a tryst. Being single again would not be a problem. In fact, the idea had immediate appeal. No more guilt about neglecting someone at home while I worked late.

At that moment a sterile cot at work seemed infinitely preferable to our unmade bed—had he ever slept here with her? It was probably teeming with adultery germs. I took a shower, packed a few things, and headed for the door.

I'd almost made my escape when the phone rang. My stomach clutched as always at a late-night call. The voice blared in my tired ears like a fire alarm. "Madeleine, where in heaven's name have you been? I've been trying to reach you for days. I thought you must have burned up in the attack. Are you all right?"

That was back when Mom was still living in Durham, North Carolina, the childhood home she moved back to after my father's death. At her first word, I realized that I should have called her.

"I'm fine, Mom. I don't work in the Pentagon. You know that."

"Since when?"

"Mom, the Mines have never been in the Pentagon, and, if there is a merciful Lord in heaven, never will be."

"Why weren't you at your desk?"

"I had to move to another desk. Everyone has been shuffled around. I'm sorry. I didn't realize you would be so worried. I should have. I haven't had any time to think."

"You have no idea the awful things I've been imagining here by myself."

My shoulders slumped with my guilt. Of course I should have called her.

"Where have you been sleeping?"

"A cot in the office."

"What have you been eating?"

"Lots of people brought food."

"Junk, I bet. How are you getting your washing done? Have you been taking your medication?"

Another silence. I didn't care to tell her that I had a friend pick me up a bale of underwear at Costco. I certainly wasn't going to tell her I hadn't taken my antacids in three days, that I'd been trying to call Rick to pick them up.

"I'm coming up there to take care of you."

"No. Mom, no. I'm serious, you don't have to do that. No. Absolutely not. I'm good. Fine. Peachy. Mom, I've never been better. Really."

"It's settled. I'll be there tomorrow." Click.

Even that was not the moment that I lost it.

That moment came later, as I reentered the Mines through the new entrance: a long, broad tunnel of green glass under the black night sky, strangely empty of the blinking red lights of planes landing at National Airport. At the far end of the tunnel stood the machines that scanned our Mines tags as we entered and exited. Nearby sat the neat, blue-blazered Security Control Uniformed Duty Officers (SCUDOs, we call them). Behind them was a giant American flag against the dark windows. It must have been there when I left earlier that evening, but I hadn't turned around to see it. In fact, since I had left the Mines after dark, I hadn't yet seen any of the thousands of flags that had blossomed on car antennas and front porches. This was the first one.

I started to sob. All the television images flashed across my mind. The flame, smoke, and dust when the towers crashed. This flag brought me to my knees in the middle of the tunnel. Something threatening about it. Patriotism against the backdrop of a dark, impenetrable cloud of national fear. At that moment I had a flash into the future that terrified me.

As I sat bawling my eyes out, one of the SCUDOs got up from behind the security kiosk and came down the hall toward me, while the other one stepped to the side—presumably to get a clear shot in case I got violent—and watched.

"Is there a problem, ma'am?" the young SCUDO said politely.

I sniffled and pointed to the flag. "First one I've seen since the Strikes."

"The first flag? Where have you been?"

"BD crisis center."

"You work there?"

"Yes."

The SCUDO's face was sympathetic. He offered me his hand. I took it and he helped me up. He adjusted his footing as I pulled heavily on him.

"Are you okay now, ma'am? Can I get you a Coke? You need to go to Medical?"

"No, thanks. I'm fine now."

Really, I'm fine.

• • •

Mom's still living in my basement. Bored with retirement and lit by the grassfire of patriotism sweeping the country after the Strikes, she applied to work in the Mines a month after she came up here to take care of me. She sold the house in Durham along with half of her belongings. Now my house is filled with cozy lamps on clever end tables on braided rugs. The walls are painted pink to match my mother's flowered, overstuffed furniture. Despite my protests, at every gift-giving occasion, she buys me cartloads of pastel-colored, rabbit-themed tchotchkes. In my foyer, a four-foot-tall resin rabbit butler greets visitors with a bucktoothed smile. He holds a tray in one hand and a giant ticking pocket watch in the other. My refrigerator is filled with hearty Southern foods in Beatrix Potter bowls. I have enough lima beans in my freezer to survive a siege. Everything is obsessively clean. I have no life.

Mom had spent twenty-five years teaching English on military bases, but overnight she became an expert on the Mines. The bureaucracy was her nirvana. She fell in love with the Byzantine rules, regulations, forms, accesses, and security measures. She landed in the SSS, Safety and Security Sector—where else? She checks desks to make sure that the secure (black) telephone line is at least one meter from the open (white) telephone line. She keeps a measuring tape in her purse. She has unlimited space to exercise righteous indignation. She is blissfully happy.

And I have to have lunch with her because I said I would. Never mind the terrorist threat, Mom doesn't accept excuses. My back is killing me, but I suck it up, peel myself from the wall, and put one foot in front of the other.

I see her coming thirty feet down the tunnel as we approach the cafeteria from opposite directions, walking by a long, sunny wall of windows. She had me when she was barely twenty, so she's not that old, not even sixty yet, and she looks fabulous. She's got that aging Southern belle elegance brightened with a flirtatious edge. Too bad we spent most of my formative years moving from one military base to another—I'll never have it. She's wearing a smart fuchsia suit with matching heels. I mean the heels not only match each other, they match her *suit*. Her hair is perfectly coifed, albeit a bit big for this latitude. The gray hairs earned in the classroom are covered with a honey brown wash.

Skipping "hello," she launches into a critique studded with exclamation points. "You're a fright! If I'd seen you this morning, I would never have let you leave the house that way! My heavens to Betsy, your shoes don't match! That is scandalous! Get home and change right now before I have to spank your little bottom!"

"Morning, Mom."

"I am dead serious, Madeleine, you can't walk around all day like this! It reflects poorly on your mother!"

"I can't go home."

Mom steers us into the crowd entering the cafeteria. My face gets hot, and I feel like I'm back in high school trying to pretend that I am in no way related to this woman.

"Let's get our food, then I'll meet you beyond the cash registers," I say.

"No, let's stick together."

We reach the trays and utensils, and Mom selects the cleanest-looking knife, fork, and spoon, wraps them neatly in a napkin, and places it on my tray.

"I can get my own stuff."

"The last time you got a knife with a dried spot of jam on it and you used it."

"And yet I still live."

"Don't use that tone with your mother. I'll get you water. Eight glasses a day will improve that pasty complexion of yours. I cannot believe a daughter of mine would leave her home without proper makeup. Cheeks must blush like peaches."

Mom goes to the water dispenser and begins to examine the tray of water-spotted glasses. I duck behind a crowd of hungry miners. I'm thinking, *Peaches, poppies, explosions, oh my!* How in the hell am I going to get away from this woman and back to my threat? I could walk off, but she would follow me back to my office and disrupt everyone. Best to just get this wretched lunch over with. I need mood food, maybe three pecan tarts with dark-chocolate chunks chased with a double espresso. But this would be a bad choice for lunch with Mom, who got an associate's degree in nutrition in her forties just for the hell of it. I grab one tart and take a piece of pizza from the warming table. I pay for my lunch and catch sight of Mom waving from across the cafeteria.

As I approach the table, she frowns and shakes her head.

"Pizza!" she says.

"It has meat, dairy, vegetables, and grains. Tomato sauce is full of lycopene."

She looks at me doubtfully, lets it pass. "I have a present for you!" She digs into her large fuchsia purse.

"Mom, I don't need any more rabbits, really."

"I couldn't resist! I found a Web site that specializes in bunnies! Open it! It's just the most precious thing."

I tear the paper off yet another porcelain bunny, this one with a big hole it its stomach containing a net thingie. I have no idea what it is. I give Mom a perplexed look.

"It's a scrubby keeper for your kitchen sink!"

I really hate fake rabbits, especially ones depicted wearing clothing, particularly vests. Why are all these rabbits wearing vests? What is it with the vests?

"Thanks, Mom," I say meekly, because what else can I do? My house is going to collapse under the weight of fake bunnies, but what can I do?

"I'll be late coming home tonight, so don't worry." Mom spoons some succotash into her mouth and chews daintily, occasionally flashing me a coy, close-lipped smile. In answer to my surprised expression, she swallows and says, "Even a mother should have an evening to herself now and then."

I find this strange behavior for a woman who usually complains about being left alone. I file it in my "read later" folder and change the subject. "I have to make it a short lunch, I'm meeting with some of the other BDs on the current threat."

"Oh, there's always a threat." Mom waves off my protest in Scarlett O'Hara fashion. "If you skipped lunch every time a threat popped up, you'd starve. You eat too fast. You need to slow down and savor your food. That's why you have such a bad stomach."

I spear a pepperoni slice and chew it with deliberate slowness, even though the rubbery greasiness is vaguely unpleasant and I can imagine already what it will feel like sitting in my gut.

Mom dabs at her lips with a napkin, being careful not to smudge her gloss. "You need to take a good time-management class. If you managed your time more efficiently, you wouldn't have to work late so much. You would get through your inbox every day and not have another intelligence failure."

I stab a mushroom. Mom has reduced the Strikes to a time-management failure. Thank you, Mom. I make a weak effort at self-justification. "We get thousands, *thousands* of cables a day on jihadists. I don't think that memorizing the top ten rules of time management will help me get through all of that." I knock the mushroom off my fork. I'm not going to eat it. It has a funny look to it.

"Well, it will certainly help you to get through more of it, as well as to keep your room neater, and have some time left over to improve your personal grooming."

"Maybe I can bake my own bread and take up ballroom dancing."

"Don't get sarcastic with me. Of course a working woman shouldn't try to make her own bread. But a ballroom dancing class is a good idea. Who knows, you might meet someone. Maybe Rick will get jealous and come back."

I impale a ring of green pepper on my knife and lift it to eye level. "Look at this. Limp, gray-green, baptized in pepperoni juice. It's disgusting. Who would eat this?"

"You're the one that chose pizza, and you've hardly touched it. What a waste."

"Mom, I've got a meeting. I have to run."

"You haven't eaten a thing! Are you going to go home and change those shoes?"

I wrap my pecan tart in a slick brown government-grade recycled napkin and stand up.

"This is not your standard threat. It's big, and I have to go."

She gives me that hurt-mother look. I feel a flash of guilt, then remember I'm approaching forty and still let this woman live with me.

"Aren't you going to take your scrubby bunny?"

I grab the damn thing. "See ya," I say without pausing for a good-bye peck. I limp down the hall thinking, *Fuck, fuck, fuck.*

6. A Voice with Many Names

I wake up after only an hour's nap, even though I don't go to work until this evening and I could have slept longer. I need to run through my lists again. In school they used to tease me about my lists, but they're essential to the organization and successful completion of any complex endeavor.

Perhaps because I'm tired, the past keeps rising up, no matter how hard I try to suppress it.

Green eyes. My mother had eyes the color of Islam, but she was Catholic and fond of lighting candles and making the sign of the cross. I didn't try to see her when I returned to France and enrolled at the university. She was part of the old, sinful life from which I had to separate myself, untangling my attachments thread by thread so I could devote my whole being to jihad. Perhaps she died when my father struck her. I think of her as dead.

I tried to study computer science at the university, but it held no interest for me. What fascinated me was men's minds and hearts, and how they could be molded, bent, and even broken. I discovered it first in darkened theaters at films and plays. I watched, fascinated, as emotions played across the faces of the audience. A single image could awaken laughter or sadness or fear in a hundred pairs of eyes at once, an image growing out of other images already lodged in the mind, but also somehow new and shocking. Such a thing, if it is an artful combination of the familiar and the unknown, can drive away whatever thoughts were there before. What would it take to cleanse the evil thoughts, prejudices, and lustful, greedy urges of a society? Only fear can dislodge what is old and embedded. Fear cleanses and alters. How to create fear? To raise it to a level that can transform the masses? I became convinced that this was a science one could learn, like the science of computers.

I began to take classes in theater. I learned how to stage plays, to orchestrate the movement of many players, to achieve perfection in timing. As an actor, I was brilliant at accents. I could listen to tapes and sound like anyone, an Irishman, a German, an Italian. I had a wonderful voice and presence for playing the tragic Shakespearian kings. I learned to pretend to feel what I didn't feel, to make other people react with their hearts. My brothers were skeptical, even derisive about my studies, but I convinced them that such skills would be useful, when the time came.

They have been useful, but I fear that what I did yesterday will destroy everything. I didn't particularly crave that one man's fear, so I crept up behind him and slaughtered him kindly, with a sharp knife. It is fear on the mass scale, not the individual, that fascinates me. I didn't want to kill him, but there was no choice. He saw something he shouldn't have.

7. Doc

Maddie appears at the opening of my relatively spacious corner cubicle—relatively spacious in the sense that I can swivel in my chair without mashing my patella against the file cabinet. Few BDs can make that claim. With no windows in the vault, my cluttered corner is rather like a dead end on a back alley where the eddying wind has dumped a heap of scrap paper.

I direct a questioning glance at Maddie, who delicately shifts her weight from one leg to the other. Her feet often ache—hallux rigidus left over from her time on pointe. She wraps a strand of loose hair around a tiny thumb and tugs.

"Well?" I say.

"I thought of another way you could help me," she says. "But I couldn't ask . . . someone of your senior status. . . ."

"Status as well-paid deadwood?"

"Doc, you are hardly deadwood. That last research paper on extremist ideology should be on every apprentice BD's reading list."

"Cut the fulsome praise. What do you want, Maddie? If it involves spending time with your mother, you may not ask."

"It doesn't. It's just that I need a double espresso from the Starbucks to go with my pecan tart and I told Mom that I had to get to a meeting, so I couldn't stop to get it, and I can't go back down because she might see me."

"So you'd like me to be an accessory to lying to your mother because you're too much of a coward to tell her the truth?"

"Exactly. Also, I'd like you to come to our brainstorming session. I need to get the people who follow the cells together with the ones who cover techniques and finances to see if we can figure out what some of the new code words mean."

"Will any managers be present?"

"Hell no, we need to be productive."

"I'll be back with your double espresso shortly. Don't you ever eat anything healthy?"

"How many mothers do I need in this building? Besides, what's that?" She points to my CD-ROM drive, which, like all such drives in the Mines, has been disabled to prevent people from downloading and removing information, part of a losing battle against technology. I now use the CD holder to hold cookies so I don't lose them among my papers. At this moment there is a giant oatmeal raisin cookie there.

"Oatmeal has been proven to lower cholesterol. Besides, I ate lunch first, did you?"

"Okay, okay. Get me a venti latte with two percent and two shots of espresso. That covers the dairy food group." She hands me a five. "And be sure to tell Wynona it's for Maddie. She makes mine extra special."

"Wynona?"

"The barista."

"Barista?"

"Just get my coffee, Doc. And don't forget to tell Wynona it's for me. That's very important."

• • •

Yes, there is a Starbucks in the Mines. Ours sells only beverages, no clever mugs with Latin phrases, espresso machines, or bags of beans, but you can still obtain a variety of pretentious concoctions distantly related to coffee—the way a lemur is distantly related to a human. Coffee with caveats. I stand in a long line and listen to people roll off their lengthy orders, which must specify size of cup; percentage of fat; whether milk be of the cow or soybean; flavor and number of pumps of syrup; presence or absence of whipped cream, sprinkles, sugar, and a partridge in a pear tree.

It's my turn. I refuse to say *venti*. There is nothing wrong with the English word *large*.

"Yeah, hon?" the woman behind the counter says. Involuntarily, I take a step back. She is tall, flushed, and meaty rather than obese. She is vigorous—almost violent—in her movements. Her hair has been exposed to too many chemicals and radiates from her head in a nightmarish blond-streaked pouf. Her name tag reads WYNONA.

"Large latte with two shots."

Wynona points to a stack of cups. "You mean a venti?"

I swallow hard and hold my ground. "I mean a large."

She huffs and points. "This size?"

"Yes. I spent three years in Rome. Do you know that real Italians would laugh themselves silly at the coffee here?"

"Whoop de do fer you." She bangs the old grounds out of the filter and starts to steam the milk. "I'm from Manassas. Never been anywhere. My big treat is going to Burton Oil Park for a double-header, but since the murder, I'm half afraid to even do that."

I know this tiresome woman would like me to ask her about the murder. She's one of those people who loves to dwell on the most lurid news of the day. I refuse to indulge her taste for the macabre. I have more important things to consider than one random killing. I merely stare at her.

She shrugs and gives up any further attempt at small talk. "You want any whipped cream?"

"No. Oh, and by the way, this is for Maddie."

"You should've said so right off." Wynona dumps the latte she has just made down the sink and starts over, much to the dismay of the man standing behind me. In a moment she presents me with another latte, which is presumably more special than her earlier effort.

"That will be four ninety-five."

"For a cup of coffee?" I hand over Maddie's five, shocked.

"No, for a venti latte, two shots. Have a nice day, hon."

When I first entered the Mines we all drank from one cracked coffeepot in the corner of the office—ten cents a cup. We had one jar of nondairy creamer. The contents had to be chipped loose. I used the same Styrofoam cup for a month or more. Now that Starbucks is here, there's no such thing as a coffee mess. Apprentice alchemists who can't afford a house pour their money into this place. Appalling. Absolutely appalling.

I walk back to our vault, working myself into a geriatric grumble about changes in the Mines. Then I remember that I can't exactly call the apprentice alchemists spoiled. While I was paying my ten cents for a cup of coffee, I shared a nice office with one other alchemist. I went home after eight hours. I could afford to buy a house on a Mines schedule-9 salary. Those things are out of the question today. I suppose I should grant them their pricey coffee concoctions. What else have they got to live for?

• • •

The meeting is in the large conference room of our vault. Only a handful of alchemists show, despite Maddie's urgent e-mails. She leans in the doorway gnawing at her tart and glaring at the clock. At five after she says, "Well, I guess this is it."

Maddie sits down next to me. "Where's Vivi?" She names an old friend of hers, the second most experienced BD after Maddie herself. Back in the days when Hezbollah was the topic of hot policymaker interest, it was largely female alchemists who defied their managers to devote time to the obscure financier who would later become the Chieftain.

A painfully young alchemist with pale, flawless skin leans forward and opens her mouth. As she hesitates, I notice a gold ring in her tongue. Ten years ago you could have strip searched every alchemist in the Mines and not found a single body piercing—other than the occasional ear—and no tattoos. Now looking down this conference table I see both. No matter that the tattoo is a Latin aphorism concerning vigilance, I still find it appalling.

The young lady, whose name is Kristin Russell if I remember correctly, speaks. "Vivian got a tasker from Beth Dean at Pent-COW and can't come."

PentCOW, or the Pentagon Council of the Wise, is an advisory body created by this administration to produce premasticated intelligence that can be more easily digested by the President than the stuff that comes out of the Mines. They also serve to keep us from doing our jobs by laying on so many taskings that we have time for little else.

"So, Kristin, what does Dean want now?" Maddie asks.

"She's asking about Britain's experience in Afghanistan in the nineteenth century."

Maddie pops the last of her tart into her mouth, makes a face, and swallows. "So Vivi is off writing history while bombs are ticking. What does Dean think we are? The Library of Congress? Doesn't she have staffers with access to Google? Where are our *cojones*-free managers? Who accepted this tasking? Who assigned Vivi of all people?" Maddie brushes crumbs off the table onto the floor and leans forward, eyes sparking. "Why can't somebody look that woman in the face and say, 'In the face of a major terrorist threat, do you really want to tie up one of our most experienced terrorism experts in historical trivia? Why don't you read a book on it? It would be good for you. In fact, why, all these years after invading a country you know squat about, have you not read this stuff?' Who is Dean's briefer? I have half a mind to—"

"Maddie," I say under my breath, "it's pointless to waste your energy on indignation. All it does is roil the gastric juices."

"I'd like to roil Dean's gastric juices with an outboard motor,"

Maddie whispers to me. Out loud she says, "Thanks for coming." She opens a tattered government-issue spiral notebook. "I don't know everyone here, so let's go around the room."

Except for Vernon Keene, the alchemists in attendance are young, most with less than two years experience in counterterrorism. Vernon was an ex–Empire analyst brought over after the Strikes, so he qualifies as a veteran. I feel a bit of sympathy for the young ones. For the first year or two, being a BD is like falling down the March Hare's hole. Names and the meanings of code words shift like sand under your feet. There are countless characters named Abu Muhammad or Abu Ali. Each man trails a string of aliases. Terrorist groups emerge, split, and rename themselves. The downpour of slag is unrelenting.

"I'm Brad Allen, BSWAS." (That's Base Special Weapons and Activities Subshaft.) The voice is curt, and the face self-assured and supercilious. Young master Brad has taken the head of the table, despite being the most junior apprentice in the room. He is leaning back, one foot propped up on the table, no materials for taking notes. Evidently his brain retains everything without the jotted reminder. He has brought a bag of Doritos, which he is chewing loudly. "I'm not here for the brainstorming session. My face boss sent me here to ask why you're having this meeting. This is really our turf."

Oh dear.

Maddie begins speaking with exaggerated slowness, as if explaining to a toddler how to tie a shoe. "I am having this meeting because as a senior alchemist it is my job to make sure that nothing falls through the cracks. We are under a major terrorist threat, and we can't afford to talk about turf. You could get your ass blown off defending your turf."

Brad cracks an unpleasant smile. "I'm not worried about getting my ass blown off."

"You should be," Maddie says.

"We rolled up the problematic cell," Brad says with swagger in his voice, as if he had personally wrestled the terrorists to the ground and cuffed them. "Besides, who anointed you senior alchemist?"

Maddie speaks more slowly, deliberately. "I was warning about the Chieftain before anybody else thought he was a threat. Back when he was just a rich Arab financier investing in the Afghan jihad. You know that background reading folder that they handed you when you walked in the door? I wrote most of it. I was covering the Chieftain back when your biggest accomplishment was growing pubic hair."

The young alchemists' mouths form a ring of tender O's around the table, Vernon snickers, and I cover my face with my hands. Maddie never used to say things like this out loud, but recently she seems to have crossed over some restraining line and now she doesn't care what she says.

"And yet the Chieftain is still with us," Brad says.

Maddie doesn't blink. "If you don't want to attend this meeting go back to your face boss and tell him I'll stop by his desk later this afternoon for a friendly chat. If you do want to attend this meeting, I suggest you sit up and take notes, and quit rocking back on that chair before you fall over and crack your skull."

Brad makes an abrupt move to stand up. Too abrupt. The back legs of the chair skid out with a screech and he goes over backward, his head striking the wall so sharply it leaves a dent. Two alchemists jump to his aid. Maddie leans over and whispers in my ear, "Life rarely provides such instantaneous satisfaction. That was way better than an orgasm." My face turns hot. Maddie laughs. I try to analyze that laugh for signs of incipient madness.

After Brad stomps out, introductions continue. A look of severe impatience comes over Maddie's face. Nonetheless, she pushes ahead.

"I called this meeting because I'm seeing a lot of things that scare the hell out of me, both in the slag and in this office. I believe there's a major terrorist attack in the offing, one that was probably moved forward after the Lahore arrests. We're not prepared to cope with the aftereffects of a big attack, much less avert it." Maddie faces a ring of skeptical faces and takes a deep breath. "Let me lay out my evidence."

This she does, methodically ticking off points with a sharp movement of her index finger in the air. "The term *holy swarm* has appeared three times recently, but we don't know what it means. The same with *red cloud*, which was used by a graduate of Camp Toxic. We do know that *dance* means an attack and we are seeing it in conjunction with the first two terms. We've also heard facilitators talk about *the poison river*, our own Potomac. Anybody worried yet? Oh, and as you all know, the chatter has dropped off to nothing in the last few days, which means the countdown may have begun."

Several young alchemists stop fidgeting and let their coffee grow cold. "We've left ourselves dangerously vulnerable," Maddie says. "Forgotten veins everywhere. Some dangerous operatives and facilitators have dropped off the radar screen. People who were plotting before the Strikes. I've been going through the old slag. I made a list, and I'm going to send each of you back with the names that fall under your accounts."

Kristin is the only one with the nerve to talk back to Maddie. "You were just complaining about BDs doing history," she says, "and now you want us to go back to the slag heaps from years ago? We have more than we can read from yesterday."

Maddie glares at her with undisguised hostility. "The support teams for this attack—if that's what we're looking at—weren't put in place yesterday. They've probably been around for a decade or more. So we have to go back to lost veins."

"We don't have any lost veins in chem subshaft and I have another meeting," says Vernon. "So, if you'll kindly excuse me—"

"Not so fast." Maddie holds up her hand. "I have a number of names for you." She points to a sheet filled with small, spidery handwriting. "For example, here's a guy, Abu Muhammad al-`Attar. He attended Camp Toxic and then to flew to Europe. We lost him. He was a member of a North African cell that was actively plotting right before the Strikes. We nicknamed them the Perfumers in honor of al-'Attar. Where is he now? What's he up to?" Maddie thrusts the paper at Vernon.

"Oh, I knew about him," Vernon says. It's his standard answer to everything. "He's not active anymore."

"Terrorists get blown up, but they rarely retire altogether," Maddie says. "That's why 401(k)s have never been popular in the terrorist world. Even with all the people they lose to bombs and bullets, the Base has a much lower turnover rate than this section of the Mines. He has more of his pre-Strikes personnel than we do. You can't dismiss someone who has apparently been inactive for a few years."

Vernon takes the paper reluctantly and slips out the door. I judge the odds of him actually following up on Maddie's leads are slim.

The other alchemists grow visibly uneasy as Maddie passes out her lists. "I don't know if I can justify this to my face boss. It will take time," someone says.

"And if a bunch of human beings get blown up because you didn't do it, can you justify it to your conscience?" Maddie responds.

Looks are exchanged. This remark seems to strike the young alchemists as somewhat unprofessional, too emotional, perhaps a bit unbalanced. I'm starting to wonder myself about Maddie's balance. Lately she strikes me less like an alchemist on top of her game and more like a ballerina spinning out of control. *Hmmm*, that sounds sexist even to me. I'd better watch myself.

Back at my desk I scan the paper Maddie has given me, my list of things to check out: a suspicious connection here, a meeting there, a sudden disappearance somewhere else. All of it could be significant or none of it could be significant. I feel a wave of homesickness for my days as a Russian specialist. So much less information to sort back then. So much more of it made sense.

I have always been a great lover of Russian literature, but my tenure as a bomb dissector has led me to reconsider Chekhov's admonition: "If in the first act you have hung a pistol on the wall, then in the following one it should be fired. Otherwise don't put it there." How sensible and neat. How it satisfies our psychological needs. And how it leads us to false conclusions, false expectations. This is how the art of bomb dissection differs from the art of fiction. In fiction there is a pistol above the mantel and it must go off. In our world, there is an AK-47 above the mantel, a basket full of grenades on the table, a half kilo of plastic explosive under the couch cushion, ricin in the candy dishes, and sarin in the air vents. And none of it is significant, because in the end it is the pistol hidden in the drawer that kills you.

8. A Voice with Many Names

I've been in this small room too long and it has made me entertain thoughts I should have banished long ago. No point in regretting the slaying. The Poppy was angry, but I had no choice and it can't be undone. I'll deal with the consequences as they occur. I can't afford afford a moment of doubt. I make a few assignments to the brothers and walk outside. Whenever I need to "screw my courage to the sticking place" as the lady would say, I make the trip south into Virginia and drive past the mansions of the powerful. I never see people in the sterile, clipped green yards, not even children playing. The minister of defense lives over there, in the house with the turrets. His deputy is two blocks away.

I drive carefully and obey the signs. I can't afford the smallest traffic violation, especially now. I burned everything after the slaughter, but there are always traces. I had to go to great pains to cover a moment of carelessness, and it has taught me that there can be no more carelessness. No moments of hesitation. Only courage.

It buoys my courage to catch sight of the entrance to the Mines, located among the tacky mansions of the rich and powerful. I slow as I pass so that I can take a long look down that road, to where the guards stand. I do it because I can and because it calms me. They live behind a razor-wired fence, while I'm free. I know where they are. They can't say the same for me. Are they afraid? It makes me laugh again to think of it.

"Hi, ya'll. Hot enough fer ya?" I call out, but the windows of my car are closed and no one can hear me. I laugh.

After I leave the Mines behind, I go about some late, necessary errands. I approach the ATM machine and remove only a modest amount of cash, enough to buy some more strontium salts, just to make sure there is enough. I buy only small amounts at a time and never from the same place. I have purchased supplies from one end of this country to the other. The movements of my body are slow, deliberate. My fingernails are clean, my face shaven, my plaid shirt ironed.

If someone approaches as I go about my business, I give a friendly smile, speak in an American accent, a Southern accent. It makes them smile because it's so incongruous with my face. That is the role I chose to play when I came here, a brilliant choice, I think. I'm a good old Southern boy, whose mother came from one of those "furrin" countries—hard to tell which from my mongrel features. I'm a boy with some foreign blood who was raised a proper redneck. I actually met someone like that once and knew instantly that this would be my story. The accent was easy enough for me to acquire and my Southerner is an easygoing soul, a man of few words. I even drive a pickup with a SUPPORT OUR TROOPS ribbon on the side, right next to the Jesus fish. I chose the name "Junior." It is a constant source of amusement to me.

I finish my transaction and get back on the road. I smile and wave a thank-you to the driver who allows me to merge.

The only thing I fear is failure. I repeat the instructions I've made for myself: Walk without footprints, act without hesitation, pray without ceasing. Death will be the final purification. I found my safe anchor in the Koran, in prayer, in all that is good, and pure, and holy. It quieted the discordant noise of my brain.

Never has our faith been under such a grave threat. I'm not a violent man. I'm an artist, an actor. I take no pleasure in the sight of blood, but blood is my paint. And this country of infidels is my canvas. I have learned to see the beauty of terror. I must act. No one can sit on the sidelines and hope to reach Paradise. The final battle is upon us. We aren't fighting for today, for ourselves, but for all eternity.

9. Doc

I stay at my desk into the evening, working on Maddie's assignments. The more I think about it, the more I think she's right: There's a cell out there we lost track of and they're planning an imminent attack. They're hiding somewhere in the slag under fake names. They took a trip, went to a camp, or met a known terrorist and somewhere it is recorded in the intelligence record, among millions of such details. If it happens, you will wonder that we couldn't see it, that not one of all our experts could trace a line from point A to point B to point C. Points as numerous as stars.

You can understand nothing of the Mines if you don't know the nature of slag. With my poor, old, computer-tired eyes, I tend to print more of it than the younger people, who are apt to read from the screen. I've mentioned slag before. It is the term for the daily influx of intelligence from human and technical collection. It includes the output of the spy satellites and other electronic eavesdroppers, selected foreign press, reports from the sharpers, the diplomatic service, the Internal Investigative Organ, and military attachés, even the occasional blind Bahraini soothsayer. I don't know how to describe the size of the slag heaps. They pile up hour by hour in an unending, unpausing stream, as they have for decades. Thousands of reports a day, millions a year. Everything in the slag heaps is in capital letters as if screaming for attention.

It takes training to read a piece of slag. To get to the text of the reports one must scroll down through a bizarre cryptic shorthand. EARSPRING, COCKTAIL, and BRASS TACT, for example, describe the origin for the report—here the National Audio Collection Agency, the diplomatic service, and Military Intelligence Service, respectively. PINNOCHIO, FLAKE, and PRINCE describe the level of reliability of a human source. TRICKLE, STREAM, and HURL describe how prolific the source has been. HOMEAPP, NOGREEN-GRAZER, and NOZIT are controls that limit the distribution of the document. NOFUSE, RIPETOMATO, and TAILFIRE indicate the urgency of the information. And so on. This gabble of words and numbers—written haiku-like with a few words a line—runs for two-thirds of a page or more.

Once you get to the meat of a report, you often find it tainted. The source may be a suspected fabricator. Information which appears to corroborate another report may actually be "off the merry-go-round," meaning one source or intelligence service is merely quoting, not corroborating, the original report. The information may be too neatly tailored to what the source knows the U.S. government wants to hear or wants to believe. This is termed "doping the baby" and was a specialty of certain ambitious Iraqi expatriates who were angling for a U.S. invasion of Iraq. Beth Dean at PentCOW treats those reports like gospel truth. In sum, tainted reports come in many forms, but sometimes, in with the dross, they contain a nugget of truth. So they cannot be ignored entirely.

Slag is like the Bible: by picking some bits of information and ignoring others, you can make any argument you please. A good and honest alchemist will weigh all the evidence, or at least all the evidence that one pair of human eyes is capable of taking in. Sometimes, however, there emerges what we call a "hired pen," the ass-shaking prostitute of the Mines, the alchemist who will make the argument that the policymaker wants to hear. This may be done as the result of pressure—applied to managers and transferred to the lowly alchemist—or it may merely be a venal desire for career ad-

vancement or even simply for praise. Alchemists are sorry crea-
tures who work long hours and hunger for some recognition.

Sometimes, when I work late and everyone else in the vault has
gone home, I can hear a rustling of paper in some other part of the
room, a small sound that I can never quite locate. I am with those
that believe it is the ghost of that old Boss of Mines, Vaughn Sutter
Wayne. He was a lummox of a BOM, bigger than life and fond of
throwing his weight around, moving, shaking, manipulating things,
tweaking history. For him the end always justified the means, and
slag was useful more for justifying the end than for getting at the
truth. They say the old man is still sifting through the piles of paper,
removing select items, which he believes the world should never
see, altering other reports. Occasionally, he is said to slip in something he has forged himself. I don't doubt it.

So this is the slag, and somewhere, deep within its vast piles,
are the few slivers of information that—if put together and inter-
preted correctly—will lead us to the particular nest of vipers we
are seeking.

10. Maddie

It's still early in the evening and Mom said she would be out until late. She was wearing a slinky little black dress. Gladys James in a slinky black dress? Could she be seeing someone? I think about my dad, but then I quickly shut all such thoughts out of my head. It's her life. I should just enjoy the fact that I have an evening to myself, but these days a quiet night at home, alone with my thoughts, quickly turns unpleasant. All my thoughts lead back to the threat.

Holy swarm. I've heard a lot of code words in my time, but something about that one freaks me out. It popped up again today in a tape released to al-Jazeera by the Chieftain. "We will darken the sun above your heads like a holy swarm." A go signal?

Swarm: a large number or body of insects in motion; a great number of bees, led by a queen, which migrate from a hive together and seek another. *Is this a bio threat? I doubt that they would use the word that literally, but it's always a possibility.*

Swarm: a moving crowd or throng; a multitude of people in motion. *Lots of things they could do in a crowd.*

Swarm: to collect and depart, as from a hive, by flight in a body; to appear or collect in a crowd; to throng together; to congregate in a multitude; to be crowded; to be thronged with a multitude of objects in motion; to team. *Swarm of what? Jihadists? Planes? Germs?*

Social swarming. The rapid gathering of people using technologies such as cell phones, pagers, and instant messaging. *Could be used as a terrorist tactic.*

I switch on the news to see what's being reported. I invite Abu Bunny into my lap. I need his calming influence, especially after she appears on screen. The dreaded Dr. Beth Dean of PentCOW, the Prez's so-called expert on terrorism. She was one of the biggest advocates of invading Iraq, and she's been the biggest critic of the Mines.

"To use the words of the President," she says, smiling, "we must fight terrorism one country at a time."

I give her the finger and start talking to the screen, another bad habit I've developed since the Strikes. "Dingbat. You'll never break international networks one country at a time. They're countryless. You concentrate on one country, they just move. Can't you get that into your head? This isn't the Cold War anymore with its Iron Curtain keeping everyone neatly in place. It's networks, not countries. You call yourself a terrorism expert?"

Her toothy grin is undimmed by my insults. She has a blond helmet, the requisite triple strand of Republican pearls, and a coat of war paint not quite thick enough to mask a large scar on one side of her head. It looks like she melted there. Briefly, before the Evil Empire collapsed, Dr. Dean worked in the Mines as an alchemist and that's when she apparently acquired her scar. I don't know how you get injured writing papers. All sorts of rumors circulated, there was a big lawsuit, and now nobody will talk about it. Anyway, she left and she hates us and peppers us constantly with annoying, often irrelevant questions, which we must duly answer.

No matter what the interviewer asks her about, she shifts the conversation to Iran in a way that makes me nervous.

The doorbell rings. I've ordered pizza to take advantage of Mom's night out, but when I get to the door, instead of an ingratiating college kid angling for a tip, I find my ex-husband, Rick.

"Aren't you supposed to be in Bangkok?" I say without bothering to disguise the displeasure in my voice.

"Is that any way to say hello to a man who has traveled thousands of hard miles to see you?" He smiles broadly and steps inside without being invited. I resign myself to a ruined evening. Rick looks good, of course. Kind of like a war correspondent: lots of swagger, khaki, and pockets. He still has those ex–Navy SEAL muscles that I fell in love with. The gray at his temples and lines around his eyes soften his face and make it more approachable. It annoys me, because I know my own face looks sharper, warier, even scarier. Nothing sagging but nothing relaxing either.

"Hard miles?" I say. "You traveled at government expense, business class, and you probably had four whiskey sours on the way and got the telephone numbers of half the flight attendants. What brings you here? I know it wasn't me."

Rick whips his right hand from behind his back and presents me with a bunch of yellow roses. "Yellow for a somewhat threatening situation," he says with what he probably believes is a charmingly sheepish expression on his face.

I take the bouquet warily. "Why are you here, Rick?"

He examines my face. "You're not the least bit happy to see me, are you?"

"Should I be?"

"Well, you used to love me. A great deal, as I recall." He's looking around now, quizzically. "It looks like Beatrix Potter had an orgy here. What the hell is this?" He points to the huge butler rabbit by the door. He gives the rabbit's pocket watch a push, and it swings back and forth. "Trying to hypnotize visitors?"

"Rick, state your business and get out."

He holds up his hands. "Hey, don't get mad at me. I'm not the one responsible for you living with your mother, unless heartbreak led you to it." He shakes his head and laughs, quietly at first and then louder. "I never would've believed you would allow this."

I raise my middle finger. "Rick, thank God you've been out of the country, otherwise I would have gotten a repetitive motion injury from flipping you the bird."

"I told my old man that I should've just written you a letter, but he insisted that I come and tell you in person."

Thanks a bunch, Doc, I think. I wait to hear what Rick has to tell me, but he says nothing. "Well?" I finally say.

He makes his voice soft, pitying. "I'm sorry, Maddie, but I'm getting married again."

"So?"

"So? Aren't you a little bit sad? You loved me."

"Not as much as you loved you."

"I try to be sensitive and thoughtful and this is what I get." He points to my middle finger, which is still raised and will continue to be raised until he is out of my house.

"Don't let the door hit you in the ass on the way out."

"Fine. I'm outta here. You're so cold, Maddie. So cold."

" 'Bye, congratulations to you and condolences to your bride. I hope you didn't pick some poor little Thai girl who was desperate to come to the United States."

He backs down the sidewalk. "No, actually, she's tall, blond, and Swedish." Turning around, he almost runs into the pizza delivery man.

"In honor of my wedding, I'll pay for your pizza." With a flourish, he hands the boy a few bills, tells him to keep the change, and heads for his car.

I don't even care to know how Rick met a Swedish bride in Thailand. I take the pizza from the delivery boy. I put it in the refrigerator—I've lost my appetite—and consider feeding the entire bunch of roses down the garbage disposal, but the stems would jam it. So I rip off the blossoms, feed them down the disposal, and throw the stems in the trash. I've handled the situation with as much maturity as it deserves.

After the Strikes, when I confronted Rick with my knowledge of his affair, I didn't get angry. He called me "eerily calm" when I told him our marriage was over. We faced off in this room across a blank field of builder-grade neutral carpet—two people who had signed a mortgage together and somehow never made a home. I went over my prepared talking points: drivers behind the breakup, bleak prospects for reconciliation, and proposed division of property. He seemed offended that I wasn't crying. He got all dewy-eyed and his lip trembled.

I said, "Is that the pout you use to haul in a grouper?"

The lip stopped trembling. That was it. I couldn't stand to stay in the same room with the scuzzball. I told him I had to get back to work, and I left.

I sit back down in front of the TV set. It's been a while since Abu Bunny and I have had an evening to ourselves. I almost feel like this is my own house again, except that it's too neat, conventional, and too freaking pink to be my house. And of course it's too full of fake bunnies. Where's my collection of model detonators? Mom must have tossed it. Doc's right. I should boot her buns out. She's active, healthy, and capable of managing on her own, but she cries every time I suggest she get her own place.

"Do you think I should kick her out, Bunny?"

Abu Bunny has sympathetic eyes. He blinks. Of the two of us, I spend my day chasing down rabbit holes and existing in the human equivalent of a hutch, while *he* has my house to himself. I'm the one who thinks for a living, but he has endless time for contemplation. But when I need a bunny to keep me company, he is reliably there—perfect in his bunniness. On the whole he is a much more satisfying companion than Rick, who was grossly imperfect in his husbandness and never there when I needed him.

"I won't kick Mom out," I admit to Bunny, "because she's my mother and gave me life and changed my diaper and held my head over the toilet while I threw up." Maybe I'm not a natural woman or maybe I just have a weak stomach, but the whole idea of having responsibility for some other human being's bodily functions for several years is repellant to me. Even if it were my own adorable flesh and blood. The fact that I'm not willing to go through that for a child makes me more beholden to my mother for doing it for me. If I cleaned up some kid's puke, I would expect big things in return.

I'm tired, but I'm really not ready for a return trip to the poppy fields of sleep yet. I flip the news channel back on. Mercifully, Dr. Dean of PentCOW is no longer on the screen. They've moved on to the sensational murder of the week. I normally don't have a taste for this sort of thing, but then I realize that this victim is someone I have a connection to, in a fleeting way. He's thrown me a half-dozen or so bags of peanuts. I don't even like peanuts that much, but back when I was married to Rick, I would get a bag every time we went to Burton Oil Park. I did it just to see Pete, the Peanut Man, lob the nuts over a whole section of seats right to my hand. Amazing arm and amazing flair. He threw peanuts overhand, underhand, over the shoulder, and even through his legs. I never saw him miss his target. Geez, why would someone murder the guy? Feeling sick, I cut the TV off and wonder if this latest bit of nastiness will find a way into my dreams. What day of the week is it anyway? I consult the bunny calendar on the wall and see that it is still Tuesday.

I hear Mom's car in the drive. I figure it can't be a date if the gentleman isn't picking her up and dropping her off. My mom would not stand for anything so modern as meeting up with a guy somewhere. She must have gone out with some women friends. That would be a good sign, maybe an indicator that she's ready to pursue her own life and get the crap out of mine.

11. A Voice with Many Names

A long day, but the doubleheader isn't over. I must keep selling my wares until the last pitch. I'm tired and it's hard for me to play the fool, when I would like to tell these people what I think of their lives and their culture. The couples here have no sense of decency. They grab each other in public, in the middle of a ball game. Girls sit on the boys' laps, and boys touch whatever they want to touch. I avert my eyes and feel sickened. Sometimes I call out to them, "Hey, y'all, get a room!" Their surprise at my incongruous accent ruins the romantic moment. I laugh.

I had a curly-haired girlfriend when I was at the university in France. She was a romantic and watched too many movies. She used tears and sighs in an effort to control me. It made me want to break her small, upturned nose. It made me understand how my father could strike my mother. I try to remember that blow was necessary to end my old life. I used to imagine my girlfriend lying in the place of my mother, wearing a flimsy lace nightgown and bleeding from the lip. My girlfriend said she would kill herself if I left her. I left without hesitation. She was a woman and there was nothing divine in her nature.

I thought I would die blowing up the U.S. embassy in Paris. My girlfriend worked there, and that's why I pretended to love her. I longed to purify myself in the same conflagration that killed her.

But then they laid the embassy plot aside and sent me to Yemen to train. Then they sent me here.

The Poppy was here first and had already made many preparations. Sometimes he gives me a bit of plastic explosive, some wire, or a detonator to carry with me to work. He does it so I'll become accustomed to it, so my face will betray nothing when the time comes. Through my carelessness, the Peanut Man saw the detonator. We were moving boxes of Styrofoam containers in the supply area when I reached up to a shelf. My shirt rode up, and he saw the detonator taped at my waist. It had to be done quickly. I felt no rancor toward the man. I am only angry with myself for endangering the operation.

Tonight is the first home game since the slaughter. A Tuesday night game. A moment of silence in honor of the Peanut Man at the seventh inning stretch. I lower my eyes and see a young man's hand slip into his girlfriend's clothing. No decency. No respect. Then the moment is over, and people resume shouting their orders at me.

The women I see around me now are little more than obscene mannequins, tackier than the French women. Some of the young ones try to flirt with me as I take their money and count out their change. I hand over soft drinks, hot dogs, and hamburgers. Junk food for junk people. "Ya'll take care now," I say. They giggle in delight. My accent puts everyone at ease.

These shameless girls will die loudly, in an undignified manner. Their lives and deaths will count for less than the pennies I drop into their palms.

12. Maddie

Vivi!"

She doesn't hear. She's thirty feet ahead of me, walking down the BOM Tunnel, the long corridor where starchy portraits of our defunct forefathers hang in gilt frames. The government doesn't hire the best of artists. Not a single portraitist has achieved a natural cheek color. One Boss of Mines glows like a nuclear peach. Another's face appears brushed with Pepto-Bismol. The SCUDOs have put up chrome stanchions and blue velour rope to separate the gloominati from us grubby miners. The tunnel runs along one of the courtyards. Across from the portraits is a wall of tall windows looking into a courtyard. Sunlight from the windows alternates with shadow like piano keys.

"Vivi!"

She stops in the sunlight, in front of the portrait of Vaughn Sutter Wayne. I hurry in her direction, envying her long legs. She's nearly six feet tall, but she wears flats and stoops as if trying to make herself less conspicuous. She's always dressed as if going to church in the 1960s: neat pastel suits, low heels, lace collars. If I were as tall as Vivi, I would wear neon colors and big, loud, rude clogs. I'd have 1980s shoulder pads out to there, and I would have a blast towering over my bosses. Vivi is far too sweet. It's unhealthy to be sweet in this place.

"I really wanted you to be at my meeting yesterday," I call, "I need to talk to you."

"What's up?"

I take a few seconds to catch my breath after I reach her. I glance over my shoulder to see the painted Vaughn Sutter Wayne caressing a globe in an oddly intimate, proprietary gesture that reminds me of a guy fondling his girlfriend's rump. There are two types of miners, the ones who think Wayne was the greatest BOM ever, and ones like me who think he stands for everything that can go wrong with the Mines. He oversaw it all: cooking the intelligence to suit the policy-makers' taste, backroom deals with the Esteemed Legislative Body, playing fast and loose with the laws governing intelligence collection.

"If you don't mind," I say, "let's move in front of Barton's portrait. Vaughn gives me the creeps. Sometimes I swear I can see the eyes move."

"Sure," Vivi agrees. "Barton was crazy, too, but in a kind of sweet way."

Barton was the one who was replaced after his secretary found him curled in a fetal position under his desk, sobbing. He has a wistful expression in this portrait. He must have been drugged out of his mind when he sat for the artist.

Vivi sweeps a lock of pale hair from her eyes and gives me a questioning look. I notice a deep scratch across her chin. I point. "What's that?"

"Accident. Sophie was just playing."

Sophie is her possum. Vivi is a licensed opossum rehabilitator. Yes, there really is such a thing. They even have a national organization. Vivi is the treasurer. I shake my head. She is the world's biggest bleeding heart, but also a damn good bomb dissector.

"You're going to end up rabid one of these days."

"Actually, opossums rarely contract rabies because of their low body temperature—"

"Vivi," I cut her off before she can launch into one of her favorite subjects. "I need your help. I'm convinced we're on the verge of another major strike, and I can't get anyone to listen. Everyone thinks that cell we rolled up in Lahore took care of it."

Vivi takes a deep breath. "I believe you. I don't like all of the terrorist movement we've seen lately. An awful lot of Base associates on the move. And it's suddenly too quiet."

"Exactly. Way too quiet, which makes me scared that this thing is out of our reach already."

If they're not communicating, we can't hone in on them.

Vivi looks down at her feet and bites her lip. "I don't think I can go through it again. I really don't."

"Remember before the Strikes, we were looking into a cell of North Africans who were planning something in the U.S.?"

Vivi looks up as if startled. "The Perfumers cell."

"Exactly."

"Doc was working with us on that cell. Nothing came of it."

"Right, it was one of several plots that were underway before the Strikes. The Base chose the most promising—flying planes into the towers—and set aside the rest. I think the Perfumers' plot has been reactivated. An hour ago I found a report from 2000 in which one of the Perfumers refers to 'holy swarm.' Now the same words are popping up in the slag again."

"I didn't know anyone from that cell was still alive. When they dropped off the screen, I assumed they got killed by a daisy cutter in Afghanistan."

"That's what I thought, but then Vernon Keene—you know the ex–Empire chem guy?" Vivi looks blank. "You know, shaves his head, permanent leer, wears black turtlenecks?"

"Oh, that guy. He gives me the creeps."

"Same here, but he came through for me. I asked him to check up on the head of that old cell, Abu Muhammad al-'Attar. It turns out that he now goes by the nickname 'the Poppy,' which really freaks me out, because I had one of my wizard dreams about a poppy field."

"Oh, not the wizard dream." Vivi, unlike Doc, takes my dreams seriously.

"Yes, and it was horrible. Anyway, Vernon thinks he's found the Poppy alive, well, and saying things like 'the Bear is gathering honey for the holy swarm.'"

Vivi frowns. "The Bear was the Perfumers' favorite money launderer and Abu Muhammad al-'Attar was their explosives expert."

We pause as several summer interns flounce past in tops skimpy enough to distract entire sectors full of men from their work. They disappear around a corner, and I continue in a low voice.

"Right. He had some training in chemical weapons, too. Spent two years in Camp Toxic. That's why it makes me nervous when we hear them talking about a 'red cloud.'" Camp Toxic was the BD's nickname for a terrorist training site near Jalalabad headed by a former chemistry professor from Egypt. We bombed it out of existence after the Strikes.

"So where is the Poppy these days?"

"We have two conflicting reports: one saying that he's in 'the land of the mad dogs' and one that he's 'by the poison river' living with a brother who appears to be a new member of the cell."

"Here?" Vivi turns her gaze eastward, as if she could see through the walls of the Old Shafts Building and the trees that line the parkway by the river. We figured out last year that the "poison river" had to be the Potomac, although there are analysts at Wright-Pat Air Force Base who contend that it's the Cuyahoga—an effort to beef up their budget, I suppose.

"My guess is that other operatives are with the Poppy."

"And the Poppy will probably leave on the eve of the operation. What does the Internal Investigative Organ think?"

"The Organ thinks I'm overwrought, as usual. Look, Vivi. Could you get away from your subshaft for a few days to help on this?"

"I'd love to, unfortunately Beth Dean is not letting me breathe between taskers. And I don't want to have to work this weekend, because I promised to take Josh to the Renaissance Fair. He wants to get his face painted like last year."

Josh is the son that Vivi was pregnant with during the Strikes. "Can't his father take him?"

"His father takes him everywhere. I promised him I would take him, and I've broken so many promises to him lately."

"Well, I could make sure you don't have to work Saturday. And someone else can answer Dean's questions for a change."

A SCUDO walks up to us. "Ladies, we're clearing this tunnel. Presidential visit. You'll have to go this way." He points back to the direction from which we came.

I glance around and see more SCUDOs moving long, deep blue curtains into place at the east end of the tunnel. Vivi and I obligingly step over the blue rope that has already been stretched across the way.

The SCUDO calls to us. "If you want to see him, you can go around the building and wait in the crowd by the main entrance."

"There's a crowd?" I ask, incredulous.

"We're assembling one now. You'd do us a favor to add a couple more happy faces."

"Sorry, we're busy."

"Thanks anyway," the SCUDO says pleasantly.

"I don't remember any presidential visits being announced," Vivi says.

"They don't announce them ahead of time anymore."

"Really? They won't announce a visit to the Mines ahead of time? He sneaks into his own security service?"

"If you were him, wouldn't you?"

• • •

Before returning to my office, I stop by the Starbucks for a caffeine jolt. I haven't talked to Wynona, my favorite barista, for a few days. She gets on my case right away. I'm the only customer, so she doesn't mind telling me what she thinks.

"Who was that puckered old goat you sent down here yesterday? If he don't think he's too good to piss in the pool."

"Oh, that was Doc. He's a sweetie."

"Hmph. Stuck-up sweetie, if you ask me. I spit in his latte, then I found out it was for you and had to dump it and make it all over again."

"Thanks for that."

"Don't mention it, hon." She rolls her eyes. "Especially not to management. Double espresso?"

"Yep."

I watch her make it and wonder how long the espresso machine will hold out the way she manhandles it. I like Wynona's style. It takes a big personality to pull off big hair like that. She told me she has a set of puckered lips tattooed on her left butt cheek to signify that the world in general can kiss her ass. She thinks three-quarters of the people in the Mines are intolerable stuck-ups, and I don't doubt her estimate. If I were in her position, I'd probably spit in a few lattes, myself. I lean against the counter and yawn.

"Look at you yawning. Did you have a hot date last night?"

"I wish. I haven't had a hot date in the last fiscal year."

"Poor baby. I've had three, and I'm married with a kid."

"Really? Well if that doesn't depress me. Let's talk about something else."

"What do you think about poor old Pete, the Peanut Man? Don't that beat all?"

Wynona loves sensational news and baseball, so it figures that this would catch her imagination. I'm not particularly interested in talking about it, so I answer vaguely, "I saw something on the news last night."

"The murderer is still out there. Not even a suspect yet. Evidence all burned up. The murderer poured out a few gallons of the cooking fat they use on the fries and set the whole room afire. Lucky it didn't spread too far. But imagine poor Pete, getting fried to a crisp like a chicken nugget."

I try not to imagine it. I have enough violent images in my life without dwelling on those that are not part of my job. I pay for my latte.

"Gotta get back to the office," I tell Wynona. "Talk to you later."

13. Vivian

We bomb dissectors measure time by the Strikes. It is plus five years now, but everything we are and everything we do is still about the Strikes. What is it they say about fighting the last war? We're still preventing the last attack. We measure ourselves by our failures before and after the Strikes. I'm appalled to discover that I'm smaller than I ever could have imagined.

It's hard to explain what the Strikes did to our memory and our sense of time. The day the planes hit the towers feels like yesterday. The day before the planes hit the towers feels like a million years ago.

When Maddie mentioned the Perfumers' cell that was so active before the Strikes, it was like she was dredging up petrified bone from some Ice Age monster. My stomach turned over when I realized that bone could still be alive and attached to flesh-and-blood terrorists. I'd forgotten about the Perfumers, completely forgotten them. The Strikes wiped them out of my mind. How could that happen? We were all so concerned about a follow-up attack, but there were so many taskings at the time and I wasn't getting enough sleep, and I was worried about my pregnancy and my sick foster possums.

And yes, possums may be a strange subject to raise in this context, but they pretty much explain who I am and why I'm having such a hard time. I got into possum rescue because I can't stand to see anything suffer. It started out when I found an injured baby. I couldn't let her die, although I had to go through this long training and licensing procedure in order to keep her. Then that led to other possum rescues, because if I said no to taking one in it would die and I couldn't bear to have that on my conscience. So, I'm a possum rescuer—doesn't that sum it up nicely? Obviously, the sort of person who rescues possums is emotionally ill-equipped to deal with terrorism on a daily basis. I didn't start out with the idea of having this as a career. I had a double major in international affairs and psychology. I can't remember now what I was planning to do with that or whether I even had a plan at all. Purely through being an accomodating person and going where I was assigned to go and doing what I was assigned to do I ended up as a bomb dissector. Whereas the typical BD is choleric, argumentative, and opinionated, I am timid and tractable. But I know my stuff and I work really hard.

But I let the Perfumers slip through the cracks. It's really not an excuse that I gave birth to my son Josh right in the middle of all the commotion. It was my job to keep track of that cell. What happened?

• • •

Only a few hours after the Strikes, I was starting to scream at people. I've never been a screamer. After the Strikes, all I wanted was to do my job. I knew I had only a short time before the baby was born. A mountain of things cried out to be done. Tracking down the Perfumers was chief among them. Unfortunately, I wasn't allowed to do that or anything else I considered critical. It made me crazy. I wanted to stomp my feet and say, "Look, I feel like an overinflated balloon. I'm a first-time, thirty-seven-year-old expectant mother, and I shouldn't even be here. I'd rather be home stenciling pandas on the nursery walls. If I have to be here, let me do what needs to be done!" Of course I didn't do that, but I wish I had. A lot of us knew that something was wrong with our response to the Strikes. We should have all had temper tantrums. But instead we were good soldiers.

I had five days in the Mines after the attack and before Josh's birth. Looking back, I can't separate those days into five units, they run together, with me doggedly punching the down arrow key, scrolling, never reaching the end of the page. Meanwhile, my unborn son was showing an early aptitude as a field goal kicker, attempting to send a large fibroid in my uterus through my pelvic bones. It hurt so bad that a couple of times I yelled "Stop it!" out loud. Then I burst into tears, because I was yelling at my baby before he was even born. I cried a lot during those five days, perhaps because of the shock of the attacks, or because my hormones were out of whack, or because I knew my husband was just throwing paper towels over the possum poop and not really cleaning it up, or because the smell of stale pizza kept me on the verge of vomiting.

Or maybe it was because I was caught up in the most bewildering response to a terrorist event I'd ever seen.

To be fair, some necessary things were done. A compendium of evidence linking the Base to the Strikes was finished up at 2:00 A.M. on the third morning after the attacks, and shortly thereafter disseminated in both classified and unclassified form. But other than that, management was making criminally poor use of our few experienced alchemists. We should have been concentrating on the Base, not Iraq.

I don't remember which morning it was, but shortly before 8:00 A.M. on a day not long after the Strikes, I was called into the sector boss's office, probably the smallest, darkest sector boss's office in all the Mines, because BDs have no pull here. Maybe that's why BD sector bosses were generally in a sour mood. Perhaps I spent too much time in undergraduate school on Freudian psychology, but I think that for some managers having a small office is as bad or worse than having a small penis. Ben Burden, our boss, probably suffered from both problems. He was a slight, stooped man with a habit of jerking his chin upward and inhaling sharply, as if he had scented an enemy. Ben flashed me a quick smile that could easily have been mistaken for a grimace and made a spastic gesture toward a low upholstered chair by his desk. The fact that Ben was attempting to smile made me suspicious.

"If I sit in that chair, you'll need a crane to get me out," I said. It was true, but I also wanted to remind Ben that I was in an advanced state of pregnancy. I had a feeling from the way he wouldn't meet my eyes that he was about to give a highly undesirable assignment, and I wanted him to feel as bad about it as possible.

"Sorry," Ben said. "Let me get you a straight chair from the conference room." He disappeared. I reached into my pocket for a handful of cherry Tums and was about to pop them into my mouth when I noticed a tall Starbucks cup on Ben's desk. It annoyed me. I craved coffee. I hadn't had any real coffee for months because of my pregnancy. Even if I could drink it now, I wouldn't have had the time to run down the hallway to buy it. Here Ben had taken the time to stand in line at the Starbucks. He had been home sleeping, while I had been there all night with barely enough time to go to the bathroom. Speaking of which, I suddenly realized that I needed to go again. This made me angrier. I don't know what got into me, but I quickly pried off the lid of his steaming latte, dropped in the cherry Tums, replaced the lid, straightened up, and assumed a look of innocence as Ben came back into the room with my chair. It was the petty revenge of the powerless, but it settled my stomach more effectively than if I had swallowed the Tums myself.

"Here you go," Ben said, as he pushed the chair toward me.

"Thank you so much." I lowered myself into the seat with a theatrical grunt.

"Have you been here all night?" His voice was oozing fake empathy.

"Where else would I go?"

"Did you get any sleep?"

"Have you ever tried to sleep on a narrow canvas cot when you're eight and a half months pregnant?"

"Can't say that I have," Ben said with a gruff laugh.

"Actually, I thought I might go home as soon as the Boss's talking points go up to the Main Shaft. My husband is calling every five minutes, threatening to drag me home." I didn't add that he was also threatening to wring Ben's neck for piling so much work on me—and for leaving him with the job of trying to get Clavamox down the throats of four possums twice a day with only two hands.

I saw a panicked and disapproving look come into Ben's eyes. "But Vivian, you're our most experienced analyst on Iraq."

"Lucky for me the towers were hit by the Chieftain, not Saddam." I made an attempt at a smile. Surely Ben was not serious.

"We shouldn't jump to conclusions," Ben said.

"I've been immersed in this stuff for over a decade," I said, as I searched my pockets for more Tums. "I'm pretty sure I'm not jumping to conclusions."

"Have you looked into the Iraq angle in the last few days?" His voice had an accusatory edge.

"No, I've been doing what you told me to do: jumping from one tasker to another and writing talking points and three A.M. updates and doing everything on earth but delving into the slag on the Base and its associates, like I should be doing."

"The VP is taking us to task for not doing our job on Iraq." Ben had a look of deep disappointment on his face. I tried to feel some sympathy for him. He took a deep draw off his Starbucks and his expression grew petulant.

"I told that woman no syrup," he said. "This tastes like shit. Excuse my French. Anyway, the VP is wondering why we haven't done our homework on Iraq."

I thought, *For the same reason my counterparts in December 1941 weren't doing their homework on Iraq. Baghdad didn't bomb Pearl Harbor and they didn't fly a plane into the towers.* Out loud I said, "We don't have enough people to track down information on the known perpetrators, much less some mythical Iraq connection.

Why aren't they asking us to look into Saudi connections? That's a rich vein."

"Don't change the subject. Forget the Saudis. We're not going there. We have to do an assessment on Iraqi ties."

"By 'we' you mean me?"

"You're the Iraq expert."

"Six months ago you pulled me off of Iraq to help out the Base Subshaft."

"I didn't mean for you to drop Iraq entirely."

"How could I do both?" Was I supposed to clone myself? I could only engage in one form of reproduction at a time.

"Vivian, the VP wants the assessment on his desk by the day after tomorrow. You're going to have to do a deep drill on the connections and have the draft to me by noon tomorrow."

"How does one do a deep drill in a few hours?"

This "deep drill" thing had become a buzzword among our managers: "Take a day and do a deep drill on such and such."

"I do have some good news for you," Ben said with his grimace of a grin.

I braced myself. From Ben, good news and bad news had a remarkably similar impact.

"You'll like this. It's what you've been asking for for years." Ben took a three-foot-long roll of paper from behind his chair and unscrolled it across his desk. I squinted. The print was small and my eyes were tired. It looked like the diagram of a terrorist network.

"What is this?"

"The new Central Counterterrorism Supersector. The CCSS. We're having graphics design a logo. I asked them for something red, white, and blue."

"Original."

"You'll have all the help you need. We're getting a hundred new alchemists by this afternoon. They can take over those taskings and talking points you've been complaining about."

I stared numbly at the diagram, thinking, *Who came up with this? Did anyone consult any real BDs?*

"Why is Maghreb Subshaft off over here?" I whined. "Their guys are all connected to European cells, which are being covered way over there." I point at a box on the opposite side of the chart.

"It was done by a team of very experienced senior managers."

"Experienced in what?" Certainly not terrorism. The diagram was huge. "Where are these people coming from?"

"Everywhere. Offices are coughing up whole subshafts." Ben looked pleased.

"Who is going to train these people? It takes years to make a good BD."

"We're going to put one veteran in each new subshaft. You'll be in the Iraq Subshaft."

God help me. "So I'm supposed to be training new BDs who know nothing and writing an assessment for the Veep and I haven't had any sleep and my possums are sick and my water could break at any minute?" It was on the last clause that my voice began to rise above its normal volume.

"Don't be gross, Vivian. It's not like you to be so negative. You're a team player."

"Ben, we have things we need to do *now*. We're letting the real conspirators get deep underground while we prepare policymakers to meet the press. Suppose the Base is planning follow-up attacks?"

"I'm not asking you *if* you want to do this assessment. I'm telling you to do it."

I had frightened myself by standing up to Ben as long as I had. In the face of a direct order, I quickly reverted to my good-soldier persona. "Okay, I'll go back to my desk and get started." As I hoisted myself out of the chair, I saw another quiver cross Ben's face.

"Um," Ben said.

"Yes, what else?"

"Your new desk is in . . ." Ben consulted the diagram. "Room eighty-two, E shaft, Old Shafts."

"What? I have to write an assessment and move all my stuff at the same time?"

"The new Terrorist Tactics Subshaft is moving into your space this morning, but I'm sure you can get away with moving the bare minimum until you get the assessment done. Oh, and the new head of the CCSS is making the announcement in five minutes. We need to be there."

• • •

I emerged from Ben's office into a sea of largely unfamiliar faces filling the reception area. I noticed some looking around with distaste at the ratty, windowless BD vault. Others appeared to be suffering a mild form of shock at having been ripped from their comfortable regional offices, window cubicles, familiar subject matter, and more or less regular hours. I looked around for the new uberboss and, with some relief, spotted Joseph Price, a senior manager with experience in Arabic affairs. Not the worst choice they could have made. Not the best, but not the worst, which is really the best you can hope for in the Mines.

Joe raised his hand to quiet the crowd. With his thin frame, white hair, and beard, he had a Biblical presence. *Parting the Red Sea will be the least you're expected to do*, I thought. As the noise subsided, Joe launched into what he surely intended as a stirring, morale-lifting speech.

"I don't believe we had an intelligence failure here," he began.

Puh-leeze. I couldn't listen, besides, I had to go to the ladies' room. As I pushed my way through the crowd I bumped into Maddie, who was also abandoning the group.

"Why are you still here?" she said. "You look like hell."

"Thanks, same to you." Her hair was full of static and what appeared to be potato chip crumbs. She had on a loose sacklike dress, the kind she wore when her stomach hurt too badly for her to tolerate a belt. Her posture was somehow out of whack.

"I had a dream about flying monkeys and fell off the cot and threw my back out."

"Ouch," I said. "I thought I was in bad shape."

"And I just found out I have to move to the sixth level in B shaft."

"B shaft! I'll be way over in E shaft in the Old Shafts Building. This is terrible. We've sat next to each other for ages. We're a team."

"Oh, shit. I need to work with you. I want to hash out a theory I have."

"Can't do it. Ben just assigned me an assessment on the Iraqi connection to the Strikes. Meanwhile, I have to get to a bathroom or I'm going to explode."

"What fucking Iraqi connection?" Maddie was shouting. "The Chieftain thinks Saddam is a dirty apostate. I swear this administration is trying to keep us from doing our jobs. Yesterday I got a tasker from Dean at PentCOW asking whether we were sure that the Ramsi Yousef we have in jail is actually the real Ramsi. Do we have DNA samples from today and from 1990? I don't know. Do you happen to have any of his old hairbrushes in your desk, Vivi?"

"Yeah, you'll find them between the urn with Jimmy Hoffa's ashes and my family-size bottle of Maalox. Look, I'll talk to you after I get back from the bathroom."

Maddie suddenly howled with pain and clutched at my shoulder. "Oh, my back kerchoinged. Oh, God it hurts."

"Can you walk?"

"I'm afraid to move."

So Maddie and I stood there, frozen, while my bladder continued to fill. I don't know how long we would have been there, except for a sixtyish woman I'd never seen before who came scurrying up to us. She was wearing hornrimmed glasses, slacks, and Reeboks. Her straight gray hair was clipped at a no-fuss chin length and her eyes were direct and matter-of-fact under brows that seemed perpetually raised. She smiled at me and it made her face beautiful despite or perhaps because of the age.

"Oh, my dear, when are you due to drop that baby? You should be home with those swollen ankles up. Is there anything I can do to help you? My name is Fran, I got moved over here from the Ex-Empire Sector this morning. They tell me I'm going to be in the Iraqi terrorism branch. Don't know a thing about terrorism, but I have a way with computer searches and can catch a newborn if necessary."

I think it was the use of the word *drop* in place of *give birth to* that made me warm up to Fran so quickly. *Drop* is the term we used on the farm and her use of it made me think she was the sort of practical, down-to-earth woman who could, indeed, catch a newborn and deal with the bureaucracy simultaneously. She had a calming presence.

Maddie and I introduced ourselves. It turns out Fran had also abandoned the morning pep talk.

"I've known Joe since he was an apprentice alchemist. I was his mentor. He loves to hear himself talk. Nobody else gets much out of it. I'm serious, what can I do to help?"

"I hate to ask this," I said, "but I really have to get to a bathroom and Maddie can't move because her back is out. Could you take over holding her up? I'll be right back."

"Of course you have to pee! Here," Fran slipped herself gently under Maddie's shoulder in my place.

"Just prop me against a file cabinet and leave me," Maddie said. "Better yet, shoot me."

I missed the rest of Maddie's theatrics in my rush to get to the ladies' room while I still had the chance. When I got back, Maddie and Fran were inching their way slowly and painfully toward our cubicles, or what used to be our cubicles.

"Do you mind running searches?" Maddie was saying to Fran. "I have a list of names that I haven't been able to get to."

"I don't mind at all," Fran said, "but they haven't given us access to the terrorism database yet."

Maddie and I groaned. What use were a hundred new analysts who couldn't get into Auger?

"Well," I said. "I do have some hard files. I guess I could have you go through those for what you can find. Of course, I have to move everything."

As soon as she got to my cubicle and saw my photos, Fran exclaimed, "Oh, you have possums! I had one growing up. They're so cute!" I knew I had a fast friend. Fran loaded my boxes, while I grabbed up everything related to Iraq I could lay my hands on. We got a cart, and she pushed it down the hall for me, lecturing me the whole way on why I should be home in bed.

"Vivian, this is your first baby. Why let them abuse you? I'm not even a BD, and I know Iraq wasn't behind the Strikes."

"It's a vice presidential request."

"Oh, he and his buddies just want to go bomb something. You would think after all the thousands of years of human civilization, men could come up with a more creative approach to problems. I used to think the old goats started wars because they couldn't get it up anymore. But then Viagra ruined my theory."

Fran made me laugh out loud. I was in a better mood by the time I arrived at my new desk in the Former Banana Republic Sector.

"Oh, my God," I said, "I can see a window." I wasn't next to the window, but a sliver of sky was visible from my cubicle.

The foul mood returned, however, as soon as I set about the task of finding links between Iraq and the Strikes. I dumped a stack of court proceedings against Iraqi jihadists into Fran's lap. Then I tried to log on to Auger and discovered it was inaccessible from computers in this sector of the White Mines. I picked up the phone and dialed the help desk. After ten minutes of the "Surprise" Symphony, someone finally picked up.

"Hello."

"Hi, I work in the BD sector. I just got moved to E Shaft and I need access to Auger."

"Have you, like, lodged a request on the MMD database?"

"I don't have time. I have a vice presidential tasking."

"I have to, like, have the request in the database or I can't process it."

"I need to get on Auger *now*."

"Okay, I'll try, but I need the serial number off the back of your CPU."

"My CPU is way under my desk and I'm eight and a half months pregnant."

"You need the serial number?" Fran whispered. "I'll get it." She got down on her hands and knees, and crawled under my desk. She found the number and I relayed it to the help desk.

"You say you're in the BD sector? The computer you're on belongs to the Former Banana Republic Sector, so, like, someone in that sector has to make the request."

Fran took the receiver. "I know where your office is and I'm coming down there and I'm going to sit in your lap until you get this done." She hung up and looked at me. "They think I don't mean that literally. I'll be back shortly." She headed off with a purposeful stride.

I had Auger up and running within fifteen minutes.

• • •

Fran turned out to be a speed reader with a keen sense of what was relevant and what wasn't. She sat on a stack of boxes with a cup of chamomile tea and a yellow highlighter and devoured page after page, offering up to me only what I needed to see, and making the occasional off-color joke. I started printing long cables from Auger, and she devoured those, too.

"How is it all these guys are named al-Masri?" she asked.

"Al-Masri just means the guy is from Egypt."

"So Mohammed al-Masri is like—"

"It's like saying Bob from Canada. It doesn't narrow things down."

"I don't know how you keep these guys straight. I take it then that al-Libi means from Libya?"

"Right, and al-Zarqawi is from Jordan."

"I have a lot to learn."

• • •

By that evening, it was clear that there wasn't a case to be made against Iraq. I wrote up what little there was in the way of linkages, noting inconsistencies and the dubious reliability of the sources. I slipped in a few paragraphs pointing out how the Base had no need of Iraq to pull off the Strikes. Ben wouldn't like that. I sent the first draft around for coordination—the excruciating process of allowing everybody and his brother to weigh in with an opinion. I gave a deadline of 9:00 A.M. the next day. I was too tired to go home, so I set my alarm for 8:50, and curled up on a blanket on the floor. I awoke to the smell of a cinnamon bun that Fran had brought me from the cafeteria, along with a carton of milk. I logged on my computer and found an inbox full of nasty grams from fellow BDs asking me why I was off chasing Saddam at a time like this. I made a few adjustments to my paper and sent it off to Ben.

Ben must have finished the paper at exactly 10:15, because that's when an instant message flashed across my screen. "This won't do. Need to see you NOW."

Fran accompanied me down the hall. "I have a feeling," she said, "that the baby could come at any minute. I have intuition about these things."

I laughed it off—he wasn't due for nine days—but I was happy to have her come along. A walk to the New Shafts Building was beginning to feel like a camel expedition across the Sahara, and I was the camel. I noticed people giving me looks of concern and imagined that they were speeding up so they wouldn't be around should I suddenly extrude a slimy newborn onto the floor. Fran and I made the trip more slowly than we had the day before. My body felt heavier and somehow unstable.

"Has it really only been a day since we were walking this hall in the opposite direction?" I asked Fran.

"Seems like half a lifetime to me, but I like the excitement. Nothing big has happened in my office since Yeltsin climbed up on that tank. As soon as I learn to keep my Abu's straight, I think I'll like it."

I didn't tell her that after all these years I still had trouble keeping my Abu's straight.

• • •

When we entered Ben's office, he was holding my assessment with two fingers, out from his body, like it was a dirty diaper. It looked like he had slept on his face the wrong way.

"Have you been eating raw rhubarb for breakfast?" Fran asked.

"Who are you?" Ben said, as Fran helped me settle in the straight-backed chair that was still in Ben's office.

"Fran Monroe. I've been helping poor Vivian. I can't believe you gave a woman who's about to give birth such a ridiculous dead-line."

"Is there some reason you need to be here?"

"Fran has been a great help," I said. "She ought to be here. She's in the new Iraqi Subshaft, and this will help her understand the issues."

Ben said something under his breath, but didn't press Fran to leave. "I just got off the phone with the Boss of White Mines. I bought you another twenty-four hours to rewrite this paper."

"I don't think I'm going to find anything in the next day that will change my conclusions." And I didn't think I could stand one more day of crashing on a worthless paper. My insides felt like they were shifting. My back hurt like crazy. I wanted to lie down.

"You're the one who said that no one can do a deep drill in a day. I'm sure you didn't find everything. If we give the Vice President an answer like this we'd better be damn sure we've researched it thoroughly."

"Ben, I don't think I can make it here another day. I need to go home and lie down."

Ben gave my bulging stomach a look of severe irritation. I could see the mental struggle in his face. On some level, he knew he should treat me humanely. On the other hand, his managers routinely treated him like a puppy who'd piddled on the rug.

"Of course I'm concerned for your health," Ben said, "but I don't have a choice here."

I leaned forward to make an argument, but Josh made the argument for me. I felt something explode inside. I instinctively jumped up, and liquid trickled down my legs to wet a circle on Ben's carpet.

"There goes her water," Fran said. She reached across Ben for the phone. "I'll call Medical. Give me your husband's number, Vivian. I'll call him, too."

"Oh, God," Ben said. "No, not now. This is terrible timing. Could you jot down a few notes before you leave?" He grabbed a notebook and pen and held them out to me. His hands were shaking.

I doubled over and groaned. I was frightened and in pain, but at the same time strangely elated. I was getting out and there wasn't a damn thing Ben or the Vice President or anyone else could do about it. There was nothing *I* could do about it, so I didn't need to feel guilty. I could even yell out loud if I felt like it.

"Aaaaaaargh!"

My bellow backed Ben against the far wall. He dropped the notebook and the color drained from his face. It was immensely satisfying. I suddenly realized that I'd always harbored a secret desire to scream at work. So a few minutes later, when the next contraction came, I gave it all I had.

"Aaaaarrrraaargh!"

If we had had windows in the BD Sector, I would have shattered them.

At that point, Medical came rushing in and two nice nurses helped me into a cart with flashing lights. Between contractions, I sat like a queen on a palanquin as I was whisked over the marble floors of the main corridors. I howled at the florid visage of Vaughn Sutter Wayne, who raised his smoking pipe to me and patted his globe. I wouldn't have to return for six months. Ben had signed off on the maternity leave before the Strikes. I thought of the last view I had of him before they took me away: He was staring down at his wet carpet with extreme disgust. The beeping, flashing cart passed Maddie in the hallway, and I caught a look of envy on her face.

"Good luck!" she called after me. "You lucky dog!"

I howled.

• • •

So now Maddie wants me to drop everything and work on this threat, and I know I'll end up working the weekend, despite her promise. And I'll miss Josh's Rennaissance Fair. I've already let him down twice in the last month. I forgot to pick up a gift for his best friend's birthday. I was the only mother who didn't bring in something for the school's May Day Celebration. I have been letting him down steadily for the last seven years. So what's the right thing to do here? Let down my country or my son? Great set of choices, as usual.

14. Vaughn Sutter Wayne Musings from an Unquiet Grave

Cave dwellers, that's what they are. Terrorists are not a proper enemy for a superpower. Not enough hardware. The Evil Empire stretched across eleven time zones pitted with missile silos. Now that was an adversary, an enemy you could wrap your mind around. The enemy in the mind is more important than the enemy on the ground. He's a part of us and spurs us to greatness.

What makes the alchemists think *they* decide who the enemy is? They're glorified support staff. A decision that vital must be left to great men. The world stage is not a court of law judging guilt or innocence on the basis of a few fingerprints. It's a place for great men to leave their footprints deep in the soil. We decide who the enemy is.

15. Doc

I've found some interesting information on that Perfumers cell. I'll go to check it out with Fran Monroe, whom I remember fondly as Fran Fletcher, but that time is ancient history and doesn't merit discussion. In our day-to-day dealings, she always greets me with a smile of recognition—as instantaneous and bright as it was all those years ago—but no sly knowing look or other indication that we were, ever so briefly . . . but I digress. Taking my cue from Fran, I behave in the most businesslike manner in her presence.

I am still fond of her, however, and it's hard to restrain myself now, because she's under threat. Not under something so abstract and statistically rare as a terrorist threat, however. This morning the office sent around an e-mail congratulating the newly promoted Mines Schedule-14s—and Fran's name wasn't on the list again. Even worse, I heard a rumor that they've put her name on the bottom-10-percent list. In a way that's meaningless, because BDs are in such short supply it would take an extreme case of incompetence before they got rid of one. But still, if Fran ever found out that she was on that list, she would be devastated.

I long to leap to her rescue. In a way, I admire Fran more now than I did when she was young and gorgeous. She was torn from her familiar accounts in the late stages of her career. It's hard for a nonalchemist to understand what that means. It's your identity. You live it and breathe it. Suddenly you're told the government doesn't need an expert on that anymore, they need an expert on terrorism. You'll need to read in quickly. You're briefing German liaison Thursday.

Fran has acquitted herself admirably as a BD. Her cubicle is papered in bedsheet-size link charts, crammed with meticulous detail in eight-point font. Multicolored lines connect operatives, financiers, logisticians, passport forgers, other cogs in the terrorist machine. Whenever she gets hold of a head shot, she glues it to the chart in the appropriate place. Movies depict the Mines looking like the headquarters of The Sharper Image, with people surrounded by streamlined, high-tech gadgetry, everything glinting in a vaguely bluish light. I wonder what Hollywood would think of Fran, in her Reeboks, glue stick in hand, updating her chart.

She hasn't seen me yet. Most office collaboration is done online, but I prefer to visit Fran in person. It's a harmless little self-indulgence that means nothing. As I wait for Fran to finish with her glue stick, a young female alchemist comes up behind me and says, "Fran, why don't you import the photo in your file and reprint it?"

Fran doesn't turn around. "I did import the photo, but there's no reason to kill a tree every time there's a little update. You think because I'm an old lady, I don't know how to import a photo into a link file, don't you?" Her voice is uncharacteristically cross.

"Oh no, I didn't think that." The young alchemist slips away, saving whatever question she had for later.

In truth, Fran is a wizard with the computer. I'm in awe of her skill, for I hate the recalcitrant things with a passion, and they hate me. I offer my arm to Fran as she steps down from her chair. She flashes me a smile, but doesn't meet my eyes. She's embarrassed that she hasn't gotten her Mines Schedule-14 after all these years. I can see it in her eyes. It breaks my heart.

"I came to tap your expertise," I say cheerily. Fran has a photographic memory. All the energy she once put into studying Evil

Empire military hardware, she's now directed at tracing terrorists. She's a resource for the entire supersector. One phone call to Fran can save an afternoon of computer searches. But Fran hasn't produced an intelligence assessment since she's been a BD. She never particularly enjoyed writing long papers, and was never particularly good at it. Unfortunately, writing papers is what gets you promoted in the White Mines. Never mind that Fran has made invaluable contributions to a hundred other assessments.

"If you can find any expertise to tap, you're welcome to it," Fran says.

This comment isn't like Fran.

I speak hesitantly. "I have a few names of gentlemen from North Africa. . . ."

"Gentlemen? You mean terrorists?"

"I suppose *gentlemen* is the wrong word. Excuse me. I misspoke." What makes me speak so formally with Fran? How stupid could I sound?

"Doc, you're such a gentleman yourself, you forget that some people aren't. Is that the list of the names?" She points to the paper clutched in my moist hand.

"Yes. Yes. I thought you might possibly know the third one from the top, the one called 'the Vortex.' We lost track of him after the Strikes. He was the recruiter for a North African cell—the one we called the Perfumers—that had been planning a U.S. attack before the Strikes. He worked with an imam from Egypt. The imam showed up in Iraq after we invaded. He was there with an unidentified man, who I believe might have been the Vortex. They went on a recruiting spree. I haven't seen anything more on them since."

Fran takes the paper and frowns at it. "Yes, I remember the imam. I'll look into this."

"Thank you," I say.

Then I stand there looking stupid until Fran says, "Anything else I can do for you? Do you need this paper back?"

"No, it's a copy."

"Okay, I'll get back to you when I have something."

"Thanks, again."

• • •

It's 2:00 A.M. and I can't sleep. I've tossed and turned so much that my cat, Molotov, has abandoned my bed for a pile of dirty laundry in the corner. If word got to me about the bottom-10-percent list, how long will it be before Fran hears? I get up and pad about the kitchen in my bare feet, back and forth between the refrigerator and the table. What could I possibly do to help? Finally, I pull on my clothes and drive to the all-night Giant.

Their flower stock is not as fresh looking as I might wish, but through careful selection, I manage to piece together a bouquet of pink and yellow rosebuds, with some white daisylike things thrown in. It still doesn't look quite right. I add some ferns. As I'm stuffing this into a paper cone, I realize I need a vase. I select the least tacky one. I wipe it clean with my handkerchief as I stand in line at the checkout.

Fortunately, the Mines is a twenty-four/seven operation, and so there is nothing strange about my showing up before dawn. I park under a pole light and arrange the flowers in the vase. I don't want to run into anyone I know, so I go through the basement and up a back stairway, rather than down the main corridor. I check the sign-in sheet on the door of the vault and am alarmed to see that it is already occupied. I work the combination as quietly as I can and step inside cautiously. The early morning workers are evidently in their cubicles. No one sees me sneak back to Fran's desk, bent over so my head will not show above the cubicle partitions.

I set the vase in the middle of Fran's desk and fill it with water from her teapot. I want her to think it is from some junior alchemist she has mentored. She must never suspect it came from me. I tear a yellow sticky note off of her pad and write, "Tks 4 the help :)."

• • •

The next morning my radio alarm wakens me with the news that there is yet another horrendous tie-up on my route into work. Alternative routes are already backed up for miles. So here I sit at my kitchen table, having a second cup of coffee and a second toaster waffle.

I don't often see my kitchen in the morning light. I sleep in on weekends. Sunbeams show up the cobwebs and dust. I should probably get a cleaning service, but it pains me to pay for something I could do myself, even if I am never likely to do it. Especially when sleeping in on weekends solves the whole problem. Or I could get blinds to keep the sun out.

How long has it been since Rebecca and I divorced? It was 19— Good God, it's been nearly a decade already. I would call that an enduring, successful divorce. I bought this townhouse after the split. It has a fireplace. Rebecca got everything else but my books. I paid a neighbor's son to build in bookshelves in every available space. I bought a bed, a reading chair, and a lamp from Ikea.

I picked up Molotov at the pound, an orange tabby. We had a great deal in common: His first home didn't work out either. He scratched the furniture and sprayed. I was never quite sure why I got kicked out. Molotov is congenial company and lends the fireplace an air of distinction. As far as I'm concerned, that compensates for the shredded chair. Books, fireplace, comfortable chair, cat. It's all I need. I'm perfectly content. I do not perceive a thing missing from my life.

I have the coffeepot and toaster right in front of me. Rebecca would never let me keep them on the table, where it's convenient. She insisted on a useless centerpiece of silk flowers. She kept the toaster on the counter, hidden under a quilted toaster cozy as if it were some shameful apparatus. The coffeepot was likewise under cover in a sort of appliance garage in the corner of the counter. I like having the toaster and coffeepot in front of me, so I can have seconds without getting up. Molotov likes that, too. He curls up to nap between the two appliances, where it's warm. His whiskers twitch when the toast pops, but he doesn't wake. It makes a comforting still life: toaster, coffeemaker, jar of superb marmalade from my last trip to London, pleasant sprinkling of crumbs, cat. What more could a man want?

I hope Fran liked her flowers. I hope it made her realize how valuable she is to the office, despite what the career panel may think. I hate it that I can't get in to the office on time this morning, but my absence should ensure that no suspicion is cast in my direction. I can't afford to make a fool of myself at this stage of my life. No, I just want to make Fran feel better.

My phone rings. It's probably my face boss wondering why I'm late.

"Hello, Doc? This is Fran."

I'm too dumbfounded to answer her. How could she possibly know it was me?

"Doc, are you there?"

"Yes," I stammer.

"Are you coming in today? I found something really interesting on your guy."

"I'm coming in. I'm just waiting for the traffic to clear a bit. A truck jackknifed on the toll road and spilled a load of glass jars of honey."

"Right. I heard about that one. When you get in, give me a ring. Your friend, his pastor, *and* at least *forty* of their little boy scouts abruptly disappeared nearly two years ago. The families haven't heard from the scouts."

"Oh dear, that's not good. Forty? That's a huge number. I'll be in as soon as I can." I put down the phone. She didn't mention the flowers.

16. Maddie

I'll be late for my meeting with Harry. I'm stuck in traffic and the traffic is in turn stuck in honey spilled by a semi that jackknifed near the Weihle exit.

I'm starting to hate this guy in the black Hummer sitting next to me. He's not turning off his motor, even though we've been here for over an hour and nearly everyone else has. He has two SUPPORT OUR TROOPS ribbons. Maybe I hate him because he's sucking on a Starbucks. I didn't bother to make coffee before I left the house, and I'd die for a cup now. He'll regret that venti when he has to pee. I'll enjoy watching him squirm.

I know what the policymakers will say when we tell them about this threat. Give us a time and a place. Actionable intelligence. Those are the buzzwords. Well, I've got news for you, Mr. Policymaker. You can jump up and down like Rumpelstiltskin and scream "Actionable intelligence!" until you're blue in the face, but you won't get a time and a place. Never. That goes by word of mouth, by the courier whom the Chieftain has known half a lifetime.

"Ms. James, this list of possible targets is so large as to be meaningless. Can you narrow it down?"

"Not with any confidence, sir."

"Might they hit one of our embassies again?"

"That's certainly a possibility."

"Which embassies have they surveilled?"

"I can't think of any that they haven't."

"What? Well, what are the most recent ones?"

"They do most of their surveillance two years before an attack. You can't judge by the most recent incidences."

"This doesn't help me. I need actionable intelligence."

"I'm sorry, sir."

Mr. Policymaker, can you say "global insurgency?" It sticks in your throat. Things are getting past the point where we can help you. No matter how much money and new personnel you fork over, it won't be enough for what's coming. The Mossad is probably the most adept agency in the world at counterterrorism, but can they stop terrorism in Israel? Tracking down a single terrorist is an astoundingly difficult task. Tracking down an ever growing army of them is damned near impossible. The Base has trained armies of mujahidin, holy warriors, not just a few terrorist operatives. But don't worry, when things blow up, Mr. Policymaker, you can always blame me. Remember, there are no policy failures, only intelligence failures. Sleep well. I wish I could.

It's going to happen again. Soon.

What could *holy swarm* mean? *Red cloud*? We either figure it out, or the terrorists fail on their own, or I hear those words in my brain for the rest of my life.

I spent half of yesterday trying to concentrate on one individual, mapping his contacts, the places he's been, and the things he knows. His wife is a cousin of one of the Manila plotters. He learned about crude chemical weapons in Afghanistan. He has a brother in the Saudi internal police. He spent time in Somalia with a U.S. citizen who now has a pilot's license and disappeared while under surveillance in Oregon.

I try to keep focused, but I keep running into things and people that also need to be tracked down. I need more people.

The Hummer guy with the Starbucks is opening his door and

getting out. What's he doing? He's walking over to the bridge pylon. Good God! He's unzipping! He's urinating in public! I will not let this pass. Where's my cell? What's that nonemergency police number?

"I'd like to report a blatant incidence of public urination."

"Can I have your name and location, ma'am?"

"Madeleine James. I'm on the Dulles Toll Road, between the Reston Parkway and Wiehle exits. The guy got out of a black Hummer, license number—"

"Toll road? You know there's a big accident there."

"Really?" I can't keep the sarcasm out of my voice.

"Traffic's been stopped for an hour at least."

"No kidding."

"The poor man probably couldn't contain himself any longer."

"He could have urinated into his empty Starbucks cup and not exposed himself to half of Fairfax County."

"Ma'am, the officers are real busy this morning handling half a dozen accidents in addition to the big one on the toll road. You know there are bigger problems in the world than a man peeing. I wish we could help you with this but—"

I suppose I shouldn't hang up on the police department, but really. Oh, look. Here he goes, zipping up and calmly walking back to his vehicle, which is still running.

I shouldn't do this—the guy might get violent—but some greater power seems to be rolling down my window.

"Hey, you. I hope that hummer is big enough to compensate for that little dick."

He flashes me the finger and gets back in the Hummer. No fight. I'm disappointed. I could have taken him.

• • •

I manage to reschedule the one-on-one meeting with Harry later in the day.

Harry and I go way back. He was my face boss in the mid-nineties. He was the one who told me to quit wasting my time on the Chieftain and get my buns back to work on Hezbollah. Then he went to the Evil Empire Sector for a few years before coming back to the BD world after the Strikes. At some point during that time, he joined an evangelical Christian church and started scolding me for my language. Despite his in-your-face Christianity, Harry is the biggest liar I've ever known—bigger than Rick, who does it for a living.

On the surface, Harry is glib and pleasant. He never hesitates, even before the most difficult questions. He merely makes up an answer. Upper management is impressed. So impressed that they chose Harry to represent us at the hearings on the Strikes. Harry Esterhaus in blue suit, white shirt, red tie, and flag lapel pin. Harry who wasn't even with the BDs at the time of the Strikes.

"Of course, I had left the office two years before the Strikes," he said at the hearings, both to exonerate himself and perhaps to suggest that had he not left, things would have been different. "I was brought back on September twelve."

And now I have to swallow my pride and appeal to Harry for help. Toward this end I have worn a modestly unflattering suit, plastered my hair back tight, and buttoned my blouse to the top. I'm demure as hell. I'm radiating fustiness, as if I've walked straight out of a Baptist fellowship hall. It took a supreme effort of will, but I pinned an enamel flag in my lapel.

I walk up to Harry's long-suffering secretary, Sheila.

"What kind of mood is he in this morning?"

Sheila is gnawing on a bagel. She rolls her eyes and points to a tape dispenser in her inbox. I give her a quizzical look, and she motions for me to wait until she's finished chewing.

"Asshole," she manages to say through the bread. "Without saying a word to me this morning, even hello, he comes out and drops this in my inbox. I finally figured out that it was empty, and he wanted me to fill it. Asshole." She reaches in her drawer, takes out a new roll of tape, and slips it in the dispenser. "Take this to him when you go and tell him to stick it where the sun don't shine."

"Sure thing, Sheila," I say.

"Wait a minute," she says. She takes back the dispenser and rips off the little piece of plastic that makes it easy to find the end of the tape. Then she sticks the end to the roll and goes over it several times with her fingernail. She hands it back to me. "This drives him nuts."

I find Harry with his head of thick gray hair bent over a book, probably his devotional.

"Good morning, Harry." I hand him the tape dispenser.

He perks up when he sees it. I detect a moment of blankness when he looks at me. Then he seems to remember our meeting. "Sit down, Madeleine."

Harry moves the tape dispenser so that it is parallel to the edge of his obsessively neat desk. "I spoke to your mother just the other day," Harry says. "She's a lovely woman. She worries about you and the path you're taking in life."

"Yes, lovely, but I came in this morning to talk to you once again about the possibility that a major, multiple-site, mass-casualty terrorist attack is in the works."

"Family is deeply *important*," Harry says in his soft, gently chiding, proselytizer-with-his-foot-crammed-in-your-door voice.

"I'm concerned about the families of the people who might get killed in the next attack." I can see that keeping the conversation on track will not be easy. My eyes light on a curious new object on Harry's desk: a rock.

Following my gaze, he says with pride, "It's Jerusalem stone."

"What's that?"

"Stone from Jerusalem."

I'm sorry I asked. "Getting back to the threat—"

"Footprints in the sand," Harry says. He turns the rock so I can see the footprints. "Do you know whose footprints they are?"

I take a stab at it. "Vaughn Sutter Wayne's?"

"No." Harry turns his paperweight back around with a frown.

"Something is going to blow up, Harry. I think the Base is returning to a plot it abandoned in 2001."

"How many times have we seen this over the past few years? How many times? Of course we should always be concerned and vigilant—*vigilant*—but I don't see anything *particularly* alarming in this, *particularly* since we rolled up that Lahore cell."

"The Lahore arrests may well have prompted them to move the timing forward. We're seeing a sudden increase in movement among—"

"Your mother was in here the other day doing a security check. She mentioned to me you have a tendency to get *overexcited* about things. She thinks it would help if you would start coming to church."

I keep my voice calm and professional. "I don't see how someone can get 'overexcited' about the real possibility of a major terrorist attack."

Harry is trying to find the end of the tape. He holds it up to the light and discovers it. After a few futile efforts to pry the end up with his fingernail, he reaches into his pants pocket and pulls out his pocketknife. On the random chance that it will work, I grit my teeth and try to employ telekinesis to move the blade toward the veins of his wrist. No luck. Finally, he pries up a corner of the tape. He replaces the roll in the dispenser.

"Madeleine, Madeleine, Madeleine." Harry shakes his head.

"Harry, please. I've compiled a list of recent threat indicators." I hand him the top sheet of the stack of paper I have brought with me. It's a glossy, color-coded matrix I worked up with the help of the graphics staff. Harry likes things with color.

Harry has the infuriating air of someone humoring a child. "The red is what?"

"The red represents indicators that suggest a threat to the U.S. mainland. There's a key on the right side of the matrix."

"And the blue?"

"Those are threats to U.S. interests abroad. The key explains the colors."

"And the orange?"

"As you can see from *the key*, those are threats to major cities, such as Paris or London."

"So you're telling me that you can't really *narrow* this down much."

"I think the D.C. area may be a target, because of the mention of the 'Poison River.'" I pass him the next sheet of paper. "I'm not sure what the others will be. I need help. I'm asking you for five alchemists for a canary crew. Just five." I hand him the third sheet from my stack. "I need Doc Hartman and Vivian Fields for their knowledge of the Perfumers cell, Vernon Keene on chemical and special weapons, Fran Monroe on networks, and Kristin Russell on financial links. If we could get someone in from the Black Mines and someone from the Internal Investigative Organ, too, that would be great. And of course we'll need space where we could work together."

"Is that *all* you want? You're asking for a lot. You know our resource constraints. Maybe I could get you three people part-time. No dedicated space. That's what we have networked computers for."

"Part-time means no time. You know how that goes. Bosses promise they will leave people time to work on the canary crew, then they load them up with so much stuff I never see them again. I have to get people out of the line of sight of their bosses."

"This is a busy place, Madeleine. A busy place."

I'm thinking, *No shit*, but I don't say it. "Should an attack occur, five alchemists and a back room won't look like much in retrospect, especially to the Mines Oversight Committee."

Harry's shaggy brows twitch. I push my advantage. "If the attack doesn't happen, nothing is lost. We will have gained insight into threats that are real, whether the bomb goes off now or five years from now. Back in 1996, I begged you for one extra alchemist to work with me on the Base. You said no." Now I'm playing dirty. I wonder if this man suffers even an ounce of guilt for underplaying the threat back then.

"I doubt if it would have made a difference," Harry says. His voice is quieter than normal. "Okay, I'll give you those five, subject to the approval of the relevant face bosses. But there's no way I can get the Organ or the sharpers to cough up a body. Forget that. But tell Sheila that your group will have the small conference room until further notice. Anything else?"

"Nice rock."

17. Vivian

My child, other children, all children. How do the dividing lines get drawn? I'm thinking about this and miss what my husband Jeff is saying. He snaps his finger in front of my face, which angers me.

"Where are you, Viv? Listen to me. Please don't join this canary crew, or whatever it's called," he says. "Please." I know he's saying it out of love, but there's a note of accusation, as well.

We're arguing about my work again. The argument is so stale that I could play my part in my sleep. We're sitting in the cluttered kitchen of our extra narrow starter townhouse—all we can afford, since I'm the only breadwinner—and I feel like the walls are closing in on me. We decided when Josh was born that Jeff would be the one to stay home with him, because my job paid more and we needed the money for medical expenses. Jeff was blue-collar, a roofer who was my high school sweetheart. It didn't do his ego any good to become a stay-at-home dad. Now he complains that I work too much, but with Josh's therapy and operations, we still have trouble paying all of our bills. But Jeff still looks square-jawed and handsome, while anxiety has etched lines on my face.

I take a deep breath and keep up my end of the argument. "I think Maddie's right. An attack is in the works."

"But why do *you* have to be on the team? Aren't there plenty of people to do that now?"

"It's just that I have experience with this particular cell. It would take someone else a week to read in, and we don't have the time."

"What about time for your son?"

"You know I love my son more than anything."

"Not enough to put him first. He's been talking about Mommy taking him to this Renaissance Fair for weeks."

"I'll take him," I say through clenched teeth. Jeff is being manipulative, fighting dirty, and I feel the thread holding our marriage together cutting through my skin.

"You know that if you join this canary crew it will get canceled. It's happened too many times. And what about your own health? You're not going to cancel your tests tomorrow for this team, are you?"

I have a CT scan scheduled for tomorrow, because of some abdominal pains I've been having.

"No, I'm still going to have the tests, but I should join the canary crew. How will I feel if someone else's child dies because I couldn't spare the time?"

"Don't you think it's about time you put Josh first? It's like the damned possums." Jeff gestures at Sophie curled up in a box in the corner. "It's crazy to have this tiny house full of wild animals. You're too damn kind. You try to save everything and it's pushing us to the edge. It's damaging us."

I'm about to answer back, but Josh walks into the room. Or rather he limps into the room, dragging his right foot. He was born with spina bifida. He has some paralysis in the right leg and uses a brace. His case is relatively mild, but has required two surgeries and much therapy.

I've read a study relating maternal stress to increased incidence of spina bifida. My pregnancy coincided with the awful months leading up to the Strikes, when we all knew that something big was coming but couldn't stop it. Was his birth defect the result of my stress? Every time Jeff and I have an argument, I feel that implication in the background. It wounds me and I lash out. I know he loves me, and I love him, but. . . .

• • •

I come in Thursday morning and tell Maddie she can count me in. Maybe I do it because Jeff made me angry, or maybe because of the deaths yesterday.

"Four marines were blown away yesterday," I say to Fran. She's once again helping me load boxes, this time with files I will need for the canary crew. "Those boys had no idea what they were getting into when they raided that house. It was a nest of seasoned muj, veterans from Chechnya. Rocket-propelled grenade launchers, automatic weapons. They had everything. Those boys had no idea." I give my box a kick and feel childish. "We knew who was in that area. Somehow we didn't get word to the marines, or they conducted the raid without giving us a heads-up. Something went terribly wrong."

"Again," Fran says. We continue to pack in silence, loading our boxes into a wire cart.

Pushing the cart down the long tunnel and listening to the high-pitched screech of a crooked wheel, I find myself getting as angry and bitter as Maddie. While I was on maternity leave, I listened to war fervor building as the administration started making a case against Iraq. I couldn't believe what was happening. There were no ties between Iraq and the Strikes. None. The only so-called evidence was reports from some defectors with highly dubious motives, and a flaky source covered in red flags. If it weren't for Dr. Elizabeth Dean and PentCOW, no one would have taken such "evidence" seriously. But people who should have known better were afraid to look unpatriotic by opposing the tide. I came back early from my maternity leave to write an assessment of what would likely happen if we went to war in Iraq. It wasn't a difficult paper to write. The conclusions were hardly farfetched: insurgency, sectarian violence, possible civil war, a recruiting boon for the terrorists, a new generation of U.S.-hating muj schooled in the streets of Baghdad, Fallujah, al-Basrah. I had seen the same things happen earlier in Afghanistan, Chechnya, Kashmir, Bosnia, and elsewhere. I knew how the muj worked, how they used ample donations from the Gulf (read Saudi Arabia) to move combat units into a country, organize, distribute night letters, incite local resistance. I'd seen it all happen over and over again. It was an easy paper to write, but, as it turned out, an impossible paper to publish. It never got through the management chain, although it reached the Boss of White Mines, Sharon Pendergast, who was the first woman to be in charge of all the Mines' alchemists. Sharon was nice enough, it's just that she reserved her sweetest smiles for those in the supergrade ranks.

"The President doesn't want to hear this."

Those were the actual words that came out of her mouth. "The President doesn't want to hear this." She slapped my paper down on her teal leather desk blotter, which matched her other desk accessories and picked up colors from the Renoir print, *The Boating Party*, a scene of brightly dressed bohemians eating, drinking, and laughing down at all the bureaucrats who passed before them. Sharon gave her blotter an extra slap with her fingers and shot me a look of exasperation and disappointment.

"Since when do we only write what the President wants to hear?" The words came out before I could choke them back. Career suicide. Sharon was known for being intolerant of criticism and having a long memory. Regular abuse by the Vice President had not improved her personality. Moreover, she personally approved or vetoed every promotion and job change above the Mines Schedule-14 level.

Sharon glared at me, because I was right, but she wasn't going to change her mind. "We're going into Iraq," she said. "It's a done deal."

"Can't we at least go on record with our analysis of what's going to happen?"

"Your opinion of what's going to happen."

"Based on years of observation."

"Not fact."

One of the biggest strategic errors of our time, and the Mines elected to sit on its hands, to write feel-good intelligence for the insecure policymaker. After the meeting, I went into the ladies' room and threw up. Then I gave up and did what I was told. The paper didn't get out.

Since that time, I've had the grim task of watching my predictions come true, thinking about my responsibility to other people's children, and rethinking the ethics of being a "nice girl." While Maddie gave everybody hell, I was Pollyanna. My upbringing and instinct led me to smooth things over, come up with compromise language, be the dependable soldier, not rock the boat. For most of my life I thought that I was doing the right thing, but now I have serious doubts.

Sharon Pendergast was a nice girl in her own way. She wanted the President to be pleased with her. She wanted to be liked among all the daddy figures. Her biggest enemies were those who made a fuss, showed their discontent, gave her bad news to pass to the big boys, who raked her over the coals. She was the worst sort of person to occupy the post of White Mines Boss after the Strikes.

And maybe I was the worst person to be a senior Iraq analyst. I should've made a stink. The results may have been the same, but I should have made it much harder for them to do the wrong thing. I think I would sleep better now.

I had to watch a video of a beheading yesterday. We were trying to identify the people involved. I can't stand to see any creature suffer. And I had to watch a beheading.

It's my job.

• • •

Almost immediately after I move myself into the canary crew's new quarters, I have to leave again for my medical appointment at a

Fairfax clinic, another attempt to try to find out what's wrong with my stomach. So here I stand trying to swallow a thick white cocktail of barium. The texture is like wet ground chalk, and my gag reflex is kicking in.

"Do I have to swallow all of it? I'm not sure I can."

The nurse gives me an encouraging smile. "Sure you can." She sounds like my son Josh's teacher: relentlessly, aggressively cheery.

I look down into the cup. It's still half full. My back is up against a cold metal plate. The nurse is buckling me to it. I close my eyes and take another big sip of the viscous liquid and quickly clamp my mouth shut against the nausea.

"We'll be ready as soon as you get that down, Mrs. Fields. Take your time. We don't want it coming back up again, now do we?"

No, we don't. We really, really don't. It would be the only thing worse than drinking it. I take another sip and start shivering violently. It's cold in here and I'm wearing only a thin cotton hospital gown. I think of my clothes waiting for me in the dressing room: pale blue seersucker suit I've worn so many times I'm sick of it, pantyhose with a small run sealed with clear nail polish, boring beige underwear. I have to put those clothes back on and go back to work when this test is over with. Another sip. Clench teeth.

The nurse leans forward and looks into my cup. "Two more sips and you're there." She turns to adjust a menacing piece of machinery that hangs from the ceiling.

The barium pools heavy in my unstable stomach. I feel like I'm walking a tightrope. If I make a misstep, I'll be sick. Very sick. Another sip.

"One more. You can do it."

I want to ask the nurse if anyone has ever thrown up on her, but I'm afraid to talk. One more sip.

"There! Good girl!" The nurse takes the cup. "Now we're going to tilt you around a bit so we can get that barium to slosh around and coat your stomach. Then we'll take pictures."

Tilt? Slosh? If it were Maddie here, she would say, "Are you fucking kidding?" I won't say that out loud, but I'm thinking, *Are you fucking kidding?*

The table I'm strapped to begins to move with a mechanical whir. By the time it has finished moving, I've lost the will to live.

"Are you under any stress?" the nurse asks.

"Some," I manage to say.

"Well, you have reflux." She points to the screen. "See how the white is rising up into your esophagus? That acid is causing the pain you feel. We'll have to do an upper endoscopy. Do you know what an upper endoscopy is?" She sounds like Mr. Rogers.

I nod. Maddie had one a month ago. The nurse unbuckles me from the table and allows me to return to my clothing. On the way out of the dressing room, I bump into the next patient in line. I almost don't recognize Sharon Pendergast in the mint-colored hospital gown.

"Oh, hello," I stammer.

She gives me a rueful smile. "We should set up a kiosk to do these tests at work. I just ran into the Vice President's briefer in the waiting room. I can't imagine what happened to *his* stomach."

"Yeah," I say. "We should have a pickle barrel full of antidepressants with a scoop."

She laughs and slips past me into the room with the barium and the moving table.

When I am finally dressed, I walk outside. The heat slams into me. In the frigid air-conditioning of the clinic I had forgotten the unseasonable swelter of the mid-May day. I stand, swaying slightly with a wave of nausea. Then I move slowly, slowly toward the car. I unlock it and lower myself to the seat. It's an oven. I hurry to start the car so I can turn on the air-conditioning, but the motion pushes me over the edge. Suddenly my dashboard is covered with barium. I'm trying to clean it up with a stack of Happy Meal napkins and some wet wipes, when my cell phone rings. I should ignore it, but I'm a good, conscientious girl.

"Hello."

"Hi, this is Carol L." I wince and move the phone farther from my ear. Carol is Beth Dean's briefer. Her voice is loud, and spills out in rapid, staccato sentences. "Hope it's not a bad time. Need your help. Got an urgent request from Dr. D." She won't use last names over the open phone.

"Another urgent request?"

"Same issue as last week, slightly different wrinkle." This would be purported ties between the Base and Iran.

"How can it be urgent? She's asked the same question thirty-three times—not that I'm counting."

"You know Dr. D. She doesn't like to wait. Can you do a draft for the exclusive pub by close of business?" The "exclusive pub" is the PIU—President's Intelligence Update.

"I'm on Maddie James's canary crew now. I'm not supposed to be following Iran. Couldn't you use the answer I gave her last week?"

"She didn't like that one. Gotta make it look like you've put in more effort. Harry said I could ask you. Please, I don't have anyone else who can do it so quickly. And at least you don't have to deal with her in person."

Yes, I am thankful for that. "Okay. I'm on my way back to the Old Shafts Building. I'll have it for you as fast as I can."

"You're such a sweetie, Vivian."

I am so deadly tired of being a sweetie.

· · ·

Fran agreed to see my Dean tasker through the editorial process so I could attend Josh's kindergarten concert. Jeff and I sit side by side in undersized chairs as we watch the children playing a rambunctious rendition of "Oats, Peas, Beans, and Barley Grow." They're using a wide variety of improvised percussion instruments. Somehow I know the song will stick with me for a long, long time. My vision starts to fade around the edges, the sign of an approaching migraine. Throughout the concert, Jeff quizzes me in a whisper about my medical tests and makes threats against the lives of my managers and Dr. Dean. I guess he's being supportive, but his anger doesn't help my stomach.

It's time for the finale. The children come out waving small plastic American flags. At this age they channel all the abounding energy and enthusiasm of their young, healthy bodies into any pleasant task they are given. They wave their flags as if they are trying to wipe the air clean of a swarm of gnats.

The migraine is getting closer and my vision continues to tunnel in, so that now I can only see a few bright faces at a time, surrounded by darkness teeming with pinpricks. There is my Josh, with his dark curls and long eyelashes. He is a sensitive child, smart, funny, and loving. The children sing "God Bless America." A mother sitting near me wipes away tears. The children finish and each one runs forward to present a flag to his or her parents. I think of white-gloved hands reverently folding flags into triangles and presenting them to mothers. All those mothers in Iraq who've lost their children, all for a big mistake, a gust of hubris that blew foul. I knew what was going to happen, but I didn't stand against the wind.

The program is over and all rise to head for the parking lot. I'm still sitting down, and my vision has narrowed to almost nothing.

"Viv?" Jeff says.

"I can't see anything. I have a migraine." Jeff should be used to my migraines, but it always spooks him when he realizes that I am temporarily blind, even though it will only last an hour or so. He bends over and gently takes my arm, and I stand. It makes me shaky when I can't see.

"Viv," he whispers in my ear, "you don't have to do this job. I've been thinking about it. I don't want you to do it any more. I'll go back to work. At least stay off this canary crew."

"No," I say, and I'm surprised how firm my voice is. "It's my job."

18. A Voice with Many Names

A better day today. The police have finally arrested Jason Beer in connection with the slaying of the Peanut Man. I was expecting it to come sooner. Jason is another vendor, an ignorant and ill-tempered man. He and the Peanut Man had a less than friendly rivalry. Before I set the storage room on fire, I took the Peanut Man's wallet. I emptied it of money and later hid it in Jason's motorcycle. All of our vehicles were searched that day before we went home. No one likes Jason and no one will vouch for him.

No game this evening, so I strengthen my resolve by driving past bars, strip joints, and brightly lit malls. After the slaying, I gave the money from the Peanut Man's wallet to a homeless man on the street. "Peace be upon you, brother," I said. He was too drunk or stoned to respond. Know thy enemy. My enemy is fat and arrogant and cowardly. He assumes I'm stupid, especially when I play the good old boy. My enemy defiles Allah with his words, his deeds, his garish and immodest manner of dress, his selfishness. Seeing him strengthens my will. I know him so much better than he knows me. I'm beneath his notice. He's afraid to meet my eye.

"How can they hate us?" I've heard it on TV, overheard it on the street. People have walked right up to me and said, "How can you hate us?" I've learned that fat older women are most likely to do this. I can spot them from across the room and know which one will approach me. It doesn't happen so much anymore. It occurred more right after the Strikes. I answer in my polite drawl, "Why, I don't hate you, ma'am. I'm mad enough to spit, myself." They always smile, thinking I am one of them.

"How can you hate us?" It is all I can do not to laugh in their faces. They can't see themselves as others see them, and that will be their death. I long to watch their complacence, their arrogance, their insolence dissolve into fear. It will happen in an instant. It will spread across ten faces, a hundred, a thousand, then millions across the country. I don't crave their blood, I crave their fear, as they craved ours at Abu Ghraib.

19. Fran

Maddie picked me for the canary crew! I'm thrilled! It makes me feel useful and wanted. You don't know what that means. My old Evil Empire colleagues, Vernon Keene and Doc Hartman, are on the team, too. The Mines is such a small world.

Until the Strikes, I'd spent my whole career in the Evil Empire Sector of the Mines, which, of course, is now the Ex-Empire Sector. Things move slower there, always have. After a while, alchemists and sectors begin to resemble their targets. The Ex-Empire Sector was big, proud of being big, and jealous of its territory. The sub-shafts that covered the Caucasus were as cantankerous as warring tribes. So after the Strikes, when a bunch of us were told we were moving in with alchemists who covered terrorism, it scared me. Would they be crazy like terrorists? Meeting them didn't calm my fears. They were running around with no sleep, unsure what would happen next. Even sweet Vivian had a wild look.

I'd worked Evil Empire, Ex-Empire affairs for fifteen years, not counting the time I took off to raise my kids, Alan and Kimberly. All that time I believed in the threat. I worked the military side, which was a trial for a woman, because a lot of the men were arrogant, crude, and have a mile-high opinion of themselves. I was an expert on conventional forces. I knew the order of battle, the military doctrine, the state of health of the troops, and whatnot. Then all of a sudden, when the Empire went belly up, none of it meant diddly. So it was nice to be needed again after the Strikes.

The only problem was that working counterterrorism brought me into contact with Dr. Beth Dean again. Sometimes the world is too blamed small. I suspect it was Beth Dean who kept me from being promoted. She complained about my briefings, when they were perfectly fine briefings. Nothing wrong with them. Maddie says we're always fighting the last war and preventing the last terrorist attack. Well, in the bureaucracy, you're always dealing with the last grudge. I suppose what goes around comes around. Beth Dean is head of PentCOW now, the Pentagon Council of the Wise—as if that isn't the unfunniest joke in town. They specialize in sending out snotty memos questioning Mines' analysis, saying Iraq was behind the Strikes, and other foolishness. She's a prostitute, plain and simple. All she wants to do is suck up to the President, throw her weight around, and get revenge just because she thinks we tried to kill her back when she worked in the Mines.

Well, maybe we're not entirely innocent on that last point, but she violated the window rule. Of course, that was no excuse to do what we did, but it got people to thinking, and that's never a good thing.

The window rule is based on seniority. There are six desks in each row, and you keep moving back until you get the window cubbie, which is eight inches bigger than the rest, and you have space on the sill to put an electric teakettle or a model of a T-72 tank or what have you. It took me nearly two decades to work my way to the window. Like everybody else, I had to start out sitting at the other end of the row, in the noisy desk by the copy machine. Not that I minded, because that was back when my hair was Titian red and everything was firm. I was single and knew what good posture could do for an angora sweater. All the young men stopped to flirt on their way to the copier. Even Doc had a crush on me. Then I committed the regrettable error of marrying Ed Monroe.

I'd moved two desks back by that time. Then I got pregnant and took a few years off to raise Alan and Kimberly. Seems all I remember from those years is sitting in the school parking lot drinking Sanka from a thermos, doing crosswords, and listening to "Cracklin' Rosie" on the radio. I don't even like that song. I don't remember why I didn't switch the station.

I came back to work when Ed left me for this hot young up-and-comer, Sharon Pendergast—same one who now signs off on promotions, which is the other reason I didn't get my MS-14 even though her affair with Ed didn't last. What did I tell you about grudges? Anyway, I had to start again back at the copy machines, but I worked my way back until I was next in line for the window. Then one Tuesday morning Quentin Traxler had a coronary at his desk right after he had turned on his electric teakettle. The teakettle started to shriek, and I yelled for Quentin to cut the blasted thing off before he steamed down the ceiling tiles. It kept shrieking. I looked around the partition and there he was, sitting back in his chair, head hanging to the side, mouth and eyes wide open. The tea bag dangled from his hand. Red Zinger. I knew he was gone from the surprised look on his face. I'd never seen Quentin surprised by anything. His favorite expression was, "There is nothing new under the sun." Well, there's nothing new about death, but it surprised Quentin.

It felt strange, moving into Quentin's desk before his chair was cold. I'm speaking figuratively. I'd never sit in his actual chair. The man cut wind like a Clydesdale. I switched his chair for mine. I packed up his model transporter-erector-launcher to give to his widow. I went over everything with cheesecloth and spray disinfectant. I polished the window until it shone. I closed my eyes and felt the sun on my face.

That window cubbie turned out to be hot as an oven in summer and cold as a witch's tit in winter, but I didn't complain. I asked Mines Maintenance if I could have a space heater, but they said it would be a fire hazard. So I cut the fingers off an old pair of cashmere gloves so I could type and it was fine.

Then one day our boss, Harry Esterhaus (same Dirty Harry who's now head of the BD sector—see what I mean about a small world?), started bragging about this Beth Dean he'd hired, who had a Ph.D., as if a Ph.D. would teach you what you need to know to get by in this crazy place. The day she arrived, Harry called us together by the microwave, where he had laid out a box of powdered doughnuts and WELCOME! paper napkins—like the Pope was coming to visit.

She waltzed in like she thought she was the Pope or maybe Henry Kissinger. Now if she wasn't one high-maintenance babe: Mikimoto pearls, Italian heels, and enough Obsession to stun a skunk. Her hair was bleach blond and sprayed solid. She was skinny and had on a green suit with shoulder pads out to there and a long narrow skirt.

Vernon Keene whispered, "This must be Death Bean."

"*Dr.* Beth Dean," she said, when Harry introduced her without the title. Nobody uses titles in the Mines. Even the Boss of Mines goes by his first name. It's tradition. Beth gave Harry one of those smiles that show the gums above the teeth, which I think is too revealing.

Harry grinned back at her. "Dr. Beth Dean has a Ph.D. from Georgetown in military affairs. She taught advanced theory of conflict at Bryn Mawr."

Vernon snorted and whispered, "Advanced conflict at Bryn Mawr is when they can't agree whether to ice the petits fours in pink or green." I laughed. This floozy wouldn't know a Kalashnikov from a cucumber sandwich.

Beth Dean exposed her gums again and pivoted like a trained poodle in a skirt. "Where's my office?" she said.

Do you believe that? "Where's my office?" Vernon laughed out loud. Other people giggled into their hands. Harry blushed. "I'm afraid only managers have offices. You'll sit here." He gestured toward the cubbie by the copy machine. Beth Dean's upper lip shrank away from her teeth and she got that look on her face that my cat

Pearl gets when the vet takes her temperature with a cold rectal thermometer.

"No," she said, "I must insist on an office." She stomped her bone-colored heel on the floor, where it got caught between the gray carpet squares that were peeling up because of a leak in the sprinkler system. Beth Dean looked down. "This is a safety hazard! This carpet is mildewed. I've never worked in a place so lacking in aesthetic appeal."

"This is the government," Herman Greene said as he leaned against a doorjamb with his gut sticking out about a foot. "People who use words like *aesthetic* usually don't last long."

"Actually," I said, "the color is called muted ecru. I asked for dusty rose, but they gave us all muted ecru."

Vernon smirked. "The good thing about government service is job security. Once you get in, you can count on being in these muted ecru people cartons for-fucking-ever."

Harry glared at us and started to jabber about space constraints, lack of renovation funds, and other nonsense that wouldn't mean a thing to Beth Dean, who wasn't listening anyway. She was clucking and peering over partitions like she expected to find a plush, peacock blue corner office hidden behind a file cabinet.

"This won't do," she said, when Harry tried to steer her into the cubicle by the copier. "Absolutely not." She planted her feet. Harry should have canned her right there, but instead he invited her into his office to "talk privately about this issue."

As soon as the door shut, we all started to talk at once.

"She has to go," Vernon said. He pounded his fist on the table. Vernon talks tough. He has a shaved head and a droopy black mustache and wears leather jackets, but he's an alchemist, for heaven's sake, so you know he would never *do* anything. Sheila—Harry's secretary, who used to date Vernon—told me he keeps pictures of naked women with live snakes wrapped around their bodies in his bottom desk drawer behind his gym clothes, which is why she dumped him. Then, of course, there were the bayonets. They hung all over his cubbie walls—he had snuck them in past the SCUDOs. I found his bayonets strange, but otherwise Vernon appeared to be a perfectly nice, polite man. So when he said, "I think we ought to kill her before she spawns," I laughed.

Twenty minutes later, Harry appeared and crooked his finger at me. I followed him to his office and sat down. He started fiddling with his tape dispenser, tearing off little pieces of tape and sticking them to his stapler. Finally I said, "Harry, did you call me in here to watch you waste an entire roll of the taxpayers' tape, or did you have something else on your mind?"

"Francine." Fran is what he usually calls me. "Francine. Every time I try to change something I hear people say 'But we've always done it this way.' Do you think that's a good excuse?"

I tried to meet his eye, but he kept turning his head. I wanted to remind him that change isn't always good, despite the fact that every new manager thinks they've discovered it like cavemen discovered fire. Sometimes change is useless and stupid and causes more trouble than it's worth. But all I said was, "No, Harry."

Harry started folding and unfolding a green Q401 slip. "Francine, I know we have always done seat assignments by seniority, but that doesn't make sense when some people come here with a great deal of experience and education."

"We have a bunch of Ph.D.s already. Half of them are useless."

"Only eleven percent of our alchemists are Ph.D.s and the Main Shaft wants to raise that to fifteen percent. Based on her impressive educational credentials, Dr. Beth Dean merits an office, but we don't have one for her. It would be a shame to lose her. . . ." Harry trailed off, and I knew he was waiting for me to volunteer my window seat. I was trying not to cry. The one thing I have maintained throughout my career is my dignity. Why should I make it easy for him? I squared my shoulders.

Finally Harry said, "Francine, I'm going to give Dr. Dean your cubicle."

"Yes, sir." I held my head high as I went to the copy machine and gathered up some empty boxes to move my things. Beth Dean walked over smiling and said, "Thank you so much. I can't get by without sunshine."

"What makes you think I can?" I said.

After she left, Vernon came by to ask me what was up. I told him.

"The bitch!" he cried. "The miserable, L'Oréal-caked, overperfumed bitch! I'll kill her!"

I was gratified at how mad he got on my behalf and how mad everybody got when they heard what happened.

Beth Dean went out for a two-hour lunch and came back with a big bag from Nordstrom. She unwrapped silk paisley scarves to drape over my muted ecru partition, a marble desk set, and a Murano glass paperweight with exploding blood-red bubbles. She plunked that down in the very spot I used to keep the pencil holder Kimberly made in the fifth grade by covering a tin can with felt.

Vernon told her something was missing. "Can I borrow this paper?" he said. He grabbed the crumpled tissue and went back to his desk. He returned with a badly wrapped package.

Beth Dean blushed. "You are so thoughtful." Then she unwrapped the bayonet.

Vernon pointed to a brownish stain. "Blood. It's hard to find them with the original bloodstains. I would only part with this treasure for a pretty lady like you. My feelings will be dashed if you don't display it prominently." He bowed.

Beth Dean's smile froze, but she thanked Vernon.

Herman ambled over. "I'd give you one of my model tank-buster rockets, but a lot of women think they're too phallic. You have anything against phallic things?"

Beth Dean didn't know how to answer that.

"All the men here are like that," Sheila said, "despite the sexual harassment seminars. Get used to it."

So Beth became the office pariah on her first day. She wasn't the worst pariah ever: That would be Warren Wasserman, a.k.a. the

Unapisser. He urinated in thirty coffeepots before they caught him. But even he didn't start urinating in coffeepots on his first day.

Beth Dean didn't even need a job. She was rich. She left academia thinking she could enter government service and immediately be put in charge of, say, the diplomatic service. I think she was expecting an office with a view of the White House. So even though she got the best desk in our vault, she didn't appreciate it. She complained to Harry that she was cold and he signed a waiver to let her have a space heater. When she griped about spending her own money—as if she couldn't afford it—he arranged for Mines Maintenance to buy it. Then she started in about the glare on her computer screen. If you insist on sunshine, then you'd better expect glare, is what I say, but she acted like it was a big fat surprise that the two go together. She finally installed sheer curtains at the window—this time on her own nickel—because even Harry couldn't get Mines Management to pony up for sheers.

"She'll put in a hot tub next," Vernon said. It was a Monday, and we were waiting for a pot of coffee to stop dripping. She was in her cubbie, sipping hazelnut latte from her private espresso machine. "Time for plan B." Vernon pulled a small glass jar from the pocket of his blazer. He held it between thumb and index finger at eye level. It was filled with dark powder. "Ground castor beans." He tossed the jar towards the ceiling and watched our eyes follow it. Vernon snatched the jar from the air, and his teeth flashed in a grin. "Think of the irony. Death bean for Death Bean."

Sheila laughed. "I bet it's nutmeg."

Vernon raised an eyebrow. "Only one way to find out."

"Oh, it's harmless," Sheila said.

Vernon grinned, took her hand, and slapped the jar into it. "You believe it's nutmeg, go sprinkle it on her lunch." Sheila tried to hand the jar back to Vernon, but he pushed it away. "If it's nutmeg, what are you afraid of?"

Sheila didn't like working with Vernon. The trouble with working in a place with job security is that eventually you have to learn to put up with an ex or two—ex-lover, ex-husband, ex-friend. If you're pretty and have bad judgment, you end up with so many ex-whatevers that it's hard to avoid all of them. So you spend your days sitting five feet from someone who once spent ten minutes licking behind your knee (she was drunk when she told me that, which is why I love the annual holiday party).

"It's not castor beans," Sheila said. "You don't have the guts."

"If it isn't castor beans, then there's no harm in sprinkling it on her food," Vernon said. "You're the coward."

Sheila was fuming. "You're an asshole, but I don't think you're capable of murder. I don't mind sprinkling it on her lunch." She opened the refrigerator, took out a plastic container, and pried off the lid. She looked at Vernon, and he winked at her. She sprinkled on the powder, replaced the lid, and put the container back in the refrigerator.

It bothered me all morning. Would Vernon really poison Death Bean? We'd be guilty if it did happen, because we knew and didn't stop him. The stuff might not actually kill her. I knew castor beans were used to make ricin, but I didn't know if merely grinding the bean was enough to kill. Maybe it would just give her the runs. What would I tell Kimberly and Alan if I got fired for this? Then there's the whole sticky morality thing. Is taking somebody's cubicle a capital offense? Probably not. At eleven o'clock I got up from my desk and checked to make sure she was still in her cubbie. I snuck the cod balls out of the refrigerator and scraped off the powder. When I got back to my desk I should have felt virtuous, but I was so depressed I ate half a bag of mini Snickers.

I was so down that I didn't notice anything wrong at first. Then I smelled something burning, something vaguely electrical and rubbery. There was a popping noise behind me, and then an ear-piercing shriek. I jumped up and turned to see flames blossoming in Beth Dean's sheers. I backed toward the door as Beth tried to stagger out of her cubicle. She was tangled in the wire from her headphones, which had caught on her chair. Her sprayed hair was sparking like a torch. Behind her, flames rose from stacks of paper. "Help me!" she yelled and looked at me like she expected *me* to do something.

I'd saved her skinny ass once already that day. I'm not Mother Theresa. I grabbed the pencil holder Kimberly made for me and headed for the door.

"Maybe we should throw something over her," Herman said. He was looking over the top of his cubbie with as much interest as alarm. He was an explosives expert and loved to watch things burn.

Sheila screamed, "Harry, Death Bean's on fire!"

Beth Dean broke free, pushed past me. Harry met her with his jacket spread like a bullfighter. He whipped it over her head and pushed her to the floor. The rest of us ran for the door as smoke filled the office, fire alarms sounded, and the sprinkler system went off.

"Can you believe the sprinkler system actually works?" Vernon said.

"Shut up and quit blocking the door," Sheila said.

• • •

We huddled outside the building. Light rain fell as we watched the firemen. The ambulance had left. "Act of God," Vernon said. "God got tired of her and—*poof*!—got rid of her."

I whispered in Vernon's ear. "That stuff in the jar?"

"Came out of my pencil sharpener, and I put it through my coffee grinder." He took off his jacket and offered it to me. I tried to decline, but he put it around my shoulders.

"They shouldn't have given her the space heater," I said. "That caused the fire."

"Act of God," Vernon said.

About that time, Doc Hartman pushed through the crowd and asked me if I was okay. Such a doll. I could see he'd been worried about me, even though by this time he'd been married to Rebecca long enough to be staying late at night to work, like men start to do when they're not anxious to go home.

"Just fine and dandy," I said.

"Oh, well, very good. Just inquiring," he said in that wonderful awkward way he has. Then Rebecca came looking for him and he scuttled off.

Beth Dean never came back here. She'd learned her lesson. If you want a good job and a nice office, you need to fork over a lot of money to a winning political party. She's a so-called expert on terrorism now, not that she knows anything about terrorism, or even that she knows her butt from a hole in the ground. These days it's ideology and bank account that matter, not expertise.

20. Doc

The light is red. I idle in the far left lane, waiting to turn into the Mines compound to begin my second day on the canary crew. I'm the third car in line, the same position another miner occupied when a holy warrior gunned him down. Out of habit I leave nearly a car length between me and the bumper ahead, in case a new holy warrior should appear, and I must maneuver my way out. Spring flowers bloom by the memorial bench. The light changes and I make the turn, past the brick guardhouse built after the shootings, through a dappling of yellow sun and blue shadow. I maintain the posted speed, five miles per hour, as I snake through the serpentine course outlined by orange cones and tire slashers. I drive under the radioactive materials detector and present my Mines tag to a SCUDO shouldering an AK-47. He swipes another detector over it and waves me on. Inside the electrified fence a Humvee sits on its haunches. A red light turns green, and the pavement swallows up a concrete barrier. I rumble over it. I spy a rare empty space on the perimeter road and park. I stroll past concrete terrorist barriers planted with pansies and slip through the metal posts installed to prevent vehicles from driving up the steps of the main entrance. I enter the building, treading over the Mines seal. As I punch in my code, the Mines tag machine sucks in my tag, regurgitates it, then sucks it in again as I am about to take it. The words "Call SCUDO" pop up on the screen, but the SCUDO is already at my elbow, having seen the problem on his monitor.

"I bent over my coffee mug yesterday and the tag went in. Must have deactivated it," I say in explanation as he pulls the tag out. "Gave the coffee a bad taste too."

He examines the stained, tattered corners, lays the tag on the machine, and irons it flat with the side of a pocketknife. He goes over it several times and hands it back to me.

"Try it now."

I do so, and the orange bars blocking my path retract. I step through the machine and raise my eyes to the marble inscription high on the south wall: "Ye shall know the truth, and the truth shall make you free."

Odd, I don't feel free. And I'm not sure I've ever come close to the truth.

• • •

"Ye shall know the truth, and the truth shall make you free." Elegant words, but hardly apt. If I had to pick a more fitting epithet for this place, it would be "What goes around, comes around." It applies to covert actions, to the tiniest details of personal and bureaucratic life.

For me, "what comes around" comes in the form of a grayhaired lady still wearing her Mines tag on a lanyard her son Alan made in the fourth grade: Francine Fletcher Monroe. Maddie has chosen both of us for her canary crew. So Fran and I are together again, in one small conference room. My heartbeat grows erratic at the thought, even though she bears little resemblance to the Francine Fletcher I met while standing in line for my first Mines tag photo a few decades ago. That Fran had elaborately coifed, flaming red hair and wore a sweater that showed off a Hollywood figure (back before Hollywood grew anorexic). She had freckles.

I was thrilled when I found out that we were both headed for the Evil Empire Sector. Of course she was headed for the military side and I the political, but she would be just across the hall. In coming years, I would have ample opportunity to see her stride down the hallways, shoulders thrown back, high heels clicking. I always said a shy hello, which she returned with a wide, bright smile that flicked on and off as quickly as a light turned on accidentally. I admired her ambition. She started as a secretary, went to night school to get a degree in military affairs, and became an alchemist. It was a bigger task to be taken seriously among the overwhelmingly male military analysts, but she worked steadily at that, even while dating at least a third of them.

I spent two years trying to work up the nerve to ask her out. I was the stereotype of a Mines alchemist: slight, horn-rimmed glasses, precocious bald spot, reserved to a ridiculous degree, brow invariably furrowed in thought. She tended to ladle from the faster-moving waters of the gene pool: ex–Navy SEALs, up-and-coming bosses, and the like. These were men who could teach her how to take apart and reassemble a Kalashnikov or snag a trip overseas. She was eager to learn everything she could about her assigned subject matter. What could I teach her? How to parse a sentence or read the lineup on the Kremlin wall.

Whenever I could manage it in my alchemy, I would throw in a line about the military so I would have to walk across the hall and coordinate it with her sector. They would invariably make me remove the sentence, but it gave me the chance to stroll past her desk and get a whiff of her perfume. I learned the name of it by accident, when I overheard a woman ask her about it: White Shoulders. I wonder now how the young alchemists court these days. All the coordination is done electronically, where you can't see the face, much less smell the perfume.

I never did ask Fran out, but I spent one evening with her, the most exhilarating, unexpected, atypical night of my life. This was before she married that abominable careerist, Ed Monroe. We were having a big sector move from the fourth level to the fifth. They were moving us from our civilized two-person offices into a vast cube farm. By Friday afternoon we were all required to pack our things into boxes. The movers would come on Friday evening to take everything to our new spaces. The movers weren't cleared, so the call went out for volunteers willing to earn extra money monitoring them. Easy money for a young alchemist. Fran and I were among the first to sign up. We changed into jeans in the restrooms—hers were breathtakingly tight—and Fran pulled her hair into a ponytail.

I was assigned to one group of three movers and she to another. All night we passed each other going up and down the halls and the freight elevator, following the carts of boxes. First we nodded to each other, then Fran added a wink, so I winked back. Then we went on to waves, salutes, little jumps, flapping our arms like chickens, whatever we could think of to make each greeting different. If one of the movers would turn, we would immediately get dead serious. I always turned around once she was past to catch a glimpse of her retreating down the hall, ponytail swishing, hips swaying. Then she turned and caught me watching and burst into laughter. We added that to the game. We were being silly and juvenile, and I never enjoyed an evening so much in my life.

The move was complete around midnight. Fran and I lingered on after the movers and other escorts had left.

"Well, I guess we had better lock up the vault," I said. "Then I'll walk you out to your car." I planned to wait until we pushed our way through the heavy glass doors of the main entrance, then ask her out for a drink as we walked around the building under the blooming pink magnolia trees.

"Who knows what evil lurks in the Mines parking lot after midnight?" Fran said. Then she got a mischievous look in her eye. I was about to set the alarm and initiate the vault closing procedure, when she said "Wait" and crooked her finger, beckoning me back toward her new desk. I followed in something of a fog. I had to remind myself to breathe so I wouldn't keel over. Fran's lipstick was the color of a blood orange.

Fran plopped down on the floor next to one of her boxes and began picking at the edge of the packing tape with a beautifully polished nail, the same color as her lips.

"I have a pocket knife." I felt manly fishing the knife out of my pocket and snapping it open. I slit the box with one smooth motion.

Fran flashed me a smile, reached in and pulled out a bottle of Smirnoff. "Every good Evil Empire alchemist should keep a bottle of vodka at her desk, don't you think?"

Officially, alcohol wasn't allowed in the building. Along with firearms, recording devices, photo equipment, and animals, it was on the list of forbidden items posted at the front gate. As I quickly learned, however, the Mines have rules and "rules." The alcohol prohibition was a "rule" that was and still is broken on a regular basis by everyone from the lowliest junior miner to the BOM. Don't try to bring in a firearm, however, that's a *rule*. You might get shot.

Fran handed me the bottle to open, and went back to scrounging in the box. She pulled out a couple of plastic drinking glasses and a cucumber.

"A cucumber?"

"I always have a cucumber with vodka. When I went on my tour of Moscow, we were staying by Red Square. My last night, I couldn't sleep, so I went out for a midnight stroll by the Kremlin walls, even though it was winter and snowing and I just about froze my buns off. I got called over by two guards, who motioned me to come inside the iron gates. Boy was I scared. Here I was a miner, and two goose-stepping Kremlin guards were shutting an iron gate on me. The short one pulled a bottle of vodka out of his coat, and the tall one pulled out a dirty glass and a cucumber. It was the short guy's birthday, and he wanted me to drink with them. So we stood there drinking vodka and chasing it with bites of cucumber. We lit our cigarettes at the eternal flame at the tomb of the unknown soldier at the base of the Kremlin wall."

"Isn't that sacrilege?"

"I asked them about that. The short one shrugged and said, 'He's a soldier, I'm a soldier. He would understand.' So now I always have a cucumber with my vodka, and I always drink a toast to Yuri and Sergei. I often wonder whether they ended up in Afghanistan or someplace awful like that."

Fran held out the glasses, and I poured a shot into each.

"That's not how the Russians drink vodka," Fran said. "They fill the glass."

I had never had that much vodka in my entire life, but I didn't want to admit that. I poured the glasses full. Fran took hers and raised it to mine. "To Yuri and Sergei, wherever they are. *Na zdoroviye.*"

"Na zdoroviye," I repeated, and we drank.

"Let's take a tour," Fran said. She hopped up without spilling a drop of her vodka, and I followed as she wove her way through the cubicles. "I'd like to come in here with a few gallons of paint and spruce up these walls. Dusty rose would be nice. Bright colors stimulate the brain."

I mumbled assent, but the truth was that my brain—along with certain other parts of my anatomy that don't bear mentioning—was already overstimulated.

Fran bit into the cucumber and then offered it to me. I don't like cucumbers, but suddenly that particular cucumber struck me as delicious and full of meaning. I bent and nibbled it from her hand. Then I took a large sip of vodka. My knees grew wobbly as we continued our tour, up one row of cubicles and down the next.

Fran stepped into one of the offices and snapped on the light. "This is Perkins's office."

Perkins was the sector boss, an irascible, humorless, arrogant old toad, but a smart, highminded toad for all of that.

Fran brushed her fingers over his desk. "Cherrywood. We get dented metal. You know we ought to *do* something in here. Something he'll never know about, but something that would make him crazy if he did know about it."

"Like what? Stick chewing gum under his chair?"

Fran laughed, a somewhat out-of-control laugh, I thought.

"Or maybe I should leave something for him."

"The rest of the cucumber?"

Fran laughed again, so hard that she spilled some of her vodka onto Perkins's carpet.

"There," I said. "We've left something for him. Maybe we'd better leave it at that. You know I'll have to initial the door when we lock up, so he'll know I was the last person here."

"No, I'm going to leave him something else. And don't worry, he'll know it wasn't yours." At this Fran reached under the back of her T-shirt and unhooked her bra. As I stared, she reached into one sleeve of her T-shirt, pulled down the strap and slipped it over her hand. Then she reached into her other sleeve and whipped out the bra in one swift motion. "*Voilà!*"

Nothing ever devised by Harry Houdini could have stunned me as much. I couldn't take my eyes off the bra, a lace-and-satin number that matched her lips and nail polish. Then I saw her nipples under the thin cloth of her T-shirt. I took a swig of vodka to calm myself.

Fran opened Perkins's lower desk drawer. "Perfect. It's full of empty hanging files." Fran selected one and slipped the bra into it. "Do you have a pen I could borrow?" I handed her one from my pocket with my hand shaking. Fran filled in the label on the folder and turned it so I could see what she had written: INDISCRETIONS. "I'll file it in the back. I don't want him to find it right away." She replaced the folder and closed the drawer. Then she hopped onto the desk and smiled like the Cheshire cat. "Think how much fun it will be knowing it's there, and imagining Perkins pulling it out one day, hopefully when *his* boss is in the room."

Try as I might, at that moment I couldn't even remember what Perkins looked like. All I could think of was Fran, and how much fun it would be to kiss those blood orange lips.

Fran patted the desk next to her. "Come sit by me. You're too shy."

I'm too reserved a gentleman to describe what happened next, except to say that on that night, I was not a reserved gentleman. And when it was over, the excitement, the vodka, and the illicit thrill of besmirching Perkins's cherrywood all conspired to make me . . . regurgitate. After all these years, it remains the most painful memory of my life. Fran tried to console me. She had pushed Perkins's trash can under my head just in time.

Thus ended my affair with Fran Fletcher. I could barely meet her eye in the halls after that. A few years later she was married to Ed Monroe and I made my own dreadful error by marrying Rebecca. I nursed my heartbreak by throwing myself into the issue of Evil Empire activities in the Third World. As the years passed, I saw that their activities and capabilities were declining. So I wrote what I saw. That's when I ran up against the thick brick wall of Vaughn Sutter Wayne. "Not your job to say our enemy isn't dangerous," he once told me. Funny, I thought that was exactly my job.

21. Vaughn Sutter Wayne
Musings from an Unquiet
Grave

Never liked the alchemists—wussy pussies, all of them. No *cojones*, no experience in the field, no idea of how the game is really played. Desk jockeys with nothing in their jockey shorts but lint. Self-righteous mice.

Started my career in the field: France, World War II. Arrived by parachute at night, the only way for a self-respecting sharper to make an entrance. Broke both ankles, but still managed to haul in three groupers the first month. Took risks big-time, drank some memorable wine, laid a lot of foreign nationals without having to fill out forms about my contacts. Didn't answer to bureaucrats in Washington. The organization was small, but agile, virile, and dangerous.

Took the helm of my alma mater in the eighties. By then, the Mines had become shy and flabby, a bloated, self-satisfied, politically correct caricature of itself. Tried to put the testosterone back into the place. Kicked a lot of ass. Forced some early retirements. Drank a lot of Manhattans with members of the Esteemed Legislative Body in the interest of beefing up the budget, big-time.

Put the alchemists in their place. Thought they were the knights of the almighty truth, did they? They tried to tell a story different from the one the President wanted told. Never understood that truth is like raw material, like ore, it's how you shape it and how you use it that gives it value. Men are ruled by myth, not fact. Truth isn't meant to go on public display in its raw form. It must be forged to fit the greater purpose.

The greater purpose was to break the back of the enemy, the Evil Empire—can you think of a nobler cause? For that we needed money, big-time appropriations from the Esteemed Legislative Body. And the alchemists tried to say that the Evil Empire threat was receding in the Third World. Nobody appropriates money to counter a receding threat! You must have an enemy to get anything done in this world. Idiots didn't understand.

The Evil Empire was the hydra, and the President crushed it, no thanks to the alchemists. If they'd had their way, they'd still be analyzing the lineup on the Kremlin wall. They called that a job. More like taking charity from the taxpayer. The real men were out in the denied areas, three steps ahead of the KGB, running groupers who risked a bullet in the back of the head in the Lubyanka.

If I couldn't die in the field, then the only place to die was at my desk in the Mines. My only regret is that doughnut, the indignity of it. The utter indignity.

22. A Voice with Many Names

Sunlight from the window catches the powder and makes it sparkle. There is so much beauty in what I do. As the day grows closer, my mind is growing steadier. The past is receding. I'm leaving the individual behind and becoming only a jihadist, one of a legion of brothers. My hands are steady as I pour the powder gently into the funnel. I'm proud that I have wasted nothing. I dedicate every grain to the glory of Allah.

There is only one God. The infidels, with their Father, Son, and Holy Ghost, are polytheists. They have many gods and respect none of them. Not even the evangelicals, despite their conspicuous piety. They use their faith for their own selfish ends. I now use their faith, too. I had a Jesus fish put on my own truck. I laugh every time I see it. It fits with my Southern accent, my role. It came in handy when the police were searching vehicles after the Peanut Man's death. They noticed the fish, the Christian literature I had stashed in the truck, just in case. They were taken in by my accent, by how anxious I was to help them find whoever killed the nice Peanut Man, by my goodwill.

I despise the infidels. They respect nothing, honor nothing, keep nothing sacred. Not even their own souls, bodies, beliefs. They bathe in our precious oil, the wealth of our holy land, while our children die, our people suffer. They are profligate in a hungry world. I must allow no sympathy for them. Weakness is evil. I must resist the evil of inaction and think only of what is good: jihad. *Our* faith, *our* people cannot survive if *they* flourish. If we don't defeat them, they will leave nothing of this earth, and we will starve trying to glean their ravished fields.

23. Doc

Busy morning. The canary crew moved into the small conference room yesterday, and now things are switching into high gear. I'm a little afraid of the what-ifs to come. What if I had followed up on that operative's cousin? What if we had pushed the Internal Investigative Organ harder to get information on that facilitator? What-ifs are like thorns, the effort to get them out of your skin drives them deeper.

We dubbed our room "the canary cage." Logistics set up computers on the table, and the six of us sit around it, elbow-to-elbow, like a grim PTA committee. A large pipe from floor to ceiling goes right through the center of the table. We can hear the occasional trickle of water. "Like sitting by a mountain stream," Maddie says sarcastically. The backs of our chairs are up against the wall and we must squeeze to get in and out of our seats, being careful not to knock down the link charts, maps, and chronos we have taped on the walls next to a framed photograph of Confederate spy Belle Boyd, the room's only permanent decoration.

Fortunately Maddie chose only relatively thin alchemists for the canary crew. Besides Fran, Vivian, Maddie, and me, we have Vernon Keene, a chem expert from special weapons. Maddie will have him looking into what the "red cloud" might be. Vernon barely fits. His beer gut scrapes and shakes the table every time he sits down or gets up. The final member of our crew is Kristin Russell, in from the finance subshaft. She's the one with the tongue piercing. Despite that, Kristin is one of the stars among the newcomers, an amazingly sharp and nimble-minded young lady who looks like she should still be hanging out at the mall with high school girls, even though she is old enough to have acquired two master's degrees: one in international finance and one in comparative religion, a killer combination for a BD. She's rail thin and has short platinum hair that apparently was cut with a Weedwhacker. Vernon, the bald goat, is besotted. Me, I'm mystified by the new standards of beauty. This fascination with curveless women suggests to me a disturbing tendency toward pedophilia.

My standard of beauty is Fran. She sits directly in front of me across four and a half feet of fake wood conference table. Our two computer monitors come between us, but I catch sight of her frequently when she leans over to consult with Vivian or to grab a printout. It is unbearable. I see the same unique mix of playfulness and intensity, a charming determination to do the job thoroughly and right, the same sly humor, the same forthright eyes that look through any effort at pretense. I fear those eyes.

I'm fortunate to have that ass Vernon here to demonstrate how a man can humiliate himself in front of his colleagues, wiping out any respect that he might have earned through his years of education and experience. Vernon tries to play footsie with Kristin under the table. Sometimes he accidentally touches my foot.

"Vernon," I say sternly, "kindly keep your feet to yourself. Don't mistake this canary cage for *La Cage aux Folles.*"

"Don't flatter yourself, Doc," he growls, and shifts in his seat, shaking the table and sloshing coffee from my full cup onto a stack of printouts.

"And perhaps you could switch to Bud Light for a few weeks," I say as I clean up the mess.

I see a slight smile ripple Kristin's lips, but she keeps her eyes riveted on her terminal. She's going through slag at an amazing clip, pausing only to answer the instant messages that appear at the upper right-hand corner of her screen. Her fingers are a blur on the keyboard as she types an answer, then continues her scanning of cables. Multitasking, they call it.

I notice Vivian sit up straight and begin to chew on her lip, a sign that she is about to speak. She doesn't do so often. She is thoughtful, hesitant to share ideas in their early stages.

"Any chance *red cloud* refers to something from the Koran?" she asks.

Kristin shakes her head and responds without slowing her typing speed. "I've never come across *red cloud* in my reading of the Koran or the hadiths. *Black wind* appears in some of the more apocalyptic hadiths, but no red cloud."

Vivian turns to Vernon. "What toxic chemicals are red?"

"Most are colorless."

"Any code words that might refer to a delivery system?" Vivian asks.

"Bat," Maddie offers. "I've seen two references to bats."

"Something that flies out of a cave and bites people. Sounds like a terrorist to me," Vernon says.

"Maybe just something that flies: plane, helicopter."

"Bat might suggest a night attack," Kristin says.

"It might suggest a dozen other things, too. I don't like playing guessing games with new code words," Fran says. "We'll never guess. Better to pinpoint cells and roll them up before they can do anything."

"We have to throw around ideas," Maddie says.

"I'm sorry," Fran says, "of course we do."

Everyone gets quiet. Fran is right about focusing on people, not plot. Maddie has me looking at three possible members of the Perfumers cell. She has given Fran the recruiter, the Vortex, and his imam.

Fran speaks slowly, thinking out loud. "As near as I can figure, the Vortex recruited forty or fifty men in Iraq. They left the country in 2004. Around the same time, we got reports of men showing up for 'special training' at camps in South Africa and the Philippines. Later, it looks like the South Africa and Philippines trainees met up in Yemen and spent another six weeks training together there. I've been trying to find something that would indicate that the men the Vortex recruited in Iraq were the same ones who later trained in South Africa, the Philippines, and Yemen."

"And?" Vernon says.

"I think I have it. One of the Iraqi recruits changed names when he went to Africa, but somehow continued to draw money from the same bank account."

"Geez, forty or fifty? That's one big operation," Maddie says. "Trying to pull off an operation with that many has got to be a coordination nightmare. And a risk."

Vivian points to the wall, where Maddie has tacked up her list of definitions of the word *swarm*. "Look at that last definition, *social swarm*, gatherings coordinated by cell phones, BlackBerries, whatever. If a bunch of teenagers can become adept at swarming, then certainly a group of highly motivated operatives can."

Maddie taps her pencil on the desk. "Anything else, Fran?"

"Not yet."

The room gets quiet as we all go back to our lists, chronos, and scribbled notes.

I'm focusing on a Perfumer with the nickname "Snail." We acquired some information on a passport forgery operation that indicates he may have entered this country two years ago. I've been working with the Internal Investigative Organ to see if we can pinpoint what part of the country. I've found conflicting information on whether he's still here or in Europe. The more I work, the more I'm convinced Maddie is right: We're on the verge of a major attack. I wake up every morning wondering whether today will be the day when we abruptly switch gears from threats to forensics.

The problem with scanning endless documents is that it doesn't occupy one's full attention, but allows a portion of the mind to wander. Where are these people who've dropped out of sight? Are they saying their final prayers, cleansing their bodies, anointing themselves with Western colognes and deodorants so that they will in no way stand out from their victims? The martyr videos were probably made weeks or months ago. Surely they are imagining how their images will be aired before the rapt eyes of young boys, who will follow in their footsteps. If they succeed, they will be venerated, immortal. It is powerful motivation.

The terrorists have blind, consuming faith in a vengeful God. They've vanquished doubt. They are storm troops of a global army of righteous anger. We wallow in doubt, whatever faith we have daily shaken by the actions of our own government, as well as those of the terrorist. From our vantage point, we have the unique opportunity to be frightened by both sides.

We are six ants tunneling through a mountain of sand that may collapse on us at any moment. I've never felt so small.

I am ruminating on such things when a familiar voice interrupts.

"You know, Doc," Fran says, "you should get instant messaging. It's a real time saver."

I experience a moment of panic whenever Fran addresses me directly, but I cover it up with a veneer of what I believe to be friendly gruffness. "Or a time waster," I say.

"Only a time waster if you don't use it correctly. It's great for asking a question of someone else in the office."

"What about that reliable invention, the telephone?"

"But with instant messaging, you can tell if someone is logged on before you even make the query."

"You can?"

"Oh, Doc, you're such a Luddite. Of course you can tell. You pull up the list of IM users and pick out, say, the bio expert who happens to be at his desk. Saves phone messages and saves time if the person isn't in."

"Well, perhaps that could be useful, but I don't have the time to figure out how to do it."

"Takes two minutes," Fran says. Before I know what is happening, she is up from her seat and squeezing herself around the periphery of the room. She rests her left hand on my shoulder as she leans over my terminal. She punches the keyboard, bringing up a series of boxes with cryptic messages. I am amazed that she doesn't hesitate before she hits Accept or No or some other mysterious choice the computer has offered. I am amazed that she is not interrupted by error messages. I am amazed that she still wears White Shoulders.

"Type in your Mines system password followed by two spaces and your entry code followed by an underscore, then the last two digits of the year you entered underground."

"What?" For a moment I draw a blank. I feel panicky. My mouth is gaping like that of a fish short on oxygen. I have advanced degrees from Harvard. I work the *New York Times* crossword puzzle in ink. But I am profoundly, incurably stupid when it comes to computers and their requirements.

Fran explains slowly. "Your Mines system password, the one you use to get into Auger. Two spaces. Your entry code is the one you use to get into the building. Underscore. Then the last two digits of the year you entered underground. It's simple."

It takes a supreme effort on my part to focus on these instructions and carry them out. Fran looks away as I type my password.

"Finished," I say. I hold my breath as Fran submits my request. I get the icon of the little miner industriously wielding his pickax. He stops and smiles. A speech bubble tells me my request is accepted. No error messages. No red light blinking on the miner's hat. This is a miracle. Nothing I have ever requested on the computer has been accepted without error messages. I look up at Fran in disbelief and admiration.

"Welcome to the twentieth century," she says, patting my back. "You're not ready for the twenty-first yet, but you'll get there."

I think I detect a slight squeeze before she takes her hand from my shoulder and returns to her seat. With an effort of will, I go back to my searches. A small box pops up in the corner of my screen. Message from Fran: "Nice tie!"

I can feel the blood in the capillaries of my face boiling. I quickly hit the X to remove the message from the screen before someone sees it. I see Fran peek from behind her monitor. She seems to be suppressing a giggle.

Another box pops up: "Go back to work, I won't bother you any more." I X that one off the screen. Where was I? North Africa.

24. A Voice with Many Names

I bought them from the school supply aisle in the grocery store: packages of colored markers and pencils. I've drawn everything out in great detail, over and over again. I've assigned a different color to each man, so he'll know his place, what he must do and when. I've drawn diagrams, storyboards, and—for my own pleasure—detailed renderings of the planes.

The Poppy has given me final instructions and is preparing to leave. After so much slow preparation and patience, things will begin to happen quickly. I feel the excitement of waiting for the curtain to rise. The whole world fills the audience. Their screams will be more gratifying than applause.

My thoughts are interrupted by the demands of children. I sell them food and take their money. "Ya'll be good, now!" Then I clean my hands with antibacterial wipes—I buy them by the case. Children are so dirty. I have learned to hear in their laughter the cackle of the Dajjal. They are, none of them, innocents. They are already spoiled, greedy, grasping for whatever is sweet or greasy. They will take it from my hands like tame birds.

25. Maddie

I hate that fucking little miner icon with his dufus mustache, potato nose, and red pickax, which moves faster or slower, depending on how overburdened the servers are. Hate him. I'm trying to do a search and he's been banging with that pickax for ten minutes and now each stroke takes several long seconds, like he's thinking about where he should strike. The rock. Hit the rock, stupid. It's the same rock you've been hitting since we all went onto the MWE (Mining Work Environment) computer system. What's the holdup? I'd like to tell him what he can do with his pickax. Why can't we have an hourglass or a spinning disk like other people? No, we have to have a stupid little miner with a pickax, the most annoying thing I can imagine.

Vivi says, "Anybody else got the miner?" and I know before I hear the chorus of yeses that the whole computer system is about to tank and will probably be down until afternoon.

The miner puts down his pickax and sits with his head in his hands, the light on his helmet blinking red. We're hosed.

My entire canary crew leans back and we look at one another.

"Well," Fran says, "I just printed out a stack of slag. I'll be happy to share." She starts to collate the stack into separate reports and staples each one with a firm slap of her palm. "You know, Maddie, I would love you to meet my son, Alan. I think you two would really get along well."

Red lights and warning sirens go off in my head. Shit. I hate it when women try to introduce me to their sons. They're always losers. My brain races for an excuse.

"Oh, I'm dating someone," I say. I pray that Vivi has the sense to keep quiet.

"Well," Fran says, "Alan is a wonderful man. He's an Air Force demolitions expert. Good, secure job."

"Oh, Maddie loves those Special Forces types," Vivi says.

I kick her. "But threat analysis is my first love," I say and grab a report from Fran's stack. I draw a TAILFIRE on the Snail.

"Here, Doc, I believe this is your guy." I reach across the table.

"Thank you, ma'am. May I offer you a purported sighting of the missing cargo plane?"

"Really?" I perk up as I reach for it.

"Don't get excited, the source also claims to have recently seen two dead hijackers."

"Sigh."

"And Elvis?" Vernon says.

"I'm sure if he perceives that the U.S. government is interested and willing to pay, he will also see Elvis," Doc says, "barefoot, drinking tea with the Chieftain, and carrying an old Evil Empire rifle inscribed 'Takin' Care of Business.'" Doc picks up his mug of vile coffee with one hand, while the other clutches the report on the Snail. His forehead crinkles in concentration, which makes his thick, gray eyebrows spiky and puckish.

"Any word on his location?" I ask.

"No, this is the response to some questions I sent out to the field. The sharpers have queried their sources, but there isn't much new." He skims down the page. "Wait, I didn't know this. He's fluent in French. Hence the moniker 'Snail.' Who's focusing on the U.S. embassy Paris threat?"

"Me," Kristin says. "Does he have a name other than the Snail?"

"Abu Mohammad, surprisingly enough, and probably a few more we don't know about. Oh, and here's another odd fact: He went to school in Paris, where he was a theater major before he dropped out."

"A theater major?" Vernon says, incredulous. "Not chemistry, biology, computer science, any of the other approved preterrorism majors?"

"No," Doc says. "It says *theater* right here."

The door of the canary cage is closed, because we're working with a particularly sensitive vein of compartmented data, meaning we had to sign a paper and watch a hokey, archaic-looking video— made only last year—on the dangers of loose lips (which is in no way a guarantee that we will be allowed access to all the information we need to see). We have a PLEASE KNOCK sign on our door, largely because anyone opening the door too wide and too fast slams it right into the back of my chair, which makes me jump and shriek. And I mean shriek. Whenever somebody startles me I emit an involuntary, absolutely bloodcurdling shriek, which has the effect of scaring the bejeezus out of everyone else in the room.

Most people respect our sign, but, of course, managers are not most people. Signs and instructions posted by cube dwellers are not for *them*. So Harry ignores the sign and barges into our room, carrying a stack of papers and a Starbucks venti. The door wangs my chair soundly, I scream—think Janet Leigh in *Psycho*—Vivi screams, Doc grabs his heart, the muscles of Harry's hand involuntarily clench, the lid pops off, and the venti caramel macchiato with extra whipped cream spews out like a geyser, raining down on me, Kristin, Vivi, and the front of Harry's pants.

"Are you crazy?" Harry asks. "What was that? I just bumped your chair."

I ignore his question. I'm more concerned about Doc, who is still clutching his heart.

"Are you okay, Doc? You're not having a heart attack, are you?"

Fran is already up and making her way around the table.

"Get out of my way," she says brusquely to Harry.

"I'm fine," Doc assures us, but his face looks flushed. Fran is already loosening his tie. She reaches down to loosen his belt buckle.

Doc jumps like he's been goosed and lets out a girlish "Oh."

"Relax," Fran says. "I'm not molesting you, I'm just making sure you can breathe easily. Vivian, call Medical."

"I'm fine. I don't need a doctor."

But Vivi is already on the phone.

"There are too many people in this room," Fran says. "Go outside, so Doc can get air."

Doc tries to protest, but chairs scrape and the table shakes as everyone rises and tries to squeeze out at once. Harry, still clutching his largely empty Starbucks cup, backs out of the canary cage. He has that vacant, rabbit-eyed look on his face that managers get when the situation is going out of their control.

"Someone should call his wife," Harry says.

"He's been divorced for years," I remind him. I look down at my dress. I've been baptized with sticky caramel macchiato from bodice to hem. There is caramel macchiato in my hair. Even worse, I know that this caramel macchiato has spit in it. I know, because I pointed Harry out to Wynona one day as a primary source of misery in my life, and she promised to spit in his coffee for me.

Harry clears his throat, and I know that my day is about to get worse.

"I came by to tell you, Maddie, I have a tasker for you from Dr. Dean that's due this afternoon."

"Harry, you promised that we wouldn't be taken off this threat."

"It concerns the threat. Dean heard that we had a canary crew up and running, and she wants a summary of everything we know about connections between the current threat and Iran."

"That's easy. No connection. Period. Zilch. She's an idiot."

"Are you sure there's no connection?"

"Haven't found a thing. That's what 'No connection. Period. Zilch,' means. I'll phone her briefer and tell her that."

"She wants it in writing. I want it in writing, too. Otherwise she'll go to the principals with a story she doesn't have right. I want this memo sent to all the principals simultaneously. Otherwise we're asking for trouble. And I don't want it to look like we're blowing her off with an off-the-cuff response. Do a deep drill."

"Can't do it under that deadline. The servers are all down."

"Come on, Maddie." A wheedling note creeps into Harry's voice. "Poll the alchemists."

"Auger isn't the only thing down. We have no wordprocessing capability, no way to send anything to the PIU staff, no way to get any material cleared for publication. I'd have to spend half the day walking the piece around for coordination or reading it over the phone. I would have no way to check the database to see who's cleared to hear it. The alchemists who have to coordinate the piece would have no way to check any facts. Her briefer is going to have to call her back and negotiate a more reasonable deadline."

"Dr. Dean doesn't like to negotiate and she doesn't like to take no for an answer. We can find you a stand-alone computer to work on and we just won't coordinate it. Fudge the wording enough, and you won't have to clear it." A gruff, impatient edge creeps into Harry's voice as he suggests two major violations of Mines etiquette, which would buy me enough ill will from both the White Mines (the coordination issue) and the Black Mines (the clearance issue) to last for the rest of my career.

I'm tempted to give Harry Doc's standard answer to an unreasonable request: "If you want it bad, you'll get it bad." Instead, I say something even more damaging to my career. "Harry, I can't make this deadline under these circumstances."

He quickly lets me know what I've done. "Madeleine, you've tried twice already to make the Senior Alchemist ranks. You have to understand that it takes something special to be a Senior Alchemist, something extra, a determination to get the job done no matter what the obstacles. You have to demonstrate that or you'll never make it over the bar."

He has no right to discuss my career in front of my colleagues. I'm furious. I take one step forward to bring myself solidly into Harry's personal space.

"If this were a national emergency, I'd find a way to do it if I had to use a stone tablet and a pickax, but it's not an emergency. It's a rich, spoiled political appointee who likes to throw her weight around and has come up with another wacko theory to distract us. If I piss off three-quarters of the office on this trivia, I won't have their support when it counts. Don't you dare accuse me of lack of determination. I'm tired of paying the price because some briefer or senior manager hasn't got the balls to say no."

We're squeezed into a cramped space outside the canary cage. We're surrounded by cubicles, but I hear no sound of typing, no voices on the phone, no chairs scraping, or humming. I think I hear the sound of people listening. Does listening make a sound? I think it does, a hollow whoosh of words being sucked into eager ears. The rest of my canary crew—minus Doc and Fran—are backed up against the cubicle partitions, trying to pretend they don't hear every word. I know they, and the people in the cubicles, all think the same way that I do. But nobody says a damn word. I suppose they have big D.C.-area mortgages and credit card payments.

Then I hear a sound approaching, the *woo-woo-woo* of the little siren on the white motorized cart sent by Medical. The cart stops outside the vault door and I push past Harry to buzz a doctor and nurse inside. Vernon holds the door to the conference room open wide. I look in and see that Fran has managed to get Doc to lie down on the conference table, although his head is up and the opening door has caught him in mid-protest. Fran is taking his shoes off and massaging his feet. In short order, Doc is whisked away. Fran insists on going with him.

Harry glares at me, says, "I'll try to get your deadline pushed back a few hours." He stomps off to his office.

Amber Minnick steps out of her cubicle. She's a veteran alchemist brought over from the Near East Asia Sector after the Strikes.

She sidles over to me and whispers, "When I saw the people in white coats, I thought they were coming to take you away for psychiatric evaluation."

"Do you think what I said to Harry was crazy?"

Amber shakes her head. "Reckless, yes. Crazy, no. I couldn't agree with you more. Thanks for saying it."

"Thanks for your silent support."

"Hey, I'm a single mother trying to make my next promotion before her daughters reach college age. And Harry is vindictive in that burning, fundamentalist Christian sort of way."

"Yeah, I know. I feel lonely, that's all. Out there and exposed."

"Use vinegar on that dress tonight and leave it to soak. Harry looks like he wet himself. The coffee splattered perfectly. I hope he has some high-level meetings scheduled for today."

26. A Voice with Many Names

Last night I dreamed of birds, flight, victory. In my dreams, I had already reached Paradise, shed my sinful self, and become, for the first time, clean and whole. I met those fallen in the struggle, and they embraced me, greeted me as an equal. My mother was there, because my deeds bought her entrance, despite her candle lighting. From Paradise, the destruction of the Infidel was a glorious sight. Explosions bloomed across his land like poppies.

My dreams were beautiful, and I wanted to lose myself in their abstraction, but I awoke to discover from the radio that the police have released Jason Beer. He was able to prove that he was elsewhere at the time of the Peanut Man's death. So the police will be looking again, asking questions. I live separately from the other men, and that was a good decision. If they come to search here, they will find nothing incriminating, nothing a good old boy named Junior wouldn't own. I won't visit the other house again. The preparations have been made. The men know what to do. Even if I'm arrested, they'll be able to carry out the operation without me. But the thought of living beyond this operation and not achieving my dream brings me enormous pain. I've measured out a portion of the powder into a capsule for myself, if it comes to that.

27. Doc

I sit in a paper gown on a bed in the Fairfax County Hospital emergency room. A white curtain makes a flimsy shield between me and the rushing, preoccupied staff. It must be close to midnight. The nurse who knows where my pants are located has become as elusive as a Base operative. Nothing is wrong with me, except that my ass is cold, and my self-respect is in tatters. I knew it wasn't a heart attack, and the doctors have confirmed that after subjecting me to an electrocardiogram and a battery of other tests. When you're sixty-one, no one believes you when you say you're not having a heart attack. They cart you off to the emergency room if you burp. I am perfectly healthy, but I fear the humiliation will prove terminal.

I hear a disturbance outside the curtain, the sound of voices. I call out, "Hello? Hello? I need some help in here!"

"I'm coming!" It's Fran.

A nurse raises her voice. "I told you that you can't go in there."

"Bullshit, I'm in," Fran says as she pushes through the curtain.

I clutch a paper sheet over my bare, hairy legs.

The nurse looks at me as if I were a truant child. "Didn't they tell you that you can go home? We finished with you hours ago." Someone calls her name, Ann, and she is off before I can ask about my pants.

"Hey," I vainly call after her. "Where are my clothes?"

Fran laughs. "Don't you know they always put them under your bed?" She squats down and I hurry to push the sheet under my legs so she won't get the unflattering view from below. She straightens up, a blue plastic bag in her hands, and laughs again. With an index finger, she smoothes her soft gray hair behind an ear. I remember that gesture from our old days in the Evil Empire Sector.

"What's the big deal? I've already seen you naked." Fran gives me her radiant smile.

"You remember?"

"Of course, I can picture you like it was yesterday. You weren't completely bare naked. You never did take your socks off."

There it is, out in the open. My humiliation is complete, total, breathtaking. How can she take advantage of me at such a time? I am, as everybody tells me, a sweet old man. Damned sweet. I don't deserve to have my youthful foibles aired at such a time.

"Can't you leave me with one shred of dignity? Here I am wrapped in paper like a dead halibut, having been ridden out of work on a glorified golf cart, with my boss and my colleagues gaping. As it turns out, I abandoned my post and made a spectacle of myself for nothing. I *told* you it wasn't a heart attack. I have the cardiovascular system of a thirty-year-old. Did you hear what my blood pressure is? One-ten over sixty. My cholesterol is one-sixty. It was your doing that I ended up in this place, and now, when I am vulnerable, you bring up that supreme embarrassment."

"I didn't think it was so bad."

"Bad? I threw up."

"Oh, I don't remember that part."

"Really?" I swallow my shame enough to look at her. She's on the verge of laughing.

She hands me the blue plastic bag. "Here, put your pants on. I'll wait outside."

"You didn't have to stay with me all this time."

"Somebody has to drive you home."

• • •

When Fran said she would drive me home, I honestly thought she meant my home. I didn't notice at first that we weren't headed in that direction. We passed a Mattress Warehouse, a Target, a Home Depot. I didn't realize that it was a different Mattress Warehouse, a different Target, a different Home Depot than the ones you pass on the way to my house. All the while I babbled on about nonsense, unable to make myself shut up. We talked about her car. She has one of those Mini Coopers, a red one with a white top. Still annoyed with her for all she had put me through, I made some stupid comment about midlife crisis cars and how I had thought only men bought them.

"I love my Mini and I don't care what you call her," Fran said. She caressed the dashboard in a way that made me oddly jealous. "I bought her last June, and I will celebrate her first birthday with a cake from Giant Gourmet. Something decadent with chocolate, raspberry liquor, and oodles of whipped cream. She's the first car I ever bought new in my life. My ex would never let me go car shopping with him. Said I would probably pick based on color. So when I went to the dealership last year, I walked up to the sales manager and said, 'Show me the red ones. Fire engine red and polished like an apple for the teacher.' He looked at me and said, 'Ma'am, I think I know exactly what you would like.' He led me right to this little lady, and it was love at first sight. I've never been so happy with a car. Who says picking by color is stupid? The way I look at it, I put in my time driving a station wagon—complete with fake wood sides and Kool-Aid–stained upholstery. I kicked up my heels when I was young, then I did my years as a doormat—first at home and later at work—and now I'm in the mood to kick up my heels again." Fran put her foot down on the accelerator, taking the next curve at an unladylike speed.

"Fran! Easy!"

She laughed and eased up on the pedal. "Why shouldn't I have some fun? My cardiovascular system is still perking along nicely, too, thank you. I've been taking yoga for eight months now. You should see how I can bend. I can do a split. Flexibility is something that you don't have to lose with age. For a while there I was giving in to being old, but lately I've started to feel that there are a lot more things that you don't have to lose with age." With this, Fran winks at me and reaches over and squeezes my knee.

Despite the fact that highly qualified medical personnel have subjected my cardiovascular system to a complete diagnostic rundown and declared it fully operational, I feel as if my heart muscle is about to implode.

"Where are you taking me?" I'm embarrassed to hear panic in my own voice.

"I thought you shouldn't be alone tonight, so I'm taking you to my house." Fran smiles at me benignly, as if she were offering me a cup of tea.

"My heart is totally fit," I assure her.

"Excellent! That's why you shouldn't be alone."

"But . . . I have to feed my cat, Molotov."

"He won't starve in one night. Don't you leave kibble for him?"

"Yes, but he expects his can at night."

"He'll live."

Suddenly I miss old Molotov, the most agreeable, nonthreatening companion a man could have. He doesn't mind my quirks, and I don't mind his. For example, despite being neutered, he has an odd, ongoing, amorous relationship with a stuffed Snoopy dog that once belonged to my ex-wife. It had somehow gotten into one of my boxes when she sent me packing. She came by to get it and saw him biting it on the neck and moving it into position and she had a fit, said it was revolting, and she didn't want the toy back. And Molotov doesn't mind my crankiness or the fact that I like to have my toaster on the kitchen table. My thoughts are making no sense, but, inexplicably, I attempt to express them to Fran in the most halting, stammering babble.

"The thing about old people is that you get bent into a certain peculiar shape." I illustrate this by twisting my hands into two gnarled forms. "And then you can't unbend again. That's why love is for the young. There is no way two bent old people can fit together unless they've grown crooked together." I bang my hands together to illustrate.

Fran smiles and raises an eyebrow. "Yoga," she says softly.

We're driving through a neighborhood in Vienna, I think. Suddenly Fran pulls into a driveway in front of a split-level and shuts off the motor. She takes my hands, which are still bent into a theatrical illustration of my idiotic thoughts. She begins massaging the palms with her thumbs. Then she starts on the fingers, manipulating them, gently working the joints. I run out of words to protest. She places my hands back in my lap and gets out of the car. She is halfway down the walk before she turns to say, "Well, are you coming or are you going to sit in the car all night?"

As I meekly follow her up the walkway, I still have an urge to warn her about my quirks, particularly the ones Rebecca disliked the most.

"I'm still using a comb I bought at Woolworth's sometime in the nineteen-fifties," I say.

"Well, why not, if it still has most of its teeth? I don't believe in replacing something that's not broken." Fran's key clicks in the lock and we are inside. Something brushes against my leg. Fran reaches down and picks up a plump gray cat with a white nose blaze and necklace. "This is Pearl." Fran rubs Pearl's ear and the cat closes her eyes and purrs.

"Would you like something to drink?" Fran asks. She carries Pearl into the kitchen, and I follow, thinking how much Fran and Pearl resemble one another, soft and cuddly. Then I'm arrested by the sight of the kitchen table.

"Your toaster is on the table!"

Fran looks at me oddly. "Where else would it be?"

"I thought all women liked to have their toasters in those silly appliance garages or under those ridiculous quilted cozies."

Fran squints at me. "You still have issues with your ex-wife, don't you?"

"Not really, but she's the only woman I've ever lived with, so that's all I know."

Fran shakes her head and places Pearl down gently on the table—the table! She pops a can for Pearl, and once again I feel guilty about poor old Molotov waiting for his chicken and liver.

"So," she says. "You never told me what you wanted to drink."

I don't want to put Fran to any extra trouble. I try to guess what she is going to have.

"Were you about to fix tea?" I say.

"Tea? I was about to get the vodka out of the freezer, but I would be happy to fix you tea, if that's what you'd like."

"No, no, vodka would be fine."

She pours.

"*Na zdoroviye.*"

"*Na zdoroviye.*"

28. Maddie

Yesterday sucked, but today is not looking too crappy thus far. Traffic was light on the toll road—I couldn't figure out why, until I remembered that it's Saturday—and the cute SCUDO smiled at me this morning when he ran his detector wand thingie over my Mines tag at the gate. Something exciting about flirting with a guy wearing a semiautomatic weapon. A frisson of pleasure rippled right up my spine. Then I ran into Harry in the hall coming in, and he gave me some good news: Dr. Beth Dean is off on an unannounced visit to Iraq, so the deadline on the tasking is postponed until further notice. Life is good. Well, not *good*, but definitely not as crappy as I was expecting.

I slip into the canary cage and find my crew in early, minus Fran and Doc. Their absence doesn't worry me. Vivi had already called me to say that Doc was released from Fairfax Hospital. I'm so grateful to Vivi for coming in on a Saturday. She wasn't going to, but then right before she went home last night an intercept came in that said, "The children dance first." It really shook her up. So she had Jeff take her son to the Renaissance Fair today.

"Morning, folks," I say cheerfully. "I don't have to do my tasking! Yay! Harry told me Dr. Dean is in Iraq! Maybe she'll meet a terrorist."

No one smiles back at me.

"She already has," Vernon says. "Car bomb blew up her hotel. Harry's been with the BOM, preparing him for testimony, so he probably doesn't know yet."

An awkward silence. I take a reluctant inventory of my humanity. I've just been speaking ill of the possibly dead. In fact, I was wishing her dead, and now she might actually *be* dead. If I were a good person, I'd be feeling rotten right now, but am I? Honestly, no. This woman has been such a pain in the ass. Really, an incredible pain in the ass. I can't help thinking about all of the work she has kept us from getting done in the past and how much we could do now if suddenly those pesky taskings ceased.

I suppose I really am a rotten person.

"Turn the sound up," Vernon says.

I turn to see a familiar scene of smoke, and rescuers digging through rubble. I punch up the volume, until we can hear the correspondent giving the body count. Seventeen dead so far, thirty wounded, undetermined number missing. No word on Dr. Elizabeth Dean. The correspondent refers to her as "the President's top expert on terrorism."

"She doesn't know shit!" Vernon roars at the screen. "My rottweiler knows more about terrorism than Death Bean!"

According to the correspondent, the hotel was struck by a suicide bomber driving an ambulance full of explosives. The perpetrators probably belong to the Base. It occurs to me they aren't doing as much remote detonation as they used to. I'll have to look into it to see if my impression is correct. Recruitment is so hot, suicide bombers are probably easier than remote detonators. The camera pans to a pair of Iraqi civilians carrying away a cloth-covered body.

"Number eighteen. That could be her," Vernon says. "You know she never did give me my bayonet back. I only gave it to her as a joke. I wonder if I could get it from her widower."

I have no idea what he is talking about.

"Don't say anything yet," Kristin says, "you might jinx it."

"Any of our people with her?" Vivi asks.

"Not that I know of," Vernon says. "She doesn't trust Mines staff . . . for some reason."

We watch the screen for a few minutes. We should be getting back to work, but it's hard to look away. Then CNN switches to another story, and we reluctantly turn to our monitors.

"Are you going to do that tasking for her?" Vivi asks.

"I think I'll hold off a bit."

It's another fifteen minutes before CNN returns to the scene of the bombing.

Vivi points to the screen. "Breaking news! Turn it up!"

The volume goes up in time for us to hear the correspondent say, "A government spokesman has confirmed that Dr. Elizabeth Dean, the head of the Pentagon Council of the Wise, was unhurt in the explosion. Her room was not in the part of the building destroyed by the blast. She has been taken to a secure area in the Green Zone."

Vivi grabs the remote and hits the power button. The screen goes black. She lobs the remote across the room. "Fucking incompetent terrorists! How hard can it be to find out what part of the hotel she's in?"

Sweet, gentle Vivi has broken the ice. It's the first four-letter word we've ever heard out of her. After a moment of shock, we all pile on.

"Idiots!"

"Can't they do anything right?"

"They must have had bad intelligence."

Vernon gets a gleam in his eye. "Hey, does the administration inform the Mines before they take these unannounced trips? They must."

"If I were them, I wouldn't."

"That was probably our last chance," Vernon says. "I bet she won't go back to Iraq."

The room gets quiet, and we each pursue our separate veins of information. The next time I look up, it is already ten o'clock. "Has either Fran or Doc called in?" I ask. "Fran's usually in by six o'clock."

"Oh my gosh, how can it be ten o'clock? No, she hasn't called in. Technically we should have reported that to Safety and Security Sector two hours ago."

"I don't think the two-hour rule applies to weekends," Kristin says. In the Mines, you have two hours past your regular reporting time to call in if you're sick or can't come in for some other reason. After that, SSS goes to your residence to check up on you.

I volunteer to try them both at home. I dial Doc's number first. No one picks up.

"You're sure he was released last night?" I ask Vivi.

"Yes, early. They said his tests checked out fine. Try Fran, she may know something."

I dial Fran's number and it rings six times before someone picks up. Instead of Fran's voice, a familiar male voice gives me a woozy "Hello." Then I hear Fran whisper in the background.

"You picked up *my* phone, you silly thing!"

"Oh!" The woozy voice is now full of alarm, as if the receiver has suddenly gotten hot. There is a clattering, then the line goes dead. I hit redial.

"Hello?" This time it's definitely Fran.

"Good morning, Fran, it's Maddie. Are you sleeping in?"

"Oh my goodness, look at the time! My alarm clock didn't go off."

"So how is Doc?"

"Well, I drove him home from the hospital last night, and he seemed fine when I left him at his door. Hasn't he come in to work yet?"

"Fran, I just dialed your number not two minutes ago and Doc picked up." My colleagues around the table look suddenly alert. Eyes widen. Vivi mouths "What?"

"You must have dialed Doc's number by mistake," Fran says.

"But when I called you just now, I hit redial. Besides, I heard you whispering in the background on the first call. I think I heard bedsprings, too."

There is a long silence on the other end of the line. The full attention of my colleagues is directed at the innocent-looking phone. Jaws are hanging open about a mile.

"Fran?"

"None of your business."

"Well, no one picks up at Doc's house. Shall I send in Security?"

"No," Fran snaps. "Your canary crew will be fully staffed again within the hour." Click.

"Did I hear you right?" Vernon says. "Doc spent the night with Fran?"

"That certainly appears to be the case."

"It's probably perfectly innocent," Vivi says. "She probably wanted to make sure he was okay. I'm sure he stayed in a guest room."

"No. They were in the same bed. I'm sure. Doc said 'Hello'—it sounded like he was hung over or at least that he had been sound asleep—then I heard bedsprings and Fran whispered 'You shouldn't have answered my phone!' and Doc hung up."

"Holy shit, the old guy scored." Vernon pounds the table with his fist. "If that isn't the most depressing thing to happen all week."

"No," Vivi says. "Dean's survival is the most depressing thing, this is . . ." She searches for a word. "Surprising?"

"Shocking?" I suggest.

"Somehow unsavory." Kristin makes a face.

"Not unsavory," Vivi says. "They're a cute couple. Doc and Fran—how adorable! Why do you say unsavory?"

"They're so . . . old. I mean I wouldn't want to see anybody over thirty-three naked. *Eww.*" She stops abruptly, evidently remembering that I'm thirty-eight, Vivi is in her forties, and Vernon is probably pushing fifty. "Oops," she says and claps her hand over her mouth.

Vernon scowls. I can see that the news really has ruined his day. I feel no small empathy. The idea that Fran now has more of a sex life than I do doesn't flatter my own ego. But I have bigger things to think about.

"Red cloud," I say. "Concentrate on red cloud."

I pull up the electronic database that holds the archive of the Daily Threat Roster, the DTR, pronounced *deeter*. Much of the stuff in the DTR is crap from people calling in to the Organ. Someone who looks Middle Eastern is seen taking notes at a railway station. An elderly lady in Cleveland thinks suspicious activities are taking place in the kabob joint down the street. A woman calls in to say she thinks her ex-boyfriend from the United Arab Emirates is a terrorist—there should be a special column just for all the ex-boyfriends and -husbands who are now believed to be terrorists. It all makes the DTR. I set my brain on speed scan and plow through weeks' worth of this drek, looking for something that might be connected to the code words.

Finally, I come across that little piece on model airplanes. I remember seeing it when it first appeared a few months ago, and querying the Organ for more information—they pooh-poohed the threat. According to the report, a hobby company executive had called the Organ to report that within the space of a week, two small toy stores he had never heard of before—one on the East Coast and one on the West—had placed huge orders for a radio-controlled (RC) model airplane called the Sky Shark. The executive thought that the planes might have some sort of terrorist application. He said they have the longest range of any RC planes in the industry. Moreover, in each case the voice ordering over the phone was impatient and defensive. Something about it didn't seem right to him. Could RC planes be the holy swarm?

"But did the Organ follow up?" I say out loud.

"No," Vernon says. "I don't have any idea what you're talking about, but I'm willing to bet my lunch money that the answer is no."

"I'll bet mine, too," Vivi says.

"Hey, I'm not taking bets on this one. I'm talking about that piece on the RC planes."

"Actually, I agree with the Organ on this one," Vernon says. "I looked at it with them when the first report came out. It's bogus. There is nothing terrorists can do with those things. They couldn't carry enough chem or bio matter to kill a cloud of gnats."

"What about a lot of them?" I say.

"Still couldn't," Vernon says. "Besides, it would take too many operatives to fly the things."

"They've trained a lot of operatives," I remind him. "There could be more than the ones we know about. Probably are more."

"Even if you managed to fly a hundred over a crowd, it wouldn't do squat."

"Did the Organ check out the toy stores? Were they real?"

"Yes, Maddie," Vernon says wearily. "They checked them out and they were real."

Nevertheless, I go to another database and pull up the original report that the DTR blurb was based on. I find the names of the toy stores: Village Toy & Hobby and ToyWorks. ToyWorks is located nearby in Maryland. I stand up and grab the phone book from the top of a file cabinet in the corner.

"You don't trust me?" Vernon says.

"No. I don't trust you or the Organ." I dial the number listed and get a recording. "The number is no longer in service."

"Maybe they went out of business," Vernon says.

The other store, Village Toy & Hobby, is located in California. I get the number from the long-distance operator and dial.

"Surprise. Another recording. Number no longer in service."

Vernon sits up in his chair. "I'll call my contact at the Organ and get them to revisit this. But I still don't think these things have a terror application."

Just as he picks up the phone, the door bangs into my chair and I shriek.

"Jesus, Maddie." Vernon covers his ears. "You're going to give me a heart attack."

It's Harry again. He hasn't learned to knock, but at least he's not carrying any hot beverages. Harry leans over my shoulder and speaks in an undertone. "Maddie, you know the Mines will pick up half the cost of counseling if you want to address this screaming problem."

"Harry," I whisper back, "I've been going to a Mines-cleared shrink for two years. You've been signing off on the paperwork. Believe it or not what you see here is Maddie on drugs already."

Harry clears his throat and straightens up. My colleagues make a show of being absorbed in their work, but they have undoubtedly heard every word. I don't care. I've never hid the fact that I go to a shrink.

"Well, anyway," Harry says, "I came to see about that Dean tasker. She wants it to read on the flight back from Baghdad."

Shit. "I've found no evidence of a link to Iran, and I have a lead I need to pursue."

"After you finish the tasker."

"Harry . . ."

"After you finish the tasker. I need a draft by three so she can read it on the plane home."

Damned incompetent terrorists.

29. Doc

They will call us a cute couple. Vivian will look at us dewy-eyed, as if we were unweaned kittens. A man strives a lifetime to earn respect only to end his days not being called "distinguished" or "erudite" as he had hoped, but rather "cute." Yet this doesn't bother Fran.

Fran is unburdened by modesty, at least in front of me. She stands in her closet door surveying her clothing options and wearing only a damp towel, which threatens to slip off at any moment. I have pulled on yesterday's clothes and now I have nothing to do but keep an eye on that towel, waiting despite myself. Fran still has a lovely womanly figure.

"Doc, why don't we just go in together? It's not 1956. Nobody cares."

"No, you must take me home so I can change and drive in separately."

"A waste of time and gas."

"I have to feed Molotov. The poor old boy isn't used to missing his can."

"Okay. I'll go through this charade for the sake of your cat. But are we going to go in separately every time we spend the night together?" She takes a skirt and blouse out of the closet and turns. Her towel slips off. For the first time it sinks in that I am going to be spending many, many nights with this woman and probably the rest of my life.

"We're going to end up married, aren't we?" I say. The thought induces a state of awe.

"Of course." Fran sounds as if she never has doubted it.

Somehow the question has already been decided before I even knew it was a question. Yet the thought is more comforting than alarming. Nevertheless, I'm an alchemist and feel compelled to lay out the obstacles. Amazingly, however, no obstacles to our happiness immediately come to mind. Family objections? Our parents are dead and our children are grown. The introduction of a stepparent is unlikely to produce psychological damage in children in their thirties. Financial issues? Fran and I are fiscal conservatives with ample savings. Miscellaneous difficulties?

Molotov. He is accustomed to a one-cat household.

"Our cats won't get along," I say. "I would never give up Molotov."

"And I'd never give up Pearl. They'll learn to get along."

"I don't know if an old cat will change its ways." As if she has understood the conversation, Pearl flicks her tail. She is curled into Fran's pillow, looking with sympathy and mild contempt at those of us foolish enough to spend our days less pleasantly.

"My Pearlie isn't old. She's only nine. She'll make sure that your Molotov behaves himself. She doesn't take any nonsense. She'll keep him in his place."

And Fran will keep me in mine, but this doesn't bother me. I've run out of objections.

After Fran drops me off at home, I open my door to find Molotov seated at the opposite end of the front hallway, facing the wall. His tail is flicking and he doesn't respond to my voice. As I turn to close the door, I see several streaks near the bottom. Molotov has been spraying, leaving yellow graffiti to protest his forgotten dinner.

I go into the kitchen and listen to the messages on my answering machine as I open Molotov's chicken-and-liver dinner. He pads into the kitchen and sits in the corner, facing the wall to wait, instead of curling around my legs as usual. There are two messages from Maddie. The last says, "Congratulations, Doc. I knew you were a stud muffin. I'm truly happy for you, but, please, get your hot little buns in here ASAP. I think I'm onto something." I'm glad no one but Molotov is here to see me blush.

30. Maddie

I whipped out Dean's tasker in three hours flat. If Harry wants any changes in it, I'll smash his Jerusalem rock paperweight over his Jerusalem rock head. I'm out of patience with that man.

I don't usually leave my desk during the day, but the canary cage was getting close and I need to clear my head, think. I'm on my second circumnavigation of the Mines compound, walking as fast as I can, trying to get blood rushing to my brain. When did summer get here? It's hot. I used to walk every day at lunch, but I've gotten out of the habit. Too bad, it opens up your mind, lets the dust out and the fresh air in. A light breeze is ruffling the wind socks hanging above the parking lot. I stop a moment to consider them. They're a new addition, added after the Strikes. In case of a chemical attack, they're supposed to tell us which way is upwind. I wonder how many miners have enough common sense to understand the concept of upwind.

The socks indicate a slight shift in the wind toward the southeast. My thoughts shift. Wind dispersion. Red cloud. Holy swarm. Model airplanes. Vernon says they can't do anything, but he would only know the chem side. I need a bio expert for the canary crew. I'm going to have to go back, hat in hand, to Harry. Worse, I have to ask for Bonnie Weathers. Bonnie is fussy and snappish. Ever since her divorce, she's indulged in a high-whining orgy of self-pity and

Entenmann's chocolate-covered doughnuts. She's put on at least forty pounds, mainly around her middle. All of it has to fit behind my canary crew table, because she's a world-class expert on airborne diseases, in addition to being a world-class hypochondriac. She'll be a world-class pain in the ass, but I have to beg Harry for the pleasure of her company.

The wind begins to gust. I continue my walk around the compound. A swarm of planes could cause mass panic. Well-placed, well-timed mass panic could cause mass casualties. Vivi tells me her family raised poultry, as well as cows on their farm. One night they were repairing the electrical lines, and someone dropped a hammer and it hit the metal roof of one of the poultry houses. The birds panicked, piled together six high, and four thousand of them suffocated. An effective mass-casualty attack using only a hammer. Panic can be like an explosion. It's all in placement of the charge and the direction of the force.

But I'm letting my thoughts wander, falling into the trap of trying to guess the plot. I remind myself that you never guess the plot. You concentrate on the people, find them, roll them up. And then there's the place. That's the hardest, because of the deliberate disinformation. Lately it seems like they're throwing code names for various cities into their conversations almost at random. One day it's *the city of the poison river* and the next day it's *land of dogs* or the *pigs' sty*. The cities connected to those code names may have changed as well. *The city of the poison river* may still be Washington or it may be New York now.

Before I left the canary cage, I gave each of my crew an angle to research. I hope I'm not sending them down rabbit holes.

It's a healthy walk around both the New and Old Shafts buildings. The compound is well landscaped, pretty except for the terrorist barriers, the orange cones, wind socks, the radiation detectors, and the razor wire on the fences.

And the goose guano. Not a deliberate defensive measure, but I imagine that any terrorist running over the grounds might well end up sprawled on his back. The slippery crap is everywhere. Back when I started at the Mines, we had no Canada geese on the grounds. Now more come every year, as if to mock our increasingly elaborate defense against intruders. The geese amble across our lawns, parking lots, and roads, snarling traffic and pooping their little brains out.

Something startles a half-dozen geese and they take flight. I watch them do a slow, low circle over the nearly empty parking lot. A flock of geese. A swarm of RC planes. I imagine a crowd somewhere: Fourth of July on the Mall, a Metro station at rush hour, Disney World any day of the week. Model planes appear, fly low like these geese. They release . . . what? Anthrax? Sarin? How hard is it to aerosolize anthrax?

Stop, Maddie. One could spend all day thinking of creative ways to kill people.

• • •

When I get back to the canary cage, I find everyone hard at work. Doc and Fran don't glance up at me as I enter. Too embarrassed. I shouldn't say anything, but I can't help myself.

"My God, you two make a cute couple."

"Adorable," Vivi says. "Absolutely adorable."

Doc slaps down a report. "Stop! Cease and desist. I will not be dismissed as adorable. If you want me to remain on this canary crew, Maddie, you will avoid all such infantile terminology. I am serious. One more word, and I'm off the canary crew."

"Yes, sir," I say meekly.

A leer crosses Vernon's face. "You sure are cranky for someone who got laid last night."

"Vernon," I say. "We need Doc and we will respect his wishes."

"Thank you, Madeleine," Doc says.

Vivi suppresses a giggle, and I shoot her a look of warning. Fran purses her lips, trying not to smile. I change the subject to something safer.

"I've decided that we need a bio expert on the canary crew, so I'm going to ask Harry for Bonnie Weathers." I pause for the collective groan, which is quite theatrical. Vernon bends over and bangs his forehead against the table. Doc shakes his head slowly and sadly.

"I know Bonnie can be difficult to deal with."

"She won't fit," Vernon says. "Doc jokes about my beer gut, but when that woman squeezes into her seat, we won't be able to exhale."

"Vernon," I say sternly, "I'm going to ignore that politically incorrect outburst. Suck it up. We need Bonnie."

Vivi reverts to good-soldier mode. "Bonnie does know her airborne diseases."

"That's because she thinks she has all of them," Vernon says.

"Suck it up, I'm going to see Harry. In the meantime, Vivi, could you be a sweetie and write up a PIU article on the RC planes?"

31. Fran

Last night we slept at Doc's house, because he said Molotov couldn't take another night by himself. I wasn't happy about abandoning my Pearlie. She'll scratch my chintz love seat while I'm gone. She always does something to get back at me when I disrupt her routine.

I hope we don't have to spend too many nights at Doc's. He has hardly any furniture, but books are stacked everywhere. It's enough to bring on an attack of claustrophobia. I didn't dare ask him when the last time was that he laundered his sheets. And I think his cat sprays. Still, it's nice sleeping with a man again. I hate to think how many years it's been.

We got up before the sun this morning so we could be in to work bright and early to make up for yesterday. Doc's in the shower now. He sings in the shower. That took me completely by surprise. I didn't think he was the type, but he has a beautiful baritone. He sings what they used to call Negro spirituals. I could listen 'til the cows come home.

The singing stops, and Doc peeks out of the bathroom. He has a towel wrapped around his waist. I'm already dressed. Even though it's Sunday, and everybody wears jeans to the office on weekends, I have on my nicest suit, a raw-silk number I bought to brief the Speaker of the House and haven't worn since. It's my favorite color: dusty rose. I even slapped on some lipstick and blush and broke out the curling iron. If I say so myself, I look fetching. I can see Doc thinks the same. It is so much fun feeling like a sexpot again. Makes me want to go out and buy a pair of stilettos, but I would probably break my stupid hip. Maybe I'll do something about this gray. I miss being red-haired.

I see an awkward look come over Doc's face. He needs to get dressed, but that would mean he'd have to drop his towel, and here I stand. He's such a silly about nudity. I wonder if I should torment him by staring or whether I should be nice and excuse myself from the room. I should probably be nice. The man is going to be my husband, after all, and being nice to him is a habit I should get into. But tormenting him is such a kick. I can't help myself. I give him my best May West voice.

"Is that an IED in your towel or are you just happy to see me?"

• • •

Took me fifteen minutes to convince Doc it would be plain silly for us to go in separately, since our fling is hardly a secret now. We drive up to the gate together and present our badges to the SCUDO. Somehow this little ceremony makes me feel our relationship is official. As he holds out his badge, Doc dips his head to avoid the SCUDO's gaze. You would think he was packing a trunk full of plastic explosive, instead of a sweet little lady wearing a drop-dead gorgeous suit.

As we walk down the tunnels together, Doc hangs back, like he's pretending that he's not really with me. When we reach the canary crew door, he hesitates.

"They'll make fun of us again," he whispers.

"Nonsense, you backed them down yesterday. They won't say a word."

"Maybe you should go in now and I'll wait a few minutes."

"Where are your balls?"

"You know exactly where they are."

"Sure do, honeycakes. Now open that door."

Doc knocks softly to warn Maddie, then opens the door. We squeeze inside and head to our opposite sides of the table. Our colleagues mumble "Good morning" and keep their eyes down. Only Vernon glances up briefly, long enough to catch my eye and wink. I sit down and log on to the computer. I feel so professional and sharp in my silk suit and pumps! Then I see an e-mail from MinesHumRes@WhiteMines. Human Resources Sector. The e-mail was sent Friday afternoon, but I guess I've been so busy that I overlooked it until now. I think at first it must be notification that I've gotten my latest time-in-grade pay increase. But, no. . . .

> This e-mail is the official notification that during the last Performance Examination, you were rated in the bottom 10 percent of all Mines Schedule-13s. Your face boss should have already informed you of this fact in person. Given that we are not currently faced with the need to reduce personnel, this bottom-10-percent rating will have no impact on your employment at present. Nevertheless the Executive Committee has decided to inform those on the list so that they can work with their face bosses on ways to improve their performance rating.
>
> Sincerely,
>
> Alfred B. Hereford
> Director, White Mines Human Resources Sector

I feel my face go numb. Bottom 10 percent? I was sure last time I would get promoted, and instead they put me in the bottom 10 percent? Am I that worthless?

An instant message from Doc pops onto the screen: "What's wrong????" Oh dear, I didn't mean to let anything show on my face, but I need Doc's sympathy right now. I highlight the text of the e-mail, paste it into an instant message, and send it back to him.

Doc reads the screen and pounds his fist on the table. He yells "Bastards!" and the rest of the canary crew jumps in surprise. He tears out of his seat and heads for the door. I get up too, to find out where he's going. I catch up to him out in the hallway.

"Doc! What are you doing?"

"First I'm going to give your face boss a piece of my mind for not talking to you in person, then I'm going to do the same to every manager who was on that evaluation committee."

"Doc, no! I'm all right." I've never seen him so angry. His cheeks are purple and flecks of spittle hit me in the face as he talks. Suddenly I *am* all right. This man loves me, and nothing else matters. I smile at him, a real smile. I put my hands on his shoulders. "As long as I have you, I'm all right. I'll ignore this. I'll stay with Vivian through this threat, then I'll retire, collect my watch, my flag, and my pension and walk out. I'll do as I please the rest of my life."

Doc looks at me intently. "Just let me talk to your face boss."

"Doc," I say, "it's Sunday. Remember? She won't be here. Really, I'm just fine and dandy."

"Are you sure? I want to make this right."

"I'm sure. If anyone has a talk with my managers it will be me. I'm not some little girl you have to protect. And by golly, if I talk to them, they will know they've been talked to."

My love touches my face. "Would you like me to drive you home for the rest of the day?"

"No, I'm going back to work."

Doc lowers his voice. "I never told anybody this, but I was on the bottom-10-percent list once, way back when I irritated Vaughn. They didn't notify people then, but I found out. Nearly killed me. I admire you for taking it this way."

I let him in on one of my favorite theories. "Men's egos are more delicate than women's, more exposed. They swell up too far and too fast and then, if you say 'Boo,' they shrink like they've been doused with cold water. Kind of like men's—"

"Never mind, dear." Without glancing around to make sure the corridor is empty, Doc gives me a peck on the cheek and offers me his arm. "May I have the honor of escorting you back to the canary cage?"

"Certainly."

32. A Voice with Many Names

The police found the knife. It was one I bought in Munich while on vacation from the university. A fine German blade. Not as large as is traditional for the method of *dhabh*, but large enough to kill efficiently. I didn't carry it with me at all times, but I had it that day. I had sharpened it that morning. Allah told me I would need it. I was reluctant to give it up after the slaughter, but it would have been insanity to keep it.

So we've moved the operation up yet again. It will take place during the next scheduled game.

I have removed all the furniture from this room and put it down by the Dumpster. I have scrubbed the walls and floor and placed my prayer rug in the center of the space. I wipe my hands. A beam of sunlight finds the rug in the late afternoon and warms my neck as I bend toward Mecca. I have washed, ironed, and folded the clothing that I will wear. It waits on my suitcase in the other room. Nothing must mar the simplicity of this room, the purity of my purpose. No distractions.

33. Maddie

Monday. Theoretically, when you're working seven days a week, Monday shouldn't suck any more than any other day. Yet it so does.

We've barely settled back into our chairs to begin the wretched day when the door flies open, banging smack into my chair. I put all of my frustration into a shriek. I whip around, expecting to see Harry, but it's Bonnie Weathers in an aubergine suit, looking like an eggplant.

"Is that any way to greet me?" she snaps. She has a whine to her voice and a wounded look on her face. She's packed on about thirty pounds since the last time I saw her, but she's compensated by adding more makeup and dying her short, spiky hair a shiny black, which turns her into a middle-aged-goth-bureaucrat eggplant.

"I'm sorry, Bonnie," I say. I am determined to make this work so I paste a smile on my face. "Welcome to the canary crew."

Bonnie looks around doubtfully. "This isn't where we sit, is it?"

"You see us sitting here, don't you?" I say.

"I agreed to be on this crew because Harry was so insistent that you needed my unique expertise, but I want you to know I have conditions."

"Okay," I say slowly, "shoot."

"First, I need to be out of here by four thirty in the afternoon to take my daughter to rehearsals. She's in the Fairfax theater group, one of the youngest members they've ever accepted. She's playing the lead in *Pollyanna*."

I'm still smiling, but I can feel the corner of my mouth begin to twitch. "No problem," I say, but I'm thinking, *Screw* Pollyanna.

"And I want to get credit for being on this canary crew. I assume you'll be writing award recommendations for us when this is over?"

"Well, that will probably depend on whether anything blows up, won't it?" I'm no longer smiling. I tell myself that this woman knows her stuff so we have to put up with her, but my God. . .

"And I would like to work at my own desk."

Several canary crew members give me significant looks, but I shake my head. "No. I'm sorry, but we do a lot of brainstorming and we need you here. We have a place for you." I point to the empty chair next to Kristin—this is how I'm getting back at Ms. Russell for being young and cute and smart.

"I'm going to go talk to Harry," Bonnie says. She walks out and slams the door.

"Jesus," Vernon says, "can't you let her work at her own desk? That whine gets old fast." He gives me a pained and pleading look.

"No, I want her here. You have to put up with her. Consider it a sacrifice for your country." I place my hand over my heart. "Think of the Nathan Hale statue out front. Your only regret should be that you have but one Bonnie to tolerate for your country."

Vernon gives me a sour look. "I always thought it was screwed that we have a gibbeted amateur spy as our institutional icon. Of course, it's probably appropriate. Or maybe we should have a great big bronze ass in a sling out front."

"Get back to work, Vernon."

• • •

An hour later, Bonnie is back, carrying a cardboard box. She slams it down without looking at any of us. She pushes it across the table toward her chair, scattering piles of paper. Fran grabs her tea so it won't slosh onto her link charts. Then Bonnie takes the empty chair next to Kristin. As she sits down, the whole table moves toward the opposite wall.

I start to give her a quick orientation. "What we're focusing on now—"

"Would you let me settle in?" Bonnie snaps. She shifts in her chair, and the table shakes. She pulls her box closer and begins taking things out. First comes a giant-size box of tissues.

"I have terrible allergies." Bonnie sniffles and honks into a tissue. "It's so difficult for me this time of year. I'm allergic to tree pollen, particularly oak. I'm also allergic to mold and cats. If anybody has a cat, please be sure to brush your clothes before you come here in the morning and dry-clean frequently. Otherwise, I will be sneezing my head off." She looks around and her eyes stop on Doc.

"Is that cat hair on your sleeve?"

"No," Doc snaps. "It comes from one of the many women I sleep with."

Vernon nudges him and winks.

"The hair on my sleeve is rabbit," I say.

"And mine is possum," Vivian pipes in.

Bonnie looks appalled. "I'll have to call Medical and have myself tested for those allergies."

"We're under an imminent terrorist threat," I remind her. "You're just going to have to sneeze for a few days."

Bonnie starts to respond, then shakes her head and goes back to her box. She has brought silly things, the type of stuff we all keep on our desk, but who else would bring it to a crowded canary crew table? A three-inch-tall Big Ben clock in brass. A "stress buster" squeeze ball with a big smiley face. A ceramic aromatherapy dispenser. I clench my jaw as Bonnie pours three drops of lavender essential oil into the evaporating bowl.

"It's close in here," Bonnie says.

I promise myself that I can kill her after this is over. I just have to put up with her until this threat is resolved.

Bonnie begins to hum "The Muffin Man" and pulls a small lamp out of the box, a purple one with dangly beads hanging from the shade. She pushes aside a stack of TAILFIREs to make room for the thing, and I take a deep breath. Everybody else but Bonnie is watching me, even though they're pretending not to. They think I'm about to explode.

Bonnie twists around to look for an outlet, and the table bucks and shudders. I can't take it anymore. I get up, grab *The New York Times* from the stack of papers on top of a file cabinet, and exit the conference room, closing the door behind me. I roll the newspaper tightly and attack the closed door, hitting it once, twice, then a half-dozen more times fast. Then, still feeling too close to committing a homicide, I walk downstairs to get myself a nice, calming double espresso.

. . .

Wynona greets me with the latest news about the Peanut Man murder.

"They got the autopsy results back," she says as she bangs the old grounds out of the basket. "Somebody slit his throat before they burnt him up. Damn near beheaded him."

"Beheaded him?" I say. That sparks a professional interest. I've done a lot of work on beheadings.

"Damn near," Wynona says. "Didn't go through the neck bone, but they said it was a real clean cut. Leastways the poor man probably didn't suffer long. Must've bled out like a hog."

Wynona hands me my espresso, and I head back upstairs with the words "bled out like a hog" stuck in my brain.

When I get back, I grab the rolled-up newspaper that I left on the floor outside the canary cage and open the door. As my colleagues watch apprehensively, I put down my coffee and slowly unroll the newspaper, iron it flat on the table with my palm, and replace it on top of the stack on the filing cabinet. I give Bonnie a long, steady look.

"Are you quite ready to begin?" I ask.

"You are certifiably insane," Bonnie says.

"Yes," I say. "I am insane . . . volatile . . . quite possibly danger-ous. So the safest thing for you to do is to bear with me, while I brief you on the ongoing threat and the role I would like you to play on the canary crew."

Bonnie holds her tongue through my briefing. Everyone else looks quiet and somber. It's good to remind the crew of the serious-ness of this situation.

34. Vivian

Mom, Sophie pooped her carrier," Josh says, just as I detect the foul odor. Monday evening and we're stuck in Beltway traffic, in sight of the Mormon Church, with its odd, Disney-style towers. It's raining. I've gone five feet in ten minutes. I was way late picking up Josh from his play date and Sophie from the vet because I was trying to get that PIU article on the RC planes through an unholy coordination battle with the Base Subshaft. They finally BLIPed it, arguing that it was too far-fetched. I think the truth is that it contradicts their line of analysis that the Lahore arrests scuttled an impending terrorist attack.

I glance behind me. Josh is holding his nose. I feel guilty that his classmates are probably home playing while he is stuck in a car with his mother and a possum and a mound of possum poop. It's raining too hard to open the windows.

"I'm sorry about the smell. What did you do in kindergarten today?" I ask, because I can't think of a more compelling question to get my son talking. I want to hear his voice.

Josh lets go of his nose and rattles off his activities with weary nonchalance, "Alphabet puzzle, string painting, music time, nap.

"What did you do?" he asks. He turns his beautiful eyes on me. Without being taught, he knows that the essence of politeness is to show interest in the other person. I'm constantly amazed by him.

I make a quick mental inventory of my day, trying to pick out the things I can safely tell a child. Research on terrorists involved in aerosolization of toxins? No. Watching an old Base training video where they kill dogs with poison gas? No.

"A new lady came to work with us today. She hums 'Do You Know the Muffin Man' all the time."

"I don't like that song. Do you?" Josh's voice is measured, thoughtful, serious.

"No."

"Can't you tell her to stop?"

I think about this for a minute as the traffic, briefly, speeds up to seven miles per hour.

"I don't think she can stop. Some people have to make some sort of noise all the time. If they're not humming, they're drumming their fingers, or blowing their noses, or creaking their chairs."

"Oh, like Jarod. He sits in front of me. He takes Ritalin. Maybe the work lady should take it."

Part of me is appalled that my little boy can pronounce the name of this drug and even confidently prescribe it. What did I know of prescription drugs at his age? Nothing. I probably knew aspirin and cough syrup and that was it. Another part of me wonders if Ritalin would help Bonnie. I imagine slipping it into her coffee. The traffic has come to a dead stop, and I see a possum hit at the edge of the road.

"I have to check for babies."

"Oh, Mom, not again."

"I have to. If there are live babies in the pouch, they'll starve."

"Be careful, Mom. Really, be careful."

I put the car into park, jump out, and cross the wet pavement in front of a beer truck, waving to make sure he sees me. The squashed possum turns out to be a male. I drag him farther off the road, so no other animals will get hit trying to feed off the carcass. I'm back in the car in seconds, soaking wet. I use an antibacterial wipe from the glove compartment to clean my hands. I start crying, because the dead possum probably didn't die instantly, and because I'm a rotten mother, and because I feel like there's another big attack out there, about to happen at any second.

"Aw, Mom. Don't cry." Josh sounds like he is about to cry himself.

I wipe my eyes and pull myself together. The traffic shows no sign of letting up and we are within a few feet of an exit. There's a toy store off of this exit. Jeff and I are a bit short on cash this month as usual, especially with Sophie's unexpected bills, but I need to make up for missing that Renaissance Fair.

"Want to go to ToyMart?" I ask. "It's cool enough today to leave Sophie in the car and we're not going anywhere anyway. I'll let you pick out something small."

Josh's eyes brighten. "Toys? Really?"

"Really."

I put on my signal and start to edge my way around the beer truck.

• • •

ToyMart is numbingly vast. We pause inside the door, and Josh chews his lip as his eyes roll across aisles exploding with technicolor plastic hustlers vying with each other for his attention. I can see that he's overwhelmed, and that I need to offer a direction. I make a quick decision to combine work and motherhood.

"Would you like to look at the model planes?" I say.

A smile breaks across Josh's face. I take his hand and we head for the hobby section of the store. I don't expect to find the Sky Shark. The model was discontinued shortly after the suspicious orders were placed. Maddie has been trying to find one for study, but none of the toy stores she's called thus far have it in stock. So I'm amazed to see a large box labeled Sky Shark on the highest shelf in the model plane section. Josh settles down on the floor to examine a small model helicopter, while I motion to a store employee for help.

The employee, a kid named Troy, brings a stepladder. As he reaches for the box, I avert my face from the unseemly gap between his baggy low-rise pants and his T-shirt.

"These are way cool," he says. "You're lucky we have one. The only reason we have this one is that the box was shoved behind some other stuff until I found it this morning. These are absolutely the best, longest-range ones going. They discontinued them, because they're about to come out with a model that goes even farther. But that one will cost more, too." Troy looks too young to be working, but obviously he has developed some expertise, as well as considerable enthusiasm, on the topic of RC planes. He starts to tell me about all the extras I will want to buy if I buy this plane, including a rechargeable battery pack, adapter, flight box, and so on and on. I can see this is an expensive hobby. I glance at the price on the box. Ouch, and that's without extras. Too rich for my blood.

Josh looks up and his eyes widen. "Wow!" He gives me a look of wondering gratitude that makes my stomach turn over. "You mean I could get this one?"

"Well, maybe when you're . . ." I hesitate and stand in stunned silence as Troy hands him the box, which is almost too big for my little son to handle.

"It has a four-and-a-half-foot wingspan," Troy says. "And a cargo hold with servo-operated doors. It's three by two and a half inches. You can carry paintballs in there and do carpet-bombing runs. Way cool."

"Wow!" Josh says.

"This is hardly a child's toy," I say, but no one is listening to me. I don't want my child to have this dreadful thing. Why did I bring Josh here? I wasn't thinking straight. I look at the picture on the box. The Sky Shark is electric blue with a snarling shark face painted on the nose.

"How much weight can it carry?" I'm thinking of the terrorist applications.

"Thirteen ounces."

Is that enough to do damage if it's a toxic chemical and there are numerous planes? Maddie has been trying in vain to get authorization from Admin to buy a Sky Shark if she finds one. If I buy this plane, there is no guarantee I'll be reimbursed. If I buy this plane, Josh will have to have it.

"This is the coolest thing I've ever seen," Josh says.

I feel a cold lump forming in my stomach. Apart from the cost, I don't like the idea of my son owning this thing with its futuristic iridescent gun turrets. Suppose he develops a desire to be a fighter pilot when he grows up?

Josh begins to imitate the fire of machine guns. "Rattatat-tat-tat-tat."

We lost a pilot last week over Fallujah.

"If you want one of these you'd better get it now," Troy says. "We've ordered the comparable model, but it won't be in for another six weeks. And it's more expensive. Like I said, we wouldn't have this one in stock except it got pushed to the back of that shelf. If I had the money, I'd buy it."

Josh is running his fingers lightly, reverently over the photograph of the plane.

"How can a plane with a four-foot wingspan fit in that box?" I say.

"It comes unassembled," Troy says, speaking slowly as if I were an idiot.

Of course, it comes unassembled.

"How long does it take to put it together?"

"Not long," Troy assures me. "And the wings come off, which makes it easy to carry around. You just take off the rubber bands, disconnect the aileron servo wire, and lift the wing right off."

Easy to carry around. That would be convenient for terrorists.

"This is way too complex for a child to fly," I say.

"Use a buddy box. That way you have two controllers. The adult would do most of the maneuvering, but I bet this kid would learn fast."

A buddy box. That would definitely make it more usable for a terrorist operation.

"Daddy and I could fly it," Josh says.

"I assume the buddy box is extra?"

"Yes."

It's all gabble to me. I hate this thing, but I'm going to have to buy it. I can't ask the government for reimbursement, because I'm going to have to give it to Josh when we're done. I've already built up the expectation, because I'm too much of a wimp to say no. I've missed out on so much of Josh's life that I can't bear to disappoint him again. Jeff is going to kill me when he finds out what this thing, this wildly inappropriate gift for a five-year-old, costs. I haven't even told him yet what Sophie's vet stay cost.

"I'll make you a deal," I tell Josh. "We'll buy this, but you have to wait a week to get it. Mommy needs to use it for work, because we're learning about planes."

Josh considers this odd request, but he's learned not to ask questions about Mommy's work. "That's all right," he finally says, and his face radiates joy.

35. A Voice with Many Names

All that is left is what is to be done. It has been set in stone, like the words of the Prophet, peace be upon him. I have no family until we are reunited in Paradise, in the shadow of our swords. Jihad is now obligatory for every Muslim. The Chieftain has explained. He has answered all of my questions and put to rest all of my doubts. I have spoken the prayers, the words of the Koran, the hadiths, over and over until they are more real than the sunshine, the trees, and the faces around me. I have already left my life behind. I will not waver. *Bismillah Allahu Akbar.*

36. Maddie

O h, dear God," Fran says.

We all look up from our screens when we hear the tone of her voice. She shakes her head.

"Just got an intercept. It says 'the Poppy has gone home.'"

"Shit. You know what that means," I say.

"No, I don't. You're all talking gobbledygook," Bonnie says. "What does that mean?"

Bonnie has only been with us since yesterday, but Kristin is the only one of us still able to speak civilly to her. She explains in a level voice that reminds me that our youngest member is also the least quirky and most professional-acting member of the canary crew.

"It means that there may be an attack in the D.C. metropolitan area in the next couple of days. The Poppy is a bomb maker and facilitator. Those types always leave the staging area right before the attack. We had a report a few weeks ago that the Poppy was by 'the poison river,' which we believe is the Potomac, although there's always a chance that they've changed the meaning of the code word."

Vernon grabs the phone. "Better call my guy at the Organ."

Bonnie's face turns pale. "It could be us they're after." She starts to rise.

"Sit!" I say. "There are plenty of targets in this area. If we work fast enough, maybe none of them will get hit. Vivi, what time did the smithies say they would be ready for a test flight with the Sky Shark?"

"One o'clock. We're meeting them at Goose Scamper Park."

Vernon puts his hand over the mouthpiece of the phone. "I tell you it's a waste of time. Time we can't afford to waste right now."

He could be right, but I stand my ground. "We're going to pursue this, Vernon. You can stay here and coordinate with the Organ. Doc, please draft something up for the President."

I sent the Sky Shark Vivi bought yesterday to the smithies for assembly. They're a whiz with models, and I found a couple who are RC plane fanatics. I've called in a dozen smithies to watch the test flight and brainstorm on what the terrorists might do with an RC plane, or dozens of RC planes.

Incredible. I called in a dozen people and fifteen show up at the softball field at Goose Scamper Park, right next to the Mines. All men. The only women are the ones on my canary crew. I guess I never thought to offer the boys toys before. They've come out of the woodwork like curious rats. Maybe I should offer free Hot Wheels at my next brainstorming session, but then I'd have alchemists going "Zoom, zoom" on the conference table.

It's an overcast day with a light wind scattering the few remaining Bradford pear blossoms. Overcast is good. I'd hate to have some foreign spy satellite catch a bunch of Mines alchemists with an eensy-weensy unmanned aerial vehicle. Our only witnesses are a dozen Canada geese taking a slow stroll across left field and a lady sunning herself on the deck of one of the neighboring mansions. One of the smithies holds the Sky Shark, while the rest of the men crowd around, caressing its blue wings, and making sportscaster remarks like "Way cool" and "Awesome."

Vivi rolls her eyes and comes over to whisper in my ear. "The scary thing is the terrorists probably did the same thing when they got their shipment. How do they say 'way cool' in Arabic?"

"I don't know, but we'd better make sure nobody walks off with this thing. It's been a long time since I've seen lust in a man's eye, but I still recognize it."

"Don't worry, I spent way too much money on it. If anyone tries to make off with it, I'll wrap myself around his ankles and scream," Vivi says.

The Sky Shark takes off and the geese take flight as well. The smithy at the controls says, "Watch this!" and directs the plane on a chase of one poor goose. The men laugh in delight as the bird squawks.

"Stop that!" Vivi yells. "It's my plane and you're not going to use it to torment innocent animals."

The controller gives Vivi a dirty look, mutters something unintelligible, and breaks off the chase.

The test flight has the men drooling and moaning as if the Sky Shark were a naked woman gyrating around a pole instead of a toy plane doing a slow, low circle over a softball field. Frankly, I don't see what the big deal is, but the men's eyes are following the plane with hypnotic concentration, heads moving in unison. The same slack-jawed, stupid expression has come over each of their faces. Meanwhile, the women shake their heads.

The smithy sends a signal to open the cargo doors of the planes, and a weighted ball falls out. Then he starts to put the airplane through more complex maneuvers. As he completes a loop-the-loop to the cheers of the men, Vivi runs across the field. She loses one of her shoes and almost falls, but regains her balance with a windmill maneuver.

"Be careful with that!" she shouts. She grabs up her shoe. Now she is hopping on one foot, shaking the shoe at him. "No loop-the-loops."

"I have to get a feel for its capabilities."

"Terrorists aren't going to be putting it through loops. It's my plane. No loops!"

"Aw, come on!" another man says. "We're not going to crash it."

Vivi stands her ground. "No, absolutely not."

Fran leans over. "It makes me miss my playground mother days. Of course, my kids were a lot cuter than these old goats."

The smithy lands the plane and inserts a heavier ball into the cargo hold. The Sky Shark takes off again, but its flight is more labored until it drops its payload.

Soon men are begging for their turn at the controls, testing out the buddy box, and doing another loop, which infuriates Vivi.

"No, I think we've all seen how it flies," Vivi says.

"It's time to reconvene indoors and discuss what could be done with this," I say. I'm thinking that Vernon may be right. All of this is a big waste of time. These planes may have nothing to do with the attack.

I get a chorus of boos from the men.

"Guess what," I say, "we're not here to play. I'll see you in the canary cage in ten minutes."

The smithy at the controls gives me a dirty look and brings the Sky Shark in for a landing.

"I'll take it," Vivi says as the smithy starts to walk away with it.

"If you insist," he snaps.

37. Doc

Wolves and warning. How to negotiate the thread that stretches between crying wolf and failing to warn? Warn too often and no one listens. Fail to warn, and reap the bloody consequences. I've always maintained that the terrorists deliberately manipulate the psychology of warning. Before the Strikes we had intelligence that the attack would occur on one date. We warned. The terrorists pushed the date back. It happened again. We warned and the date passed quietly. By the third time, the policymakers were rolling their eyes at us. The people we write for are extremely impatient. The people we write about are infinitely patient. It doesn't take long for warning fatigue to set in. A state of high alert is costly and cannot be maintained indefinitely.

With this in mind I set out to draft an article for the President. I can guess his frame of mind. Last week he stood on the Mines' seal at the front entrance and crowed about his administration's great success in assuring our safety. He pointed to the roll-up of the Barcelona cell as evidence that his policies were working. He even implied that advanced interrogation techniques had played a role. They had not. The intelligence was from intercepts. The administration is so willing to torture to ensure our safety, but the scenario they talk about never happens in the real world. Under their scenario, we pick up a terrorist, torture him until he tells us about an imminent terrorist plot. Using this information we foil the plot. There are a few problems with this scenario. For one, the prisoner will lie, or give us enough truth to sound plausible and lie on the critical details. Even in the unlikely event that he tells us the truth, his cell would have changed the details as soon as a member was arrested. The only hope is if the cell doesn't find out about the arrest immediately. But somehow, under this administration, word of every arrest is leaked immediately so that they can claim a success. They are willing to torture to ensure our safety, but unwilling to forego good publicity for the same end.

I have grown into a very angry old man.

38. Maddie

We return to the canary cage to find Doc and Vernon red-faced and muttering. Doc has been getting grief from the President's briefer about sending up yet another "imminent attack" warning, and the Organ has been yelling at Vernon for not having more specifics on venue or modus operandi.

"Retromingent numbnuts," Doc says.

"Assholes," Vernon says.

"What does *retromingent* mean?" Bonnie asks. She really should learn when to keep her questions to herself.

"It means backward pissing," Doc barks.

"How does that apply—"

"Bonnie," I say, "help me move these chairs so we can fit everyone into the room."

Only four of the smithies and technical analysts who watched the test flight have come for the meeting. I'm severely annoyed, but I realize that more would not have fit into the canary cage. As it is people are standing crushed along the walls. I shush the eager boy talk that surrounds the Sky Shark, which is sitting at the far end of the table directing its painted snarl at me.

"You're the technical experts, you're the creative people," I say to the smithies. "If you were out to kill a bunch of people with a fleet of these things, how would you go about it? Don't hold back because you think an idea sounds stupid. I want to hear everything that pops into your heads."

Bill, the smithy who was controlling the Sky Shark, speaks up. "I'd put a miniature fogger on it and disperse anthrax. Find a big enough crowd and you couldn't get enough Cipro to take care of everybody."

Bonnie clears her throat and sniffles loudly. "Well," she says. She pauses to pour a packet of turbino sugar into her tea and stir it with a tiny, ornate silver spoon. She looks around the table with a smug smile as she stirs, cocking her pinkie at a delicate angle. Her hands are plump, but amazingly small and tapered. She replaces the spoon on the saucer of her flowered bone china cup. "I can tell you've never worked with *Bacillus anthracis*. It is extremely hard to weaponize. Only the U.S. and Russia can do it. You need large centrifuges to wash the spores before you attempt to aerosolize them. Even if they did manage to sicken a few people with an unrefined strain, local supplies of Ciprofloxacin should be more than adequate to handle it." Bonnie gives us another smile of superiority and takes a sip of her tea.

I don't like to have ideas shot down so cavalierly. "Well, you're not as familiar with the Base as we are. The Base had well-developed anthrax production capacities. And are you sure there's not another country besides the U.S. and Russia that can weaponize anthrax? We're not the only countries in the world with large centrifuges. Any big pharmaceutical company would have them. Wouldn't it?"

Another smithy speaks up. "I'd use a binary chemical weapon. Easier to handle. All you would do would be to tape the vials together, then drop them on the crowd. They break, the chemicals mix, and boom: You get a toxic cloud."

"It's not as easy as that," Vernon says. "It would disperse too rapidly. For amounts as small as those planes could carry, you'd need an enclosed space."

"Fly them into a subway station à la Aum Shinrikyo."

"I think you'd lose your radio signal," one of the smithies says.

"What about VX gas? A cloud of VX gas?"

"Only a few countries have it. It's hard to handle and generally it's a liquid, not a gas. You have to heat it to very high temperatures to release a vapor," Vernon says. "If they've managed to get hold of VX, I don't think they'd use such a suboptimal delivery system for it."

"What about launching these things?" one of the smithies says. "How do you surreptitiously launch a bunch of these things if you're aiming to do this in a crowd, which I assume is their aim."

Bonnie puts down her tea and leans forward, "To get back to bio weapons—"

"Wait, let's deal with the launch issue first."

"I think we have to figure out what these things are going to carry."

The brainstorming session is lurching about in fifty different directions, as these things tend to do. The only mouth not moving is the one on the Sky Shark, frozen into its snarl.

39. Jibril ibn Faraj

Abu Muhammad al-Dhayany

The Snail

Jean Moreau

Junior Smith

I prayed for this calm. For six innings, I have done my job unerringly, not even miscounting the change. The moment is almost here, when I see the detective who questioned me earlier standing near an exit. He looks at me. Then I notice other policemen nearby. I feel a rush of elation, because the plan is about to spool out and they are too late to stop it. I choose the prettiest child I can find as my gift to Allah. I give her a free hot dog. Smile.

40. Maddie

I glare at the snarling Sky Shark. I'm about to open my own mouth to try to bring the meeting to a more productive order, when the room goes suddenly quiet, all eyes riveted on the television set, which is behind me.

"Turn up the sound!" Vernon barks.

As Vivi reaches for the remote, I twist around to get a view of the screen. I'm appalled to see another Sky Shark coming toward me, this one soaring over the heads of a stadium crowd. I see the image for a few seconds before the sound comes on. Screaming, unearthly screaming.

The announcer's voice, raised to a panic pitch. "My God, we're under attack."

"No!" Vivi says. Her shoulders slump. She covers her face with her hands and repeats, "No, no, no, not again."

A somewhat calmer voice in the news studio cuts in, "Once again, for those just tuning in. We have breaking news from Burton Oil Park, can you tell us what's taking place?"

"They're gassing us. Model airplanes are gassing us."

One of the stadium cameras switches to a picture of a small child going into convulsions as her mother screams for help. The crowds are stampeding for the exit tunnels.

"That makes no sense!" Vernon yells at the screen. "Those planes are too small!"

I shake uncontrollably as I watch pandemonium take over. Then the sound of one explosion, two, three. Flame and black smoke rise from the entrance tunnels.

"They're killing us!" the on-site announcer screams. "They're killing us! Oh my God, blood . . ."

Vivi gets up. "Let me out of here." She tries to squeeze behind Bonnie. "I'm going to be sick, let me out of here!" Bonnie attempts to move away, but not before the contents of Vivi's stomach erupt over her lap and keyboard.

"Oh my God, oh my God, oh my God." I don't know who is saying that. Perhaps me. I look down at my hands and see blood under my fingernails. I've been scratching my face.

"Mute it!" Fran shouts. She has her arms around Vivi's shoulders and is helping her finish vomiting into a trash can.

"No!" Vernon shouts. "I have to hear this. And smithies, get out of here. Watch it from someplace else. We need to work."

The announcers are shouting. "People are being trampled to death. No one knows where to go. Oh God, we can see everything from this booth. . . ."

Bonnie flees the room to clean herself off. Vernon, Doc, and Kristin type away, trying to pull up more information. I'm doing nothing. I'm paralyzed. Some minutes later, when the door slams into the back of my chair, I can't scream or flinch. I'm made of rubber.

Harry opens his mouth to speak, but his eyes light, first on the vomit on the floor, then on the Sky Shark. He points to it. His hand is shaking. "That's it. That's what they used. What in God's name are you doing with that? What did you know before these attacks?"

I take a deep breath and try to switch into the automatic pilot mode that served me so well after the Strikes, but my voice is shaky, hesitant.

"We tried to get out a PIU on the planes, but—"

"Where did those planes come from?"

"There was a report in the DTR a few months ago about large purchases of RC planes. We were following up on it."

"Months ago?" Harry asks, dumbfounded. "Months ago and you're just now following up on it? Fran, I want a detailed chronology of everything this task force has done since it was stood up. Vivian, I want a write-up of everything we know on these attacks. We'll need talking points for the BOM, ASAP. Maddie, you come with me. I want you at my side when the President calls to find out how the hell we let this happen." Harry starts out the door and then turns. "And Vernon, put your jacket over that thing." He points to the Sky Shark. "I don't want people asking why we had one sitting in our office at the same time they were killing people."

41. Vivian

Sit quietly. Don't move, Viv, or you'll get sick again. Sit quietly and think rationally. Put the facts down and get them into order. Order. Reason. Blow the smoke away. The first step toward making some sense of it, if sense can be made of such a thing. Fight back the confusion and the chaos. Put it into the correct sequence. Get the chronology straight.

Time: 3:45 P.M. Tuesday.

Venue: Burton Oil Park. Major-league baseball game.

Sequence of events: During the seventh inning stretch, approximately fifty radio-controlled airplanes appear over the walls of the stadium. No panic yet. People think it's entertainment. Within a minute, planes begin to fly low over the crowd and drop red smoke bombs. Several children in the crowd go into convulsions. A camera picks out one of the children and the image appears on the stadium's large screen. Who decided to put this on the screen? The crowd begins to panic and rush toward the exits. As soon as the exit tunnels fill, suicide bombers positioned near three of the exits detonate bombs. The stampede reverses itself, with multiple casualties. Local authorities inadvertently heighten the panic when they land a helicopter on the field.

Casualties: Can't get the numbers straight yet.

It's time to tally up the losses. Corral the confusion into neat columns. Wipe the soot from the faces of the dead and arrange them in rows by time and manner of death. It's your job. Do not cry. That's not your job.

42. Maddie

Nineteen hours since the attack, and the sun must have come up, but I can't imagine it. No one in my crew has gone home, even for a change of clothes. The air is sour. My aching brain can't produce a word to describe our collective mood. The worst part for me is the foul bodily familiarity of it. My eyes, my head, my stomach, have felt this way before. The memory is an echo that sends back a fresh wave of pain with every breath.

Last evening a courier brought video from the stadium, images too graphic to show on TV. Our stinging eyes alternate between the slag and the sight of people dying from compression asphyxia, explosions, and poison gas. This must be the most thoroughly documented terrorist attack in history. Every angle. How many are dead? The numbers are all over the map. The overall death toll appears to be in the high hundreds, but the local health system and morgues are in chaos.

The crew communicates with words that are as few and softly spoken as possible, except for Vernon. He won't shut up, and he's talking far too loud for this tiny, cloistered space. It's like he's on some kind of upper.

"It makes no goddamn sense," Vernon bellows for the fortieth time. He throws down his pen. "I can't think of anything that the terrorists could put in those planes that would cause instant convulsions and death. Thirteen ounces per plane? The timing doesn't work, either. And that bright red smoke—none of it makes sense. The Russians don't have anything that deadly, much less a bunch of jihadists from the caves."

"You're culturally biased," I tell him. "Don't underestimate the Base. Don't think they aren't smart and sophisticated." I'm beginning to raise my own voice. I want to scream at Vernon. He's arrogant and obnoxious and he smells sweaty.

"Don't accuse me of that, I know they're smart," he says, "but they can't have the capability to do this." He picks up his pen and begins to twist it apart, put it back together again, twist it apart. . . .

"Well, they did it," I tell him. "Argue with that."

"I am arguing with that."

I see Fran and Doc exchange looks and pointedly bury their heads deeper in their work. Kristin's fingers continue to work the keyboard at blinding speed. Vivi actually puts her hands over her ears. Bonnie is wearing earphones. None of them want any part of this unproductive argument.

"Let's just let it be for a while," I say to Vernon.

We've found out a lot in the last nineteen hours. In the background of one video, you can see the controllers sitting in the highest seats of the stadium, each one surrounded by a few thuggish friends. Some of those guys are in custody. The others melted away in the confusion. The planes were launched from the roofs of a line of derelict row houses near the stadium. One team did the launching; then, when the planes cleared the outfield fence, they switched control to guys with buddy boxes in the upper seats. They coordinated everything with Bluetooth gadgets hooked over their ears. Authorities searched the row houses and found RC plane flight simulator programs on all the computers, with spatial data on the stadium loaded in so they could practice exactly what they had to do.

"It stinks to high heaven in here," Vernon grouses. "Vivian, what did you have for lunch, anyway?"

I'm annoyed that he's hounding her. She still looks ill. Vivi doesn't answer. She's bent over photographs obtained from the Organ, staring at a copy of the charred driver's license photo of someone named Junior Smith, of all things. They found his body plastered on the walls near one of the exits. I can guess what's going through her head. She's trying to figure out how he could have done it. It's her psychology background, I suppose, that makes her want to understand. Me, I don't care. I'm just glad he's dead. If I could kill him again, I would.

At the top of the hour the morning newscast does a wrap-up, so I grab the remote to turn up the sound. The newscaster reports that more than six hundred people are "believed dead in the chemical attack that took place yesterday a—"

"What did they die of?" Vernon yells at the screen. "Asphyxia, explosions, heart attacks. Why are you calling it a chemical attack?"

"A half-dozen children did die from chemicals," I remind him. "That's been confirmed."

"No, it hasn't," he snaps back.

"Are you blind? We have video of them gasping and dying," I yell. I can't take any more of his superior, dismissive tone. At this point I would rather shoot him than spend one more minute crammed into this closet with him.

"It wasn't an airborne chemical."

"Then what was it? You explain to me how those people died. Those children." I see Vivi flinch, but I press my point. "They were all children who went into convulsions. They would be the ones most vulnerable to an airborne chemical."

"Like I've told you, they'd be the ones most vulnerable to anything." Vernon flings down the pen he was pointing at me and it skitters across the table and falls to the floor next to Kristin. She keeps her eyes pinned to the screen and doesn't say a word. She has the calm I had after the Strikes. I recognize it. She doesn't realize it now, but she'll pay for it later. I feel a moment of pity, then I return to my argument with Vernon, which is moving beyond a polite, professional difference of opinion.

"And why only a dozen out of the forty thousand people there?" Vernon says.

"Isn't a dozen enough for you?" I counter. "What about all the people who are sick?"

"Of course they're sick. Just like the thousands who showed up at hospitals after the Tokyo sarin attacks. That many people couldn't possibly have been exposed. It was psychosomatic."

I glance over at the TV and see a Sky Shark on the correspondent's desk. I turn the sound up another notch. The anchorman seems proud of it. "BSNBC has obtained a radio-controlled model plane identical to the one used in the attacks."

"How did they do that so fast?" I ask no one in particular.

Vernon reaches across the table and rips his jacket off of our Sky Shark. "If BSNBC has one, I'm not going to hide ours. Screw Harry. Maybe looking at it will give me an inspiration."

"Looking at it makes me ill," Vivi says.

Bonnie stretches and takes off the earphones she's been wearing all morning. She's oblivious to the fact that the cloying perfume she splashed on to cover the smell of vomit on her skirt has raised our antipathy toward her to a new level. She turns to Vernon. "Have you made a list of airborne chemicals they could have used?"

Vernon jumps down her throat. "How many times do I have to tell you people that it's not an airborne chemical?"

"Well, it's certainly not biological, and there's no need to be uncivil to me." Bonnie pouts. "It has to be chemical. Nothing biological could cause convulsions that quickly. And what about the odd color of the smoke? What toxin is that?"

"Nothing toxic. Probably strontium nitrate, the same thing they use in fireworks."

"Why color it?"

Vernon rolls his eyes as if amazed by her ignorance. "To freak people out, of course. To create waves of panic to push forty thousand people over the edge. They did it brilliantly. First the planes, then the red smoke, then the sight of children gasping—which appears on the big stadium screen—then the planes rise into the sky and crash into the crowd, then the explosions. Did you see how the bodies were lined up? For the most part they weren't crushed against walls. Those lines are where a crowd moving in one direction met a crowd moving in another. It was orchestrated for maximum casualties."

"And your point is?" I interrupt, not caring to hear it all again. Vernon sits quietly for a minute, staring at the ceiling, obviously thinking big thoughts.

"Let's look at those tapes of the children dying again."

"Oh, no," Vivi says, "I can't. I simply can't."

Vernon reaches for his wallet and pulls out a ten. "Here, go get yourself some breakfast on me. Keep the change. I need to review those tapes. Come back in half an hour." His voice is kind.

Vivi hesitates. Fran snatches the ten and stuffs it in her hand. "I'll go with you. I don't particularly care to see those tapes again either."

"I'm in, too," Kristin says. "I need a few minutes out of this room."

Doc stands up. "I don't see the point of watching them again. I've had my fill."

"Well, if it's a party . . ." Bonnie says.

Vernon looks at me. "Aren't you going?"

I shake my head.

Vernon waits until the door is closed to slip the tape into the VCR. I watch as he fast-forwards and pauses to watch yet again the death of a little blond girl, about five years old. "Look at this," he says. "Do you notice anything odd about this girl?" He freezes the frame.

I look closely at the child, whose eyes are rolled back. "She has something yellow on her cheek."

"Mustard. She was eating a hot dog. She's about to gag some of it up." He unpauses the picture so I can see what he's talking about. "Notice anything else that looks strange?"

"Her face is very pink."

"Cyanide."

"Cyanide gas? I can see a red haze. One of those bomblets must have landed right there."

"But look, people next to her are unaffected."

"But the little girl gasps, like it's in her lungs."

"That's what cyanide does. It cuts off your ability to absorb oxygen. So victims gasp, whether they've ingested the poison or inhaled it."

"Then what was in the planes?"

"Nothing," Vernon says. There is an excited, almost happy look on his face. "Don't you see? They were just blowing smoke, so to speak. They carried little, if any, toxic substance. They were there to raise the level of panic, to remind everyone of the planes crashing into the towers. The hot dog killed her." He sits back, looking enormously pleased with himself.

"So the vendors poisoned people?"

"Select people, children—lovely photogenic children yet—who would respond rapidly and reliably to the cyanide. Looks like they picked them out, poisoned them, then directed the planes to fly right over them with the smoke bombs, which, in turn, quickly attracted the cameras."

I sit back and try to absorb Vernon's theory, all the while hating him for his sudden high spirits. The door opens, and the rest of the canary crew appears.

"Aren't you back early?" Vernon says.

Kristin rolls her eyes and assumes the sarcastic demeanor of a teenager. "Uncle Harry saw us playing hooky in the cafeteria and yelled at us. He asked us what the hell we were doing taking a coffee break."

"I hope you told him to stick his caramel macchiato up his ass."

"It crossed my mind."

Vernon can hardly wait until everyone is settled to explain his theory. Suddenly he seems to be in a great mood. I see their faces express skepticism at first, but he slowly wins them over. He wraps up his spiel with a flourish. "I'm confident that they'll find that the vast majority of deaths resulted from the human stampede. That's perfect for the terrorists, because they can say we were killed by our own fear. They've always called us cowards."

Vivi rubs her face. "How . . . how could they think of something like that?"

Vernon has a ready answer. "My guess is that they were originally planning to put something toxic in the planes, but found out it wouldn't work well enough. When they examine those planes, they'll find nothing but traces of strontium salts. In fact, I'm going to call my contacts at the Organ and see if I can be there when they examine the planes."

Vernon picks up the phone and dials. Some of the piss goes out of him when he gets put on lengthy hold, but his bizarrely fine mood soon returns, so much so that he begins whistling the theme song from the old *Andy Griffith Show.* The rest of us stare at him, dumbfounded. Finally he notices the hostility and stops in mid-whistle. "Hey," he says, "what's wrong with something cheery to break the tension? Am I the only one in this room who loves his job?"

"Yes," I tell him. "You are. Are you fucking crazy? You love this job, and I'm the one seeing a shrink? We just failed to stop an attack. People died. Children died. How the bloody hell can you love this job?"

Vernon shrugs. "I can't help it. This is real. This is our Great War, and we're on the front lines. Why would you want to be anywhere else?"

43. Vivian

I'm on the phone with my son, explaining why I probably won't be home in time for dinner again. He listens quietly and says, "We ate a long time ago." The conference room clock is broken and I forgot my watch today so I motion for Kristin to show me hers. It's Josh's bedtime! He must think his mother is crazy. Maybe she is. I should have anticipated his next comment, but it catches me off guard.

"My plane killed the people. I saw it."

I take a deep breath. I wish his father hadn't let him watch this thing on TV. "It wasn't your plane. It was the same kind of plane. It was a big coincidence." There is a long silence on the other end of the line. I try to think of the right words. Then Jeff is on the line.

"Can you take that damn thing back to the store?" he says.

I assure him that I can, although I doubt they would take back an assembled Sky Shark now. Neither is the office likely to reimburse me for an object that made its awkward, incriminating appearance a few hours before the attacks.

I hang up and sit still until the urge to burst into tears has passed. Despite the lower body count, I'm taking this attack harder than the Strikes. My mind, my body, my heart are all rejecting the reality of it. I'm having trouble doing my job. I've had to go to the ladies' room several times for a cry. I can see that Maddie and Doc are having problems, as well. Kristin, Fran, and Bonnie are fine. Vernon is as happy as a toddler in a wading pool. Only the veterans are faltering. Maybe BDs are good for only one big attack close to home.

Everything about this attack is sick, demented. The final results from the toxicology reports aren't in, but Louis Townsend, the guy who is conducting them, agrees with Vernon that the dead children were probably poisoned through their food. Vernon is glowing with satisfaction, and we are sick of him.

We've found out that Junior Smith is a dual citizen of France and Yemen named Jibril ibn Faraj, a.k.a. Abu Muhammad al-Dhayany, a.k.a. a half-dozen other names. He was a theater major. He was adept at staging extravaganzas. He won an award for producing a student opera. It surprises us that he blew himself up. It seems that such a gifted planner would be too valuable to the organization, but perhaps he couldn't resist the drama.

What haunts me is the video of the children and their parents. I see the fear, disbelief, desperation on those parental faces. The people are different, the reactions remarkably alike. I feel close to them, barely a hair away. They won't show the most graphic images on TV, but they show the reactions, the horror. What are these images doing to us? The Chieftain is changing us. What freedoms will we exchange for the safety of our children? I can feel his long fingers wringing my sore heart. I have a bitter taste in my mouth, as if I had been poisoned.

I ought to be home with my son. He saved me after the Strikes by choosing that time to be born. I need to save him now, because he's shaken. I can hear it in his voice, but I can't leave.

44. Maddie

*C*olossal, unbelievable, mammoth, historic intelligence failure. I've scribbled a list of the adjectives applied to the term *intelligence failure* by various TV commentators. That list is stuck to my monitor. I should have the words tattooed on my forehead. The terms *intelligence failure* and *Maddie James* are synonyms. The blame game has begun and I'm looking like a goat. You don't get any brownie points for almost stopping an attack. When people are maimed and killed, someone must be blamed, and generally, the ones who are blamed will be the same ones who tried hardest to prevent it. It's what happened after the Strikes. What's about to happen now. I see the signs everywhere.

First, there is the expression on Harry's face when he sees me. *You let me down,* it says. *You let those people down,* it says. *You let your country down,* it says. Out loud, he says, "The Mines will take the fall for this. We may be reorganized out of existence." I let the Mines down. This is the only one that doesn't bother me. Perhaps the Mines should be reorganized out of existence.

Second there is the collation of the written record, a task that has now fallen to me. Everything we have written on this threat, everything we have said to policymakers. Did we adequately warn? Did we take the necessary measures, task the right collectors? The public might be surprised that such questions take precedence over the question: What might the terrorists do next? If there is one hard lesson I've learned in this town, it's that ass-covering trumps national security every time.

Third. Esteemed Legislative Body hearings. They're coming. I guess I'd better brush the rabbit fur from my suits. The Mines don't like to put peon-level employees on the stand, but I suspect that this time I will have to take center stage.

• • •

I read through the additional information that Doc has managed to obtain on the Snail/Junior/Jibril since the attacks. He was half French, but the fact that he spoke French turned out to be irrelevant. Nevertheless we wasted time looking at a possible Paris embassy angle. The fact that he was a theater major—the thing that we laughed at—turned out to be significant. He orchestrated this ugly bit of theater, the timing, the entrances, the exits. That's the thing. Sometimes things are completely irrelevant. Sometimes seemingly irrelevant things are critical. I read on and discover that his mother was a chef and his father was a halal butcher. Only then do I remember Wynona's words, "bled out like a hog." I feel physically ill as I realize that the Peanut Man was killed according to the method of *dhabh*, and the Snail was the murderer. Those words had stuck in my mind, but somehow I couldn't connect them to anything until too late.

Perhaps it's time for me to quit. My mind isn't nimble enough anymore. Leave this job to the Kristins of the world.

How long before I can shut my eyes and not see the painted grin of the Sky Shark? Right now, I can't imagine that time ever coming.

It is all I can do to focus on my work. I'm collating the reports I've found, putting them in chronological order, digging out all the distribution lists and attaching these to the end of each report. Then I'll type up a list of the reports with a summary sentence of each and Xerox ten copies of the stack. Secretarial work, but we don't have enough secretaries to do it anymore. Consequently, three days after a big terrorist attack, one of the office's most experienced BDs is

Xeroxing. But it doesn't matter anymore. I've come to doubt whether I'm capable of a greater contribution.

The door bangs into my chair, but I've lost the ability to scream since the stadium attack. I expect to see Harry, but it is the other person who never bothers to knock: my mother.

"Madeleine! You haven't returned any of my phone calls. I was starting to wonder if you had collapsed. Have you eaten today?"

"Yes," I say. "I ate a good lunch."

"Two pecan tarts," Vivi says.

Snitch.

"I knew it! Well, I'm going to fix that! I took the day off again and I've been cooking and baking all morning. I brought enough for everybody."

"You are so good to us, Mrs. James!" Vivi says. For some odd reason, all of my colleagues call my mother Mrs. James, even though every other person in the Mines goes by his or her first name.

"We are most grateful for the excellent comestibles," Doc says.

My mother beams as she pulls a cart as far into the room as it will go and begins to unload foil-covered casseroles and platters. These are passed directly over my head to the waiting arms of my colleagues, who push aside stacks of papers and other debris to make room for the feast.

When everything is unloaded, my mother hands out wet wipes and little packages of plastic cutlery. "You folks eat. You need to keep up your strength. I'll be back for your dishes later." Mom kisses the top of my head and exits with her cart. A second later she's back. "I almost forgot to give you the condiments!" She sets down a wooden condiment caddy painted with pink bunny rabbits. The door closes again.

Vernon raises the foil on one of the casseroles. "Does your mother have some sort of lima bean fetish?" he says.

"It's a Southern thing," I say. "Eat it and don't complain."

"What's this?" Kristin asks as she lifts the foil on another casserole.

"Cheesy hominy bake."

Kristin looks doubtful. "Explain hominy to me again. Is it a carb?"

"Just eat it," I snap. "Eat it all or she'll interrogate me on what was wrong with it."

My colleagues exchange looks and dutifully dig in.

"I love Southern cooking," Bonnie says as she spoons out a large dollop of cheesy hominy bake. "I appreciate your mother even if you don't."

"Don't appreciate her too much or the opposite sides of this table will have to take turns inhaling," Vernon says.

A minute later the door bangs into my chair again. I don't flinch.

"Yes, Mom?" I say without turning around.

"Madeleine, I forgot to ask you. When will you be home tonight? Late?"

"Yes, late, probably very late. Very, very late."

"Okay. I won't bother you again until you all are finished. *Bon appétit!*"

"Thank you, Mrs. James!"

I have nothing to live for. Nothing. Life is one big sucking, stinking morass. One humongous intelligence failure of historic proportions. No love life. No outside life. Career down the toilet.

Vivi tries to pass me a platter of country ham, but I wave it away.

"Come on, Maddie, eat something. Your mother was so sweet to do this. The ham is a little salty, but there are biscuits to put it on."

"If we have to ingest all of these carbs—not to mention the saturated fat and sodium—then you should, too," Kristin says.

"Pass me a brownie."

• • •

Three hours later, I haven't accomplished shit. I'm so antsy, I can't seem to properly alphabetize my list of reports. I'm tired and wired and can't stop yawning or chewing my nails. My shrink approved an increased dose of my latest selective seratonin reuptake inhibitor, but it's not working. I still want to kill the other people in this room, despite the fact that a couple are dear friends. Even dear friends get old if you're cooped up with them too long. Doc, my witty, erudite, goodhearted old colleague, has bad breath, and his coffee smells vile. Vivi has a tendency to go soft and weepy and talk about motherhood, the last subject on earth I care to discuss. Then there are the people to whom I'm less attached. Fran is a priceless researcher, but when she plays footsie with Doc under the table or winks at him, it is a bitter reminder that my own love life has tanked. Of course, she'd be happy to fix me up with her very own perfect son, Alan, but I'm not that desperate. While Fran is a reminder of one of the ways I've failed, Kristin is a reminder of all of them. My jealousy is compounded by the fact that she is bright enough to already have plans to leave the Mines before she turns into me. Then there's Bonnie, who sucks on her food before swallowing it and whines endlessly. Vernon is just vile. Vile, sleazy, and insufferable when he's happy.

Under these circumstances, it would be justifiable homicide.

Doc catches me in the middle of another yawn. "Go home, Maddie, you're not doing yourself or anyone else any good. Go to bed and turn off your alarm clock. Harry can wait for his compilation of reports. It's not a life-or-death matter. It's just an ass-covering exercise."

I say a silent apology to Doc for wanting to kill him a moment earlier. He's right, and, for once, I'm going to listen to him.

"Okay, I'll go home."

Doc looks stunned. "You never take my excellent advice."

"I'm going to start taking it."

"You look too tired to drive. Let me drive you, I'm feeling fine," Vivi says.

"The last time I rode with you I ended up with a lap full of naked baby possums you scooped out of a roadkill." I shiver at the memory. "I can drive myself."

I squeeze myself out of the room and breathe deeply as I make the trek down the long hallways, out the door, to the far end of the Mines' acres of parking lot. It's about three o'clock in the afternoon, and the traffic on my way home is relatively light for a . . . a what? Friday I think. I notice that several cars have half-size baseball bats wired to their front grille. Red-and-white-striped baseball bats with a blue grip. This must be the symbol for the stadium attack. How do they produce this drek so fast? Too much.

When I get home, I see Mom's Lincoln in the driveway with a baseball bat attached to its grille. I'd forgotten that she said she was taking the day off. Never mind, I'm going straight to bed. I'm too tired to talk to anyone except Abu Bunny.

I find the front door unlocked and it sets me muttering. I keep telling Mom that this is not her genteel, upper-class North Carolina neighborhood. We have rapists, gangs, and crazed ex–federal employees. Women should lock their doors.

They see me before I see them. By the time comprehension breaks over my numb mind, they are grabbing for the crocheted Afghan draped over the back of the couch. For some reason he reminds me of a meerkat. His thin body rises out of the sofa with alert and danger in his tiny eyes, his twitching whiskers, and all the frail flesh of his body. I'm surprised at how small he looks naked. Small, boiled, and pale.

"Maddie, turn around! Don't stare at us," my mother says.

But I can't move. My mind is still trying to right itself. I can't remember the last time I saw my mother naked or even in her underwear. I didn't even know what kind of underwear she wore. She didn't run a casual house when I was growing up. Sure, she was a flirt with men, but she always told me that baring too much flesh was tacky. Now I see a flaming red lace bra and matching bikini panties draped over the back of a chair. Bikini? She always made me wear white cotton panties with a big elastic waistband. This soft, white, dimply naked woman cannot be my mother. But she is. I've caught my mother and my feckless boss Harry on my couch.

Somehow this is worse than finding out that Rick was having an affair.

"You're supposed to be compiling the intelligence record," Harry says, but it is a weak, almost apologetic complaint. It's hard for a man to project authority when his paunch is on display, an odd paunch the size of a rock Cornish game hen, the only fat on his skinny body.

When the initial shock wears off, I find myself in the same cold, decisive frame of mind I experienced after the Strikes. I speak slowly, firmly, and do not take my eyes off the pair cowering behind the loosely crocheted pink afghan, which covers far too little. "Harry, you are going to get out of my house now. Mother, you are going to take what you need to stay in a hotel until you find your own place. Then we can move the rest of your belongings. In particular, I want you to take this couch and any other piece of furniture that Harry has touched with his naked ass. I want you to take all of my toilet seats. In fact, I insist that you take them with you today. If you don't, I'll have them sent to your hotel by courier. I'm not kidding. You do not live here anymore. This does not mean I will refuse to speak to you. You are still my mother and still a part of my life, but you will not live here anymore. Understood?"

My mother nods. Tears run down her cheeks. They ruin her mascara, but they have no impact on me. I turn to leave, but there is one last thing I need to say. I turn back just as Harry is reaching for his pants.

"Harry, my apologies. I've misjudged you all of these years. I see you *do* have balls." I point, and Harry shrinks back toward the couch.

• • •

I don't know where else to go, so I go back to work. I try to stroll in as if nothing has happened, but my colleagues sit back in their chairs, and Vernon says, "What in the hell—? Did someone club you over the head?"

"What makes you think something is wrong?"

"Your mouth doesn't usually hang open, for one. And you have that postal look in your eye. Maybe we should frisk you."

"Yeah, Maddie," Vivi says. "You look a bit, for lack of a better word, *deranged.*"

I sink into my chair. I can't keep anything from these people. They practically live in my underwear. I can't stand it. A BD should be permitted one good cry per major terrorist attack. This is mine. The dams burst. I blubber, sniffle, drool, howl. Soon Vivi is hugging me, Fran is smoothing back my hair, and others are patting my arm. I can't stop crying. I have no self-control left. It all comes out.

"Harry . . ."

"What did he do?" Vernon asks.

"Harry . . ."

"What did he assign you to do now?"

"Harry . . ."

"Come on, we can't help you if you don't tell us."

"I caught Harry on my own couch . . . having his way with my mother."

"Fucking her, do you mean fucking her?" Vernon bangs a fist rhythmically against his palm.

I nod.

"You say *fuck* four hundred times a day and now you switch to 'having his way with her'?" Vernon says. "This is one for the shrink."

I cry louder. I'm almost howling now.

"You saw it?" Vivi says. "You actually saw them doing it? Naked? Harry, Captain Kangaroo Harry, naked? This has got to cause permanent psychological damage."

I'm choking on my own tears and can't answer.

"Do you have to call him 'Daddy' now?" Vernon asks.

I try to strike him, but he leans away and Doc grabs my arm and holds on tight.

"Calm down, Maddie. Your mother's a grown woman. You have to let her make her own choices, even if they're bad ones."

I calm myself enough to answer him. "That is so fucking lame, Doc."

Doc shrugs his shoulders and looks at Fran as if to say, "I tried."

"Here," Fran says. She takes Doc's place by my side and puts her arms around my shoulders. "Maddie. Did you kick her ass out of your house?"

"Yes."

"Good girl. One problem solved. Now we just have to figure a way to get those awful images out of your head."

"So does he have a minuscule dick?" Vernon says.

Fran swats him. "You're not helping."

"I want to know."

"You have so many unhealthy interests, Vernon," Kristin says.

My tears are starting to dry up. "It's on the small side."

"Excellent," Vernon says. "By the way, Maddie. Why did you choose to come back to the office after you saw these gruesome sights?"

I'm surprised by the question. "Where else would I go?"

Vernon shakes his head. "Come on." He stands up and motions for me to follow him. "The rest of you get back to work. I'm taking Maddie out for the afternoon. Don't worry, my intentions are entirely honorable."

Vernon has exactly the sort of vehicle I feared he would have: a shiny black, oversize, gas-guzzling pickup truck with those stupid extra tires on the rear.

As I try to climb gracefully into this behemoth, I ask the obvious question. "What are the extra tires for? Killing more squirrels on the parkway?"

"Don't get politically correct on me, Maddie. I'm trying to help you."

"Help me what?"

"Get a life."

"I've got a life. I'm an experienced, highly trained intelligence professional who has dedicated her career to going after the hard targets."

"Quit reading the recruiting posters and look in the mirror. You're a wreck."

"Thank you for that observation."

"I'm not trying to be a hardass, I'm just trying to help. You catch your mother and your despised boss getting it on in your very own flowered davenport and the only place you can think of to go is back to work? That's not normal. That's highly abnormal. Do you exist outside of work anymore?"

I let that question pass over my head as we exit the compound and merge into traffic. I focus on the flow of cars immediately around us and deliberately lose track of where I am. I'm adrift on vehicular currents in the middle of nowhere. Where would I go? What does this hypercrowded suburban landscape offer? I could get a mattress, a Starbucks venti, a manicure, or a tan. Then I could do it all over again twenty or thirty times without hitting the same store twice. I could knock on the door of any one of a thousand townhouses that look exactly like mine. How many of them have naked bureaucrats on their sofas? I shudder to think.

"Get the picture out of your head, Maddie," Vernon says. He must have detected a shadow of revulsion on my face. "Think about something else, anything else. Who are your closest friends outside of work?"

"Don't have any real friends outside of work."

"Anybody you spend time with who's not connected to the Mines?"

"The gastroenterologist and the orthopedic surgeon. I guess the shrink is Mines cleared, so he doesn't count. I should dump him. The orthopedic surgeon hands out better drugs."

Vernon makes a sudden, harrowing turn across oncoming traffic and pulls into a small parking lot in front of an aging strip mall. He waves his arm toward a sign that says OLDE VIRGINIA BREW PUB.

"This is my home away from the Mines. They all know me. They're talking about naming a beer after me. This is the sort of place you need to go after you've seen your boss screwing your mother."

"No, Vernon. I think I really need to check myself into a mental hospital."

"Shush. Come on." Vernon hops out of the truck and comes around to help me out. I don't know about this place. It looks like a dive, but I let him lead me inside. Coming out of the sunshine, it's very dark. Lots of dark wood, fake antique signs on the walls. Vernon chooses a somewhat sticky varnished table near the window.

The waiter walks over. "Vernon, what brings you out on a Thursday afternoon? What will it be? We have a new batch of your favorite, Beltway Brain Basher."

"Sounds good to me."

"And the lady?"

"Ice tea, please," I say.

"Jesus," Vernon says. "You just caught your mother naked in the arms of your equally naked boss and you order ice tea?"

"I'm not in the mood for beer."

The waiter says, "Whoa! Your mom? Your boss? Really?"

"Thanks for broadcasting my humiliation to the world, Vernon."

The waiter holds his hand over his heart. "I won't tell a soul, on my honor. How about a Scotch on the rocks? We have Glenlivet single malt."

I perk up a bit. "Why, that would be lovely, thank you."

"Isn't this better than stewing at work?"

I look around. As my eyes adjust to the darkness, I recognize the Mines boss for alchemist retention, two smithies I met once in a training course, and three retired Middle East experts.

"Vernon, everybody here either works or has worked at the Mines. You call this getting away? It's like a Mines off-site. Even if nobody here was from the Mines, a bar isn't the answer for me. I need to find some other place to go outside of work."

"Let's see." Vernon frowns in concentration. "You have an artsy-fartsy side, don't you? You could go to a museum or Wolf Trap or the Kennedy Center."

"I've written attack scenarios for all of those places. Kind of takes the pleasure out of an evening of the arts when you know how vulnerable the ventilation system is."

"Maybe you should get out of counterterrorism for a while. It's warping your brain. Besides, I get the sense that you're not enjoying it anymore." Vernon leans forward, switching into a tone of fatherly concern. "You're letting it get to you. For me, becoming a BD was like getting a new lease on life. I like explosions." He simulates an explosion with hand gestures and vocal effects. "*Fwoooom! I* loved the firearms and explosives courses. A total blast—*fwooom!*— no pun intended. I get the feeling, though, that women don't enjoy it as much." The serious tone returns. "Not that women don't make great BDs—you really do, but you tend to take the death and carnage thing too seriously."

"You don't take death and carnage seriously?"

"Well, sure I do. Death and carnage are bad. Very bad. I'm not a total hardhearted slob, but I've learned to keep things in proportion. Sure it looks gross to see body parts strewn all over the place, but you have to remember that all of these people are going to die eventually anyway. We all die. It's part of the great human condition that we share."

Vernon seems to sincerely believe he has said something profound. He takes a sip of his Brain Smasher and belches. "What I'm saying is, you should either learn not to take things so hard or you should go be a political alchemist on some nice quiet little country. Pick a country with good food, great climate, safe water, and scenic countryside. Take as many trips there as the government will pay for. Be wild. Get a suntan between embassy briefings."

"Suppose I want to change my life entirely?"

"Wouldn't that be a change?"

"No, leaving the Mines would be the only change that would really be a change."

"Where would you go? DipServ? Defense? Not the Organ, for God's sake. You think the Mines are a pit—so to speak—all of those places are worse."

"What about leaving government altogether?"

"Oh, you can't do that. You have too many years in. Your retirement would be toast. Although, if you went to work for a contractor like Managotech, it could be lucrative enough to make it work. They would snap up someone with your experience and clearances."

"But if I signed on with them, I'd end up right back in the Mines, consulting."

"But you would be getting paid better and work fewer hours."

"But I'd be doing the same job."

"Well, what do you want that you can't find in a government job?"

"Joy?"

"Phooey. I don't know what your alternatives would be, other than finding a sugar daddy." He looks me up and down as if assessing my probability of success.

"How about taking a job that pays less and provides more satisfaction? A job in some part of the country where everything isn't ridiculously overpriced?"

"Don't be stupid. You're not going to give up good pay and great benefits to go teach kindergarten in Appalachia."

"That wouldn't be enough of a change from counterterrorism. Small children scare me." I finish off my Scotch, and realize that I drank it faster than I should have. I can't suppress a burp.

"Another one?"

"No, if I have one more, I'll have to crawl out of here. Bars aren't the place for me."

"Would you like to go somewhere else? Name it and I'll take you."

"A hardware store."

"A hardware store?"

"I need to buy new locks for my doors and new toilet seats. I don't suppose you could help me install them?"

45. Doc

It has begun, and it is so much like the last time that I am already heart-weary and filled with disgust. Theater. The attacks were theater and the aftermath is theater, with stage sets and scripts and tragic monologues. The President's handlers must have been up late into the night devising a scene to rival the famous speech atop the rubble after the Strikes. This attack presented greater difficulties for the image makers. Not much rubble. Not to mention the fact that it happened not a week after the President's latest declaration that he had made the nation safer. Pose the great man with a toy plane with painted teeth? It lacks dignity. Pose him at the stadium? It's still undergoing an intensive decontamination. So they called in the model builders, some of the same folks who put together the Sky Shark, and they built an entire Iranian village to scale on the White House Lawn and surrounded the President with saucer-eyed children in a politically correct range of skin tones. The canary crew—minus Vernon and Maddie, who are still off somewhere—sits subdued as the President gravely informs the nation of the perfidy of its enemy and the seriousness of the threat that remains. Dr. Dean stands in the background, holding a photogenic two-year-old. Our illustrious leader caresses a child's head with one hand, then removes the roof of one of the small buildings to reveal a chemical weapons facility complete with centrifuges, tanks, and tiny scientists in white coats. Saucer eyes widen further. Do you see where this is going?

"Turn it down before I vomit," Vivian says, and I comply quickly with her request. We've learned not to take such threats from her lightly.

We're quiet. Not only did we fail to prevent another terrorist attack, but we inadvertently handed the President *casus belli* for a war with Iran. They've been planning this war for months, but they lacked a justification to go in. Is it possible that this could happen again so soon? Are memories so short? I don't think they will get away with it this time, but I didn't think they would last time, either.

Vernon doesn't know yet. The word came in an hour ago from a friend of his at the Pentagon. All of the Sky Sharks involved in the attacks have been destroyed—taken out to a military base in the desert and blown up—purportedly because of the danger they posed. More likely before someone can discover that there was nothing in them, no state-of-the-art, fast-acting, and deadly chemical devised by the Iranians.

The sound is turned off, but I can see the members of the Esteemed Legislative Body striking poses on the television screen, looking both grave and indignant as they seek a target for their righteous anger. I can lip read the words *intelligence failure.* That emphatic *f* presses the lower lip against the upper teeth, dimples the chin, makes jowls more prominent. It's an angry bulldog look, and I predict the Mines will soon feel the teeth.

There are no policy failures, only intelligence failures.

What I have yet to see on the screen are the toxicology reports from the children. Louis Townsend told Vernon the results would be ready by now. Why aren't they being reported? It might quell the rising national panic to know that the victims died from common poison and not some mysterious substance from a tiny plane. What is reported over and over again is that not all the Sky Sharks bought last year were used in the attack. Dozens of them are still floating around somewhere, unless they crashed them during training flights, which is quite possible.

Vernon returns after an absence of nearly four hours. By this time, Fran and Vivian have gone home for a well-deserved rest. Kristin is sipping a Starbucks and writing up a response to Dr. Beth Dean's latest inquiry. Bonnie is chewing on reheated pizza and drafting a Situation Update (SitUp, in Mines cant). A night crew will arrive in another two hours.

"What were you and Maddie doing all afternoon?" I ask Vernon.

"Changing her locks and replacing her toilet seats. The woman had no toilet seats in her house! I asked her how that happened and she said 'Don't ask.' So don't ask me, because I don't know. What's new?"

I hesitate to give Vernon the news, for I fear that his reaction will be violent. "The army has destroyed the Sky Sharks, citing a danger to public safety."

Vernon is silent for a full minute, as if he can't quite take in the meaning of what I've said. The rest of us hold our breath.

"What danger? There was nothing in them!"

"They're still reporting that the children were killed by something in the planes."

"The hell they were. What does the media say about the toxicology reports?"

"Nothing. Absolutely nothing."

Vernon's mouth is set to form the letter w—perhaps to say *What?* or *Why?* or *Who?*—but he ends up saying nothing. He picks up the phone. "Louis, this is Vernon Keene in the Mines, I spoke to you yesterday about the toxicology reports, and I was wondering if you would fax me a copy. . . . What? . . . What do you mean your initial reports were wrong? . . . Who redid the test? . . . Redo the test yourself. . . . Well, why did you let them take all the tissue samples? . . . Can't you get more? . . . Can't . . ." Vernon puts the receiver down, snatches the print of Belle Boyd off the wall, and slams it over his knee, breaking the frame in half. "The bastard hung up on me."

"He's repudiating his original report?" Kristin says.

"It appears so. He doesn't want to talk about it."

"They're not conducting further tests?"

"He has no remaining tissue samples and the bodies of the children have been cremated, at the government's request."

"The government can't just step in and cremate somebody's kid," Kristin says.

"The Minister of Defense himself went to their houses to explain that it was a safety measure, that the bodies posed some sort of danger. It's ridiculous. Why aren't there experts on TV saying how ridiculous this is?" Vernon rubs his hand over his bald pate, a characteristic gesture, which leads one to think that his head has achieved its shine through this constant polishing. "In all my years in the Mines, I have never seen anything like this. Suddenly black is white and white is black and we've all fallen down Alice's rabbit hole."

"Been down that hole before," I say. "Welcome to the tea party."

"That's all you have to say? You're just going to roll over on your back and let yourself get screwed by these people?" Vernon takes what is left of Belle Boyd and throws it across the room. "Because I'm not. It's not going to happen this time."

46. Vaughn Sutter Wayne

Musings from an

Unquiet Grave

A shadow of its former self when I died. Less than a shadow, now. The Mines are weak, timbers shaken. Their imminent demise vibrates in my own powdery bones. Dust to dust. Nothing survives time, wear, and unwaning scrutiny from the Esteemed Legislative Body. Damn shame. They ought to let us do what needs to be done. We know what that is.

It's the reformers. Don't understand the business. And the media. Understand only their own whining. Don't have the hard decisions to make, the tough moral choices. Sit on the sideline and whine, second-guess, and offer hindsight. Don't understand that sometimes there are no good choices. You do what you have to do to keep the country safe. Can't stay squeaky clean and morally pristine and get the job done. Do what you have to do and then live with it and keep your damning fucking mouth shut. Whole country of whiners. Want to see into the Mines. Don't like it when they get a look. Don't like what it takes to keep a democracy safe. Don't offer any better solutions, only hindsight and censure. Want their freedoms and want to be perfectly safe. Somebody gets hurt, they're hot to sue, find the guilty party, and string them up in the town square. Need it to keep their own consciences clean.

Now the Brits, the Brits understand intelligence. The only decent books about the Mines were written by Brits. They lack that American moral schoolmarmishness, the muckraking, where's-my-Pulitzer? attitude of the press, the suspicion of anything that isn't dissected in minute detail on the boob tube.

Agencies of government don't die cleanly like people. Limbs are attached to other bodies—sometimes backwards—and survive attenuated, damn near useless. Furniture gets moved, letterheads reprinted, and a shiny new agency seal is struck with that same old raptor in a fresh pose. Where will my portrait hang? Where will our club of tough men convene? The walls of some museum?

Perhaps they can't kill the Mines altogether, but they can chain it out in the sunshine until it goes blind. Then where will we be?

47. Doc

W e're already dead. It certainly smells like death in the Mines, but there has been no obituary, playing of "Taps," or cannonade at sunset. Not even a powdered doughnut. Miners still stream through the entrances every morning looking purposeful, but the Mines I entered so many years ago is dead beyond resuscitation.

I always believed that the highest purpose of intelligence was the prevention of war. The Mines fulfilled that purpose back when we were facing off against the Evil Empire. While the whole country wallowed in collective madness during the fifties, building bomb shelters and finding Communists under every rock, the President was steady. He didn't cave in to fear and do something stupid. He knew that there was no bomber gap, no missile gap, and that, indeed, we were ahead of the Empire. That's because the Mines built the U-2 and the satellites. We could watch their airfields and missile silos. We stole their military doctrine and knew they had no plan to strike first. We cleaned their clock without firing a shot. We calmed fears. But that was back when we had preemptive intelligence. Now we have preemptive war.

If the current administration had been in place back then, we'd all be sitting on sandbags now, licking out Spam tins.

Some years ago the emphasis in the intelligence community

shifted toward "support to the war fighter," which means giving the Pentagon more of what it wants, and paying more attention to conducting war than preventing it. Never mind that the Pentagon has its own, bigger, intelligence apparatus. They want control over it all.

The Mines could have told the President exactly what would happen in Iraq if only we had had the courage to do so. The Mines could have told him *before the fact* that invading Iraq would fan the flames of global jihad. Instead, we waited until it had happened, until the whole world was saying it, to come out and—timidly, apologetically, pathetically—say it ourselves. Instead of providing the insight that might have prevented war, we allowed ourselves to be bullied into providing an anemic *casus belli* based on flaky sources. Sources we didn't believe in ourselves. Of course the President wouldn't have listened to us if we had told the truth, but we might have saved our institutional soul. If there is such a thing.

The high bosses are so proud of their access to the President. They would do anything to protect our foot in the door, because not every President has let us in. But we've paid too high a price for face time. We learned the fine arts of self-censorship, watering down, and fudging. We told the President what he demanded to hear, instead of what he needed to hear. We fell victim to our own fears.

Now the drums beat for Iran. Will the Mines stand back and let the President say Iranian chemicals were behind the stadium attack? Of course we will, because we are already dead.

48. Vivian

Seven o'clock on the first Monday morning since the attacks, and I'm walking due east, approaching the New Shafts Building entrance. The sun is directly behind the glass tunnel at this time of day. The entrance is on the fourth level of the building, at the top of a hillside, with most of the structure below, hidden in the side of the hill from here. In this building you take the escalator down to enter the Mines. On a bright morning like this one, the building is lost in the glare. You can't focus on it. A light mist, from the steam plant where the documents are cremated, falls through the air. I walk with my eyes on the sidewalk. I see the jeans and sneakers of night shift workers ending their day, and the polished dress shoes and heels worn by those heading out for early meetings downtown. One pair of particularly pricey navy blue pumps and sheer stockings makes me glance up. I catch Sharon Pendergast's frown. She averts her face and picks up her pace. I stop and turn to watch her hurry off, carefully curled yellow hair bright and dead looking against her navy suit. She clutches her lock bag tight against her thigh. I want to yell, "Don't pretend you don't know me!" But I'm too well behaved for that. Still compulsively well behaved, after all that's happened.

I'm angry. She should know the ridiculous hours that the canary crew and I have been working. Would it hurt her to acknowledge me with a word of encouragement or at least a smile? She did after the Strikes. Whenever I ran into her, she said hello and asked me how things were going. This time she looked like she could have bitten me on the ankle. What's going on?

I go through the Mines tag scanners and step onto the top of the three levels of escalators in the glass-walled atrium. I float down past the dusty hanging models of the U-2 and the SR-71 Blackbird, as well as a Rube Goldberg contraption rigged up to direct the leak from yesterday's rains into a series of buckets on the floor. I see Harry below me, coming up the escalator. He doesn't see me yet, or more likely, he's seen me and is deliberately staring in the opposite direction. He's standing in a Napoleonic pose, but with his hand on his vest rather than slipped into it. He looks grave, as if he were viewing the battlefield at Waterloo rather than logistics's ugly duct-tape-and-plastic installation. I'm sure he knows that the whole canary crew has been briefed on what he was doing with Maddie's mom. I'm sure he'd like me to pass him without a word, but I'm too angry to give him a break.

"Good morning, Harry," I say as our paths cross, and then, because I no longer care about my career or about being a good girl, I ask, "How's it hangin'?"

He's already past, but he jerks his head in my direction and looks at me as if he's not sure he heard what he heard. I give him a sweet smile. He'll never know if he really heard what he heard. I hope it drives him crazy.

When I reach the floor of the atrium, I pass my regular face boss—my boss before the canary crew—Ellen Hughes. She's a straight shooter. We got along well. But even Ellen avoids my eyes and gives me only a cursory nod.

By the time I get to the canary crew room, I've been ignored by three more people that I know and I feel like I have a contagious disease. I open up the door and find my colleagues all in place. They look up, but no one offers a good morning. The room is strangely quiet. No one is typing or shuffling papers.

"What's up?" I ask warily.

"Welcome to the penalty box. That's our new name for the canary cage," Maddie says.

Fran swivels her monitor around so I can read the e-mail on the screen.

Memorandum for: CanaryCrew@WhiteMines
From: Harold J. Esterhaus
Subject: Standing Up New Crew

Canary Crew,

First, let me say that the following is no reflection on your hard work and dedication, which is appreciated/acknowledged by all. Per decision of the White Mines Executive Committee, however, we are creating a new crew, under Ellen Hughes, to be a focal point/ lead for all matters pertaining to the ongoing investigation/review of the stadium attack. Ellen has over three years of experience as a leader on hot-button issues and is superbly qualified to take on this task/challenge.

The current canary crew will redirect its efforts toward fulfilling requests for finished intelligence made by the new Mines Oversight Committee Subcommittee on the Stadium Attack (MOCSSA). Only **finished/reviewed intelligence** should go to MOCSSA. Please direct other materials that do not constitute DoneIntel— including drafts, chronos, notes, link charts, et cetera—to NewStadiumCrew@WhiteMines. Thank you for your work and dedication. It is deeply appreciated by all.

Sincerely/Respectfully,
Harry

"An e-mail?" I'm incredulous. "I thought that even Harry was enough of a manager to know that you don't send news like this in an e-mail."

"This is the work of a man with an extremely small dick," Vernon says.

"Well, Maddie," Doc says. "What do we do now?"

Maddie looks up, as if surprised at the question. "We *all* Xerox, collate, and staple, instead of just me. We take long lunches. We work no more than eight hours a day."

This is not the answer we were expecting. What's wrong with her?

"You're going to take this lying down?" Vernon, the ultimate cynic, seems appalled by Maddie's complacence.

"I'm taking it sitting down," Maddie says. She takes the stacks of paper next to her monitor and begins to distribute them around the table. I want to ask for an explanation, but I can see that she is in no mood to provide one.

• • •

It turns out that Maddie was wrong. We don't Xerox, collate, and staple. We just Xerox and collate. We are under strict orders not to staple. Our packets go up to the Main Shaft, where Sharon Pendergast herself scans them with a sharp eye. Only *she* determines what goes out in the final packet. She's the one who finally pushes the thick stack into an electronic stapler, which drives metal through its pages with a sound like a shot.

Three days now we've been doing this, and it's just about driven us batty.

A tink informs me that I've just received an e-mail. It's from Harry's secretary, Sheila. Sheila and I used to go jogging together, back when I had the energy. I pumped her the other day on why the canary crew was sidelined. She said she didn't know why, but she'd try to find out. In exchange for her efforts, I told her all about Harry and Gladys James. I'm usually not a gossip, but I figured Harry didn't deserve executive privilege on this one. Sheila was thrilled to get definitive proof that Harry was the hypocrite she always thought he was. She said she'd try her best. I open the e-mail eagerly.

Viv,

So far the only thing I've found out is that the decision came from pretty high up. Geez, what did you guys do? Whenever I even mention the canary crew I get a look like I've said a four-letter word. If I were you, I'd try to get off the crew so the guilt-by-association can begin to wear off. Seriously, it doesn't look good for you guys.

In other news, I found out Harry and the Mrs. are renewing their vows at a ceremony at the Inn at Little Washington. That'll cost him big bucks. Actually, it'll cost her big bucks, because everyone knows she's the one with the money. The guilt—and the fear of losing his tobacco heiress—must be eating his Saved Soul. According to a woman I know in the SSS, Gladys James has moved into a condo in Rosslyn and is moping like a teenager. Poor Maddie! If my mother screwed around with Harry, I'd try to get her committed to a convent. And I'm Jewish. Thank God Gladys is past her childbearing years.

I'll get back to you if I find out anything else. Give my best to the crew, except for Vernon, who deserves every nasty thing he gets and you can tell him I said so.

Cheers,
Sheila

Vernon wrote up his theory that there was nothing in those RC planes. His first reports never got past Harry's desk. Yesterday, he walked his latest effort up to the Main Shaft, right to Sharon Pendergast's office. They wouldn't let him see her, but the secretary promised she'd put the report on Sharon's desk. Sharon sent the paper back down with a note scribbled on the first page. It said "NO EVIDENCE TO SUPPORT THIS!" and it was underlined three times. Of course there isn't any evidence. It all burned. Did you know that truth burns? I didn't think it did, but it turns out I was wrong.

No one opens the door and bangs it into Maddie's chair anymore. She doesn't scream anymore anyway. She hardly talks. Even her body is quiet. She's quit chewing her fingernails and twirling her hair around her thumb. I feel so bad for her. I'm glad her mother is out of her house, but I wonder if Maddie eats a real meal anymore. I tried to get her to talk this morning, but all she said was, "I'm sorting." I asked her what she was sorting, but she waved me off.

I've been watching Maddie for ten minutes, and she hasn't moved. Her eyes are cast down toward the stack of papers in front of her, but she's not reading. I don't know whether she has quit taking her antidepressants or whether they don't work anymore. I think all of us on the canary crew will be okay, except for Maddie.

49. Doc

Sunday at home. It's been less than a week since the attack, but in our new status as untouchables, we in the ex–canary crew are no longer required to work long hours.

"Fran!" I call. I think she must be in the kitchen. I am in the recliner in her living room. I don't even remember making the decision to move in with her. One evening, I was talking about Molotov being upset about my absences, and she said, "Well, let's go get him" and we did. So here we both are. At the moment, he's in my lap, and I hate to disturb the old boy, so I'm yelling "Fran!" instead of getting up to go look for her.

"Yes, sugarballs?" She appears in the doorway.

"Must you call me that?"

"I promise I'll only call you that when you yell at me from the recliner. I take it you'd like another beer?"

"Well, that's not why I called you, but if you're offering . . ."

Fran disappears and returns a moment later with a cold Nut Brown Ale.

"I really don't want to be the sort of man who vegetates on the recliner and yells at a woman to get a beer," I explain to Fran before taking my first sip. "It's just that Molotov is on my lap"—here Molotov cooperates by yawning and stretching into an even more comfortable position—"and I wasn't actually yelling for a beer, I wanted your excellent opinion on something."

Fran settles into a corner of the couch, folding a leg up under herself. "Okay, shoot."

"The disappearance of tissue samples, the cremations, the whole decontamination procedure . . . I think what we're seeing is a government cover-up." I make this announcement in a dramatic voice.

"Duh," Fran says.

She's not as impressed with my powers of analysis as I had anticipated. I sincerely hope that this isn't a sign of things to come. I'm about to elaborate on my analysis when a knock at the door startles me into spilling a few drops of ale on Molotov, who is accustomed to it and only flicks an ear.

"Must be the Organ coming to haul you in for treason." Fran hops up and opens the front door to reveal Vernon. It is fortunate that we know Vernon, for otherwise we might guess that he was an escaped criminal seeking asylum. He's wearing black from head to toe, his face has a two-day growth of stubble, and the look in his eye is homicidal. Even if he were shaved and grinning, however, I would be disturbed to see him out of the context of the cubicle and in the context of my private life.

"It's a cover-up," he says, without any preliminaries.

"Duh," Fran says again. "Want a beer?"

Vernon looks at my bottle. "Is that a Nut Brown Ale?"

"I'll get you one," Fran says and disappears into the kitchen again.

"Got any chips?" Vernon yells after her. He reaches down to push Pearl off a chair, and yelps as she hisses and claws his hand.

"Sit in the couch," I advise, although in truth I'm reluctant to encourage him to make himself at home and am rather proud of Pearl for so brilliantly expressing exactly what I feel.

"I'm bleeding," Vernon complains to Fran as she returns with his beer and a bag of tortilla chips. He points to Pearl. "Has that cat had its shots?"

"Have you had yours?" Fran asks. "Because I wouldn't want Pearl to get sick."

"Sit in the couch, Vernon," I advise again.

Vernon throws himself onto the couch, props a booted foot on Fran's mother-of-pearl–inlaid coffee table, and stuffs a handful of tortilla chips in his mouth before speaking in a chip-garbled growl. "What are we going to do about this? Because we have to do something or I'm going to kill somebody."

I take another sip as I consider. Could we actually do something about this? As I entertain the notion, my pulse quickens.

"Well," I say, "first we need some evidence. What about your old buddies at the Organ?"

"Tried that already. No luck. The only thing I can think of is to start interviewing people who were there."

"Which we in the Mines can't do," I remind him.

"The first thing we have to do is give up any thought of playing by the rules. We'll never get anywhere that way."

"Maybe we need to figure out what we're up against," Fran says. "What has the administration got in mind?"

"Well, obviously," Vernon says, "they're seeking justification for some move against Iran. Probably something they already had in the planning stages before the stadium attack. Shit. Probably something they plan to move on quickly, so we don't have much time."

"Oh, dear," Fran says. "Oh, dear."

"What?"

"I was wondering why Alan showed up in town all of a sudden."

"Who's Alan?" Vernon asks.

"My son. I've told you about him a hundred times, Vernon. My son the Air Force Special Operations officer. The one I've been trying to get Maddie to go out with. He does a lot of secret stuff involving demolitions. Never will tell me what he's up to. He showed up at the door the day before yesterday without even calling first. He's in town for meetings at the Pentagon." Fran yells, "Alan. Alan!"

"We need to get the whole team moving on this. We need to shake Maddie out of her depression," I say.

"She's been like a zombie since the attacks. Can the shrink up her dosage?" Vernon says.

"Already has," Fran says. "Alan!" she yells again.

Alan finally emerges from the basement, where he has been worshipping the big-screen TV and making great inroads on my beer, while his mother does his laundry. He's a strapping, square-jawed fellow in a muscle shirt. We don't get along. He doesn't like the fact that I am sleeping with his mother. I told him to grow up, and he didn't like that either. I still remember the heartbreak I felt the first time I saw him, a bulge in his mother's stomach indicating that her new marriage was not about to end in annulment, as I had hoped. He looms in the doorway with one hand on the frame and the other clutching what is probably my last Nut Brown Ale.

"What's up, Mom?"

"Honey, how long are you going to be in town?"

"Don't know."

"Do you have any trips planned soon?" Fran tries to disguise her interest in his itinerary. "You know your cousin's wedding is in a month. Will you be there?"

Alan scowls. "Don't know. You know how it is." He gestures with his beer toward Vernon. "Another friend of yours?"

"I'm sorry, honey. I didn't introduce you. This is Vernon Keene, a colleague of mine."

"As long as you're not sleeping with him." He glares at me. "Is that all you wanted to know? Game's on."

"Yes, that's all."

"Nice meeting you." Alan disappears.

"He's not going to tell us anything," Fran says.

"Talk about Oedipal issues," Vernon says.

Fran is about to open her mouth, but Vernon snaps his fingers as if he's had a major revelation. He points to the basement door.

"Is that Maddie's type, or what?"

My heart sinks, because he's right. Alan is exactly the type Maddie goes after, which is why I don't want the two of them to ever meet.

"I've been trying to tell Maddie that," Fran says, "but I can't seem to get them together, and Doc has been no help at all."

"Maybe there is a way to perk Maddie up and get some information out of Rambo at the same time," Vernon says.

"Forget it, Vernon," I say firmly. "I am not going to have a hand in trying to fix Maddie up with anyone. Disaster. It will only end in disaster."

Vernon fishes his cell phone out of his pocket. "It's not like we can make her life worse than it already is. She's a train wreck, but we need her input on this." He fishes his Mines tag out of another pocket. We all carry a list of team phone numbers on a card that slips into the plastic holder behind the tag. He consults it and dials.

"Maddie? It's Vernon. I'm at Fran's house—um, she called me—and we have an emergency here . . . yeah, that's exactly it. His heart. EMTs are on the way. Fran is freaking. Can you come? No, come here. Don't know which hospital he's going to yet. I'll take you when you get here. Just hurry." Vernon replaces his cell phone in his pocket.

"Vernon, that's horrible," Fran says. "Suppose she has an accident rushing over here?"

"Relax, if this works we could prevent another war and you might get some Special Forces ballerina grandchildren out of it." Vernon laughs. "Camo tutus. Can you see it?"

• • •

Maddie screeches into the driveway twenty minutes later. She's barefoot and wearing an old T-shirt and cutoffs. Fran greets her at the door, and Maddie throws her arms around her.

"How is he?"

Fran points to where I sit in the recliner. I shrug. Molotov opens an eye, yawns, goes back to sleep.

"Vernon lied to you," Fran says. "Doc is fine. We were just having a little brainstorming session on the attacks, and we wanted you here. I told Vernon he shouldn't have alarmed you. Would you like a beer?"

Maddie glares at Vernon. "I can't believe you did that to me. I could kill you. In fact, I will kill you. I'll sneak into your home at night and suffocate you with a pillow. So just expect it. Every night, when you go to sleep, expect it, because it's going to happen. I absolutely will kill you. This is not a joke."

"See?" Vernon says to me. "She's perking up already."

"Maddie," I say. "We tried to suppress Vernon, but you know how he is. The thing is that we do need you. We can't just sit around and let the administration twist the stadium attack into an Iranian provocation. We could end up in another war."

"Beer?" Fran asks again.

"Something stronger," Maddie says. She shakes her head, waves her hands in the air in a way that suggests swans gliding through water . . . then the swans abruptly turn into different birds as Maddie gestures in the general direction of the White House. "I can't believe we are living this over again. It's not possible. How can people be fooled again so soon? Where are their brains? How is this happening?"

I pick up the remote and flick on the television set. "This is how." We watch a little boy blowing out the candles on a birthday cake—the local news is showing a home movie taken of one of the victims. I select another channel. This time we see the rubble of the Khobar housing complex. Another channel shows the body of a Mines sharper, turned hostage, spinning at the end of a rope. The flaming towers. A terrorist training video showing dogs being poisoned. Satellite images of Iranian chemical facilities. Blindfolded American hostages. Khomeini shaking his fist. A wall of flowers laid up against a fence blocking entrance to Burton Oil Park. Images of a child choking. The President looking grim and pointing a finger. Probably saying "I told you so," but I have the sound turned down. I hit the off button and banish the pictures as well.

"People are sitting in front of their screens for hours watching this. Do you think they can calmly process these loaded images and come up with sound conclusions? Figure out who is responsible for what? No, all they know when they haul themselves up out of their chairs is that they are frightened and something better damn well be done about this. What a golden opportunity for a President trying to reshape the world! Another golden opportunity! How lucky can a man get?"

Fran brings Maddie a shot glass and a bottle of vodka. "All I know is, I'm going to kill somebody myself if they send my Alan to Iran."

Maddie downs a shot in one gulp. "He's going to Iran?"

"I don't know. I think he's involved in something secret, but he won't tell me about it. He showed up here two days ago, and he's been spending most of his time at the Pentagon. He's a demolition expert, you know. One of the first into Afghanistan. Takes part in a lot of planning exercises. I only pray that this is just an exercise."

"This can't be happening," Maddie says. "Damn it, what can we do? What can we do?" She pours another shot and walks over to Pearl's chair. Maddie scoops up the cat, cuddles her, and settles into the chair with Pearl, purring, in her lap.

"I can't believe you picked up that wildcat," Vernon says. "She raked half my skin off."

"She's not wild, just discriminating," Maddie says. "So, do we have a strategy here?"

"Our first problem," Vernon says, "is proving a negative. There were no Iranian chemicals in the planes. Now, there are no planes, unless some scrap of something escaped the decontamination procedures. Even if we found something and tested it and found no trace of anything on it, it probably wouldn't convince anyone that chemicals weren't used."

"What about the initial tests?" Maddie says. "The guy who performed the initial tests."

"Townsend. Louis Townsend," Vernon says. "He's at a lab in

Maryland. I'll give him another call. Maybe he's feeling guilty." He takes a pad and pen out of his pocket and begins to make a list.

"What about the positives? The things that would have been present if your theories are correct?" Maddie says. "Cyanide, for one. They had to get it somewhere. And the bomblets. If they were carrying a chemical, they would have been made differently than if they were merely meant to produce a puff of smoke."

"Right," Vernon says. "They would have been as flimsy as firecrackers, probably made of paper. They would have needed paranitroaniline red to color the smoke and probably potassium chlorate."

"Things which they probably bought locally," Maddie says. "I'll look into it. And"—the swans go into motion again as Maddie thinks—"and you know what? We're not the only pissed-off people in government. You know there are other people out there who are pretty unhappy about things they've been asked to do. A few isolated unhappy people can't do much, but if we could find a number of people. . . ."

"Exactly," Fran says. "Safety in numbers. We all need to get on the phone tomorrow and milk our contacts—gently, of course."

"We also need to know how much time we have," Vernon says. "How fast is the administration planning to move on Iran? We don't want to go public before we have enough evidence, but it would be no good coming out with our information the day after they've dropped a tactical nuke on some facility in the Iranian desert. Do you think Alan really might know something, Fran?"

"It's possible, but he won't tell us. He's extremely closemouthed about his work. I've never been able to get a thing out of him, even when I was worried sick over things I thought he might be doing in Iraq."

Vernon shifts an evil eye in Maddie's direction. "Maybe he would let something slip in a moment of passion. . . ."

"No, Vernon." I slap my hand down on the arm of the chair, waking Molotov up again. "I will not let you insult Maddie like that."

"Yeah, Vernon," Maddie says, "what do you think I am?"

"My apologies," Vernon says. Then he gets up and pours her another shot.

"Maddie," I say, "perhaps you should go easy on the vodka."

"Nonsense," Maddie says, "I can drink a marine under the table." She drains her glass.

Fran gets defensive. "Alan is a fine man. I hardly think that it would be an insult to Maddie to go out with him. A lot of women would kill to go out with him."

"So what branch of the Special Forces is he in?" Maddie asks.

"Air Force."

"Really? Do they have their own coffee mug?"

"A beautiful mug. It looks like a building at night, but when you pour hot liquid in it, the building disappears and you see a Special Forces officer planting explosives."

"Cool!"

Fran calls down the basement stairs, "Alan, Alan come up here a minute."

"Coming, Mom." Alan appears in the basement door. He points to his empty bottle. "Doc, you got any more of these? These are great."

"Not bad," Maddie whispers.

Alan, unfortunately, is just the type she is attracted to. As was my wretched son Rick. For an intelligent woman, Maddie has the most execrable taste in men. My mind races into the future. I marry Fran. Maddie marries Alan. I am Maddie's father-in-law again. Alan has an affair with some Swedish female commando he meets on some top-secret mission. Maddie finds out about it and is once again sitting in my cubicle, pouring out her sorrows and downing antidepressants, lattes, and chocolate. In how many ways can history repeat itself in one lifetime?

"Alan," Fran says, "this is Maddie James, another one of my colleagues. I've told you about her before. Terrific alchemist, besides being a beautiful woman."

Maddie gives Alan a dazzling smile, and I feel my Nut Brown

Ale seething deep within my gut. Alan is giving her an appreciative look, too. I cannot let this happen, even if I have to make a supreme sacrifice.

"I'm out of Nut Brown Ale, but I have a special stash of the finest microbrews on the East Coast in the extra refrigerator in the laundry room. They're in the vegetable crisper under some kale. Help yourself."

"Thanks, Doc. You're not all bad. Nice to meet you," he says to Maddie, before he heads for my lovely beers.

"That was nice of you," Fran says.

"Not nice, I was just trying to distract him from Maddie." I turn to Vernon. "What century are we living in that you think a fine alchemist like Maddie can be used like female . . . bait to pry information out of—"

"He does seem like a nice enough young man," Maddie says.

"Just your type," Vernon chimes in.

"Maddie, where is your self-respect?"

"Relax, Doc. There's nothing wrong with me sitting down and having a conversation with the guy. I'm an intelligence officer. I'm very clever at talking people up. It's not like I would offer sex for information. Give me some credit. Please." Maddie jumps up from her chair, unceremoniously dumping poor Pearl on the floor. She's unsteady on her feet. How many shots has she had? "Excuse me, but I think I might go downstairs and try one of your microbrews."

"No, Maddie."

"Shush, Doc," Fran says. "Mind your own business. I think they would look really cute together."

Cute? They would look like a disaster, an unmitigated disaster.

50. Maddie

I've been standing outside the door for three minutes trying to get up the nerve to go in. Now I know how Doc felt walking into the canary cage after his first night with Fran. Crap. How much did I drink last night? I have no idea. I wasn't even aware that I was still interested in sex until I saw Alan in his muscle shirt. That and the vodka and the microbrews, combined with not getting much sleep in the past fifteen years . . . It's been a long time since I've been really drunk. I crawled out of Fran's basement window this morning around 4:00 A.M. and drove myself home. Left Alan snoring on the couch. He is gorgeous. A little shallow, but I don't need more complexity in my life. Maybe I'll go get a latte first and then go in. Yes, a little caffeine would make this easier.

Before I can turn to go, however, the door opens a crack and Vernon's leering eye appears.

He whispers, "Maddie, we know you're out there. We know where you've been. We know what you've been doing. Now, we need to debrief you." He opens the door wide to show a room full of expectant faces. Crap. I have no choice but to walk in and sit down. I hate the arbitrary intimacies of this place.

"Oh, Maddie, I'm so happy for you and Alan," Fran gushes. "I always knew you were perfect for each other! Didn't I tell you? Didn't I tell you this would work out, Doc?"

Vivian, Kristin, and Bonnie are trying not to laugh.

"Fran, whoa, Fran." I don't know what to say next. I can't exactly tell her that this is unlikely to be anything more than a short fling—for one thing because this guy has been so incredibly spoiled by his mother that he still brings his dirty shorts home for her to launder.

"Fran, it's too early to engrave the wedding invitations. Calm down," Doc says.

Vernon leans across the table. "So? So? As much as we would all like to hear juicy details of your sordid evening, I'm more interested in whether you managed to get any information out of Rambo."

"I'm an intelligence officer. What do you think?" Once Alan found out I had worked with his commander in Iraq, he got way more talkative than he should have. He was saturated with beer, and lulled into a false sense of security by my use of military jargon and familiarity with secret operations. Then of course there was his massive ego and need to impress me. He had to start boasting. For that type of guy, boasting is as necessary as breathing.

"Well?" Vernon prompts.

"They're planning to insert a six-man demolitions strike team through Iraq, aiming for a facility near the border. Alan is the operations officer. They'll slip across the border and meet up with a truck that will take them within three miles of the facility. They go the rest of the way on foot, carrying enough C-4 to blow the place up twice over—C-4, so they're obviously not going to try to hide the American footprint. They plan to cut the fences, set charges at key nodes, and get out, hopefully without engagement, but if they have to take out a few guards, they will. All of this is set to take place in roughly three weeks. At that point—"

I stop talking as I realize that all the blood has drained from Fran's face. Doc reaches across the table and grabs her hand. Now I know why Alan would never tell her anything about his work.

"What did you do to him to get him to spill all of that?" Vernon says. "I'm impressed. You must be damn good."

"Fran, I'm sorry. I didn't mean to upset you. I'm sure it's not as dangerous as it sounds." Even as these words come out of my lips, I realize how lame they sound. Fran has begun to cry and Vivian has her arm around her shoulder, comforting her. Jeez, I thought she would know that a demolitions expert would get dangerous assignments. Shouldn't she know that?

"I always knew he was doing dangerous work," Fran sobs, "but—"

"Look, Fran. This isn't going to happen, because we're going to prevent it." I feel terrible.

"Damn right we're going to prevent it," Vernon says. "Maddie, did you find out anything else?"

"Yeah, Alan really hates Doc."

"Understandable," Vernon says. "Just like you hate Harry. Well, Maddie, you've done stellar work. If you ever want to know anything from me, feel free to work me over good. I can take it."

I glare at him, but he only smiles.

"If they're heading out in three weeks," Vernon continues, "we'd better get moving. In your absence this morning, I've briefed the rest of the canary crew, and everyone is ready to go."

Asshole is acting like he's head of the canary crew.

"I've got some contacts at the Organ and Heartland Defense. I'll see who else is disgruntled and might be willing to talk," Kristin says.

"What can I do?" Fran says. "I need to do something or I'll go crazy with worry."

"How about interviewing some of the people who were at the stadium?" Vernon says. "I've talked to a couple of people, but I'm not very good at putting people at ease. They clam up and look at me like they don't trust me."

I can well imagine what sort of impression Vernon makes showing up at someone's door. Poor people. As if they hadn't been through enough already. Vernon starts to rub a hand over his bald head, an indication that some sort of idea is cooking.

"I can't believe that no shred of those planes survived. Wouldn't you think that some stupid kid would pick up a piece of debris? It's the sort of thing I would have done when I was twelve. And some people got out of the stadium before they set up the decontamination stations, because they were begging people on the radio to come back. I know that there are pieces of those planes out there somewhere."

"And I know exactly where they would show up," Bonnie says. A smug smile comes over her face as we wait to hear what she will say. She lets us hang for almost a full minute. "Where else? On eBay. Or somewhere online."

Who else but Bonnie would come up with the idea of shopping for evidence?

"Do you really think someone would be stupid enough to put something like that on eBay?"

"Well, if they were stupid enough to pick it up in the first place."

"Let me just look," Bonnie says. Her fingers are a blur on the keyboard. In addition to being a bio expert, she's a world-class on-line shopper.

"Well, if you find it, buy it," Vernon says. "I'll reimburse you. Meanwhile, Fran—"

The door wangs into my chair and I shriek. This is the first time I've seen Harry since I caught him naked with my mother. He has been very careful to avoid me, but now I've made him mad enough to seek me out. Red blotches of righteous indignation bloom on his sallow cheeks. He doesn't bother with any preliminary niceties, such as saying hello.

"Maddie, Sharon Pendergast says that after she turned down your request to be allowed to testify at the Stadium Hearings, you called the committee chair and had him put you on the schedule anyway."

"Yes, I'm testifying Wednesday after next."

"No, you're not. I will be presenting the Mines' testimony."

"Right. And I will testify right after you're finished—just in case you don't remember everything."

"The Mines will not allow you to testify."

"Are you going to physically restrain me?"

"We'll fire you."

"Then I'll resign first." It is a decision I made even before I phoned the Mines Oversight Committee.

"You can't do that," Harry says. He sounds lame and he knows it. He can't prevent me from resigning.

I sit down at my keyboard and type a one-sentence letter to Mines Human Resources. Believe it or not, I write them an entire sentence without any obscenities. I print it out and sign it with a flourish. All the while I am conscious of my colleagues staring at me. The canary crew is shocked. Harry looks like he would like to try to physically restrain me, but he's had enough sexual harassment training seminars to know that he'd better not lay a hand on me. I grab my purse.

"You're not thinking of your future," Harry says.

"I am. I can't imagine living with the regret I would feel if I let you distort the record. I'll take this letter down and drop it off personally at Human Resources on my way out." Before I close the door, I have to say one more thing to Harry, just to let him know that *everyone* knows about his dirty affairs.

"And Harry? Be sure to wear a condom when you screw my mother, because I don't want her catching religion from you."

I slam the door and feel good for about ten seconds, until I am out in the corridor, wondering what I am going to do with the rest of my life. I've never been anything except an alchemist, a good alchemist. It takes a lot to become a good alchemist. You have to learn the Mines and its sister agencies as well as you learn the terrorist. To make sure you have access to information, you have to cultivate the collectors—the sharpers, agents from the Organ, the cocktail sippers in the DipServ. You have to learn the oblique language of cables and develop a sixth sense for what's solid and what's flaky. You have to know where the expertise is and how to tap it. You have to know a thousand things. Things that are absolutely

useless once you walk out of the Mines. You can become an aca-
demic, but you've spent years listening to academics drone on,
knowing that they didn't have a fraction of the information available to you. It would be like voluntarily gouging out one eye.

But I can't let Harry be the public record on the stadium attack.
He'll dust off his flag lapel pin and his contrite expression and give
testimony that doesn't contradict any of the administration's asser-
tions. He's perfect for delivering Mines testimony: polite, polished,
boring, and he swallows the end of his sentences. Despite their best
efforts, people don't listen to him closely. Their minds drift. They
think about the movie they saw last night or whether or not they
left a burner on in the kitchen or what that intern looks like naked.
The canary crew will have a voice in these hearings, even at the
price of my career. I made that decision before I called the MOC.
Now I'm just carrying it out. The BD's human resources officer is
out of her office. I leave the letter in her chair.

We have long, long corridors in the Mines. How many miles
have I walked up and down these tunnels in the past fifteen years?
I don't even make an attempt to nod at any of the familiar faces I
see. They're already ghosts from another lifetime, like the shade of
Vaughn Sutter Wayne.

I decide to leave the building through the main entrance, so I
can walk one more time over the Mines seal, inlaid in marble on
the floor. I insert my Mines tag into the machine and the bar lifts. I
walk up to the SCUDO's desk. I'm surprised to see the same young
man—a little older now—who witnessed my tears after the Strikes,
when I saw that enormous flag.

"Ma'am? Can I help you?"

"Yes." I slip my Mines tag chain over my head and hand him the
whole jangling mess: the chain, tag, Pentagon badge, security fob,
and the safety whistle issued to us so we could blow for help, should
we somehow end up under a pile of rubble. "Take this for me, please.
It's too heavy."

He looks at me in surprise as I turn. I glance at the letters engraved high on the south wall: YE SHALL KNOW THE TRUTH, AND THE TRUTH SHALL MAKE YOU FREE. Then I glance at the memorial stars, and say good-bye again to a couple people that I knew. I listen to the sound of my heels clicking over the marble surface of that eagle, remembering how proud that sound used to make me feel.

51. Doc

Cameras are in place. Senators adjust their ties in the doorway before they take their stately walk to their chairs. Young aides and interns, drunk with pheromones, crawl over their ego-bloated masters like bees on the queen. I look up to the high, ornately decorated ceiling. The room is smaller than it seems on TV and filled with the momentous sounds of hushed talk and rustling paper.

Senator Westerly, the MOC subcommittee chair, gavels the room to order and launches into opening remarks. He's a tall, impeccably dressed, reed-thin Southerner, who in person looks disconcertingly older than his hair and teeth. I try to pick up a sense of where he'll go with his questioning. He hits all of the usual points. It was an enormous intelligence failure. Indeed, it was an "unprecedented" intelligence failure. Then, contradicting himself, he goes on to say that it was one of a string of enormous intelligence failures. Or perhaps he meant to say a string of unprecedented intelligence failures. He bangs his fist on the table and unveils his creative solution: We need to reform the Mines, we need to break down the resistance of the Mines to reform, we must attract better alchemists, better sharpers, better smithies. Nothing about us is good enough. He's a stubborn administration loyalist, so he tiptoes around the role of the President, who, after all, has been trying valiantly to reform this

blind, deaf monster called the Mines. Finally the distinguished
ELB member gets down to introducing the first speaker, our own
Harry Esterhaus. Maddie's testimony will follow Harry's.

Maddie, all of us, were up most of last night working on her remarks. As we did after the Strikes, we now sit in front of the families of the victims of the stadium attack, who cradle photographs
and cry softly. Fran, Vivian, Vernon, Bonnie, and Kristin. We're all
here for Maddie, and we're all afraid for her and afraid for ourselves. Maddie feels she can't let Harry testify without offering our
alternative analysis, but I think it's too early. We haven't been able
to collect enough evidence yet to prove that Iran wasn't connected
with the stadium attack. We have some, but not enough. We haven't
found anyone else yet willing to come forward with stories of
cover-up. The public is still in the throes of post-attack panic. It's too
early, and it's going to be ugly.

As we listen to Harry's testimony, we get an idea of how ugly it
will be. Two minutes into his remarks, he blindsides us.

"The Ministry of Intelligence has collected irrefutable evidence
that Jibril ibn Faraj, the operational head of the stadium attack, met
with the head of the Iranian Qods Force on March seventh of last
year in Lebanon."

We're dumbfounded. First by that word *irrefutable*, a glaring
red flag. It is a rare piece of intelligence that can be described as "irrefutable." And this piece of intelligence? The Snail and the Qods
Force? The Base doesn't need the Qods Force to operate. Their network is easily capable of carrying out its attacks without turning to
any country, much less a Shiite one.

As we sit, stunned, we hear the words *smoking gun* whispered
here and there.

Harry claims that the "irrefutable" reports come from a Mines
asset in Beirut. He also asserts that the Mines has passport and
photographic evidence of the Snail's trip to Lebanon. Evidently this
information was contained in veins so secret that we, the canary

crew, did not have access to it. Yet the Mines is now willing to make it public.

By the time Harry finishes his testimony, we have sunk back in our chairs, barely breathing. Fran holds a hand over her mouth as if to restrain herself from crying out. Vernon is on the edge of his chair and his face has gone a menacing shade of purple. Kristin scribbles notes. Bonnie's mouth hangs open. Vivian fails to hold back tears. My heart beats erratically. Maddie's face has tautened to a mask. Her testimony will be shot down and shredded in the political circus.

There's a short recess after Harry is finished.

"Maybe we should cancel or at least postpone this," I say to Maddie.

She shakes her head. "No. We may or may not have more evidence later. We have to at least try to introduce some doubt, to slow this steamroller down. I can't sit quietly this time and listen."

"There's bunny hair on your suit." Fran pulls a tape roller out of her purse and starts to run it over Maddie's jacket. "Maybe you should wear a baseball bat pin?" The purveyors of memorial kitsch have been working overtime to supply the populace with patriotic stadium attack items. The enameled baseball bat on a flag is the most popular, but there are also earrings, necklaces, hats, T-shirts, and refrigerator magnets.

Maddie shakes Fran off and goes to take her place at the table bristling with microphones.

The recess ends.

"Our next witness, Dr. Madeleine James, is a former senior alchemist in the Counterterrorism Supersector of the Ministry of Intelligence, or the Mines, as we like to call it." I had forgotten Maddie even had a Ph.D. "She resigned only last week. Dr. James has requested ten minutes for opening remarks. Dr. James?"

"Thank you, Mr. Chairman, and members of the committee."

I told her to use the word *esteemed* to modify *members*, but she has forgotten or else it is a deliberate omission. In either case, it's a bad sign.

Maddie continues. "I requested permission to come before you today for three reasons. First, on behalf of myself and my colleagues, to apologize to the families of the victims of the stadium attack for our failure to prevent it. Second, to give you a view of the days and weeks preceding the stadium attack from the alchemists' point of view, outlining some of the obstacles that we encountered in our efforts to deter the attack. Third, to state that none of the alchemists involved in trying to prevent the attack has any doubt that it was the work of internationally networked terrorists, and not the work of Iran or any other state. I would further argue that the administration has attempted to deliberately mislead the public on this point, just as it misled the public into believing that Iraq was responsible for the 2001 Strikes."

Maddie pauses for breath. I see Senator Westerly's eyes narrow. He rips off a page from his pad and begins to scribble. A ripple of muscle tension passes through the rest of the subcommittee, straightening shoulders, wrinkling foreheads, twitching jowls.

Maddie's voice is choked and shaky as she begins with her apology. There can be little doubt that she has taken the weight of the thing on herself, even though so many other people share in the blame. Her voice gains strength as she talks about the days prior to the attack, how she fought to get a half-dozen people assigned to the canary crew, how she had to struggle every day to keep the crew from being pulled away to do less pressing business, how cooperation with the Organ still leaves much to be desired. When she begins to talk about the aftermath of the attacks, her voice fills the room, and her anger is palpable.

"There was *nothing* in those planes," she says. "We called the labs and they told us that their initial tests had turned up no toxic substances. Yet within two days, the planes had been destroyed. Why? The administration would have you believe that they contained something so toxic, so dangerous, so concentrated that it could be carried on a toy airplane and dispensed through the air to kill children instantaneously. They would have you believe that the substance is so advanced, that it could only be the result of a concerted effort by a state bent on our destruction. Let me ask you, where are the toxicology reports on those children? Why were the bodies cremated? They were destroyed because toxicology reports would have proven that the children were poisoned the old-fashioned way, with cyanide, which could be readily obtained and placed in food sold by the vendors. We know that at least three of those vendors were, in fact, terrorists, and that one was the planner and lead operative."

I pray that Maddie will keep her voice steady. She mustn't appear to be too emotional. She must be calm, professional. Otherwise, she will be taken for a flake. She takes a long sip of water. As if she's heard my thoughts, she starts speaking again more quietly.

"The Commission on the Strikes recommended that the White Mines be more open to alternative analysis in its counterterrorism effort. Instead, the opposite has occurred. The efforts of our canary crew—and in particular our expert on chemical weapons—to put forth alternative hypotheses have been stifled from the first day after the attacks onward. Instead, Mines management, in cooperation with the Pentagon Council of the Wise, has chosen to highlight scattered reports from sources of dubious value, while at the same time, the administration has destroyed the physical evidence."

As Maddie lays out her arguments, we on the canary crew can hardly breathe. Is she being convincing? Are people taking in what she has to say? Will anything come of this?

Across the room, I catch sight of Dr. Elizabeth Dean, head of PentCOW. When her face flushes, her scar glows an angry scarlet. Nearby sits Harry. Maddie's testimony has come into direct conflict with his own, and he is quite obviously aggrieved. Beside Harry sits a large-haired woman whom I recognize from his desktop photos as his wife. She's wearing a jeweled cross around her neck. Periodically she whispers to him and squeezes his hand. I sense that there will be family prayers tonight. Perhaps they will pray for Maddie's sinful soul. On the other side of the room I see Gladys James, who spends more of her time glaring at Mrs. Esterhaus than she does looking at Maddie.

Maddie's testimony ends. The room is quiet. The families clearly don't know what to think of her arguments, which have introduced an unwanted element of complexity into their simple grief.

Senator Westerly clears his throat. "Dr. James, you make serious, and, if I may say so, rather absurd, charges against the administration. You offer no real proof of any of these claims. I have no idea why anyone would snatch such ridiculous theories from the clear blue sky. I can only surmise that they are a pitiful attempt to distract attention from your own incompetence. You, Dr. James, were the head of the team charged with stopping these attacks. Is it true that on the morning of the attacks, you and your colleagues were out in a soccer field playing with the very same model of airplane used in the attacks?" He consults his notes. "A Sky Shark?"

"Mr. Chairman. We were not playing. I had assembled a team of experts to test the capabilities of the plane to determine how it could be used in a possible terrorist attack."

"According to a resident who lives next to the soccer field, you were using the Sky Shark to chase a goose. Were you testing the capability of the plane to attack a goose, or were you playing?"

"We were testing the ability of the plane to maneuver."

"Did you catch the goose, Dr. James?"

"No, sir."

There are titters in the audience and expressions of anger from the families. The senator has managed to distract attention from the real issues rather handily. He shakes his head as if he can't believe what he's hearing. When he speaks, it is in a tone of the utmost incredulity. "The ability of the Sky Shark to catch a goose was completely irrelevant. Yet the planes still managed to kill hundreds within an hour after you finished playing."

"Sir, those people weren't killed by the planes. Some were poisoned from food sold by vendors. Some were killed by compression asphyxia or explosions."

"Are you in a state of denial, Dr. James? Six hundred ninety people are dead, and you claim the planes had nothing to do with it? What were you doing with that model plane on that particular day? Why did you have the Sky Shark and why hadn't you sent out a warning?"

"We had the plane because I had seen an Internal Investigative Organ report saying that large quantities of the planes had been bought by two toy stores in July of last year."

"July of last year? When was the report dated?"

"August of last year, sir."

"Last year? You mean to tell me that you were just getting around to following up?"

"Sir, when I originally saw the report last year, I called the Internal Investigative Organ to see if they had followed up on it. They told me that there was little likelihood that the planes could be used in an attack. They said that their experts had determined that the plane would be a poor dispersal agent for a chemical or biological attack."

"They were wrong."

"On the contrary, Mr. Chairman, they were right as far as they went. The planes were useless in dispersing chemicals but highly effective in inducing panic."

"Those children who went into convulsions didn't die of panic."

"They died of *poison*," Maddie says, "but not from the planes."

I feel a hand clutch my shoulder and a voice, quivering with anger, whispers, "My daughter was gasping for *air*. Her face turned pink."

Vernon, sitting on the other side of Fran, leans over and whispers back, "That's cyanide. It blocks the body's ability to absorb oxygen. I need to talk to you. Did you smell almonds on her breath?"

A young man comes to warn us to be silent. The hand on my shoulder grips harder, then lets go.

"Getting back to this report. Why did you suddenly become interested in it again?"

"I was going back through the databases looking for something that could be connected to one of the code names associated with the attacks."

"Which were?"

"I'm not authorized to disclose that information in open session, sir."

"Very well. So what did you do when you came across the report again?"

"I called the toy stores mentioned in the report and found that both had gone out of business. That was suspicious. So we called the Internal Investigative Organ to check up on it."

"But you didn't investigate the stores any further?"

"It is the responsibility of the Internal Investigative Organ to operate in this country. We could not legally—"

"Dr. James, do not presume to instruct me about the responsibilities of the various agencies of government. I'm tired—and I think the country is tired, and I know the families are tired—of hearing people say 'It's not my job.' So you're saying you did nothing further to follow up on the report."

"No, we did. A member of my team found and purchased a Sky Shark. As I testified before, I assembled a group of experts on chemical and biological weapons, as well as model builders who would know how such a plane could be modified."

"And yet with all of these much-vaunted Mines experts crowded into a field, nobody figured out how the plane could be used in an attack."

"No, sir."

"Nor did you catch the goose."

"No, sir."

The senator has succeeded in making Maddie look ridiculous and incompetent. His sarcasm increases as he continues his questioning. Maddie's voice gets softer, and he has to prompt her more than once to speak up. Vernon clenches his fist. Vivian cries into a handkerchief. Fran mutters to herself.

A hand touches my shoulder again, gently this time. The woman behind me leans forward until I feel her breath on my neck. The whisper is barely audible. "I did smell almonds on her breath." A slip of paper drops into my lap. "Tell that man to call me."

The woman sits back as the senator moves on to the subject of Maddie's resignation.

"Dr. James. You resigned shortly after the attacks. Was this resignation your own choice?"

"Yes, sir."

"Did you finally realize that you were not competent to do your job?"

"I was no longer being allowed to do my job."

"Who was stopping you?"

"My management had taken me off the attacks and had me doing . . . archival work."

"Do you believe it was somehow unreasonable to take you off the attacks after you had failed so utterly to prevent them?"

Maddie takes a deep breath. "Given my—and my team's— background and expertise, particularly the time we spent tracking the individuals involved in the attacks, I thought it was a poor decision to replace us with people who were starting out new on the subject."

"If your background and expertise are so valuable, wasn't it unpatriotic for you to leave the Mines? Shouldn't you have stayed to help out in whatever capacity your seniors judge fit?"

Maddie takes a minute to answer. Her shoulders are sagging, and I can tell that she's very tired. "After the stadium attack, I was spent," she says. "I no longer had the drive, the energy, and the passion that I once had. I thought it was best for me to step aside, particularly if my management chose not to use my expertise."

"You no longer had the passion? You mean you no longer cared?"

Maddie throws her hands in the air. She's stepping out of her professional briefer demeanor. She has a dangerous look in her eyes, and I'm afraid of what she will say next.

"Fifteen years ago, there was a threat against the very building that we're sitting in, and I stayed awake for two days making sure you guys didn't get your asses blown off."

"And now?" the senator says. "Now you no longer care whether we get our asses blown off?"

Maddie lets out a bitter laugh. "Let's put it this way, sir. It wouldn't ruin my entire day."

52. Vivian

The night after the hearings, Vernon calls the woman who had been sitting behind us, the one whose daughter was killed in the attack. She agrees to talk with the whole team. We arrange to meet her at Fran's house the following evening.

On the way to Fran's, Maddie and I keep looking at each other. No need to say out loud what we are thinking about: those earlier hearings, after the Strikes of '01. We had sat directly in front of the families of the victims, listening to their whispers, soft sobbing, and snorts of disgust. The hair stood up on the back of our neck, and our skin crawled. We felt like criminals or fugitives in hiding. We were certain that if they knew who we were they would fall on us and leave nothing but gnawed bone. I felt a deeper fear than I did on the day of the attacks, when the planes were still in the air and we sat like a fat bull's-eye on the Potomac. We were sitting in the path of a boundless, hungry, irrational anger. It made me dizzy. Maddie gripped my arm and said, "I know."

Now we were about to face one of the victims of this new attack head on.

When we arrive, the woman is already seated on Fran's couch, sitting very still, very straight, seemingly trying to compose herself by breathing deeply. We all recognize her from the attack video, even though the cameraman's shaking hands blurred the images.

We've all seen her precious child die many times, but we can never tell her that. Fran has already poured her a Scotch.

She's old to be the mother of a young child. I wonder if, like me, she went through years of fertility tests and drugs. The thought almost makes me swoon. I have to close my eyes and compose myself before I can open them again. Her hair is streaked with gray and styled into a simple chin-length cut. She's lean and well-dressed in a dark color. She has a handsome and intelligent face, but one cheek has a large bandage, a piece of gauze taped securely. She looks to me like someone who had a good, full life until only a short time ago.

I have to take a deep breath, before I can move forward. I don't think any of us have ever had such a hard time simply walking into a room.

Her name is Caroline Abbot and she is gracious to us, thanking us for coming as if we were doing her a favor. She offers us a strong, well-shaped hand, and we shake it nervously and sit down. No one wants to push her into telling her story.

Caroline finally takes a deep breath and begins. Her voice is distorted by her taped cheek. "It hurts to talk . . . in many ways. I've lived inside a bottle, since the attacks. And I don't want out. Even though the drinking burns. I've come to savor that pain." She takes a quick sip and doesn't look up at us. She gazes into her glass, touches the rim with a finger, and says, "She thought they were birds." Her words come out shaky and thin. She sits still for another long minute before continuing in a stronger voice. "At first my daughter, Annie, thought that those little planes were birds. Maybe she was thinking of the gulls she fed at the beach last summer. When she saw them coming over the walls of the stadium, she broke off a piece of her bread and offered it to the sky. She is . . . was . . . a generous child."

"The bread," Vernon says. "Where did the bread come from?"

"It was from her hot dog bun. The vendor gave it to her for free. He said it was a prize for being the prettiest little girl in the stadium. I don't usually let my children eat junk, but Annie begged."

"How much of it had she eaten?"

Caroline considers. "A third, a half, enough so that she already had mustard all over her face." Her voice breaks and she takes another deep swallow. "Then she realized that what she had thought were birds were really toy planes. She lowered her hand to her mouth and ate the bread herself. She never took her eyes off those planes. She wasn't frightened. She was delighted. All the children were excited. My son was whooping and cheering. Everyone thought it was some sort of show the stadium had arranged for the seventh inning stretch. No one realized at first that anything was wrong." Here she looks up at us as if to ask for understanding. "The mind tries hard to accept things as normal for as long as it can."

"Yes, Mrs. Abbott," Maddie says. "We're all like that."

Caroline fixes her eyes on her glass again. I notice that her eyes and the Scotch are the same color, a liquid yellow brown.

"The planes started to swoop low, so low I could see the doors open up underneath and red things fall out. Like large capsules. When they hit the ground there was a puff of red smoke. Still, some people thought it was part of the show, but it upset me, because why would the stadium be bombing us? Even with tiny little bombs? I looked around and caught another mother frowning. Then I looked back at Annie."

"She had been smiling just a second before, but the smile had bent out of shape. Such an awful expression on her face. I can't get it out of my mind. Horror, pain, surprise, and a plea for help. My child was looking at death. Then one of those red bombs hit right next to us. Annie began to gasp and spit up the hot dog."

This was the point at which the stadium camera had zoomed in on the scene. We all played it over in our minds as Caroline spoke. "I thought it was an asthma attack and grabbed her inhaler. It did nothing. Her face contorted and turned bright pink. It turned pink so fast, it was like a shrimp dropped in boiling water. She crumpled. She started to convulse. Saliva rolled from her lips. I yelled her name, but the gagging and spasms wouldn't let go of her. I begged her to come back. I brought her face close to mine." Caroline stops and looks at Vernon. "I smelled almonds on her breath. I remember that clearly."

Vernon nods, but says nothing.

"All around us people began to scream, scramble, shove. It was bedlam. The planes flew straight up, then began to spiral into the crowd. That pushed people over the edge. They went crazy. I scooped up Annie, grabbed hold of Ben with the other hand, and ran too. I had to get her away from the planes and red smoke. I fell. Feet battered us, rolled us over. Someone's high heel poked a hole in my cheek." She delicately touches the bandage on her face. "I struggled to get to Annie and covered her with my body. She may have already been dead by then. I think she was. I heard an explosion, then several more. A red haze hung over everything, like hell itself. People were screaming. I didn't know that I was screaming, but I must have been, because for days afterward I was hoarse." Caroline takes a big gulp of the Scotch and turns the full intensity of her gaze on us. "Annie didn't scream. Never once, through the whole ordeal, did she scream. She couldn't. I could tell that she wanted to, but she couldn't. Her silence . . . All the noise and her silence . . . haunts me."

For several minutes, no one says anything.

"It wasn't the planes that killed her, was it? I saw the awful look on her face before the bomb hit near us. Then she started to gasp, but the awful look was there first." Tears start to run down Caroline's face, tracking across the medical tape, but she makes no move to wipe them away. "It was that hot dog, the hot dog I allowed her to have."

Vernon nods. "Do you remember anything about the vendor?"

Caroline shakes her head.

Vernon reaches into his pocket and brings out several photographs, not the ones that have been shown on TV, but others we feel are better. I want to grab them to keep him from causing that poor woman any more pain, but I'm unable to move. Vernon pushes the photos across the table. Caroline fingers them one by one, then stops when she reaches a smiling photo of the Snail. Recognition comes into her eyes, mixed with horror and disbelief.

"This is him. He, I remember now, he came and stood by us and smiled just like this. Oh, my God, I remember now. He spoke to Annie with a Southern accent. He smiled just like this. He picked her out. He picked her out and looked into her beautiful face and murdered her." Caroline raises her own face from the photos and asks us, "How could anyone do that? Take something so precious? It is beyond anything I will ever be able to understand. I will never, never be able to understand why my daughter died."

When I get home, I wake my son up to hug him. I bury my face in his soft, dark hair and run my finger over the scar on the back of his neck, where the surgeons closed the lesion over his spinal cord after he was born. I didn't protect my own child. I didn't protect those other children. Josh asks me why I'm crying, and I can't tell him.

53. Doc

A week after the hearings and what is left of the canary crew labors on, uninterrupted by taskings or management visits, because we are all now officially untouchables. It would not be an unpleasant state, actually, if it weren't for the fear that young Alan Monroe might be packing his explosives and heading for Iran any day now. Meanwhile, Maddie continues to follow up leads from the outside. Bonnie has not found any Sky Shark debris on eBay yet, but she has purchased herself a coral necklace, an almost new Roomba, and some lawn furniture. Vernon has spent all morning on the phone, talking to various miners who happened to be at the park during the attacks—Burton Oil Park is not a terribly long drive from here. Some of these people claim to have suffered some ill effects from the chemicals, but Vernon is convinced they're all hypochondriacs.

About mid-morning Kristin emits a triumphant "Yes!" and smiles. We all look up expectantly.

"On March seventh of last year—the date that Harry claims the Snail met with the Qods Force officer in Beirut—a Jean Moreau withdrew money from an ATM in Ashland, Oregon. The account was one that the Snail had used before. Jean Moreau is a name we haven't come across."

"I'll do a trace," Fran says.

"What can I do?" I ask.

Fran gives me her sweetest smile. "Could you fetch us some coffee?"

"That barracuda doesn't like me."

"Barista, not barracuda. Just tell her it's for Fran. Don't forget that. Please, honey? It would do you good to play cabana boy every once in a while."

I trudge downstairs, wondering what a cabana boy is and dreading another meeting with the fierce Wynona. At least there's no line.

"Good morning." I pull out the list that Fran gave me. "I need three lattes. One large with two percent and two squirts of crème de menthe. One medium with two percent and one squirt of amaretto. One medium with soy milk and no squirts. I will also require one large mocha with extra whipped cream. This is for Fran, Vivian, and Kristin. Nothing for me," I add, so she will not think that I drink this sort of thing.

"I remember you," Wynona says. "And nothing is exactly what you will get unless you give me the right sizes."

I waver for a moment between arguing this point and relenting. Finally I decide that all my energies should be focused on the stadium attacks, and not on making a point with some hostile, big-haired coffee lady. I meekly repeat my order, inserting the required words.

"That's better," Wynona says. She turns to hobble over to the cooler for more two percent. Hobble, because she's wearing a cast on her foot. I suddenly feel pity for her, having to stand on her feet with such an injury. I regret having given her a hard time.

"How did you hurt your foot?" I ask.

She bangs the old grounds out of the filter. "Got knocked down and stomped on during the stadium attack. Thought I was dead, sure enough. Peed blood for a week."

"You were there?"

"Never miss a game at Burton Oil Park."

"Right. I think I've heard you mention that. I'm so sorry you had to go through such a horrible time."

"Worse than horrible." Wynona fits a lid onto the first of the lattes. "I'm just lucky that my husband and kid got out okay."

"None of you were affected by the chemicals?"

"Nah. We was lucky."

"Do you happen to have anything from the attack that day? Anything you wore or picked up?"

"The authorities come and destroyed everything we had on or carried that day."

"Everything. You're sure?"

Wynona looks at me suspiciously. "You're not going to sic the authorities on me, are you?"

"No, ma'am. I don't think it was necessary to destroy that material at all."

"Me neither. We do have one thing. My stupid kid, Harley, picked up one of those red bomb things that fell. It was half burned up and still smoking, but the idiot slipped it right into his pocket. I didn't find out about it until I got home from the hospital. Found the damn thing on the dresser in his room and I thought it was trash and picked it up to throw it away, and he says, 'No, Mom, that's my souvenir bomb!' Dang stupid kid!"

"Does he still have it?"

"Yeah, he wouldn't let me throw it away."

"Don't you worry that it might have dangerous chemicals on it?"

"Well, since it had already been sitting on the dresser for a week when I found it, I figured it must be okay. But I made him put it in a Ziploc baggie, then I wrapped it with duct tape, too, just in case. And I made him wash his hands good."

"Good thinking." I pull out my wallet as she totals up the damage for my colleagues' caffeine binge. I offered to treat them, so the $18.50 hurts. "You know, I work in the Counterterrorism Supersector, and it would really help us out a lot if we could study that bomb-let."

"My kid won't give it up," Wynona says.

"Maybe we could just borrow it for a while? Maybe you could slip it out of his room for a couple of days."

"He'd notice."

"We really would like to see it."

"Well, he ain't going to let it out of his sight, so unless you want to stop by the house, you're out of luck."

. . .

So Fran and I are sharing another evening with Vernon. I'm driving. Fran has Wynona's scribbled directions and is navigating from the passenger seat, while Vernon sits in the backseat licking an ice cream cone—he insisted that we stop for soft-serve, because it was on the way. We've spent so much time with him lately, that he's beginning to feel like a son—a son who won't move away from home, no matter how many hints we drop.

"I must have talked to a hundred people who were at the stadium. Nobody picked up anything. And you walk down to get coffee, and boom, this falls right into your lap. I don't believe it. How do you get so lucky?" Vernon says.

"If only I could get lucky enough to have some time alone with Fran. Between you and Alan—"

"How is old Alan?" Vernon asks. "Still seeing Maddie?"

"They went to a concert last night," Fran says. "Maddie really looked cute. I think she's falling in love with Alan. I haven't seen her with makeup on in ages. And she was wearing a dress that showed off her legs. And cute shoes! I thought all she owned were black pumps, but these were adorable strappy little—"

"Fran, Vernon is not interested in Maddie's shoes."

"No, actually I have a huge foot fetish. I fantasize about insteps, in particular."

"Spare us. Aren't we getting close to the turn?"

Fran consults her directions. "Yes, left at the next light then an immediate right."

• • •

Wynona lives in one of those vast townhouse developments constructed with slapdash speed and bottom-of-the-line materials. She greets us at the door wearing jeans and a leather vest.

"Come on in. I told Harley about you and he said, 'No way are they touching it,' so good luck. Harley! Harley, they're here."

Wynona waves us toward a living room that is tidy, although rather unattractive, as it is decorated largely with Harley-Davidson colors and logo items. I'm no expert on color theory, but I've always thought that orange should be used with great restraint, if at all. It takes Wynona five minutes to persuade her son, young Harley, to come out and greet us.

Harley is an eight-year-old victim of the childhood obesity epidemic now sweeping the country. He clearly views himself as quite tough. He's chewing on a candy cigarette and has inked tattoos over his arms, evidently using a leaky ballpoint. He's wearing a leather vest over a Simpsons T-shirt.

"You the spies?" he says.

"Yeah," growls Vernon, who also enjoys looking tough.

"Mom, I'm going to shave my head." Harley is obviously admiring Vernon's shiny head and black mustache.

"Harley, go back and get your bomb. The people want to see it."

"I told you, I don't want them touching it. They might try to steal it."

"You don't really think we'd try to steal from you, do you?" Fran says.

"Yeah, lady, I do."

"Harley, you were smart to pick up that bomb casing," Vernon says. "Now you could play an important part in saving your country and fighting the terrorists by letting us look at it."

"Don't you want to fight the terrorists?" Wynona says. "Because of the terrorists, we almost got stomped to death and we ain't going to get to go to another ballgame for I don't know how long. Now go and get that thing before I tan your hide."

Harley stomps out and Wynona says, "Anybody want a Coke? Bud Light?"

We decline.

"Careful," Harley says when he returns, "it's deadly." He holds up the bomb casing, still hermetically sealed in its Ziploc bag and covered with duct tape. When Vernon reaches for it, he pulls it away.

"I said it's deadly. Deadly to regular people. Won't hurt me. I have powers." Harley puffs out his chest and squares his jaw.

"I have powers, too." Vernon sucks in his beer gut and puffs out his own chest.

"Were you at the park?" Harley asks. "Because that's where I got my powers. The red smoke hurt other people, but it gave me powers. That's why I'm not giving my bomb up."

"We don't need to keep it, son," Vernon says. "We just need to borrow it for a few days to test it."

"Nope. I don't want my powers to go away."

"I'll give you fifty bucks," Vernon says. "For fifty bucks, I'll rent it from you for three days."

"A hundred bucks for one day, and I'll consider it." Harley crosses his arms in front of his chest.

Vernon eyes the child as if he were a terrorist. He fishes out his wallet and finds a fifty, two twenties, and a ten. "Okay. Give me the bomb casing."

Harley looks at the money and shakes his head solemnly. "I said I would consider it, but I've decided I would rather have powers than money."

"Give me that money, and I'll get that piece of trash for you," Wynona says. Harley tries to make a break for it, but Wynona is quick, even with her cast. She grabs him and wrenches the baggie out of his hand. As he starts to scream, she swats his behind and says, "Get back in your room, or I'll have your daddy get his belt out!" Harley retreats, still crying. Wynona holds out her hand, and Vernon slaps the money into it and takes the bag. "You can keep it," Wynona says.

We make our departure swiftly as banging sounds issue from the direction of Harley's room.

• • •

"That poor child!" Fran says as we drive away. "Don't you feel terrible taking that away from him?"

"No. Hate kids. Hate 'em." Vernon is working his pocketknife through several layers of duct tape.

"You are sure that thing has no dangerous chemicals on it?"

"One hundred percent sure. Look at this." Vernon pulls the burnt casing from the bag. "Paper. You don't put dangerous, super-advanced Iranian chemicals in paper. They made these casings by wrapping stiff paper a couple of times around a dowel, hot gluing it, and stuffing the end with cotton wool and more glue. Something happened with this one. It didn't explode the way it should have. Any ten-year-old could make casings like this. I know, I used to make something similar when I was a kid. Filled 'em up with flash powder mixed with match heads, which have chlorate and perchlorate, added some sucrose, and got this really hot lilac flame. Supercool. Planted one in my sister's Barbie convertible and blew the shit out of it. With Barbie in it. Melted her head. Sis still doesn't speak to me. Bitch."

"I suppose we're lucky you didn't join the dark side," I say.

"The government has better benefits. Of course, the government may turn out to be the dark side. Anyway. Our Snail and his friends simply filled the casings with a homemade smoke bomb, which could have been as simple as potassium nitrate cooked with sugar. The recipe for red smoke is potassium chlorate and paranitroaniline red and lactose. I think I might have even seen a little red flame, so they may have used strontium salts for that. Nothing could be simpler. Kid stuff."

"That's our problem," I point out. "How do we get the public to believe that they killed more than six hundred people with kid stuff?"

"How did they get the things to explode at the right time?" Fran asks. "A simple fuse wouldn't have worked."

"Well, the detonation mechanism was probably more complex than what the average kid could come up with. There are a number of ways they could have done it. I probably won't be able to tell exactly what they did from this casing."

I line up our assets. "We've got Caroline Abbott's story, this casing, and perhaps some evidence that the Snail didn't meet with a Qods Force officer in Beirut, at least not when the Mines claims he did. I'm not sure that's going to be enough. Can we even prove that this casing came from the stadium?"

"No," Vernon says, "but I have some other ideas."

54. Vivian

The canary cage is quiet. We're concentrating on the Snail, Jibril ibn Faraj. We need to place him definitively in Ashland, Oregon, on March seventh of last year so we can disprove that fake intelligence report saying he was in Lebanon with a Qods Force officer. We have the bank transaction, but we can't prove it was the Snail, versus some other operative using one of his names.

We've learned a great deal about Jibril since the attacks and it's been a field day for the psychologist in me. He's the product of a stormy marriage, broken home, parental kidnapping, physical abuse, you name it. His school records show a student with extremely high aptitude tests and mediocre grades. He was sickly and shy as a child. He was born with a minor birth defect that was corrected with surgery—that detail kills me. He grew into a handsome teenager and a magnet for girls. He was arrested once for nearly strangling a girlfriend with a silk scarf, but she dropped the charges. I've seen his mother on the news hiding behind her own silk scarf as she tries to avoid the press. In the brief glimpses that I've had, she has an elegant figure; a beautiful, worn, tear-stained face; and haunted eyes. She refuses to make any public statement. If I were her, I would also refuse to speak. I completely understand that.

"Does anyone have any intelligence on the Snail from January to April of last year?" Doc asks.

"Nothing. A three-and-a-half-month gap. I called the Organ and the only thing they can come up with is the Mines' fake report," Vernon says. "Kristin, have you come up with any other financial transactions?"

"No, just the one from Ashland, Oregon, and we can't prove that Jean Moreau and the Snail are one and the same."

"Why Ashland?" Vernon asks. "Anything special about that place?"

"I'll search Auger," Fran says. "Vivian, can you do open source?"

"Sure." I check out the chamber of commerce Web site. It looks like a nice place: lively arts community, wineries, a chocolate festival.

"This is interesting. They have a months-long Shakespeare Festival. Maybe something a theater major might be interested in?"

"What was playing in early March?" Doc says.

I search the site until I find a schedule.

"Macbeth."

"Ah," Doc says, "the Scottish play. He would like that one. I myself played the Scottish king in college."

"Scottish king?" Fran says.

"Yes, the king whose name begins with *M*. One must never say the other name out loud. It's bad luck. No self-respecting thespian would ever do it. If I say so myself, my turn as the Scottish king garnered quite respectable reviews."

"I know I've seen that term before and I'm pretty sure it was in Auger and not in a play." Fran taps furiously at her keyboard. "If I remember correctly, it was being used to refer to an operative that we never further identified."

"Maybe another code name for the Snail?"

"Could be." Fran throws up her hands. "Oh, the dirty dogs."

"What?"

"The Black Mines pulled my access to that compartment."

"Let me try," I say. I run the search only to find that I am also denied access. Same for the rest of the crew.

"Why don't you bastards just turn off the electricity and duct-tape our door shut!" Vernon yells at the walls.

"Shh," I say, "we don't need to buy any more trouble."

"Well, I printed a hard copy when I first saw the report. It's somewhere in those stacks." Fran points to the mounds of papers that cover the conference table as well as the floor underneath the table.

We all set about searching. Skinny Kristin slips easily from her chair and disappears under the table. She sits cross-legged on the floor scanning the footprint-covered cables that have accumulated there in a disorderly heap. The rest of us work the coffee-stained stacks on top of the table. Some of the reports are completely stuck together from Harry's caramel macchiato spill.

"State-of-the-art intelligence gathering," Vernon mumbles as he pries apart the pages.

We keep at this for an hour without finding a single reference to "the Scottish King."

"Are you sure you saw those words?" Bonnie says.

"Absolutely positively." Fran's face has set into a deep frown of determination.

Fifteen minutes later we hear a shout of triumph from underneath the table.

"Got it!" Kristin says. She slithers into her chair from below, an amazing double-jointed maneuver which is easier for her than asking Bonnie to move. Vernon takes a deep breath and closes his eyes.

Kristin reads from a torn paper. " 'I bought what you requested and met up with your brother while visiting the Scottish King.' That's all there is. The other guy says 'I'll bring the packages,' and that's it."

"You can read that two ways," I say. "Either it's Jibril talking about meeting another operative at the play, or another operative referring to Jibril as the Scottish King. I'd vote for the former."

"Yeah, me too," Vernon says. "I'll call the Ear and see what else they have on the phone numbers associated with that report."

From the Ear, we find out that one of those numbers is associated with the name Jean Moreau. This is the name that Jibril was using during that three-and-a-half-month period. Vernon goes back to his contact in the Organ with this information. Soon we're able to fill in the blanks for that time period. It takes another day for the Organ to come up with flight information for Jibril/Moreau's trip to Oregon and to scan photos from the airport security cameras. And then we have it in our hands, a photo of a handsome, black-haired Jibril placing his backpack on an airport security conveyor belt on seven March. I look at the photo and think, *Birth defect. He had a birth defect.*

55. Maddie

At 7:00 P.M., Vernon's oversize Darth Vader black truck pulls up in front of my house, right on schedule. I've agreed to drive to Maryland with him to meet Louis Townsend, the lab guy. I'd rather take my car, but it's in the shop for a new alternator, a repair I can't really afford, since I no longer have an income.

Vernon has been talking to Louis Townsend by phone for days. He's convinced that Townsend is hiding something, and he thinks I can get him to talk—perhaps because I got information out of Alan so easily, but that was another matter altogether. The only thing I'll be drinking at dinner tonight is coffee. I sling my purse over my arm.

"Is that what you're wearing?" Vernon asks.

"What's wrong with it?" I have on new jeans and a nice top, which is perfectly acceptable for the restaurant we're going to.

"Not very sexy," Vernon says.

"Forget it, Vernon. I'm just coming along to talk to Townsend, that's it. Clear your dirty mind of any other ideas."

After a long, slow slog through Beltway traffic, we arrive at an Italian restaurant filled with faux-barrel-stave furniture. Fake stucco walls are lit by electric candles in wrought-iron sconces. The waiter leads us to a table where a nervous little man is nodding to himself, idly using his breadstick to draw doodles in a plate of olive oil. The table is covered with crumbs and his wineglass needs refilling. We've kept him waiting some time. He doesn't see us enter and seems startled by our appearance.

Vernon offers his hand and Townsend drops his breadstick on the checkered tablecloth. It rolls off and falls to the floor. Townsend makes an awkward move to retrieve it, then changes his mind, stands, and takes Vernon's hand reluctantly.

"Vernon Keene. And this is my colleague, Dr. Madeleine James." I've never heard Vernon use a title with anyone before, but I suppose he figures that Louis is the type who is impressed by them.

"Dr. Louis Townsend."

Dr. Louis Townsend is barely taller than me and nearly as thin. He's dressed the way the boys on my high school debate team used to dress for state competition: white shirt; nerd tie; ill-fitting trousers. He has a helmet of peppery hair that grows too low on his forehead. Rabbity eyes under a jutting brow. If I had to choose one word for him it would be *uncomfortable.* He seems uncomfortable with the situation and uncomfortable in his own skin, as if it fit as badly as his pants. I decide that it's perfectly safe for me to order a glass of wine, because there's no way in hell I would be tempted to end up in bed with this guy.

We sit, and the waiter takes our orders while Dr. Townsend fidgets.

"So," Vernon says, "we had a conversation right after the attacks. I remember every last stinking word out of your mouth." Vernon gnaws off the end of his breadstick and chews as he watches Townsend's face. He's wearing his favorite tough guy ensemble: tight black T-shirt, leather jacket, and freshly shaved head. The droopy black mustache is as impressive as ever. "By the way, nice front teeth you have. Very white. None missing. Not even a chip. That's good, because you can't even eat a breadstick with no teeth."

I roll my eyes. Vernon may be overdoing it, but it's fun to watch, so I let him continue.

"As I was saying. I remember every, single, stinking word out of your mouth after the attacks. You said that the preliminary toxicology results indicated death from ingested cyanide. I'm not

dreaming that conversation. Any effort to deny it will only infuri-
ate me further. Already it's all I can do not to shove those pearly
teeth down your throat until they come out—"

"Now, Vernon," I say in a voice of warning. I don't want him to
scare Townsend so badly that he goes to the police. Vernon gives
Townsend that diabolical psycho look he does so well. I wonder
how he can manage to go for so long without blinking. All the blood
drains from Townsend's face.

"Have you been listening to the war drums?" Vernon asks in a
low voice. "But then your children are probably too young to be in
the military, so what do you need to worry about?"

"I'm worried about paying for their college, and I can't do it if I
turn into some crazy crusading whistleblower, as you seem to want
me to do." Townsend speaks under his breath. "Someone could be
bugging us right now."

"You've been watching too many bad movies," I tell him. "The
Ear is way too busy to bother with the likes of you."

"All I want you to do is tell the truth," Vernon says. "I won't even
ask you to stick your neck out publicly. Tell me about your initial
findings. Tell me who came to get and destroy those samples. Tell
me if you know someone with a conscience who might have the
balls to go public."

"It'll all come out sooner or later," Townsend says. "Their story is
too implausible. Any real scientist should be able to figure that out."

Vernon snorts. "Oh yeah. I've already seen a real scientist or
two on TV, questioning the idea that some supertoxic Iranian
chemical was used in the attacks. You know what happens? The
media, in the interest of fairness, puts on another 'scientist' with
the opposite view. Never mind that one guy is a pillar of the scien-
tific community and the other is a crackpot, they both get equal
airtime. Then the pundits start yelling at each other. Then they
flash a few more pictures of stadium attack victims on the screen.
Then a few pictures of the Beirut bombings. Yeah, the public is
going to be able to figure out the truth from that. Right. Maybe

six months after we bomb Iran they'll figure it out and that will be way too late."

"Did samples go to any other labs?" I ask.

Townsend peers at me strangely. "Do I know you? You look familiar. Are you famous for something?"

My hair is loose, not the way I wore it at the hearings. I have abandoned the chignon since my appearance on TV, but people still recognize me now and then. "You might know me as the goose chaser, the butt of jokes."

"Right. The MOC hearings. Did you a lot of good to go public. You don't have a job now, do you?"

"No." I'm starting to think maybe Vernon should take this guy's teeth out. "But I'm not ashamed to look myself in the mirror in the morning."

The uncomfortable Dr. Townsend grows even more uncomfortable.

"So who's threatening you?" Vernon says.

"No one."

"Right. You know I was able to get hold of one of these." Vernon pulls the casing out of his pocket. It is secured in a new baggie, this time without duct tape. He removes it from the bag and lays it on the table.

Townsend's eyes widen in alarm. "You shouldn't have that."

"Relax. Do you think anyone would recognize what it is? Other than you, and you've obviously seen one of these before. A piece of paper. Interesting thing to put deadly chemicals in, don't you think?"

"They'll fire me and strip my clearances," Townsend says. "Strip my clearances so I can't get another job."

I lean forward, which causes the intensely uncomfortable Dr. Townsend to lean back in his chair. "You were right when you said that eventually it will all come out. We've already found a way to prove that the Mines faked information linking the Snail to the Qods Force. In a couple of years, a new administration will come in and the old henchmen will be removed from all the government agencies, government labs where they have done so much damage. The pendulum will swing in the opposite direction and a nasty light will shine on those who made this cover-up possible." I say this with confidence, although I'm not at all sure it will happen. But Townsend is taking me seriously. He looks ill.

"Tell you what," Vernon says. "You give us what we need now. We don't tell anyone where it came from until that old pendulum has shifted. Then, with your permission, of course, we reveal you as the silent hero."

"I'm writing a book, you know," I tell him. I'm not, but, hey, I could. I have plenty of free time. Why not? "You'll be in it, one way or another. What would you like your kids to read?"

I take a close look at Townsend, who dips his head, trying to retreat behind the defenses of his jutting brow. I know this squirmy man. I've just met him, but I know the type so well I can crawl right into his claustrophobic little skull. He is a good man as long as good is easy. He's into sins of omission, not commission. He hasn't slept well since the attacks. He's not happy with the role he has been forced to play, but all he wants out of life is to live calmly within some system, because he doesn't have the balls or creativity to strike out on his own. Unless someone pushes him over the cliff. Townsend is too upset to be able to calmly assess whether or not Vernon and I actually have the ability to make good on any of our threats. His eyes dart about the room, as if looking for a pathway for escape.

"We're not going to let you off the hook," I tell him.

"We're not going to let you off the hook," Vernon says. "Ever."

I'm used to Vernon now, but I try to look at him as if, like Townsend, I were seeing him in person for the first time. After weeks of obsessing over this attack, he has a sort of E. Howard Hunt air of barely contained craziness.

Townsend rakes his fingers through his hair. I hope he doesn't have a heart condition, because if he does, he might keel over at any minute. The waiter brings our food and wine. Townsend lowers his head and begins to jab at his fettucini, raking up a forkful and then swooping down and snatching it in his mouth with a reptilian quickness. He eats without looking up at us.

"No matter how hard you try to lose yourself in your pasta, I haven't gone away," Vernon says. "I'm still here, plotting how I'm going to screw your skinny ass to the wall."

Townsend stops shoveling, but he doesn't look up. Finally he sucks up some dangling fettucini and whispers, "I didn't destroy all the samples. Didn't seem right to me. I hid one in the lab. Mislabeled it. You're correct. It shows cyanide poisoning. Common cyanide, ingested, not inhaled."

Vernon exhales loudly. He and I had both been holding our breath. "And unlike my little casing sample here, we can match the DNA to a victim so there will be no question that it came from the stadium attack. Can you get me that sample?"

Townsend nods with resignation. "It shouldn't be too hard to get it out. They rarely check bags and packages. Once, maybe twice a year. You have to promise to keep my name out of it. I'll be under suspicion. Less than twenty people have the necessary accesses."

"We'll keep your name out of it."

Townsend relaxes a bit, as if relieved that he has finally come clean. He reaches across the table and picks up the casing. "You may be able to connect this to the attack, if it's like the one I saw." He inserts a fingernail between the layers of paper and carefully peels them apart.

"There."

I lean in for a closer look. It looks like part of an *H*.

"What is it?"

"The logo of the Hebrew Specialty Company. It's a small Maryland firm. They make excellent Kosher hot dogs. Their biggest customer is Burton Oil Park. This paper is perfect for making homemade casings. Just the right size and weight. These have never been used to wrap hot dogs. It looks like the vendor took several fresh stacks home to use as casings."

• • •

"Do you think we could actually beat them on this?" I ask Vernon on the way home. "Do you really think?"

"I think," Vernon says.

I'm starting to feel better, almost excited when, two blocks from my house, I spot the car. "Vernon, stop. That's Harry's car."

"You sure?"

"Gold BMW with a Jesus fish and tags that say PRAYZGD. Oh, and a red-white-and-blue baseball bat wired to the grille."

"That would be Harry's car. What's he doing here? Screwing one of your neighbors?"

"Or sneaking up to my house for some reason. Stop here. Park in front of him. If you back it right up to his bumper, he won't be able to get out, because he's too close to the car behind him."

"Get out and tell me how far I need to go. I don't want his paint on my bumper."

Vernon inches back until his truck is about a quarter of an inch from Harry's BMW. We get out and walk toward my house. A half block away, I see a shadowy form on my front porch. Harry is vainly trying his key. He is dressed all in black, just like Vernon.

"Good thing we changed the locks," I whisper.

"Let's sneak up on him."

Vernon and I take a circuitous path through the neighbor's shrubbery. We watch from an azalea as Harry tries my front window. Foolishly, I've left it open a crack. I wasn't thinking when I left the house. Harry looks around. He is fairly well hidden on the dark porch. He takes out a pocket knife—undoubtedly the same one he uses on rolls of tape—and slices through my screen. He flips up the latches that hold the screen in place and removes it and places it carefully next to the window. Then he pushes the window up and crawls inside.

"What should we do?"

"Give him time to get whatever he came for," Vernon whispers. "I'll tackle him on the way out."

"I hope you plan to knock the shit out of him."

"Of course. This is a once-in-a-lifetime opportunity. He's an intruder, and I'm perfectly within my rights to knock the shit out of him, even though he's my boss. This is way cool."

We wait, listening to the sound of cicadas. My legs are getting cramped from squatting behind the stupid bush. I'm afraid of getting bugs in my hair. I hate the idea of bugs in my hair.

"He wouldn't have gone out the back, would he?" Vernon says.

"We'd hear it if he did, because the neighbors keep their dogs in their backyard. I can't go out without the damn things yapping their heads off."

We wait some more. My back hurts, and I have to go to the bathroom.

"I hate the idea of him pawing around my house. What do you suppose he's after?"

"Some incriminating evidence. Maybe he left his boxers in Gladys's underwear drawer. I wonder why he didn't try to get it earlier."

"I've been home almost every night, except for that one concert date with Alan."

"Are you still seeing him?"

"Don't know. He disappears for days at a time. Off training or planning or something."

"Has he told you any more about the operation?"

"No. He regrets having told me anything in the first place. He is much more careful about getting drunk around me now."

"Shh. I hear Harry. You stay back."

Vernon creeps forward as the front door opens. He lunges. I hear an "Umph!" as the wind is expelled from Harry's lungs. Harry is down and Vernon is on top of him, punching. It occurs to me that the level of violence is gratuitous and perhaps I should step in to stop it. Then it occurs to me that I could get a punch in too, if Vernon would just move to the side a bit. Then I take a good look at the object Harry dropped.

"Oh no!" My cry of anguish is shrill enough to stop Vernon in mid-punch. He follows my gaze and whoops.

"Woo-hoo! A sex tape! That's got to be a sex tape!"

Harry takes advantage of the distraction to attempt to slither out from under Vernon.

"Don't move!" Vernon orders and lands another punch on Harry's already bloody nose.

"Please," Harry begs. "Please. Don't hit me anymore."

"Maddie, maybe you'd better call the police," Vernon says.

"No, no! It's me. Harry."

"Is that a reason we shouldn't call the police? You, Harry, are guilty of breaking and entering and theft."

"No, no police. No." Harry is whimpering. Blood is running from his nose and mouth, and his left eye is beginning to swell shut. "Please. Please. Please let me up. I think you broke a tooth. I could choke to death on the blood."

Vernon rolls off of Harry. Harry slowly stands, gingerly poking at the damage on his face with an index finger. Then suddenly he lunges for the videocassette. Vernon knocks it out of his hand. Harry hesitates a moment, then abandons the tape and takes off running in the direction of his car.

"Good idea, Maddie, blocking him in with the truck."

"Vernon, tell me that's not a sex tape. Please tell me that my mother is not on that tape. I can't handle it."

"Only one way to find out." Vernon picks up the tape. "Where's your VCR?"

"No, no one is going to look at it. We are going to throw that thing away." I make a grab for it, but Vernon holds it above his head, well out of my range.

"Maddie, do you realize what we have here? We have a way to get Harry to recant his testimony. Haven't you ever heard of blackmail? It's a time-honored technique in our business."

"No, this is my mother."

"The tape will never see the light of day. We just use it against Harry."

I can't stand this. I sink to the porch floor and curl up into a fetal position.

"No, no, no."

Vernon abandons me to my misery and goes inside. I want to throw myself between him and the VCR, but I can't move. All I can do is remain in the fetal position, whimpering. The light goes on in the living room. After a long pause, I hear Vernon begin to howl.

"It's the Baptist version of a sex tape!" he yells. "Come look at this. Don't worry. No nudity."

I peel myself off the porch floor and reluctantly go inside. On my TV screen I see Harry and my mother sitting on my couch. Harry has a guitar and my mother has a tambourine and they're singing Christian rock—badly. Very badly.

"Oh . . . my . . . God," I say. "Are they drunk?"

"Drunk on the spirit."

I watch for a minute. "Half of me is relieved and half of me wishes it were more incriminating. Sure, Harry would be in big trouble should his wife see this tape, but I don't think it gives us enough material to hold his feet to the fire."

"Wait one minute," Vernon says. He moves closer to the screen, then punches his fist in the air and lets out a yelp of triumph. "Yes! Yes, we've got him by the short hairs. See the open briefcase on the end table? Notice anything familiar?"

I lean toward the screen and instantly recognize the pale blue cover, red-striped border, and presidential seal. Recognize it even though I rarely get to see one. This is the Mines' holy of holies, the eyes-only "exclusive pub." The pub that we are not allowed to enter into any electronic database. Even the alchemists themselves are not allowed to view the finished product that they write for. And it's not just "close hold" because of Mines' secrecy, but because the President himself is adamant that no one find out what the President knew and when he knew it. This little indiscretion would not only get Harry in trouble, but the entire Mines, because the Mines is supposed to keep close tabs on every single copy.

"Holy crap," I say, "that's a PIU. The idiot brought the President's Intelligence Update along for light reading."

Vernon and I exchange looks.

"That is just so illegal," I say.

"So illegal," Vernon repeats, shaking his head and smiling.

We continue to watch through four more dreadful songs. Finally Harry gives my mom a big sloppy kiss and the tape ends.

"Harry, Harry, Harry," I say, "you are so screwed."

"I can't believe even Harry would do something so stupid. I mean, why would he take an unnecessary risk like that?"

"He did it to impress my mother," I say. "Same reason Alan told me things he shouldn't have. Never underestimate the need for a man to look important in front of a woman. Why, I bet you've done it yourself. Look me in the face, Vernon, and tell me that you've never disclosed a bit of classified information just to make yourself look like a big, important spy guy."

Vernon doesn't answer my question. "Shh," he says, "Harry is coming up the walk."

Harry appears in my door glowering. "Move your truck, Vernon."

"Oh, hi, Harry. I was just enjoying your performance."

"Look, Vernon. I could get you fired."

"Ditto. We couldn't help noticing your dirty reading material."

Harry's face turns a lighter shade of white. "What do you want?"

"I want you to go back to the MOC and ask to testify again. This time you tell the truth. You admit to suppressing evidence and cooking up that fake Beirut report. By the way, we found a way to prove that the report is fake, because we can place Jibril in Ashland, Oregon, at the time of the supposed meeting with the Qods Force officer. So either way, you're screwed."

"It could be the end of my career." Harry's voice is weak, pleading.

"Your career is toast in any event," Vernon says. "The best you can hope for now is to stay out of jail and maybe even stay married to your rich wife if you're lucky."

56. Doc

It is four weeks to the day since the attacks. Once again we collect inside the hearing room. Everyone hugs Maddie, who is having a hard time of it, even though so many things have gone our way lately. The attacks, the cover-up, and the Gladys James–Harry Esterhaus affair have filled her with what she terms "an existential nausea." Alan called her the other night, and she told him she didn't want to go out with him again, didn't want to go out with any man again. She said she was going to join a convent as soon as she could find one that accepts agnostics. Alan was disappointed. Fran is devastated.

Alan has told Fran that he's leaving for a trip in three days. I pray that what comes out in this hearing room today will prevent that trip from happening.

Senator Westerly, as bumptious as ever, gavels the room to order and once again introduces Harry, pausing to ask what has happened to the poor man's face. Harry mumbles something about falling down the basement stairs. He resigned from the Mines two days ago, to save them the trouble of ousting him. His wife, whom we only know as Mrs. Harry, is sitting nearby to lend support. Sharon Pendergast is sitting near the front. Since Harry resigned, she doesn't get a preview of his testimony and it's killing her. She eyes him with loathing. Dr. Elizabeth Dean, on tap to testify later in the day, is also in attendance, smiling and unsuspecting. She air kisses VIPs right and left. We elbow each other and nod in her direction. We find her presence enormously satisfying.

We, the canary crew, know exactly what Harry will say. We insisted on reading off on his testimony. It was quite delightful giving Harry orders, editing his flaccid prose. We did not allow him to use the passive voice. No saying "mistakes were made." We forced him to come up with a flesh-and-blood subject for every verb. He was sweating bullets by the time we finished with him. Sitting in the glare of the lights, he is a sad sack, a slumped, bruised, battered, and broken man. He is hollow eyed and rumpled, and hasn't even remembered to wear a flag lapel pin on his suit. He glances nervously toward us, but we take no pity on him. Vernon stares Harry down with an unflinching glare that is, nevertheless, almost benign in comparison to the fierce, accusatory look Maddie directs at him. Vivian is chewing her fingernails. Fran and Kristin are sitting quietly, aware that things can still go wrong. Bonnie is texting other mothers, trying to find someone else to take her daughter to rehearsal.

Senator Westerly must prompt Harry to speak.

"Chairman, members of the Committee," Harry begins in a shaky voice. "I have come here today to correct certain misstatements that I made during my earlier testimony."

We allowed him to use "certain misstatements" rather than the more accurate term "honking, bald-faced lies," which Maddie had originally insisted upon. I was not familiar with the word *honking* when used as an adjective, but I looked it up on an online dictionary, and found that Maddie had used it quite correctly. When Harry begged, however, we relented and went with *misstatements*. We're not entirely without mercy.

"I believe I testified that the Mines had collected reliable evidence that Jibril ibn Faraj, the lead operative behind the stadium attack, had met with the Qods Force in Lebanon. I testified that we had passport evidence as well as an account of the meeting provided by an asset in Beirut. Such a meeting would have been compelling evidence of an Iranian hand in the stadium attack. In fact, however, both the passport evidence and the supposed asset report were fabricated by the Special Documents section of the Mines at the behest of"—here Harry's Adam's apple bounces up and down as he swallows hard and tries not to look toward the corner of the room—"at the behest of Dr. Elizabeth Dean at PentCOW. The Boss of Mines, Brian Mason, and the Boss of White Mines, Sharon Pendergast, signed off on the forgeries."

Here Harry stops. He is out of breath, out of courage, and quite possibly out of clean underwear. The room erupts in chatter. Dr. Dean grips the back of the chair in front of her and leans forward, almost as if to lunge at Harry. I can see her mouth moving rapidly, but I can't tell what she's saying for all the noise in the room. Fran taps me on the knee. "Look, I think her hair is on fire again!" The chairman calls for silence. Harry takes a gulp of water and reluctantly continues, testifying that the Mines blocked publication of analysis suggesting that the radio-controlled planes carried no Iranian chemicals. By the time he is finished, he looks on the verge of death, while Beth Dean appears to be on the verge of murder. The chairman calls a recess. Harry flees the room with Dr. Dean in hot pursuit and her security detail and the press chasing both of them.

57. Vivian

It's been a lovely week. The hearings were just plain fun. Jeff has a job lined up for when Josh starts school next fall, so I'll be able to switch to part-time. I pour Josh's cereal and break into song, dancing across the room with the Cheerios box. "I feel pretty, oh so pretty. . . ."

"Mom!" My son is alarmed. He's used to seeing me tired and unhappy. He thinks I'm losing my mind.

I put the cereal in the cabinet, dance back across the room, and land a big kiss on his forehead.

"Mom!"

An unsuspecting Sophie waddles into the kitchen on three legs and I scoop my possum up and give her a big hug. She's also alarmed and struggles to get down. I put her back on the floor.

"Run, Sophie!" Josh advises. "Mom is crazy."

Sophie takes his advice, and moves as fast as an animal with an extremely slow metabolism can move.

I resume my song, reliving the highlights of the past few days, Harry's testimony, the positive press coverage of Maddie's testimony.

Jeff comes into the kitchen, grins at me, and pours himself a cup of coffee.

"Who's testifying today?"

"Louis Townsend. Now that public opinion is swinging in the opposite direction, he feels safe sticking his neck out. This should cinch it. We had the tissue sample tested by an independent lab. The results are totally consistent with poisoning by ingested cyanide. The DNA matches to one of the stadium victims. Not only that, but the deputy chief at the lab is going to testify about the cover-up as well."

"Wonderful. I have some good news for you, too. I was just listening to the radio in the bedroom. Guess who just resigned?"

"Well, I already know Sharon Pendergast resigned. The BOM?"

"No, but that's probably coming soon. Someone else. Who has wrecked more of our evening plans than anyone else?"

I yelp. "Dean?"

Jeff grows stern and speaks with the voice of an NPR announcer. "Dr. Elizabeth Dean, head of the Pentagon Council of the Wise, resigned this morning, citing a desire to spend more time with her family."

I crow with laughter. "Her family? Her family! Did anyone consult her family first? How do they feel about spending more time with her?" I almost choke myself laughing. I get up and go swirling around the room, singing, "I feel pretty, oh so pretty. . . ."

58. Maddie

It's late at night. I'm not sure how late. I recorded the C-SPAN coverage of the hearings and I've been watching it for hours, but it doesn't make me feel any better. I'm the only member of the canary crew not celebrating our "victory." I suppose I should be happy that the worst of the prostitutes have abandoned the Mines, that my public reputation has been restored, and that Alan's business trip to Iran has been canceled. But I can barely drag my sorry butt out of bed in the morning. I pull Abu Bunny into my lap. Poor rabbit is going to get another earful. Lucky thing he has such big ears.

"We didn't stop the stadium attack, did we? Just like we didn't stop the Strikes or the Iraq war. Your mommy still has INTELLIGENCE FAILURE tattooed on her forehead. Ever heard of a policy failure, Bunny? No such thing."

I wish I had taken a few whacks at Harry when Vernon had him pinned on my porch. That might have made me feel better. I still can't think of Harry and my mother without a major attack of reflux. The fact that Harry looks like Captain Kangaroo makes it even worse. I used to love Captain Kangaroo.

Someone sent Harry's wife an anonymous letter telling her about the affair. I'm pretty sure that someone was my mother. So now Mrs. Esterhaus has booted Harry out of the tract mansion. Mom called me yesterday and told me that she has left the Mines and that she and Harry have bought a big-ass RV and are planning on traveling around the country. She wants me to forgive her. She also wants me to sell the furniture she still hasn't moved out of my house and send her the money. I suppose I will do those things eventually.

"Mommy's mom is a floozy, Abu Bunny. A floozy."

I look around. I haven't done a damn thing to the house since Mom left. I've been too focused on writing testimony and tracking down evidence. I hate the way this place looks, all cutesy and pastel. I cut off the television and gently push Abu Bunny off my lap. I need to do something physical and I'm going to do something about this. I fetch a box of extra-large lawn-and-leaf bags from the utility room. I'll sell Mom's stuff for her, but I'm pitching everything she has ever given me as a gift.

"Bunny, you are going to be the only rabbit in the house again. I only like real rabbits."

I start grabbing up the bunny kitsch: bunny figurines, bunny clocks, bunny lamps, bunny wall hooks, bunny throw rugs, bunny table runners, bunny pillows, bunny place mats. Everything breakable, I raise above my head and hurl into the trash bag with all the force I can muster. The sound of porcelain shattering sends Abu Bunny scrambling under the couch. I pick up speed. I growl as I race around the house, seeking out and destroying fake rabbits. In the bathroom, I rip down the bunny shower curtain and pry the bunny toilet paper holder and towel racks and toothbrush holder off the wall, leaving holes in the Sheetrock. In the kitchen, I collect the bunny scrubby holder, bunny Jell-O molds, and bunny salt and pepper shakers. Finally, I arrive in the front hall. The four-foot-tall butler rabbit stands there grinning at me, his buckteeth protruding from his resin lips. Ears poke through a shiny top hat. Striped purple vest clashes loudly with red jacket and trousers. In one hand he hefts a tray complete with a DayGlo orange resin carrot, in the other he holds a ticking pocket watch. Words cannot express how much I hate this thing. Merely throwing a garbage bag over his head and hauling him out to the curb will not satisfy me. I stand staring at him, trying to catch my breath. Then I get an idea.

It's late, but I phone Vernon.

"Hello? It's me, Maddie. I need something badly, and I need you to help me."

I'm surprised at how quickly he agrees to come. Before long, I see his humongous black pickup once again pull into my drive. I meet him out on the front porch. As soon as I see the expression on his face, I realize he's misread my message.

"Maddie, I've been waiting for this. You need some love, don't you?"

"Oh God no. Sorry. Misunderstanding. My bad." I laugh nervously. "Between the Zoloft and the affair between Harry and my mother, it will be *years* before I want to touch a man again. No offense, but eww, yuck, no. But if I ever get any of those stirrings again, I'll keep you in mind . . . meanwhile . . . um . . . I need your truck."

Vernon throws up his arms and looks to the heavens. "Shit, I don't believe this. Do you know what time it is?"

"Vernon, I'm so depressed I could kill myself. But I finally figured out something that will make me feel better. Would you please help me? You owe me. Wait here." I don't want him in the house, in case he still has any funny ideas. The thought sends a shudder down my spine. I wrestle the resin rabbit across the hall and out the door.

"What the fuck is that?"

"Four-foot-tall fake rabbit. What does it look like?"

"May I ask—"

"No! Just help me get it into your truck."

He follows me to the driveway as I drag the rabbit. "You're not going to put that ridiculous thing in my—"

"Please, Vernon. Here, I'll get in the cab, and you squeeze it in next to me." I jump into his truck.

"You are the kinkiest fucking woman I have ever met. And not kinky in a good way." But Vernon lifts the rabbit and wedges it next to me between the dashboard and the seat. "Where are we taking this?"

"Mines."

Vernon starts to pull the rabbit out of the truck, but I slap his hands away and force the door shut. Vernon kicks a tire, then comes around and climbs in the passenger seat.

"Maddie, you don't work there anymore. Remember? And I'm not going to try to get you a visitor's tag in the middle of the night. And I'm certainly not going to get a tag for this freakin' rabbit."

"Don't need any tags. We're not going in. Just take me to the parkway entrance."

Vernon sits with his arms crossed. "I'm not taking you there. And you know that entrance is closed this time of night."

"Exactly."

"Maddie, what do you have in mind? I'm not liking the sound of this."

"I'm going to leave the Mines a gift."

Vernon strikes the wheel, and the horn blows. I'm starting to get annoyed at his childishness. I try to explain that what I want is really quite simple.

"All we have to do is get off at the exit. You don't even have to stop the truck. When we get to the top of the ramp, I'll push the rabbit out. You hit the accelerator, and we go right over the median and down the ramp and back out onto the parkway. Simple."

"Unless they blow my tires out. Don't they have someone there even when the gate is closed?"

"We'll be two miles away before they can even react."

Vernon pokes the rabbit with his index finger. "Maddie, this thing is holding a clock, a fucking timing mechanism. They're going to bring out the bomb squad. Then they're going to take it out to the culvert and pump a few rounds in it."

"Exactly. That's exactly what I want them to do."

Vernon throws up his hands. "Why?"

"Because it will make me feel better. Isn't that reason enough? I have had a really, really shitty summer, and taking it out on this rabbit—this potent symbol of the train wreck that my life has become—would make me feel better. Please, Vernon. I'm not asking much." I manage to squeeze out a couple of tears.

Vernon stands his ground for all of one minute before he caves. He turns the key in the ignition. "Well, this evening is turning out just great. Here I thought I was going to find out all the wonderful techniques you used to get information out of Alan Monroe, and instead I'm going to be shot by some SCUDO for attacking the Mines with a fake rabbit. You were known as the Goose Chaser. Now I'm going to be known—probably *posthumously*—as the Bunny Bomber. This operation is going to make Ted Kaczynski look like a reasonable guy."

Vernon is such a baby, he grumbles all the way to the Mines. We get on the George Washington Parkway from the Beltway.

"All right. Are you ready?" Vernon says.

"Ready."

Vernon gets off at the Mines exit. At the top of the ramp, he slows the truck briefly as I shove the wretched rabbit out the door. It hits the pavement with a satisfying *thwock*, rolls, and comes to rest with the arm holding the pocket watch sticking straight up in the air. I barely get the door shut before Vernon jams his foot down on the accelerator. It's been rainy recently, and our back wheels fishtail a bit on the median, tearing up some grass. We manage to avoid getting mired and go barreling down the ramp on the other side. Vernon doesn't even bother to check to see if anyone is in the lane before merging.

"Woo-hoo!" he yells as soon as we are back on the parkway. "That was actually fun."

"Yeah. I feel a little better."

"A little? All that and you only feel a little better? Are you sure you don't need something even more stimulating to make you feel much better?"

"No, Vernon. That will do. I'm fine. Really."

59. Doc

Today is my wedding day. I keep saying it to myself, but I'm not sure I believe it yet. I'm at an age when the largest events of my life should be surgical: hip replacement, knee replacement, bypass. Yet here I stand trussed up in a tuxedo, trimming my nose hair. My lovely bride has banished Molotov and me to the basement bathroom, so we don't see her in her dress—or Pearl in her special new collar—until the ceremony. Molotov is sitting on the commode—we keep the lid down—watching me intently. He seems amused. He is already wearing his bow tie, which doesn't bother him as much as mine bothers me. He somehow manages to maintain his dignity. I should be more like my cat.

Why should I be nervous? Fran and I have been living together companionably for months. I love her. She's my dream woman. It's a beautiful spring day. We're old. If the marriage doesn't work out, we don't have that many years left to suffer together. There's nothing to be nervous about. I hope the guests won't snigger at me for being an old fool. I've already threatened Vivian with dire consequences should she call us an "adorable couple" again.

Okay, I admit it: I'm afraid I'm going to cry. It happens sometimes. Despite decades in the White Mines practicing rigorously logical thought, I can still become sentimental and blubbery without warning. It's the apparent result of an errant gene inherited from my fluttery Georgia grandmother, Willadene.

Fran asked me last night if I really thought she had forgotten our night on Perkins's desk. Of course I thought she had forgotten it. I was too insignificant in her world.

She told me that she waited for me to call her after that night. She didn't call me because she thought she wasn't smart enough for me and that was why I didn't call. She said, "I really wasn't as loose as you might have thought, from my behavior. I had been hoping you would ask me out for months, so when we ended up together after hours, I went for broke. You were sincere and thoughtful and funny and brilliant and you really adored me. At least I thought you did, until you didn't call me back and wouldn't look at me. That really hurt."

When she told me that, tears came to my eyes. And they are back now. And I will probably blubber through the whole wretched ceremony.

Thank goodness it is to be a small wedding. Our guests will be limited to Fran's children, her daughter's husband, and the canary crew. It will be an odd affair. Fran decided that she would like all of the women present to be her bridesmaids. All of them! Fran bought and mailed every one of them several yards of dusty rose silk. I had to drive her over the entire greater metropolitan D.C. area until she found the right shade. She told them to have their dresses made up in whatever style they liked, but they had to wear the dusty rose. Fran, Kimberly, Maddie, Vivian, Kristin, and Bonnie are upstairs now, changing into their dresses. The giggling is no doubt audible throughout the neighborhood. I would not have expected seasoned alchemists to giggle so much.

Fran has kindly agreed to dispense with the most barbaric wedding rituals: throwing a garter, smashing cake in each other's faces, and pelting the new couple with rice, birdseed, confetti, organic steel-cut oats, tapioca, or whatever is the substance of choice today. Most of this idiocy evolved from fertility rituals, and I steadfastly decline to have anything as ludicrous as a fertility ritual at this wedding. I was unable to talk Fran out of having Molotov be the ring bearer, as cloyingly silly as that will be. The ring is already attached to his bow-tie collar with a tiny ribbon. Fran taught him to walk on a leash, so I will be leading him down the aisle, undoubtedly to the accompaniment of a chorus of women cooing about how cute it is.

Fran is the most alluring woman I have ever known, a goddess. Otherwise I would not put up with a second of this hoopla. Fortunately, Fran has planned a martini bar for the reception. By then I should be in great need of a stiff drink.

60. Maddie

I've never been a bridesmaid before. When all of my college friends were getting married, I was off doing graduate study in the Middle East. In my first few years at the Mines I did a lot of overseas trips too. To tell you the truth, I deliberately scheduled one or two of them so I would miss weddings. Nothing seemed so inane to me as parading down the aisle of a church smiling like an idiot. I suppose I'm not a romantic. My own misbegotten wedding had the sole advantage of being cheap. Rick and I got married in a meadow. I had no bridesmaids and wore jeans. Besides a few friends, we had a fat old woodchuck who chewed on grass as he watched us. It was all I could do to keep Vivi from "rehabilitating" him. I don't mind this wedding, though. It's fun. I had my dusty rose silk made into a tea-length dress with full skirt, fitted bodice, and handkerchief hem. It reminds me of my ballerina days.

"It's gorgeous," Vivi says. She has me whirl around so the skirt flares out.

"You look lovely," Fran says.

We're all blown away by how lovely and statuesque Fran looks in her ivory silk and lace. She's dropped a few pounds, and her figure is absolutely amazing. She'll blow poor Doc right off his feet.

Alan is here. I've avoided him thus far. He's out in the lawn having a beer. Fran nudges me and nods toward the window.

"Don't you miss my beautiful son? I know he would love to go out with you again."

"Um . . . I've been taking a kind of sabbatical from relationships, but maybe in another year or two."

"I'm not taking any sabbaticals," Bonnie says, "I'd love to go out with him. He's just my type."

Fran looks as if she wants to scream, "No he's not!" but she holds her tongue.

I smile at Bonnie benignly, thinking that her dress is really too snug. Three of us had to help her wrestle it over her head and down over her hips. If that zipper pops, there's going to be shrapnel.

"You really should get back into the swing of things," Vivi says. "You haven't added to your mug collection in ages."

Bonnie looks confused. "What do mugs have to do with—"

Vivi giggles. "You know how she got all those mugs she has? They're from all the military units she's slept with."

"From all the *individuals* I've slept with from various units. Don't make it sound worse than it is."

I didn't think Doc was going to make it through the vows. He had tears running down his face and he could barely get the words out. His cat was cute strolling down the lawn with its tail in the air. And Fran's cat wore a bow around her neck made from the same material as our dresses. The whole thing was over-the-top adorable, but we respected Doc's wishes and didn't tell him so. The only odd note was Vernon's smart-ass contribution. As the bridesmaids were all squeezing together for a photo, he ran to his car and hauled out a lifesize photo cutout he had made of Beth Dean—in a dusty rose suit, no less! He tried to put it next to us, as if Dean were one of the bridesmaids, but we wouldn't let him. The man has a sick sense of humor, absolutely sick.

The ceremony seemed to take it out of Doc. He's sitting on a bench with Vernon. A pitcher of vodka martinis stands on the ground in front of them. I walk over and sit down beside Vernon, making him squeeze closer to Doc.

"You know," I say.

"Know what?"

"You know what?"

"What?" Vernon says, annoyed.

"You know Wynona, the barista?"

"Yeah."

"She used to spit in your espresso."

Vernon looks shocked. "What?"

"Oh, yes. Every time. She spit in your espresso."

"Why would she do that?"

"Because it was too hard to inconspicuously pee in your espresso." I slap my thighs, laughing. I spit, I'm laughing so hard. It's quite possible that I'm a little drunk. I stand up unsteadily and leave Vernon and Doc staring.

"You have a sick sense of humor," Vernon calls after me.

I walk over to Fran, who is tending bar in her wedding dress, whipping up all sorts of exotic concoctions. The bar is set up under a pergola at the far end of the garden. A fifty-foot orange extension cord snakes between the daffodils from the patio to the blender.

"Pour me another Bahamama mamama." Damned hard to control the number of syllables in that drink after you've had a couple. "And don't spare the rum."

"Yes, ma'am." Fran pours with a flourish.

Vivi sits on a bridge over the water feature Doc constructed in the backyard. Her dyed-to-match dusty rose pumps are beside her and her feet are in the water. Also in the water is the Beth Dean cutout. She has been placed smack in the middle of the pond, where she stands up to her knees in water lilies.

Vivi drains her dirty girl scout, which includes Godiva liqueur and a few other high-test ingredients. "This is scrumptious!" she yells to Fran. "I don't suppose I could have another one?"

Bonnie has had three appletinis and she's all over Alan. She's playing one slow dance after another on Fran's boombox and she hasn't let go of him in forty minutes. Good for her. The jerk has been trying to flirt with Kristin all day.

I deliver Vivi's dirty girl scout and lean my elbows on the bridge railing.

"I've never seen you tipsy before," I say.

"How can you tell I'm tipsy?" She looks surprised. Her face is flushed.

"Your dress is trailing in the water."

She looks down and opens her mouth in surprise. "So it is. It's silk, and I'm not even upset. I was going to hem it to a shorter length anyway for wearing to church." Vivi points to my glass. "What about your stomach? Are you supposed to be drinking?"

"Stomach doesn't bother me much anymore. What about yours?"

"Mine either."

"How's your back?"

"Doesn't bother me much either. Must have been the muscle tension."

Vivi's face clouds over. "What's going to happen when you go back?"

I slip off my own shoes and sit down. I stick my feet in the pond and kick an arc of greenish water toward Beth Dean. Her soggy knees buckle and she collapses, still smiling, and sinks down among the fishes. When I go back, I'm going back to the Mines. Hard to believe, but I've been offered a position as the head of the new Alternative Alchemy Unit. And I'm taking it. What choice do I have? This is the only thing I know how to do.

"It will be different this time. My job will be to kick ass, shake things up, challenge the office line, and I'm good at that."

"Awful lot of ass to kick," Vivi says.

"I'll wear my pointe shoes, that'll leave some painful dents."

Vivi smiles, but worry soon takes over her face again. "Don't get your hopes up too high. You know what's happened in the past to initiatives like that. The place will try to reject you like a transplanted organ."

"I know that. Know what I'm up against better than anyone, but it doesn't matter. Hey, what can I say? It's a seething shit hole, but it's home. It's a warped place and I'm a warped woman." I give Vivi a broad smile. "Whatever happens, I plan to leave so many sugar-plum purple, toe-shaped bruises in my wake that they'll never forget me."

"When you put it that way, it almost sounds like fun."

"We'll see."

Glossary of Terms

alchemist - analyst.

Auger - electronic terrorism database.

Base, the - English translation of al'Qaida.

Black Mines - the operational sector of the Mines responsible for clandestine intelligence gathering.

BLIP, BLIPed *vb* - to judge as Below the Level of Interest of the Policymaker.

bomb dissector (BD) - counterterrorism specialist.

Boss of Mines (BOM) - the presidentially appointed director of the Mines.

BOM Tunnel - the corridor in the Mines where portraits of former BOMs hang.

canary crew - special team set up to handle a particular terrorist threat.

Central Counterterrorism Supersector (CCSS) - unit responsible for following terrorist threats.

Daily Threat Roster (DTR) - a listing of current threats.

drones - administrative personnel.

DoneIntel - finished, published intelligence.

Ear, the - see National Audio Collection Agency.

Evil Empire - the Soviet Union.

Esteemed Legislative Body (ELB) - bicameral legislature of the Grand Old Democracy.

face boss - line manager.

diplomatic service (DipServ) - the agency responsible for foreign diplomacy.

Grand Old Democracy - the United States.

grouper - foreign asset, agent.

hadiths - a narrative record of the sayings of Muhammad.

Heartland Defense - a new agency of government set up after the Strikes to defend the homeland from a dearth of agencies responsible for defending the homeland.

Internal Investigative Organ (IIO, in the Mines known simply as "the Organ") - the agency responsible for domestic law enforcement.

Main Shaft - the executive wing of the Mines, headed by the Boss of Mines.

Mines - the agency responsible for gathering and assessing foreign intelligence for the President.

National Audio Collection Agency (known in the Mines as "the Ear") - the agency responsible for the collection of audio intelligence from satellites, wiretaps, etc.

New Shafts Building (NSB) - built in the 1980s, it lies to the west of the Old Shafts Building at Mines Headquarters.

Old Shafts Building (OSB) - the original headquarters building of the Mines.

Pentagon Council of the Wise (PentCOW) - a temporary unit set up in the Pentagon to take intelligence rejected by the Mines and turn it into *casus belli*.

President's Intelligence Update (PIU) - daily "newspaper" of the most critical intelligence for the President and a few top officials.

rockslide - an unfortunate public incident involving the Mines.

slag - the daily inflow of intelligence cables, intercepts, diplomatic reports, etc.

subshaft - A small work unit focusing on a specific subject area.

Safety and Security Sector (SSS) - a unit in the Mines responsible for grounds security and developing and enforcing information security procedures.

sharper - operations officer or, less politely, spy.

smithies - technical experts who make spy gadgetry.

Special Employee Services (SES) - a unit within the Mines responsible for helping employees deal with personal and psychological problems, as well as substance abuse.

Strikes, the - the 2001 attack on the World Trade Center and Pentagon.

towers, the - the World Trade Center towers.

White Mines - the analytical sector of the Mines.